HEART WRENCHED

HOLLOWS GARAGE
BOOK 1

KATE CREW

HEART WRENCHED

Content Warnings: Sexual content (Consensual), Toxic Friendships, Non Consensual distribution of nude photographs/videos, Near Death Experience, Violence, & Explicit Language.

Nate,
Thank you for encouraging me to finish the damn book and always reminding me how strong I am.

ONE

QUINN

3 Years Ago - High school

The first time I spoke to Ransom Ward was the worst night of my entire life, and I'd hated him ever since.

It didn't start that way, though.

From the first moment I saw him, I was already hooked. His sharp jaw, dark hair, and haunting blue eyes were like a bear trap, snapping my foot and snaring me without a word.

Every day he and his friends would be in the school parking lot with their cars, and my skin would prick with the feeling that I was being watched.

So many times, I would wonder if it was my imagination, but then I would catch his eye, and the spark would reignite all over again. I would never talk to him, and he wouldn't talk to me.

Ransom and his crew circled the school like wolves, leaving most of us too scared to get closer to them. It was the rumors, mostly.

Each one that went through the school kept growing worse, darker with crazy stories about them killing a man, that they had wild parties, they would bet on street races, or use their fast cars as getaway cars in robberies.

But no matter what I heard, I couldn't help but be drawn to Ransom.

When a particularly dark rumor started, I knew I shouldn't brush them off anymore. I knew I should start to believe them.

Not that I wanted to.

No, my mind was too busy running out of control with fantasies.

I would try to brush the rumors aside and dream of who he could be, who I hoped he was. I would think about his hard body over mine, getting to run my hands through his dark hair, and the more I thought about him, the more frustrated I became. Soon, I was so annoyed that each time his face came to mind, I would do anything to push the thought away. I tried to focus on school, on my boyfriend or my friends, anything but him.

I thought I was saving myself from ruining my life. I knew getting good grades meant getting into a good school and never going back home again. It was what I wanted, and I just needed to get over the phase of my life when a girl wanted a bad boy.

But nothing ever got rid of him. I even thought of him when I was making out with the guy I dated.

I tried hard to get a bad boy out of my system by dating Logan. He was a safe bad boy in my mind. While we dated, he went from burnout to quarterback. His grades soared, and they even planned on him getting scholarships to play football. Over-all, he was supposed to be perfect.

But whether I was dating Logan or not, I couldn't help but steal a glance at Ransom every morning, wondering how he could look better each time. Him, his friends, their ridiculously fast cars - it was impossible not to be curious about them.

I wouldn't go near him, though. I wouldn't let myself fall into his bottomless pit of trouble. Instead, I turned to Logan again and again, trying to finish whatever stupid hang-up I had on bad boys and save myself the risk of going near Ransom.

I thought Logan was a decent choice for a boyfriend, but he quickly became something so much worse.

Everything was going fine until it wasn't. Until I wasn't saving myself, I was destroying myself.

9 MONTHS AGO - High school

It was the night I first spoke to Ransom.

It happened during my senior year.

Ransom and most of his crew had graduated, but I still saw them around some of the parties. At school, there was no more staring at him each day or watching them go. There were no glimmers of hope that he was looking at me, too. And as many times as I tried to tell myself they were dumb fantasies, some ridiculous part of me still hoped they would come true.

At some point, I realized he wasn't coming for me. It was no one else's job to save me from the horrible cycle my life had taken. That was when my destructive path twisted even more out of control.

Logan and I still dated, breaking up every month and then getting back together. I just stopped caring. The breakups happened in a quick second so I could move on with my life until he came back around. There weren't tears or heartfelt apologies from either of us. Instead, I went along with it, spiraling until I was out at every party, dancing and drinking until I couldn't anymore. Not wanting to go home and not wanting to stay anywhere else, every place I went leaving a bad taste in my mouth that I tried to drink away.

It was that night at the party everything shattered.

I walked in and saw Ransom with his friends, some girls hanging all over them. I had looked each one of them over, my stomach churning with something I could only place as jealousy. I wanted to be that girl on his lap, and for a moment, I thought I might take the chance to be.

I was already ruining my life. One night with Ransom couldn't really make it worse.

I had taken a deep breath, ready to walk over and take my chance, when I had finally caught his eye. Everything changed, his body going rigid as he stared daggers at me, letting me know I was definitely not welcome to come any closer.

Each moment of that night felt like a slow descent into my own nine circles of hell until I was standing at that party, a video of me playing on repeat on every phone around me.

A video of me having sex with a guy I thought was my boyfriend but was actually an asshole. A perverted asshole that recorded us having sex and sent it to everyone at school.

The room stilled around me, and the air was sucked from my lungs. I was in a prison of people who wanted to laugh and stare but not let me run. I still remembered everything, the smell of beer and weed and the music playing loud in the background, the sound of my own moans filling the air as the video played on everyone's phones.

I pushed through the crowd, going for the front door, and stumbled onto the porch, hitting a solid chest. Arms wrapped around me, steadying me before they pushed me away.

I looked up into those piercing blue eyes I had never seen that close, but black swirled through them then.

"You need to get the fuck out of here."

"I— I was," I stuttered, not sure I believed that those were the first words Ransom had ever said to me. "I know." I stumbled out again.

"Well, go faster, and don't come back," he said, anger tightening in his jaw. The look of disgust had been unmistakable.

So I ran.

I didn't stop running until I was camped out in the run-down shed behind my house, not daring to face my mother with my face tear-stained and swollen.

I stayed there for days until I was forced to come out by my best friend.

Life went on, but from that day onwards, I knew I hated Ransom Ward.

TWO

QUINN

"Aren't you *at all* excited?" Josie whined, grabbing another dress from the closet and holding it up. "This is our first week here. We should be getting out, meeting new people, seeing the sights!" She was yelling, jumping around the room in a flurry of excitement and anxiety-inducing happiness.

"The sights? We grew up twenty minutes from here," I said with a laugh.

Tonight was the welcome party for incoming college freshmen, and Josie's sole mission was to get me to go.

While I had spent the first half of senior year of high school in self-destruct mode, Josie spent her entire year working on extracurriculars and getting straight A's. It was a shock that our friendship made it out alive, but she was there when everything fell apart and helped when I needed to undo the damage and bring my grades back up enough to be accepted into college.

Even when I came to her to tell her I couldn't afford any fancy college, she had screeched in joy when she realized that meant we would both be going to the state university in our hometown. She wanted to stay near her family, and I had no other choice.

"Please, Quinn. I promise we will stay in all night tomorrow and do whatever you want if you do this."

"What I want is to hide away from anything resembling a party," I said, throwing a blanket over myself.

"Stop, you'll mess up your hair! I just spent an hour on that, Quinn. Get up!"

"Me, mess up my hair?" I held a sarcastic hand to my chest. "I would never."

I pulled the cover off and stared at her, ready to do anything to keep her happy. After all she had done for me, I wasn't going to ruin a night for her. At some point between high school and college, Josie had perfected doing her hair and makeup along with getting a new wardrobe. Now she was always ready to help me improve my style.

She had hidden away for so many years in high school, punishing herself to the corner when all she wanted to do was be her true, whole self. Now in college, she committed to being exactly who she wanted to be. It inspired me to try to do the same, even if the guilt and memories stayed with me.

In the place of old Josie was a girl who wore dresses more expensive than my entire wardrobe combined, loved every bright color available, and did flawless makeup and hair that should get her on the cover of magazines. Her family had money - like *a house at the lake an hour away and another on a beach in Florida* money. It had dawned on Josie that she could use her money to look and become popular in college. I knew it wouldn't take long to work because of how good she always looked now.

My wardrobe consisted of jeans, sneakers, t-shirts, and jackets. They were nothing fancy, but I was happy they were clean and new enough not to be too embarrassing.

Tonight, though, with my hair and makeup done and a witchy

dress that I hoped Josie wouldn't mind me wearing again, I felt different. Beautiful and more like myself than ever before.

It felt amazing.

Josie finished getting ready, looking like a disco ball in a silver, shimmering dress.

The party was on the other side of campus, so I slid on my boots as she put on a matching pair of heels.

"Are you sure you want to wear those?" I asked, pointing down to the deadly stilettos.

"Absolutely. They go perfect with this dress."

"That wasn't my concern. I don't know if I'll be able to carry you the entire way back!"

"What do you mean? I told you we were getting a ride back with Sarah."

"Sarah? Why?"

Sarah had been the resident popular girl in high school. Somehow, she and Josie had become best friends over the summer.

Josie rolled her eyes. "You realize we're friends now? She's cool, Quinn, don't be so judgmental. She is meeting us there and offered to give us a ride after, so we weren't walking home late. It was nice of her to offer. Can you please try to be friendly?"

"Hey, I've never been mean to her. It's just so weird. She bullied kids in school, and now I'm supposed to be her friend? She was never friendly to me."

"No, but just like us, she wants to leave high school behind and move on."

"Fine. That's fair. We all want to do that." I said, "But if her asshole boyfriend is there, then I am out."

Her boyfriend, Tyler, was one step away from being an accomplice in everything that had happened to me. Sure, he didn't record it, but he blocked the door so nobody else would interrupt us having sex. He helped, and that's all that mattered to me.

"I don't think he'll be there tonight. He doesn't go here, and Sarah didn't mention him coming along."

I didn't know if Sarah knew her boyfriend helped, but I found it hard to believe she wouldn't. After the authorities got involved, and then the school, someone came to the agreement that all videos would be deleted as long as the guys weren't charged. The minute Logan joined the football team, it was like a contract was signed. He was protected from any wrong-doing. They acted like the video wasn't saved to hundreds of kids' phones. The thought of the meeting still made me sick, so I tried to push it away. They had tried to blame me for every-thing, telling the school and authorities I had Logan jumped and beaten up the same night. I told him I didn't do it, that maybe it had been karma, but that hadn't gone over well either.

"I can't believe we made it," Josie said after we locked up the room and headed out.

"Made it?"

"To college!" she yelled, getting either drunken smiles or annoyed glares from people passing.

I shook my head, "I'm glad you're happy, Jos."

She pulled me in, wrapping an arm around me. "Now we need to get you happy."

"I'll get there someday. I hope," I added, mumbling under my breath.

"Someday is coming soon."

We walked in silence the entire way until we turned the corner, the madness of a house party sprawled in front of us.

I skidded to a stop. "I thought you said this was a welcome party the college was putting on."

"It is," she said with a crooked smile on her face.

"At a frat house?"

"Ok, so it is a welcome party. But it's being hosted by some frat brothers, not the college. Come on! It will still be fun."

"No, no, I don't think I should." I pulled back, but she reached forward, grabbing me by the arms.

"Pleaseeee," she said. "Please, we can go if it's terrible. I want to try it, and would be too scared to walk in alone. You've grown, Quinn. You're not going to lose control like before."

I couldn't say no with her bright eyes begging like that. "Ok, you're right, but I'm leaving if I hate it."

"Deal," she squealed, pulling me through the crowd into the loud house. The entire place reeked of stale beer, cigarettes, and sweat. The lights strobed around the room, keeping it just bright enough to blind and annoy me. I had hated parties since the night of the video. I never went to another one again until tonight.

Josie kept pulling me until we were in a bright kitchen.

"Sarah!" she yelled, running out the back door onto the porch.

"Josie!" she yelled back, pulling her into a hug. "And you came too, Quinn! It's so good to see you."

"It's good to see you, too."

"I wasn't sure if you were coming out tonight."

"Josie said it would be fun, so-" I let the sentence fall flat with a shrug of my shoulders. I couldn't relax here, couldn't have fun with so many people around that I didn't know.

The sounds of the party set me on edge. Every part of me was too aware of all the noise and people around me.

Josie and Sarah talked for a minute until a guy came up, draping his arm over Sarah's shoulders. My body tensed, every muscle going rigid as I glanced up at Tyler.

"Josie, Quinn." He nodded to each of us. "I'm surprised to see you here."

"Why?" Josie asked, grabbing my hand. "We go to school here."

"Well, you know, after everything that happened, you weren't the party type in high school, Jos," he said with a golden smile and laughed. He was one of the golden boys, the football team star, and couldn't be touched. None of them could.

"Well, I'm trying to go out more now."

"Don't go out there too much. Quinn here taught us what could happen if you put it all out there." He laughed, his stupid bro laugh making my lip curl.

Sarah hit him in the stomach, and I stepped back, needing more space.

"What the fuck, Tyler?" Josie hissed.

"Yeah, seriously. Not needed, Ty."

I could only glare. This was why I never went to another party. I would hear the comments all over school, so there was no reason to go to parties and listen to the same comments unfiltered. I had always worried about running into Logan again, too. I didn't know what I would say or do to him, but the thought of facing him made me hide away. Tonight didn't help in convincing me I should go to more parties when Tyler was still lurking around.

"I'm going to get a drink." I turned and pushed inside, feeling Josie run up behind me.

"Are you ok? Do you want to leave?"

I turned back, sadness spreading across her face. "I think I'm done for the night, but you should stay. I know you wanted to hang out with Sarah."

She chewed her lip. "No. No, it's ok. We can go. I didn't know Tyler was going to act like that."

I held my eye roll back, knowing Tyler always acted like this around me. He was always a different guy to Sarah and Josie, though.

"No, please. If you're good with staying with Sarah, I'm good. I'm getting an Uber back."

Her face scrunched again. "Are you sure?"

"Positive." I plastered a fake smile and knocked against her,

"Go! I'll get my ride now." She hesitated for a minute before nodding, "Ok, only if you're sure."

"I'm sure. Sarah will give you a ride, right?"

She nodded. "Yeah, that was the plan anyway."

"Alright, I'll talk to you tomorrow."

She pulled me into a hug. "Sorry. I was hoping you would have more fun."

"Me too, but it's fine." I hugged her back before letting her go.

I made sure she went back out before I turned and pushed through the crowd, trying to make it to the front door before any tears came.

The crowd pushed back until I started elbowing them to move, feeling suffocated against the sweaty bodies. Even out on the lawn, the whole place was suffocating. I shouldn't have come. I should have known I was done with parties like this.

It wasn't until I rounded the corner that the crowd thinned completely, and I could breathe again.

I made it down the block, but just as I stepped into the street to cross, two cars roared around the corner, their engines screaming into the night as headlights bathed me in light.

THREE

QUINN

FOR A MOMENT, I only froze in fear.

Instincts finally took over as I grabbed my head and crouched down, holding my breath as I waited for the impact.

The loud screech of tires sliding against pavement made me scream along with it as the car skidded to a stop. The front bumper was within inches of my arm. I reached out to grab it, holding on as I tried to stand and stop shaking.

"What the fuck are you doing?" A man's voice yelled as he got out of the car and slammed the door.

The other car had sped past, but this one stayed, the engine rumbling under my fingertips, soothing me as I pulled myself up.

I recognized Ransom and his car immediately. His eyes found mine in the dark. This time, though, I didn't mistake the look for anything like sympathy or relief. There was only anger.

His gaze burned through me, but I wasn't going to cower away from it this time. Instead, I matched it with my own, "Walking. What the hell were you doing? Trying to kill me?"

"You were walking in the street. How the fuck is that me trying to kill you?"

"Because you were driving like this is fucking Nascar," I

yelled. I could feel my hands start to shake, any adrenaline that had coursed through me dissipating.

"I was racing. A race which I lost thanks to you."

"Thanks to me? Pretty sure street racing is illegal, and so is attempted murder."

"I didn't try to kill you," he said, rolling his eyes. "But, legally speaking, there is no crosswalk here."

"Legally speaking, you weren't going the speed limit. I wasn't expecting anyone to be going that fast. Maybe if you leave me alone now, you can catch up."

He gave a strangled laugh. "He's won, and now I'm out two grand."

"Two grand?" I said, my eyes widening. "You were racing for two grand?" That amount of money was hard to come by, but racing with the possibility of losing that? I couldn't stop my mouth from falling open.

"Yeah, it was a quick race tonight, but I wasn't betting on losing. I needed the money for my car. Now it's gone."

"Well, go find another race. You're insane for racing a car for that much money. Who the hell has that much to risk throwing away?" My bank account had a similar amount of money, but it wouldn't be for long. My next payment was due to the school this week.

My gaze went over every inch of him before meeting his eye again. Warmth flooded through me, the heat making me clench my legs together. He looked so good. It had been eight long months without seeing him, and as much as I didn't like him, I really, *really* liked looking at him.

Ransom was the epitome of tall, dark, and handsome. His dark hair and blue eyes were hard to miss, but add in worn t-shirts, jeans that hung perfectly on his body, and black boots that looked like he could kick someone's ass, and I could never look away.

He was dark and dangerous, and I knew it. I was burned

when I tried to replace feelings for one bad boy with another. Set on fire, basically. If that's what happened with the replacement, I couldn't imagine what would happen with the real thing.

He growled and slapped his hands on his car with a huff. "Why are you out here?" he asked, looking around into the dark neighborhood.

"There was a party."

"And you went?"

"Why do you sound so surprised?"

"I didn't think Quinn Carter would ever step foot inside another party. Haven't seen you at one in a long time."

The words hit me hard. Tonight was only more proof I should have stuck to that.

"Well, I never thought I would see Ransom Ward graduated and out of jail."

He smiled, a small laugh escaping him. I tried to ignore how my stomach flipped when he smiled. It didn't seem to be something he did often.

"Touché." He surprised me even further by adding, "Get in."

It took me an extra second to register the words, "What? I'm not getting in there." I pointed to the car that had almost killed me. I wasn't a fan of fast things or dangerous things. I didn't like the risk anymore, and the jet-black car screamed *death trap*.

"I'm just driving you home, Quinn."

"Why?"

"Because I may be a lot of things, but I'm not the asshole that leaves a girl out on the dark street and then has to feel guilty the next day when her name is plastered on the news, knowing I could have prevented something from happening."

"You want to drive me home so I don't walk alone, get killed, and then you feel guilty?"

"Exactly, now get in."

He wasn't wrong. Walking home alone in the dark wasn't the best idea, and it was getting cold. This dress was not doing much to keep me warm and getting home to my warm bed faster wasn't a bad thing. It seemed the risk of walking home alone was worse than the risk of him driving me.

"I don't want you to drive too fast."

His face fell in annoyance. "What are you thinking is too fast?"

I thought it over, knowing he would take advantage of anything I said. "Anything five miles over the speed limit."

"Five miles over?" he asked, as though I said only go five miles an hour.

"Yes."

"Well then, you better get in so we make it there by sunrise."

I rolled my eyes and pulled the door open. "Dramatic much?"

"Anxiety ridden much?" He mocked back. "You don't trust me to drive my car fast?"

"Oh no. I know you can drive it fast. But I don't have a reason to trust you can drive it fast and safe at the same time."

"I can get you home at a hundred miles an hour and still get you there safe."

"Are you always this cocky?" I don't know where I was finding the confidence to spur him on, but it came so easily.

"Not always. Only when it comes to someone questioning if I can drive."

I shook my head and slid into the dark car as he slid in next to me. The car wasn't small, but this was the closest I had ever been to him. Blue lights glowed from the dash, and he turned down the radio until I could barely hear the screaming music coming through the speakers. The warmth and deep musk smell wrapped around me like a blanket. I leaned back into the seat, closed my eyes, and took a deep breath.

"When did you realize it was me?" I said, keeping my eyes closed.

"It took me a minute after I got out of the car to adjust my eyes, but then I knew."

"I hoped you wouldn't."

"Hard to forget your face," he said.

"So you immediately thought of what happened to me then," I said it like a statement. I knew what his answer would be, but couldn't meet his eye when he said it.

"I didn't mean it like that, but yes."

I sighed again. It was better than what everyone else did, lying to my face as though it wasn't the first thing that came to mind when they saw me.

"You're not very delicate, are you?"

"Listen, I offered you a ride, not a conversation about our pasts."

"Wow. Noted." I said, staring out the window in silence. I almost expected him to apologize like most people would, but he stayed quiet. It was agonizing as I tried to hold my tongue.

I pointed to my dorm as he pulled into the parking lot. "That's me. You can let me out here."

He ignored my demand, pulling up to the doors.

"Goodnight, Quinn," he said, dismissing me from the car. I almost hesitated, not wanting to leave the warmth, but I pushed open the door anyway.

"Goodnight, Ransom," I said, slamming the car door shut. "And fuck you."

I didn't look back as I walked to the door, but I could hear the car rumbling behind me. It wasn't until I walked in and shut the door that his car roared away.

One small interaction and I was right back where I started with Ransom. It was the most time I had ever spent talking to him, and I worried my imagination would run wild again, proving I should stay far, far away from him.

Even if I liked looking at him, he was exactly who I thought he was.

FOUR

RANSOM

I HIT THE STEERING WHEEL, the thud echoing in the now-empty car. I couldn't believe I had lost the race. I didn't exactly need the money right now, but I liked to race to stay on top of car repairs. It wasn't cheap to keep up with a car you beat into the fucking ground each week. I don't know how I managed to lose a race and almost kill a girl in one night, but I did it.

Quinn, fucking, Carter of all people, is who stepped out in front of my car. The girl I had come to hate during high school.

At first, it was just her car I hated, the beat-up piece of junk was shit, and most days, I was surprised it even got her to school.

One time, it rolled into the parking lot and shut off, which broke something in me. I knew Fox was the charming one, so I made him go over to offer some help with her car, but she ignored it completely, which pissed me off more. She needed our help, my help, so why couldn't she just take it? The car was junk. I wouldn't be surprised if it left her stranded every other week, and I knew she didn't live in a good neighborhood. It might have been a step better than where all of us on the crew had grown up, but it wasn't *that* much better. A reliable car meant safety and freedom. I never understood why she didn't see that. It would get under my skin every time she would pull out, and I had to wait and wonder if she was even getting home safe.

The first time I saw her, she glanced at me with such an innocent but determined smile that I felt like someone had punched me.

I was fascinated. I had sworn I was in love for a while, but the stupid thing was that I had never even talked to her.

I have always been confident with girls, but everything about her threw me off, making me unsure of myself. So I had taken the safe route for once - ignore her until I could gain the courage. By the time I did, though, it was too late.

The rumor of all rumors came out of nowhere. One that disgusted me, even though it was about me. It was all made up, but no one seemed to care, and I never learned who started it.

Every day she saw me, she was only more pissed off, and I knew she was starting to believe every word people said about me.

It was around that time she started dating Logan. The asshole pretended he was good enough for her, but he was sleeping with no less than three girls behind her back. I never knew if she didn't see it or just didn't care. She didn't seem dumb or oblivious when he did it in front of everyone at school and at parties. Then I would see them cozied up to each other a few days later.

At that point, I knew it was too late. I couldn't handle it. It was like a knife slicing into me every time I saw her look at Logan like he was the hero when he was the one wrecking her. He took every opportunity to hurt and use her, but somehow, I was always the monster. I knew the rumors didn't help, and based on the look in her eye, she believed them. How could she not?

When she would finally glance over at me again, the look would change from awe to what I could only guess was disgust. She would never look at me like she looked at Logan.

That was the moment I started trying to convince myself that

I hated her. The bitterness of never having a chance had buried itself under my skin as I realized I couldn't, and would never, have her.

It was already my senior year by then, and I had never even talked to her. I knew it was time to get over whatever idea I had about her. I had almost succeeded, but now it all came back like a punch to the face.

I pulled into the garage and hopped out, glad the lights were still on. That meant I didn't have to sit here alone and pathetic.

Fox and Dante were hunched over a car, mumbling a string of curse words.

"What's up?"

"I think the motor is blown." It was Dante's car, and I knew that feeling too well.

"Shit, sorry. We can help you put a new one in it."

"Yeah, I guess I was getting sick of this one. Never a bad time to upgrade."

"No, never a bad time for that," I said.

"What's up with you? Get your money?" Fox asked.

"No, the night went to shit," I said, pulling a rolling chair over, sitting down, and kicking out my legs. I had barely slept the night before, too, deciding to stay up to work on my car to prep for the races instead of going back home, but a tired feeling was sinking in now.

"What? You lost?"

"Lost and almost killed someone. Glad I just redid my brakes."

"Shit, what happened?"

"We were mid-race, and a girl stepped into the street. A girl you know, actually, Quinn Carter." I didn't hide my emotion now, anger rolling through me.

"No shit?" Fox crossed his arms and leaned back. "Then what happened?"

"You sound like a damn gossiping girl," Dante said, shaking his head, but I ignored him.

"I lost the race because of her walking into a fucking street and then took her home."

"That's it?"

"That's it."

"Didn't you want to sleep with her in high school?"

I hid my growl of annoyance. Fox knew damn well I wasn't just out to sleep with her. He was the one who told me to back off until I got my shit together. "In high school, yeah, not now."

A car revved into the parking lot, making us all turn. Kye pulled in, the front of his car smashed up and mangled.

"Shit, this night isn't stopping. What the hell happened to you?" I said, walking out to check it over. Kye was a good mechanic, but he was younger than us all, making him more of a little brother of the group.

"I might have fucked up a bit," he said, shutting his door and looking over the front with me.

"A bit?"

"Yeah, I was racing tonight, and things got out of control. I may have hit a certain prominent statue on a certain college campus, making it fall over." He took a deep breath. "And crack in half."

"Kye!" Fox yelled, "What the fuck, you guys? Did all of you go out and blow the fucking town up?"

"Seems like it," Dante said.

"And none of you invited me? I'm disappointed in each and every one of you." Fox said with a huge smile as he pulled open the hood.

"Do you hear that?" I said, catching a hint of something that sounded like screaming in the distance.

"Music?" We all listened. The faint sound almost sounded like it was coming from my car.

I jumped up, heading towards it as the noise got louder. I

pulled open the door to some girl's voice screaming a song and dug through the car until I found it.

Quinn's phone had been dropped between the seat and the console. I fished it out, the name Josie flashing again and again as she called.

I didn't answer, but laughed as the call ended. I didn't have to worry about forgetting Quinn now.

Fate decided for me.

If Quinn wanted her phone back, she was going to have to come see me.

FIVE

QUINN

I HAD TOSSED and turned all night, dreaming of Ransom's blue eyes and angry glare. I hated to admit to myself how hot it made me. The room was quiet as I rolled over, looking at the sliver of sunlight coming in. Josie never came home, so I assumed she had stayed with Sarah, and I was even more glad I had decided not to stay.

I pulled my iPad off the nightstand, not knowing where my phone had ended up in the night. I sent a text to Josie to check in on her and then scrolled through social media. My fingers hovered over the search bar for a full minute before I typed in Ransom's name.

There was almost nothing from him on his page, but he was tagged in enough to fill it up. Photos with his car from races he won, ones from racing events where people caught a glimpse of him, and then a few from the garage where he works. Some were next to his friends, others with girls with their arms wrapped around him. He didn't smile in any of them, a hard look etched across his face each time. I clicked out of it, not wanting to see anymore.

I browsed more until the words "street racing" caught my

eye, making me scroll down to the article posted on my college's page.

"A local street gang has caused severe damage to a statue on campus." I read to the quiet room, "Those assholes." I murmured as I kept reading.

The article went on about the damage and how they believed it would cost around twelve thousand dollars to repair.

They were idiots. That amount was more than enough to cover my tuition, and they would waste it on repairing a statue that no one liked. Then the word "reward" popped up. They were offering a thousand dollars to anyone who could lead them to the culprit of the crime.

I laid the iPad on my chest, staring up at the ceiling. I happened to know of at least one street racer that had been racing late last night, and while I didn't see them do this, I couldn't imagine there were that many people street racing at a college campus on a Thursday night.

The thought pushed back and forth in my mind. I could live off money like that for the entire school year. It could cover food, clothes, supplies, and everything I needed if I was careful. I pulled the iPad back up and clicked into my bank. I should have about a thousand dollars left after my books and tuition payment, and I planned to stretch it for as long as possible while I ate ramen and cereal. Another thousand would give me enough to even go to the cafe sometimes to buy a coffee while I studied.

Relief and excitement burst through me at the thought until my bank account loaded.

One big, negative balance stared back at me.

Relief was replaced with panic. How could I have gone from an extra thousand dollars to negative without buying anything?

It didn't take me long to figure out, though, as I clicked in further and saw purchase after purchase for visa gift cards. Each one was for hundreds of dollars until the account was drained.

My mother.

I had gone on a quick trip home the day before to grab the rest of my things and left my purse on the counter while I loaded up Josie's car with the last of what I wanted and needed. The bitch had used it to take all of my money and leave me with nothing.

Not that she cared.

By this time of the morning, she would be drunk at the casino. The money she stole from me was probably gambled away by now. I knew the gift cards would work there.

Tears welled in my eyes before I considered the reward money again. It could save me.

I didn't hate Ransom quite enough to turn him and his friends in to the police, but if they committed the crime, they should be held responsible. So was it wrong of me to turn them in?

I remembered how Ransom treated me over the years, ignoring me at every turn until he decided he wanted to judge everything I did. Like he was perfect? Anger filled me at the thought, and it was enough to make me decide.

I ripped off the blankets and searched the room for my phone, turning everything over and inside out until I realized it wasn't there. I might have dropped it last night. Now that I thought about it, I hadn't remembered seeing it after Ransom almost hit me.

More anger rolled through me. The man was infuriating enough, and now he was going to make me lose my phone when I was broke. I needed to call and cancel my card. I needed to call to turn them in and get some money back into my account.

I changed quick and grabbed my room keys, stomping down the steps and half-jogging to where he had almost run me over. I walked all over the place it had happened, but there was nothing, not even tire marks from where he had stopped.

There was only one other place it would be then.

I didn't want to do it. I didn't want to go to the garage he worked at. He would be surrounded by all of his friends, and I would be alone. It would be like walking into the lion's den.

No, no, no. There was no way I wanted to go to this garage and face Ransom again. I paced on the sidewalk, trying to weigh the pros and cons.

I wanted nothing to do with him and didn't want to lose my nerve in calling to report them. I needed the money, and I needed my phone. So there was no point in going in to report them if the money was only going to cover the phone I would then have to buy.

No, I needed to go face him and get my phone back, but I couldn't forget that I was going to call and let the police know it was them who had wrecked the statue.

I stared down the empty road, one way bringing me back to my dorm and the other to the garage.

The garage was another ten-minute walk from here. If I walked fast, this whole thing could be over within half an hour. Then I could call and report them as I walked back.

I took off, picking up my pace until the garage came into view.

I tried to ignore my nerves as my hand shook at the thought of being near him again.

SIX

QUINN

THE GARAGE DOORS WERE OPEN, and I could hear music and metal banging echoing inside. Ransom's car was parked out front, so I knew he was there. I tried to relax my tight shoulders and take a deep breath. I was going to face him again.

I had to now.

My hands fisted, and I willed them to stop the shaking as I pushed forward, walking into the garage with all the confidence I could muster.

There was no turning back.

A guy was working on one of the cars in the bay I walked into, and I recognized him as Fox, one of Ransom's close friends. He was one that would sit outside the school with Ransom every day. His head jerked up when he noticed me. If he recognized me right away, I couldn't tell, but a smile still spread across his face as he looked me over.

"And what can I help you with, beautiful?"

"I'm looking for Ransom."

Fox smiled and leaned against the car. "Are you sure? If you're having car troubles, I can help you. I think you'd prefer

my help," he said with a wink. I couldn't help but smile back at
his relaxed charm.

He was good-looking. Could someone be too good-looking?
His bright smile, a halo of hair, and sharp jaw made me think of
what I pictured the Greek god Apollo would look like. He was
always favorite of the high school girls, and since he was a touch
less threatening than Ransom, he usually had plenty of girls
approach him.

Ransom stepped out from behind one of the other cars, and I
sucked in a breath. He wore a dark mechanic's coverall that was
tight around every muscle, paired with black boots, his dark hair
wild and unkempt. If Fox was Apollo, Ransom was Hades, the
darkness clinging to him like it was born there.

"She's here for me, Fox. Back off."

Fox turned back to me. "Really? I'm a better mechanic than
him. Better racer." He stepped closer and flashed his smile again.
"I'm better than him at a lot of things, actually."

I smiled back, already liking Fox as he prodded Ransom
more, making him angrier.

Ransom came up, pushing him lightly into the car. Fox must
have expected it because he caught himself before he fell onto it.
"You are not a better mechanic or racer."

"Wow, no need to be upset, Ransom. I was just offering top-
notch service. Isn't customer service important around here?" He
winked at me, Ransom not seeing it, and I couldn't hide my
laugh. I had been so nervous about walking in here, but I was
feeling more comfortable now.

Ransom caught my arm. "Come on," he growled, pulling me
forward and heading deeper into the garage. His touch was like a
branding iron searing into me, and I didn't know if I wanted to
pull away or lean into the agonizing heat.

He stopped at a dark green muscle car in the far back corner
of the garage, the darkness covering us so far away from the bay
doors. His hand had dropped from me, and he leaned against the

hood, looking as relaxed as I was tense, but he didn't say a word, only stared, his face hardening into a frown.

The tension was too much for me to stay quiet. "I came to see if you found my phone."

"Was that the only reason?"

"Was there supposed to be another?"

He shrugged. "Maybe you came to see me."

"That sounds stalker-ish."

"You're the one who left their phone in my car on purpose."

"I did not! I even debated not coming to get my phone to avoid you. I think it's clear you don't like me, and the feeling is mutual."

"Really? I didn't know I made it so clear," he said, arching an eyebrow.

"I can put two and two together." I tried to look relaxed, but I knew it wasn't working. "So you did find my phone then?"

He didn't answer, his eyes raking over me again. His sudden interest in annoying me was starting to get on my nerves. I didn't need him looking at me like that when running into him last night felt like ripping off a bandaid. Something about him sparked my interest without a second thought. It was out of my control, and all I wanted to do was stomp those feelings out.

"Enough, Ransom. I need my phone."

"Why?"

I widened my stance and put my hands on my hips. "Why do I need my phone? Doesn't everyone need their phone?"

"Why do you need it right now?" He slid across the front of the hood until he stood right in front of me. "Do you have a boyfriend who can't stand to go five minutes without talking to you?"

His eyes were trained on me, and I felt like I needed to get out from under their gaze. He couldn't know what I was going to do, could he? Panic set in, growing deeper as I realized how much I wanted to reach out and touch him, feel his hair through my fingers, feel his lips on my neck. He was close enough that I could do it now if I wanted, the thought making me lose all train of thought.

I shook my head and narrowed my eyes. "Is that any of your business?"

"It is right now."

"Maybe I do have a boyfriend I need to call. He's probably freaking out right now, not being able to talk to me all night."

"I don't blame him. Although, is a guy really interested in you if you leave a party and he can't get a hold of you all night, and then he doesn't do anything about it? Shouldn't he have come to see you?"

"I said *maybe* I have a boyfriend. It's none of your business if I do or not."

"So if you don't have one, why do you look like you want to run out of here as fast as you can?"

"Because I do want to get out of here as fast as I can. I have no need to be here longer than it takes to get my phone and go."

His voice dropped. "Why? Can't stand to be this close to me for too long without touching me, Kitten?"

The words came out like a sin, and I knew I was immediately wet. Thoughts of him naked over me with that same voice saying a string of dirty words flashed through my mind until I replaced them with anger. Anger at him for hating me one minute and then turning me on so easily the next.

"You know what, Ransom," I said, stepping towards him, "I want my phone because there happens to be a reward for information on a group of street racers who ruined a statue last night. I happen to know a few people who were racing then, and I could use the cash, so I need my phone to make a call."

I could see him tense at my words. Anger made his jaw tighten as he frowned, and I was almost pleased with myself until his hands reached out, gripping my waist and pulling me into him. My hips hit against his with a bruising force. His lips were only inches away, and I pressed mine together, trying not to make a noise at the sudden contact.

"I think that would be a bad idea," he whispered, his eyes hardening as he stared openly at my mouth.

I pushed against him, and he let me go. "Why's that? Because you would be in trouble?"

"Because you could be wrong. Do you know for sure it was my crew or me?"

"How many street racers are running around our campus at night at the same time you were?"

He laughed. "Races usually take more than one or two cars."

"Maybe, but at least I could tell them who one of the groups was."

"If they decided it was one of us, they could wreck our business. It would ruin all of our lives."

"I'm calling. They can sort out the details."

I almost felt bad. Just a quick glance at the garage made it obvious they were busy with work. A car filled every garage bay, and it seemed like everyone was working. I didn't want to be the one to ruin someone's business, but then again, I needed money to survive.

"How will you call if you don't have your phone?" he asked with a smirk.

"Ransom!" I yelled, the noise echoing through the garage. "Give me my phone."

"Only if you agree not to call."

"That's not an option. They are offering a grand to turn you in, and I happen to be broke." I cringed at the admission, remembering the looks I would get at school when it was apparent I struggled with money. I knew they all saw it, too. It was obvious when I didn't get new clothes and drove my beat-up car. Word got around about my mother, too. So many people knew what she was up to all the time.

He scowled and glanced away. I was starting to feel bad until

I realized he could be doing it on purpose. Playing me with the nickname and touching me, persuading me not to call so he could give me my phone and not get in trouble. He knew games that I didn't, and dangerous ones at that. I couldn't fall into this trap.

"They are giving a thousand dollars as a reward?"

"Yes, and I need that."

"I'll give you a job," he said, his voice tight, like the words pained him.

"What?" I said, stepping back as my mouth dropped open.

He was still scowling. "If you don't call, I will give you a job."

"Why?"

"Because I don't need police looking into our personal business, and I know for a fact the statue...incident was an accident. The college can afford to fix it themselves."

Something on his face made me feel like he was genuine, but I couldn't trust myself to know when someone like him was telling the truth or lying.

"I'll make sure you make that much money and more. Your hours can be flexible, and I'll give you a five hundred dollar starting bonus, but you cannot call any one of us into the police."

He pushed off the car and stepped towards me but didn't say anything else for a moment, letting me think it over.

"Well, what do you think?" He wasn't close enough to touch me, but close enough that I could feel his warm breath as he whispered, "Kitten?"

The word sent a shiver down my spine.

"Stop calling me that."

He smirked like he had won, but I wasn't agreeing. I didn't think I was.

"Are you being serious? This job isn't something perverted, right? It doesn't involve any sexual favors?"

His smile fell, and eyes darkened. "No. I wouldn't proposition you to be paid for sex. I don't need to pay anyone for that."

I let out a breath. I didn't doubt that he wouldn't have to pay someone to get them into bed, but him saying it out loud uncurled something that had knotted in my chest.

After the video came out, some guys began to treat me like a toy. Like me sleeping with my boyfriend at the time and his recording it, meant I would sleep with anyone, anywhere, for nothing. Or worse, they offered me something for it. Not long after it happened, a guy from the football team offered me twenty bucks to sleep with him behind the bleachers. On instinct, I had punched him in the face, not knowing how much it actually hurt to punch someone. I must have done some damage, though, because he came to school the next day with two bruised eyes and a broken nose, and none of the football players ever bothered me again. I had been surprised my punch had done that much damage, but I wasn't going to question it.

"What would the job be, then?"

"Helping around here. We don't get a lot of calls, but we need things ordered and organized in the office, cleaned up, and things like that."

"I don't know how to work on cars."

"I wouldn't let you work on these cars. You mess up something small on these, and we could be out thousands and lose clients."

I tapped my foot, nervous energy filling me with nowhere to go. I could use the steady money, especially now that I had negative accounts, but being around Ransom so much could be agonizing. Not to mention, put me right back where I started with lusting after bad boys. I looked him over now, and I couldn't really say the lusting after bad boys stage was even over in my life. I couldn't get wrapped up in another one. I knew if it happened again with Ransom, of all people, I could fall even farther than I did last time.

"And it's worth giving me money upfront, so I don't call the cops?"

"Yes."

Ransom must have read my mind about being so close to him. "You can be in the office most of the time. Away from us out here. Plus, none of us will care if you need to study or whatever when there's nothing to do."

"And I could have a flexible schedule around classes?"

"Come and go as you please."

"Why are you offering this?"

"Because the person that hit the statue doesn't deserve any more punishments. At least not this time. Plus, we could use the help around here. We like working on cars, not organizing offices."

"Do you own the shop?"

"Not entirely. I bought thirty percent of it. Fox owns another thirty, and Luca owns the rest. He's the one who started it but is looking to retire at some point. He isn't around much anymore."

"And none of them will care?"

"Quinn, I wouldn't offer you anything I couldn't deliver on. The job's yours if you don't call to report anyone about the statue."

"Can I think about it?"

He huffed and ran a dirty hand through his hair, making it even more messy, "Fine, but you can't call until you give me the final answer."

Something about his tone made me wonder what he would do if I declined and decided to call. Even worse, some part of me wanted to find out.

"Deal."

He was still leaning on the car. His emotions masked again as I tried to figure out what he could be thinking.

"Can I have my phone now?"

He reached into his back pocket and pulled out my phone before handing it over. "Cute case."

The back of my phone showed a skeleton reaper crushing a heart in its hand. I didn't always go for anything so dark, but it felt fitting at the time. The more I let myself be myself, the more I realized that I liked those things.

"Looks like you got a bit of darkness in you, Kitten."

His face still wasn't giving anything away, but I was surprised he had had the phone in his pocket since before I came. He knew I would come for it. I guess who wouldn't come for their phone, but the thought of him sliding it into his pocket this morning unnerved me.

I grabbed the phone, my fingers brushing against his, and stepped back, "Thanks." I stood awkwardly for a moment before taking off, not quite running but not quite walking through the maze of cars and toolboxes.

Fox had stopped, a wicked smirk on his beautiful face as I went by, "Bye, Quinn," he said, and I waved back, realizing that he did know me. So many people knew my face after the video, and the thought of them getting to know me after seeing that always made me sick.

I kept my pace until I was safe and back in my dorm, the door shut and locked behind me. I flopped on my bed, staring at the ceiling as I tried to decide what to do next.

SEVEN

QUINN

IT WASN'T another hour when Josie burst in. "Oh my god, Quinn," she yelled, "I can't believe you left last night. It ended up being so much fun. I wish you would have stayed."

"Hi to you too, and yeah, I was better off coming back here. After the show Tyler put on, I wasn't up for staying any longer."

"I know. He can be such a prick sometimes. If it helps, Sarah and I both went off on him for what he said. She said he better start being nicer, or she would have to reconsider dating him. I mean, not that I believe her because they have been together for so long now, but still, she made it sound so believable. Did you end up getting your Uber? I walked out to check, but you were gone, so I assumed."

"Um, no. Not exactly." I said as she jumped down onto her own bed.

"Were you okay? Why didn't you call? Wait, what does that mean, and does it have anything to do with you not being here earlier?"

"Yes, but not in the way you are thinking."

"Come on." She shrieked in excitement, "What happened?"

I told her the short version, skipping over the part of Ransom flirting with me and my body responding in the worst possible way.

I also decided to leave out the part about one of them hitting the statue. It seemed like a bad idea to tell her at this point. She hated them and wouldn't hesitate to call them in herself. I know I had almost done the same thing, but now it was my leverage for possibly getting a job. I didn't need her to be the one to call, get the reward money, and then ruin my chances for work.

"Ransom Ward almost ran you over and then stole your phone?"

"He did almost run me over, not on purpose. I was technically in the street, and my phone dropped out of my pocket. He didn't steal it."

"And now you're what? Going to work for him?" Her face twisted into disgust, as though the idea of me working for him was nauseating.

I shrugged, "I don't know. I'm thinking about it. I need the money, and it does sound flexible, which is perfect. I mean, he felt bad about almost hitting me and was nice enough to offer me a job. It can't be that bad."

"Yeah, felt bad because he didn't want to be sued and have anyone look into his life. You'd be working at a dirty old car shop with those guys around. It's not like they are the most stand-up group of people. What if they do something to you, or you're caught up in something illegal, or they hurt you? Aren't you a little too freaked out to work there?"

"Not as much as I thought I would be. I can deal with Ransom, and the other guy, Fox, seems pretty nice."

"Fox?"

"Yeah, his friend from high school, the blonde golden boy who was always with Ransom. I guess he owns part of the garage now."

"Oh, yeah. I remember now. Fox is a stupid name. Honestly, Ransom is too."

"What?" I stared back. It wasn't like Josie to be so blatantly rude. She was bullied through high school and never seemed to want to bully anyone back. But, then again, she never liked people who didn't do what they were told, and that was the epitome of that crew.

"A dumb name, if you ask me. Like a guy named Fox or Ransom isn't going to be like CEOs or like golfing with one, you know? Could you imagine? Really though, do you think you should take a job there? Is it even safe?"

"I don't feel like they would hurt me or let anything happen while I'm there. Ransom said I would mostly be in the office while they are out working on the cars."

I knew Josie didn't have to worry about money. Her parents were on the high end of wealth. Her home was on the wealthiest road in the county, and her parents paid for every penny of her college education. She knew I wasn't in the same place, though. I didn't have the money to buy new clothes or go out to eat every night. She tried to be nice and pay for me, but I turned her down most nights, not wanting to be pitied, as I ordered the cheapest thing I could find. Lately, it meant she was going with Sarah instead of me. The sting of losing time with your best friend to another person was hard, but I knew it was my own fault. I couldn't afford to keep up with her.

"Are you worried about me working or just working there?"

She shrugged. "It seems like a waste to have you working at all when we have classes, but especially there. We've both heard the rumors, Quinn. They aren't the most stand-up group. Couldn't you try the country club? You would meet a lot of cute guys there, plus I bet the tips would be insane if you showed off some of this." She wiggled her boobs and laughed before looking at me like the answer was obvious.

Her disgust at the idea of me working at all was surprising.

"You know they wouldn't hire me at the country club, Josie." Those jobs were reserved for the rich kids, and even with Josie doing me a favor, I doubted they would give me a job.

"Fine, but there have to be other ways to get money. I don't want you getting involved with the wrong people again. Even if you don't feel like they would do anything bad, you know you can't rely on that. Look where it got you last time." She was moving around the room, changing into a new dress and grabbing her things. Anger flared, and I tamped it down, reminding myself that she was just looking out for me.

"I know. Thanks for looking out, but this is different." Somewhere in this conversation, I realized I was taking the job, even with Ransom being...Ransom. I needed a flexible job and money.

"Do you want to go out with Sarah and me tonight? We're going to some axe-throwing place and then out for sushi. She said some of the guys are coming, and they are cute." She wiggled her eyebrows and went back to fixing her hair and makeup.

I mentally added the cost of the night, hitting at least forty dollars before I stopped, not going any further.

"I can't tonight. I have a lot of work to catch up on before Monday. Especially with this job. Not to mention, I don't want to run into Tyler again."

It sucked that Josie had chosen Sarah as her new close friend, mainly because Tyler hung around them. I know Josie said she tried to stand up for me and tell him to stop, but it didn't always feel like enough. She knew what he had done and still tolerated being around him. I knew it wasn't her or Sarah's fault, but it still felt wrong.

"I get it. If you change your mind, text me, and we'll come grab you."

"Thanks, have fun."

She waved, and the door shut behind her, leaving me in a peaceful silence.

I turned over, grabbing my phone.

Ransom's name flashed across my screen with a new text. I had never added his name or number to my phone.

I clicked it open. There was just one word in a new text thread.

> Ransom: Kitten.

> Quinn: Stop calling me that.

> How is your name and number in my phone?

> I thought you might need it so I added it.

> How did you get into my phone?

> Is that important?

> Yes, and why do you keep calling me that?

> You look sweet and cute, but I know you have claws. And I know you would use them.

> It seems like a nickname I should be insulted by.

> Are you?

> I don't know.

> Then it stays until you know.

> How do you know I would use them?

> Feels like you're holding back.

> Holding back my claws?

> Holding back using them when you want to.

The next text almost gave me an orgasm where I sat, filling my mind with every dirty fantasy about him that I thought I had buried.

> Maybe I will get to feel your claws one day

The thought of getting to rake my hands down Ransom's back, the chance to see him completely naked, every muscle and tattoo on display. I groaned, annoyed that my crush had come back with a vengeance. Now it wasn't just an innocent crush on a guy across the parking lot. It was a full-blown, take-me-to-bed-and-make-my-legs-useless type of crush, which was even more upsetting. I should have learned my lesson.

I didn't even know what to say, all of it too overwhelming.

Until a different reality hit me.

Was he saying this because of the video? Because he thought I would be easy to get with, especially if we were working around each other? It was the best explanation I could find for his sudden interest in flirting with me.

> Don't cats usually go for the face?

> I guess if they feel intimidated. Do I intimidate you?

> No.

Every word I said felt loaded now, but I wasn't going to tell him the truth. He intimidated me, turned me on, made me angry, and I didn't know how to deal with any of it.

> Then I guess I don't have to worry about my face.

Moments went by before another text appeared.

> Are you going to work with us?

> I haven't decided.

> Yes, you have.

What do you mean?

I think you knew the answer before you even walked out of here. I just couldn't figure out what that answer was.

Oh, so you can read my mind?

No. I can't ever figure out what you're thinking

I could say the same about you.

Then I guess we are on a fair battlefield. So, are you?

I didn't say anything for minutes, watching the clock change as my answer sat there, ready to send. My fingers found the nerve and sent it.

Yes.

Good.

When do I start?

Monday?

I have class till two.

Fine. Come for me after.

I sucked in a breath, not able to stop more dirty thoughts from flooding my mind.

What am I supposed to wear?

I suddenly wish we had uniforms.

Whatever is comfortable and you don't mind if it gets dirty.

What if I'm late?

I worried I wouldn't be able to make it that fast. My class let out at 1:45, and the walk had to be about twenty-five minutes from the building where my classes were.

> I'll wait.

Another text came through immediately.

> I'll be nice and hold off on the punishments and spanking comments.

> Why the sudden interest in flirting with me?

> There's nothing sudden about it.

It seemed pretty sudden to me. Yesterday, it seemed like the worst thing when he had to drive me home, and now each text seemed more flirtatious than the last.

> Well, you need to stop.

> Why?

> Because we work together now. It's not going to happen.

Minutes ticked by without a response.

> I don't think it was going to either way.

I couldn't say anything else, not knowing what he meant or what I felt. If he knew it wasn't going to happen, was he really only messing with me? Maybe it was all a harmless joke, the flirting and sudden interest in me a way to pass the time and stop me from calling to turn them in. Maybe it was just them as a group. It seemed like flirting was Fox's second nature too.

I shook my head. They were a group of hot guys. Of course, they would flirt with any girl who came around. I would have to be prepared for that now, too.

I had agreed to the job, though, and now, come Monday, I was going to be stuck in the same building as Ransom. It was a good experience for me, though. I hoped to run my own business one day, and looking into a real, running one would be great. It might give me a chance to see what I like too. I had been so busy surviving for so long that hobbies had never been a priority for me. Plus, I could stay on top of homework while making money.

I tried to remind myself why I was doing this by looking at my bank account again, but the negative balance only made it worse.

Ransom had texted me again.

> For saying yes.

It came along with an app notification that he had sent me the five hundred dollars he offered as a starting bonus. If he couldn't read my mind, he was really close.

Within a minute, the money was in my account.

It wasn't enough to cover all my upcoming tuition due, but it at least got the account out of the red.

I could hardly believe it.

I had a job, the money back in my bank account, and now I had a front-row view of Ransom every day.

Even though there were downsides, it was hard to think of them as I drifted off to sleep.

EIGHT

QUINN

Sunday came and went, my anxiety climbing as I went to classes on Monday. I sat watching the clock tick by as two o'clock came faster and faster.

Before I could think about it again, my last class was over, and it was time to go. I took a deep breath and forced myself down the street towards Hollows Garage. I knew about most of the crew, but I had never met them all face-to-face, and the thought of meeting them now was making my stomach churn and my hands' sweat. I didn't know what to expect from all of them, including Ransom. They were intimidating enough from afar, but now I was going to have to see and meet them all up close.

I made the walk in twenty minutes, my stomach still in knots, but at least I would only be five minutes late on my first day. I walked in the same way I had before and ran into Fox again.

"Hey!" he yelled. "You showed up."

I froze. "I was supposed to, wasn't I?"

My whole body screamed to run, telling me I was somehow being set up. I vowed never to fall into a trap again, and now I worried that's exactly what I found. The way he said the words was like it was a trick. I stepped back, but Fox stepped forward.

"Of course. Ransom said you'd be coming to help us out, but I gotta admit, most of us didn't think you would be crazy enough to agree and show up." He smiled, his bright, god-like smile blinding me for a moment as I caught my breath.

He pulled me in, tucking me under his arm as we walked inside. "So you showed up to try to help us get our shit straight, then?"

"Something like that," I said, sending him a smile. Somehow, I didn't feel uncomfortable tucked under his arm. It felt like the older brother I had always hoped for, keeping me safe and comforted while I walked into a nerve-wracking situation.

We walked through the garage like that, his arm keeping me close as he pointed ahead.

"We were having a little meeting," he said, leaning down, "about you, actually. The guys are all in here. Scout's still in school, but she'll be here in an hour or so, and Jax is out picking up some parts. He should be back around the same time." He pulled open the door to what I assumed was the office and pulled me inside.

I found Ransom's eyes as soon as I stepped in the door. He was sitting with his black boots kicked onto the table, his blue eyes darkening when he saw me. "Look who I found wandering in off the street," Fox said proudly.

"Well damn, Ransom, you weren't lying." One of them said before turning to me, "I can't believe Ransom didn't scare you off. The guy has a scowl that would make anyone turn the other way."

Ransom glared at him then, making the guy smile more.

"That's Kye. He was on my side about you not showing up," Fox said.

"Fox," Ransom said, his voice low. "She's an employee now.

Maybe take your hands off her? Do we need to have a meeting about sexual harassment?"

Fox pulled me in close with a laugh before letting me go, "Hey, I was just happy she showed up. This place is a mess. Well, in here, at least."

"The garage is in perfect order," Kye said.

"Quinn, you've met Fox and now Kye. This is Dante." He pointed to the guy next to him, and I waved.

Dante stared for a moment. "I honestly didn't think you would show up either," he said, breaking a smile. "I didn't think he was charming enough to convince a girl to come work at a dirty garage." He turned back to Ransom. "We done in here? I have to run out."

"Yeah. We're good."

The three guys filed out, leaving me alone in the room with Ransom. I took a deep breath, trying not to show how nervous I was. He stood, giving me a better view of him. He was wearing the same mechanic jumpsuit as the other day, but it was tied at his waist, with a white tank top covering his chest. It stretched and flexed, giving a perfect view of every muscle and tattoo on his arms. I could tell he had been working all day with black marks covering every part of him.

I thought back to his texts from Friday night, and it was like a magnet in the room, forcing me to move closer to him, begging me to touch him. I wasn't lying when I said it couldn't happen, though. I couldn't let myself get closer to another guy that looked and acted like him. He fell right into the bad boy category, and I've been there before.

The room stayed silent, his eyes raking up and down my body. I wore a pair of jeans and a ripped t-shirt. It was comfortable, but I still felt like I looked good, and I had to admit, I wanted to look good right now.

"You showed up," he said, walking around the table towards

me. I took a step back at the same time, knowing if he got any closer, I would reach for him. My hesitation made him stop.

"You held up your end of the bargain. I'll hold up mine. I'm just glad it wasn't a trap," I said.

He cocked an eyebrow. "What? Why would it be a trap?"

I mentally scolded myself. I never tried to never give those thoughts away, not wanting anyone to know how insecure I was to fall back into another trap. "I've fallen into one before," I said, looking away.

He nodded. "Yes?" he asked, waiting for more.

"Yes, so I'm always watching to make sure I don't fall into another one."

He nodded again. "That isn't going to happen here."

"I don't know that."

"You do now. If anyone tries to lure you into any trap or situation that makes you uncomfortable, let me know. You will never see their face again."

"While I appreciate the thought, I don't think that's possible."

"No one here is going to mess with you, and if they did, I could absolutely make sure you never see their face again." He had stepped closer again. This time, though, he didn't seem to be holding himself back. Instead, he reached up, his knuckles running down my jaw.

I couldn't stop, leaning my head back and exposing my neck to him. A deep rumble came from his chest as he stepped back and dropped his hand, not hiding the snarl across his lips. It was like ice after heat, the loss of his touch burning my skin and the obvious loathing he had for touching me. I pulled my shoulders back. It wasn't my problem if he hated it. He's the one who touched me.

He stepped around the desk. "Let me show you around and show you what we need help with."

"Okay, yeah, let's go."

He walked me through the garage first, giving me a more in-depth look at each bay before heading back to the office.

"The books are always balanced, but we need all this sorted." He pointed to a desk with stacks of papers, each one higher than the last.

"What are all of these?"

"Part orders, invoices, quotes. I don't know. Everything in between. We need it sorted somehow."

"Got it."

"Come get me if you need anything." He went to stomp out the door but stopped and turned back. "Get me," he growled, "not Fox."

And with that, he slammed the door behind him, the music from the garage muffled.

I looked around at the mess. There was a lot to do, but I realized how hard it would be to work knowing a blue-eyed boy in boots was right on the other side of the door.

I groaned out loud and turned back to the pile. The only way I would forget about him out there was by remembering how much work I had to do in here.

NINE

RANSOM

By Thursday, I was going out of my fucking mind. Five full days of Quinn being in my space was putting me on edge. I woke up every day, and the first thing to come to mind was that I would see her that day. Excitement and dread would fill me each time, too. Then I would have to spend ten annoying minutes telling my cock to calm down.

I didn't want her around, even though I was the one to bring her there. I reminded myself this was just to save Kye from any more trouble with the police and not because of anything I felt. This year alone, he'd been arrested three times, and I knew they wouldn't go easy on him if he was arrested for crashing into the statue, not to mention the bad attention it would bring to our business.

At the pace we were going, we were making a name for ourselves by building fast cars. I didn't think it coming out that we also wrecked private property while street racing would help us. Kye's banged-up car would have to be enough punishment for now. That was the only reason she was here. I couldn't have her call the police about us. I needed to keep her here and happy until the entire threat of calling us in was gone.

CHAPTER NINE   51

The reasons why weren't enough, though, when I had to watch her walk in every day, her head down as she ran into the office. My mind and dick didn't care about why she was there, just that she was right there for my viewing pleasure. She was still scared as hell of me, or at least acted like it. I didn't think anyone could act that good, though, not all day, every day, so I had to guess that she was just hateful and scared. Then when I texted her, pushing for any sign she didn't hate me, she made it very clear there wasn't a chance in hell for me to get anywhere with her. I grabbed for a tool as Quinn caught my eye.

She had finally emerged from the office.

Her long brown hair was almost red in the sunlight, and I didn't know why the fuck she looked that good in a pair of jeans and a t-shirt. She stopped to watch each of the guys working on a car, her eyes running over them, lingering for a second and then moving on to the next. I flexed my fist around the wrench in my hand. I don't know what any of them did to deserve her looking at them so sweetly.

Her eyes fell on me, and immediately her expression turned, her lips tightening into a frown. I didn't move, didn't smile, didn't do a thing until her eyebrow cocked up.

"Problem?"

"I just realized I have been here a few days, looking over all these parts you all buy, and I still don't get what you do."

I leaned against the car I had been working on. "We build and fix cars for racing mostly, but still take non-racing cars a decent amount. Some older stuff that other garages don't want to deal with."

"Why don't they want to deal with them?"

"Old parts, old bolts, pain in the ass parts to find. We don't care. We've needed the clients and the money, so it's fine by us."

"You need the money? Based on what I've seen, the garage is doing great, more than great even."

"It is now, but it hasn't always been that way. Clawing your way up the industry isn't easy. Not many people want to take a chance on a no-name garage run by some young guys."

She nodded. "I could see that. So you guys do this all legally, then?"

My eyebrows furrowed. "Legally? Yes." I couldn't hide my smile. She really did still seem scared of us and what we did here. "What did you think we were doing?"

"I don't know. There are rumors of all the illegal things you do. I didn't know if this was some sort of chop shop or hideout for stolen items."

I couldn't hide the shock that shot through me. "You've been sitting in the office for almost a week, and you thought we were running some illegal ring of stolen cars? You didn't even say anything. Yet, you still agreed to work here?"

She shrugged, but I could see she was trying to act relaxed about it. "Well, I didn't know for sure, and I needed the money."

I clicked my tongue. "See how easy it is to fall into a life of crime? The only thing we do now that is a little on the wrong side of the law is race."

"Now?"

I shot her a devious smile. Maybe keeping her a little scared of me was the best chance to get out of this without falling apart at her feet. "We can talk about that another day."

She threw her arms across her chest with a huff. "What if I want to know now?"

"Then that's your problem, because I'm not talking about it now." I heard the edge in my voice and kept going. "You're here to work, not pry into our past."

"Yeah, you have a big hang-up about the past, don't you?"

"Maybe I don't like to rehash shitty memories." Now, I wasn't talking about the illegal things we have done. I was talking about her. "Maybe I don't like to be judged by what others say and do. I think you, of all people, would agree with that."

The hurt was visible across her face. She knew what I was talking about now. If she wanted to believe the rumors about me, maybe she should think that I believed the rumors about her.

Not that I did.

I knew what Logan had done that night and that she hadn't agreed to it. The asshole had taken advantage of her trust in him and used it against her. The only thing I had never figured out was why. Logan had already been popular, especially after joining the ring of golden boys. Half the school knew he was sleeping with any girl that would take him. It never made sense to me, but I had also never talked to Quinn about it.

I knew she was going to explode, her lips pursing together and cheeks turning red. She was mad at me, and for the first time, I was happy about it. At least her being mad this time was for something I actually did.

"You know what, Ransom? Just because I wasn't perfect doesn't mean you were. I know the rumors about you, too, so fuck off."

I took one step towards her, "You know the rumors about me, don't confuse that with knowing me, Kitten. The things I know about you are facts, not rumors. Some are even on video." As soon as the words left my mouth, I regretted them. I was so focused on pushing my own feelings away that I lost control of my mouth. I had never even watched the video. I didn't care to see it then or now.

Only curse words could form in my mind as her eyes went wide. She spun on her heel and walked back into the office, grabbing her things and storming out of the garage. I watched her stalk out, frozen in place.

"Fuck," I yelled, throwing the tool from my hand and hearing it bounce off the brick wall. "Fuck," I yelled again, turning to watch her.

I wanted to push her away from me, not hurt her.

"What was that?" Fox asked, keeping a safe distance.

"That was me fucking up and Quinn possibly not coming back."

"Ransom," He scolded, "you're kidding, right? We like Quinn being here, and she's killing it by keeping up with the office."

"Not kidding." Was all I said, running a dirty hand through my hair, ready to pull it out of my head.

"You better fix it. I'm not dealing with anyone new coming in, and having this place sorted has made my life easier."

"Fucking great," I mumbled, watching Scout's car pull in.

She walked in and stopped near Fox, looking us both over. "What's wrong?"

"Ransom scared Quinn off. She just ran out of here, and he doesn't think she'll come back."

Scout's face fell, "What? Are you kidding me, Ransom? I liked having her here!" Scout yelled, and her hands started flying as she spoke, something I knew only happened when she was super pissed. "You scare off the only other girl who has cared to come around and help us? Not only that, she's nice to me. She doesn't make fun of me and doesn't care that I hang around smelly boys all day."

The disappointment on her face was too much. Scout was young, still in high school, and just like Kye, we took her in as our little sister years ago. I would be the first to admit that most days, I forgot she was still a teenage girl. A teenage girl who, for the first time, had another girl hanging around with us. A teenage girl who was scary as hell when she was pissed.

"Hey, we're not smelly," Fox said.

"You are too," Scout said and then turned her sights on me. "You better make sure she comes back. I don't have any friends at school because I hang around you all, and what? Now I won't even have a friend here? No, you don't get to mess that up just because you used to have a crush on her and don't like her here now."

"How do you know I used to like Quinn?" My eyes narrowed as I turned to glare at Fox.

He shrugged, "She beats me up until I tell her the good gossip," he said, pulling her into him and messing with her hair.

I couldn't hide the loud huff, trying to sort out my thoughts. "Fine. I'll try to make sure she comes back, but you can't be mad if it doesn't work."

"Yes, I can." Scout pointed at me and turned, walking to her bay and getting to work.

I shook my head. "Dealing with her is getting harder and harder."

Fox laughed, "We are the ones who helped teach her to stand up for herself."

I let out a strangled laugh. "I guess we did. I just didn't realize she would turn on us."

"Hey, I'm on her side. You messed it up. You fix it."

"Yeah, yeah. Leave me alone now. I'll do what I can."

I didn't know how I was going to try to fix it. Aside from cars, I wasn't known for fixing things. Breaking them, sure, but fixing them? Not really.

I went back to work, hoping something would come to me.

The part that bothered me the most was the thought of her not coming back here felt like a knife to the stomach. I wanted her to come back, and I wanted her to not hate me.

Now I just had to figure out how to make that happen.

———

I WENT HOME HOURS LATER, showering and finding something frozen to make before calling it a day. It was ten by the time I cleaned up and got into bed. Most days that I worked this late, I passed out, but sleep wasn't coming now, and I knew why.

Once again, Quinn Carter was taking over my life.

I grabbed my phone, typing out the words I so rarely used.

> Ransom: I'm sorry.

I sent it, not knowing if she would even reply. Minutes went by, and I stared into the dark.

Quinn: Right.

> I am. I was being an asshole.

Ok.

> Ok? That's all I get?

I don't think you deserve any more than that.

> Fair. I was pushing you and then pushed too far.

A bit.

> Does it help if I let you know I've never seen the video and as far as I know, nobody on the crew has?

That does help. It's hard walking around not knowing who has and hasn't watched it. Sometimes I can tell by how they look at me, though.

> I'm not interested in watching anything like that.

At least that's one good thing about you.

> Ouch.

> I guess I deserve that this time. I won't bring it up again.

That would be preferred.

> Does that mean you'll be coming back tomorrow? I'm pretty sure if you don't, I'll be getting my ass kicked by a small, angry teenage girl.

Scout mad?

> Absolutely pissed.

Then I guess I'll come back. For her. I'm growing to like the rest of them, too.

> I'm going to guess that doesn't include me.

No, it doesn't.

> So I guess I can't say that I'd rather you be here with me?

My phone was quiet as the minutes dragged on.

No, you can't say that.

> Because I'm not allowed to flirt with you, but Fox can.

Yes.

I groaned. I hated this. I wanted to never see her again, knowing she didn't want me anywhere near her, and at the same time, I needed her in bed with me. I needed to touch her, kiss her, and find some relief from the desperation that kept growing.

> I'm thinking about firing Fox.

At this point, I was only half joking, the deranged part of me wondering if Quinn would warm up to me if Fox was gone for a while. I knew it was stupid, and I knew it wouldn't work, but damn if I didn't wonder.

> You can't fire him when he owns part of it.

> Fine, I'll ask him politely to get the fuck out until you like me more.

> We would never see Fox again.

I smiled. It was the honest response I had known was coming, but hated it. I rolled over and hit the pillow. I did what needed to be done. Quinn was coming back to work, and everyone else would stay happy now. I didn't need to text her more and didn't need to learn more about how much she hated me. As the days went on, I started to wonder if she actually did like Fox, but I didn't want to think of that possibility for too long.

> Not a good plan, then.

> Goodnight Ransom.

> Yea, yea goodnight.

I threw my phone back, and something in my mind solidified.

One night, Quinn would be saying goodnight next to me in my bed. I wouldn't stop until I was the only one she could ever dream about touching her.

TEN

QUINN

THE NEXT WEEK and a half went by in a blur of classes and working at the garage, trying to learn everything I needed to do. I had fallen into a comfortable enough routine, walking in, waving to everyone, and then shutting myself in the office.

I had had time to get to know everyone now, Scout quickly becoming my favorite. She was sweet and cute but scrappy, keeping up with the guys better than some of the guys even did. She was helpful, too, giving me tips and information when I felt dumb for not knowing what a car part was or what it did. I had managed to avoid most interactions with Ransom but had to ask him enough questions that I still had to get close to him every day.

I walked in on Thursday to all of them louder than usual. I tried to keep my head down as I walked into the office, but Fox grabbed me, dragging me against his side.

"What's up, Fox?" I asked, looking up at him.

He rested his head on mine. "Just saying hello."

I met Ransom's glare. If someone could throw daggers with a look, that was it. I debated pulling away but thought against it. If this was some sort of whose dick was bigger contest, I wasn't getting involved, so I leaned into him instead.

Fox leaned back against the car, letting my shoulders go as his hand trailed down my arm and grabbed my hand. "So Quinn, you coming with us tonight?" He swung it around, playing cute with his bright smile.

"Coming with you, where?"

"The races are every Thursday," Jax said. "We'll all head up there later tonight."

"Oh, no. I don't have to go with you guys." I dared to glance at Ransom again. His eyes fixated on Fox's hand holding mine. It made me itch to drop it, but I didn't dare.

"You work around these cars all day now. You should know what we do with them," Ransom said. His tone wasn't friendly, but it wasn't rude. I hated that even up close, I couldn't figure out what he was thinking. I always thought it was the distance of the high school parking lot that tripped me up, but even here, I couldn't figure it out.

"Yeah, you'd love it. We meet up with other racers and go for a few hours. It's fun. Plus, you could watch me race. The ladies love watching me race," Fox said.

I rolled my eyes but couldn't help but laugh. "And what? I watch you race your car once, and I'm going to fall head over heels in love with you?"

He dropped my hand and raised his in the air. "Listen, I'm just trying to warn you."

"Wow, well, thank you for the warning. I'll think about it." I shook my head at him, heading for the office and trying to avoid Ransom's eyes, but his words stopped me.

"You'll ride with me if you decide to come," he said, the tone soft in the loud garage.

For a moment, I couldn't say anything. It was like whiplash, from glaring at me one moment to telling me I was going to ride with him the next.

"I'll let you know," I said, and he nodded, his jaw flexing as he tightened each muscle.

I walked into the office, shutting the door behind me. I made it to the desk before I thumped my head down. I thought working around him would be easier, but it was proving to be a lot harder than I had planned.

Two hours went by as I tried to force myself to focus on the papers in front of me. Finally, the door banged open, and Scout walked in, dropping her bag on the floor and jumping onto the couch. She had made a habit of coming in here after school ended and before getting ready to work.

"I heard you're coming with us to the races tonight," she said with a big smile on her face.

"Who told you that?"

"Fox."

"Of course he did. I said I would think about it."

"What's to think about? Fast cars, hot guys, plus your best friend will be there," she said. I furrowed my brows, knowing she couldn't mean Josie.

"Me. Duh. Seriously though, please come with us. The guys are always swarmed by girls, but then other guys know they aren't allowed around me, or all my big brothers will come for them like wolves. So then I end up just sitting alone half the night while they race. Now I don't have my car, so I don't even get to race." She pouted, her lip sticking out with a frown.

I tried to ignore her comment about the guys being swarmed by girls. "I guess it would be cool to see everyone race." I smiled. "Are there really hot guys there?"

She groaned. "I could almost drool. There's one guy there. He drives this old muscle car, and I swear he's the hottest guy I have ever seen." A picture of Ransom came to mind, making me doubt her statement.

"Alright," I said, laughing. "I'm sold. I'll go since my best friend asked nicely."

She jumped up. "Yes. I promise it won't be boring. We'll have fun."

"I don't think it's possible to be bored around you, Scout."

Her smile widened. "Isn't that the truth?" She was heading back into the garage when I stopped her. "Scout, wait."

"What's up?

"I have a really girly question for you."

"Well, that is one statement I thought I would never hear in this office. I'm listening."

"What the hell do I wear to a night of street racing?"

————

IT WAS ALMOST seven when my panic started setting in. Everyone had left and come back, changing into cleaner clothes, and were now checking over their cars. Scout bounded back into the office just as I leaned back in the chair.

"You ready?" she said.

Ready was a relative term. I had been ready for hours, but now I was ready to sit in the chair for the rest of the night and not move.

Scout had told me she was wearing leggings and a hoodie, so I decided to wear the same. I had ran back and grabbed my favorite pair of leggings and a cropped t-shirt with a hoodie. I didn't like to brag, but the leggings made my ass look great, and I needed the confidence boost.

"Yeah," I said, trying to gather any ounce of courage I could find.

"Ransom said you're riding with him?"

"Uh, sure. Unless you want to, I can ride with whoever."

"Oh no, I don't care. I'll ride with Fox," she said, meaning it. "Kye is riding with Jax tonight along with Dante since his car broke down."

"Alright then. I guess I'll go with Ransom."

As though he had heard his name, he stepped inside, and I was losing every thought in my mind. He had on dark jeans, his boots, and a hoodie and jacket overtop. His hair was still damp from a shower and was a mess across his forehead. Every part of him screamed trouble, but my body didn't care when all it was screaming was, "fuck me".

"Fox is waiting on you, Scout." He smiled, and she smacked him on the arm, filled with excitement as she ran out.

"Is this every Thursday?"

"As long as the weather's good, yeah."

"And Scout is always this excited?"

A real smile broke on his face. "Every single week, but she's extra excited you're coming tonight."

I nodded, loving Scout and how welcoming she was to me.

"Are you ready?"

I stood, turning my back to him and grabbing my bag and hoodie.

"Shit, Quinn, is that what you're wearing?"

I glanced down. I didn't think the outfit was bad, the crop top showing a design of a knife and skull, the gray leggings going all the way down to my shoes. "Oh, no, I have a hoodie." I held it up.

"Does it cover your ass?"

My eyebrows shot up. "Is this part of your sexual harassment training?"

"No, it's just those leggings. I just mean," he drew in a ragged breath, "you look great." He ran a hand through his hair and mumbled something about causing an accident. My smile grew, and I grabbed my stuff, heading out the door ahead of him. Something in me shook, a satisfied feeling filling me that, even for a second, I affected him.

He locked up as I headed to the car. The passenger side door was open, and I didn't say anything as I got in. I had been in his car, but it all felt different now. The new dynamic changed everything around me.

The others were in the parking lot, revving their cars next to us. Ransom jumped in and leaned over towards me. I sucked in a breath as he reached up behind me, pulling the harness-style seatbelt down over me.

His hands worked fast as he clicked it together. "I figured it would be faster if I did it. We're going to lose if we don't hurry."

"Lose what?"

In the next second, Fox took off, and then Jax. Ransom looked over at me with a genuine smile. "Ready?"

"Do I have a choice?"

"I mean —" he started, but I stopped him.

"Just go!"

Part of me wanted to watch him drive, and I realized I even trusted him to drive fast. They had been racing around the past two weeks for me to know that Ransom knew what he was doing behind the wheel of his car.

He didn't need me to say it again, shooting from the parking lot and shifting the gears faster than I knew they could move. I watched his feet, pushing the clutch as one hand shifted and the other steered. It seemed like too much to coordinate at once, but he was doing it with ease.

I had never seen anyone do this up close, but I couldn't imagine he was bad at this. It didn't take long for him to catch up to the others. The car screamed underneath us, catching me off guard. I didn't think we could go faster, but Ransom did. The empty road was enough of an invitation.

He only slowed when we reached the town, not saying a word as all three of them slowed down. They turned, heading towards the end of town that I knew led to miles and miles of nothing.

"It's not much farther."

I didn't say it, but I suddenly cared even less about the races.

I could watch him drive all night, the warmth of the car more soothing than I would have thought, even at high speeds.

The thought of speed has always made me feel on edge, made me think of deadly statistics and death itself, but being in the car that was flying down the road wasn't the same. The risk-averse voice in my head quieted. The smooth skill of his hands turning me on more than they should have.

He turned down another road and hit a bump. I sucked in a breath, regretting my previous thoughts as I worried the car would be out of control in seconds. But the only thing that happened was Ransom's hand grabbing my thigh.

"We're good, just a small bump."

"Small?"

"Ok, yeah, it's a bit of a jump at this point, but I got it." And he did. The car was still moving down the road with ease, and he still held my thigh.

I stopped my hips before they could move any further. I was dangerously close to pushing them up, making his hand slip higher. I wasn't going to do it, though. I wouldn't let him have the satisfaction of knowing I actually wanted his hands on me.

He looked over with a grin, and every part of me flamed with embarrassment, hoping that he couldn't read my mind.

I didn't want to get myself into trouble with a guy like him, yet here I was, ready to beg him to move his hand higher up my leg.

He scowled and pulled his hand away as though I slapped him and put it back on the shifter.

My attention snapped away as the sound of the races filled the world around us. Engines revved, shaking the ground, and music spilled from every direction.

"Like I said, it's a lot. So just stay by one of us," he said.

I couldn't say anything as we drove up. Cars lined the road, and I lost count, but there had to be at least a hundred of them here.

"Are all these cars racing tonight?"

"Probably not. More like half, maybe." My heart raced as he parked his car next to Fox. I started to unclip the harness and was about to slide out when a girl ran up to his car. She pulled the passenger side door open and yelled, "Ransom! Want to go f—" she stopped as she saw me. "Oh. I didn't see you there."

I know she hadn't. The tint on the windows keeping me hidden. I had seen her, though. She was beautiful, almost perfect, and she wanted to see if Ransom wanted to go do something that started with a big fat F. I didn't need to hear anymore to know what she meant.

I kicked my feet out, and she jumped back.

"Who are you?" she asked, crossing her arms and frowning. It was that sentence that made me decide I didn't like her. Like she couldn't believe I was getting out of Ransom's car, like I didn't deserve to be there, like I was invading her territory.

I didn't have to respond, though, because she turned her attention to Ransom, who had jumped out of the car and came over to the passenger side. I pushed around her. "I gotta go find Scout."

"Oh, good," she said. I glanced back once. The look on Ransom's face wasn't confusing now. Pure anger covered it, and I hoped it was as clear on mine.

Not that I had any claim on Ransom.

I had no right to be mad if he was with her or if she was waiting on him. For all I knew, he was dating her or told her to come to meet up with him once he got here. I went around Fox's car and found Scout.

"I thought you said what I was wearing was fine."

Her brows furrowed, looking over my leggings, t-shirt, and hoodie. "It is?"

"Then why did some girl just come up to the car all dressed up in some cute skirt and tank top?"

"Oh, yeah, a lot of the girls wear that type of stuff. I just figured you weren't into that. Most of them do it to try going home with the guys. Sorry, I didn't know. Is that what you wanted to do tonight? I would have let you know sooner." She sounded confused, and I felt for her.

"No, I don't want to go home with anyone but Ransom." Before I realized what I had said, she wiggled her eyebrows, and I heard what it sounded like, "No!" I swatted at her arm, "I just meant for the ride home! I'm going to my home!"

"Sure, sure." She said, "I'm sorry, Quinn. It didn't even occur to me that you might want to dress up. I would be dragged back to the garage if I dressed like that, so I didn't think about it."

"No, I'm not mad or anything. I just didn't know if this was a dressier place than I thought. I am not looking for any guy to go home with, so this is fine."

We moved to Fox's car, where everyone else was standing around.

"Come on, Quinn. Ready to see a few races?" Jax asked, patting an empty spot on the hood next to him.

I kept my eyes forward, not wanting to look back at Ransom again. "That's what we're here for, right? Are any of you racing today?"

"I might," Jax said.

"I may have a few broken parts on my car," Kye said with a smirk. "I was told to keep it in the garage for another week or two as we fix it."

"I can't believe you ran into that thing." Fox said, shaking his head, "You need to get better at driving."

Kye knocked into him. "Hey, I'm a great driver. The guy I was racing tried to run me off the road because he knew I would win."

"Right, right," Fox said, hiding his smile.

"What about you, Dante? Racing tonight?"

He shrugged. "My engine is blown, and I'm not able to fix it yet. Maybe in a few weeks or something."

"Don't you guys have an entire garage filled with parts? Is it that bad?" I said, looking around.

"Pretty bad," he said, his face falling. "I'm going to walk around. I'll be back."

We watched him go, and I winced. "Did I say something wrong?"

Jax shook his head. "No, he's just been having trouble with money, and then his car blew up. He's bummed about it."

"Well, I understand the money problem."

"Yeah. Ransom said you wanted to turn us in for the statue," Fox said, seeming to think it was funny now.

"Hey!" Kye yelled. "Do you know how much trouble I would get in if you ratted me out?"

"First, maybe don't wreck your car into expensive things," I said. "And second, I needed the money! You guys are trouble anyway."

They all laughed. "Maybe you shouldn't be hanging out with us then," Jax said. "Might turn into trouble yourself."

Another race went on, and everyone went quiet to watch. Then they erupted into noise again to talk about it. I sat silent, listening to everyone go on about what they did right and wrong.

"How does it work, then? Are you guys on a team or just race each other?"

"It depends on the night. Some nights are just for fun, like tonight, and some nights, we team up against other crews. The one with the most wins the entire night, and usually, a lot of money to go with it," Jax said.

"Oh, so you're a little race team, then?" I asked.

"Little? My heart." Jax clutched his chest. "First of all, our cars aren't little, and second, we have won at least seven nights in the past year and will come back after Kye or Dante's car is fixed and kick ass."

"You guys do this every week?"

"Close," Jax said. "things have been busy around the shop, though, so we've been here a little less now."

"So you work there, but don't own a part of it like Ransom and Fox?"

"No. When they decided to sign up for everything, I couldn't wrap my head around it. They took us all on, but I wasn't up for that level of responsibility. Honestly, don't know if I am now, but I think I'd like a chance at it."

"That I can understand. I couldn't imagine getting out of high school and jumping into a business."

"I'm trying more now, but I don't know if I'm ready for all that yet. Plus, I need time to get out and find the girls. Ransom and Fox are there all the time. They are never going to find a girl that way." He smiled, and Fox turned.

"Did you just say I can't find a girl?"

"That's exactly what he said," I said, laughing.

"Alright, ass, let's go. First one to get a number wins."

"Deal," Jax said as they both jumped up and started talking over their agreed-upon rules.

I turned back, seeing Ransom stalk over toward us, the girl not far behind him. I scrambled to grab Scout. "Come on. I need to see this hot guy in a muscle car."

She laughed in delight. "Fox. We're going. Text me before you race."

Fox nodded. "Don't lose each other."

Scout grabbed my hand and held it. "Thick as thieves."

"No thieving either," he said with a wink. Ransom had made it over, and I turned, pulling Scout into the crowd to disappear with me.

ELEVEN

QUINN

"Where do we go?" I asked, still holding on to Scout.

"This way. He parks over here a lot."

I followed her around to the other side of the track, where more cars were lined up. We weaved through them until we ended up directly across from the guys' cars. I could see them all crowded back around their cars, more people coming up to talk and hang out with them now.

Ransom scanned the crowd, the girl that was with him nowhere to be seen, and I wondered if he was looking for her now.

Scout kept me close until we came across an older, blacked-out muscle car.

"Wow," I said, and Scout nodded next to me.

"I know, it's beautiful."

I walked around it, looking over every detail of blacked-out metal. You wouldn't be able to see it parked at night.

Scout elbowed me in the side and I looked up.

Scout hadn't lied when she described him. He had to be a little older than me, the shadow of a beard on his face giving a dangerous edge to his jawline. His green eyes were bright against his dark hair. Every feature of him is as dark as the car.

"Oh wow," I mumbled to her. "You weren't kidding."

"Hey, Ryder," Scout said. "I was showing my friend here your car."

"It's beautiful," I said, turning back to it and away from him. I don't know what it was, but I didn't want to meet his eye when I spoke to him.

"I could say the same thing about you."

My face didn't hide my surprise when I realized why I didn't want to look at him. He was a charmer, a smooth-talker. He knew how good-looking he was, his voice deep and soothing. It was overwhelming.

He reached his hand out. "Ryder."

"Quinn." I took his hand and shook it. There was no shock to my body, nothing electric running through me. It unnerved me even more to know that this hot guy wasn't having any effect on me.

Wasn't that what I was into? These tall, dark, and handsome guys that came off as dangerous as this guy did. I always thought it was this general type I liked, but then shouldn't Ryder be making me feel some sort of way other than indifference?

I looked back at Ransom. I could almost see his tight jaw from here as he watched me, but he turned away to the races when I met his eye.

Just the difference between how I felt when Ransom touched me compared to Ryder. It was like comparing fire and static. The night and day difference wasn't even something I could understand.

The problem with Ransom's touch setting me on fire, though, was getting burned. I needed static. I needed someone who didn't make me lose my mind or make me want to rip my clothes off with just a touch. It didn't matter how I felt or didn't feel about Ryder. I needed someone who wouldn't ruin me again.

I turned to Ryder. "It's nice to meet you."

"You too. And good to see you, Scout."

Scout gave him a smile, not falling for his charm either, but it didn't mean we couldn't entertain it.

"Are you racing tonight?" I asked, watching another set of racers lined up at the starting line.

"Maybe. Haven't found someone I want to race yet."

"So are you on a team then like they are?"

His smile faltered, and he looked at Scout with a narrowing of his eyes I didn't like. I stepped closer to her as his face changed back, relaxed and happy.

"Sorry, you don't have to say. I'm just learning about all of this stuff."

"No, no. It's okay. I'm working on it. Seeing what my options are. What about you?"

"What about me?"

"Are you on their team now? Doesn't sound like you race."

"I don't, and no, not in the way you're thinking."

"So what, are you someone's girlfriend, then?"

"Also, no, just work at the garage."

He gave a half smile. "So, you're single then?"

"Single and unavailable," I said quickly. It wasn't a lie. I was single, but I didn't feel like I was looking for a boyfriend anytime soon, especially not with Ryder.

"A beautiful girl, single and unavailable? That doesn't make much sense."

"It does when I'm not looking for a guy like you."

He gave a light laugh. "Alright then, what about a ride? Just a ride. Try out my car?"

"No thanks. I don't think that's a good idea. Now or ever."

He was friendly and hot, obviously, but I wouldn't be interested in any date with him.

He stepped closer, Scout still by my side. "Sounds like a challenge."

"Nope. No challenge, just the truth."

His phone pinged, and he checked it, texting back and forth with someone.

"Looks like it's not up to you now, darling. I do love to win a pretty prize. I gotta go." He looked up, and I followed his gaze as he stared at an angry Ransom. He looked ready to kill.

"I'll talk to you soon, though," he said, grabbing both of our hands and kissing them.

I couldn't hide the surprise and a hint of disgust from etching across my face. Scout's expression matched mine as we walked away.

"That was—."

"Weird." Scout finished for me. "I'm assuming that was specifically for Ransom to see. Come on. We need to get over there."

"Why?"

"I think Ryder and Ransom are about to race, and that isn't a good thing."

TWELVE

RANSOM

I HAD STAYED BACK, fighting with Brooke to stay away from me. I knew I couldn't let her come any closer to Quinn and the crew, or it was going to look like I did want her there with me. I didn't even know she was going to be here, yet she seemed to know I would be.

Most girls I slept with were on the same page. There was no relationship, just sex, whenever we wanted. Brooke was different, though. We had the agreement, and then a week after we slept together, she started clinging to me like fucking glue. Everywhere I went, Brooke was there. Then she would come around the garage, hanging out like her car needed work. Somehow Brooke hadn't come around lately, and I had hoped that meant this was over. Now it seemed that Quinn thought I was on my way to have sex with Brooke in my car right now. The thought filled me with a dread I wasn't expecting.

I told Brooke so many times to leave me alone, but she refused to listen. Somehow it was supposed to be flattering if a girl stalked me, but not the other way around. Minutes ticked by, and Brooke rambled on. Normally, I wouldn't stand there and listen to it, but I needed her to understand that she couldn't come around me or any of us tonight. By the time I got her to walk away, Quinn was gone from the group, her and Scout taking off like the devil was chasing them.

I made it back to the car, sitting to watch whatever race was up and waiting for Quinn to get back. She rode with me. She would have to come back at some point.

I finally saw them across the track. They weaved through the crowd, and all I could focus on was her in those damn leggings. What was I even thinking? She was fucking hot, and at a race night full of guys who would kill to take her home, of course, she didn't have to come back. She could find a ride with anyone here. The next race started, the blur of noise and air clearing my mind for seconds before I noticed she had moved and was now standing directly across from us.

And of all fucking people, she was looking up at Ryder.

It felt like high school all over again. She looked at me with such a hateful look and then went off with another guy and looked at him like he could save the fucking world. A guy who, just like Logan, was a fucking ass. I accidentally fuck up some-how, so she goes to the biggest asshole here.

The worst part was that I couldn't blame her exactly. She had every right to run over there and talk to him. It's not like I've dropped many great hints to have her do otherwise, but I hated every second of it.

Some ridiculous part of me thought we had an agreement that she was, in fact, there with me tonight. She rode there with me. I made sure she rode there with me, not giving anyone else the option to take her, and I thought it would somehow let her know I wanted her there with me.

How fucking stupid.

I turned and slammed my hand down, hitting the hood of my car, and when I looked back over at Quinn, I was surprised she was looking over at me.

I pulled out my phone, knowing how I would get her away from Ryder and keep him away without causing any problems. Hopefully.

> Ransom: Race and loser leaves Quinn alone.

> Ryder: Excuse me?

> Ransom: I want you to leave her alone. Time for a race - you ready?

I watched as Ryder said something to Quinn and prayed like hell he wasn't repeating my text because I knew it would only piss her off more. I'd never bet anything like this before, but I felt desperate at this point.

> Ryder: And the loser doesn't get to talk to this beautiful woman?

> Ransom: Yes

> Ryder: Then I'm in. How will you manage at work when you can't talk to her?

I groaned and popped the hood of my car, checking everything over. I came ready to race but hadn't been sure if I was going to with Quinn there. Now it looked like I was racing *for* Quinn.

Red-hot anger sliced through me and only got worse as I realized this ended badly for me either way. If I lost, Ryder would never stop going after Quinn. If I win, Quinn might take this as me, basically making a joke of her to Ryder and then run right back to him.

"Fuck," I yelled, slamming the hood down.

"You good?"

"No. Fuck no," I said. "I'm racing Ryder."

"Well, shit," Fox said.

I ignored him, sliding into my driver's seat as Quinn and Scout came into view. I couldn't stop to talk, though. Anything I say now would only make this worse.

I didn't even care how fucked up this was. All I could do was race and plan not to lose.

THIRTEEN

QUINN

AFTER WE LEFT RYDER, Scout pulled me back towards the guys'
cars.

"What do you mean, that isn't a good thing? Why would they
be racing now?"

"Ransom must have asked Ryder for a race, and we need to
get to Fox."

"Why? What's wrong?"

Scout's lips pursed. "They have never got along, and when
they race, things get…heated. They have found themselves in a
fistfight at the end more than once. For a while, they wouldn't
stop racing, but it was getting too hard to determine an absolute
winner. Finally, someone here forced them into a truce. They
haven't raced in at least a year."

"Why did Ransom want to race him now, then?" I asked,
yelling over the noise as we made our way back. She shrugged.
"I don't know. Let's ask Fox or Jax. It looks like those two are
both still over there."

"What are the prizes, normally?"

"Cars or money most of the time."

I saw Ransom messing with his car and then getting into

the car, but not before throwing daggers at me with his eyes. I didn't know if I was getting sick of Ransom's glares, how angry it made me to see the girl run up to his car, or just more of them falling all over him as I stood over here. It pissed me off that he wasn't just coming here for the races. It pissed me off that he said enough to make me want him when I couldn't want him. I hoped he would lose. Maybe it would knock his ego down a bit and stop him from continuing to pretend to flirt with me.

We made it back to the cars as Ransom pulled out, heading for the starting line.

The girls that had been around Fox were gone, so we slid next to him on his hood.

"Who said what to piss Ransom off?" Fox asked, looking between us.

"We didn't do anything. We were over there talking to Ryder, and it sounds like Ransom texted him asking to race. I was about to ask you why they were racing all of a sudden."

Fox looked over at me, his arms crossed and eyebrows raised. "Any guesses, Quinn?"

"No? How would I know?" I thought back to Ryder's comments about liking a challenge and a pretty prize.

He shook his head. "Well, he was pissed. He's not about to lose this race. Let's just hope he keeps his head straight enough to keep it between the fucking lines." Fox sounded annoyed, but still wrapped an arm around Scout, tucking her next to him.

"And not fight at the finish line," Scout said with an eye roll.

He didn't touch me, not that I expected him to, but I was becoming used to his playfulness. His face was hard now, though, as he watched Ransom pull up to the starting line.

The girl that had run up to us at the car before went up to his car now. A shot of irritation filled me. "What is she doing now?"

She bent over, leaning against his driver's side window, saying something to him, but he didn't seem to respond.

Scout snorted, "She's trying to be what they bet on, but it looks like she's getting rejected. Big time."

My eyes flew to her and Fox. "Excuse me? I thought you said you guys bet on cars and money."

"Some of the girls like to be the prize for the winner. It's all their choice, of course. We don't bet that. It's more something they do for fun." Fox said with a shrug.

My mouth dropped open. "And that means?"

"Exactly what you think it means," he said. It was my turn to grab onto Fox, my voice low enough so Scout wouldn't hear me while I gripped his forearm. "Ryder asked if I was dating any of you, and when I said no, he got a text and said he was up for the challenge and likes a pretty prize. He looked at me then, but I thought he was messing with me."

Fox took a breath. "Yeah, that's what I was worried about."

My heart stopped. "What does that mean? What if Ryder wins? Would I have to go with him? I don't actually have to go with him, right?" My nails dug into Fox.

"Oh hell no, Quinn. You don't have to do anything you don't want to. He's only doing it to piss off Ransom, and it worked. Like I said, we don't bet for people, and I couldn't imagine Ransom would risk anyone thinking they have a claim on you." He wrapped an arm around me, "Interesting that you're not worried about what happens if Ransom wins."

"I just - I mean, I was just —." My words cut off as their cars roared to life. Ransom's tires spun, creating a cloud of smoke before he stopped and backed up. Ryder did the same, and then they lined up.

My heart was racing, making my body shake with nerves as I stayed clinging to Fox.

I hated how much I wanted Ransom to win. The anticipation was killing me. It seemed like there were a thousand questions I needed to figure out the answer to in the next few minutes.

They both pulled up, and Ransom came into view behind the

windshield. I knew he was upset, but I hoped it wouldn't put him in danger now. The cars revved, each one doing a burnout before backing up to the starting line.

It was like butterflies burning alive in my stomach, the fluttering of nerves making me sick. He revved the car again, but this time he looked over, meeting my eye. It sent every part of me up in flames now, the tingling heat going over every inch.

The spell broke as a guy ran forward, giving them signals until his hands went up.

"As soon as he puts them down, they go," Fox said.

The guy moved, his arms swinging down as both of them took off. I could only hold my breath as I watched. It was all too fast and too slow. In seconds, Ryder was winning by a few feet. My heart dropped as he gained precious feet until Ransom's car let loose. He jumped forward, the car not missing a beat, and took off at a speed I didn't think a car should ever go.

The engines roared, and for a moment, I wondered if they would explode with how loud they whined. Ryder started to inch closer, but Ransom wasn't slowing down. His car moved with such ease that I thought he was going to win until the last second, when Ryder pushed forward one last time.

"Shit," Fox said, leaning forward. He mumbled under his breath as Ransom moved again.

They had passed the finish line, and I was ready to pass out.

"Who won?" I grabbed onto his arm, my fingers digging in.

"I think Ransom," Scout said, but there was so much question in her voice that I turned to Fox.

"Who. Won," I said, louder this time.

Fox didn't say anything until someone yelled and pointed to Ransom's car.

"Ransom won. Relax, he won."

Scout yelled, sending loud whoops into the air as she jumped up.

Fox was yelling, too, "Hell yeah."

"Oh, my god." I grabbed my chest, leaning down on the car to take a deep breath. I knew I wouldn't have to go with Ryder if I didn't want to, but the relief that coursed through me at Ransom winning was overwhelming.

Fox was saying something else, but I couldn't hear it. My thoughts were gone as I realized Ransom had won, and he had apparently done that for me in some way. Someone wouldn't go out of their way to do something like this if they weren't really flirting with me, would they?

Was he going to collect, or was it all only a ploy to get Ryder to race him?

My breath caught as his car pulled around. He stopped behind Fox's car, everyone watching as he got out and came around to us.

I was still sitting on the front of Fox's car, my feet propped up on the bumper. Ransom stood in front of me, his eyes wide and chest heaving as he tried to get his breathing under control.

"Come with me," he growled as he stepped into me, grabbing my waist and picking me up off the car. I wrapped my legs around him, the sudden loss of solid ground giving me no choice but to hold on.

I couldn't think of a reason to protest as he carried me back towards his car, putting me in the passenger seat and slamming the door. Everyone around us watched as he got in.

"Put on your harness."

I did, and he waited until it was clipped to take off, speeding off with the same force he had raced down the track. He moved through the gears, taking the car faster and faster.

"What the fuck did Ryder say to you?"

"While that's none of your business, I'll be nice and tell you, anyway." The words sounded so different from how I felt inside. "He said I was beautiful and offered to take me for a ride. I assume he meant a ride home, but who knows? You interrupted us."

"Fucking hell."

"And he asked if I was dating any of you." I saw his fingers tighten on the steering wheel.

"What did you say?"

My face scrunched. "You have nothing to worry about. Your reputation at the races is safe because I said no, that I only worked at the garage now." He had slowed down as we wound through backroads. "Why does it even matter to you what he said? I had a girl in my face the moment I opened the door, asking you to go fuck her. It's not like anyone thought I was there as anything more than your friend."

"That's not what happened." He shook his head. "That's not what I'm worried about."

With a quiet thud, his palm hit the steering wheel. "Don't worry about her. I took care of it. Hopefully. You shouldn't have been talking to Ryder."

"You know what, Ransom, fuck you. You can't tell me who I can and can't talk to. I was having a good night until you did this shit. Pull over."

"What?"

I didn't know if he actually didn't hear me or didn't register the words, so I was clear this time, yelling over the engine, "Pull. Over!"

The car screeched to a stop. "What the hell? What's wrong?"

I pulled off the harness and kicked the door open. "What's wrong? What's wrong?" I yelled, my heart hammering. The racing was too much, spiking adrenaline through me, and now this.

My hands shook with anger. "I'm stuck in the car with you! Like you have the right to tell me that I shouldn't talk to Ryder! Like you have a right to whatever bet you made with him to race. I know it was about me! And you know what? He was nice. He was just fine to look at, too, so it's none of your business if I talk to him or not." I jumped out, ready to be away from him.

He got out of the car too, his hands on the roof. "No woman describes Ryder as 'just fine.' I know what happens to any woman around him."

I rolled my eyes, grabbing my bag from the car and slamming the door, "Oh right, was I supposed to fall to my knees right there because he was so good-looking? How did you know? You actually interrupted me begging to suck his dick right then and there! That's what I do, right? Fuck off. You know what? He was pleasant enough to talk to. You're the one I can't stand being around. Can you even make up your mind if you hate me or not?" I was yelling, the sound echoing down the empty street. At least there was no one around. The woods lined both sides, leaving us completely alone.

"I don't hate you. I mean, I thought I did, but I don't. I wouldn't have asked you to work with us if I hated you. I wouldn't have asked you to come tonight, especially to ride with me," he said. "What are you doing, Quinn?"

I walked around to the front of the car, stalking down the dark road.

"You could have fooled me. And I'm going home."

I didn't care about the dark or distance. I've walked farther in the middle of the night by myself. The casino had been almost fifteen miles from our house before they built a new one, and I would have to take myself home when my mom forgot she had brought me with her.

"It's too far, Quinn. It would take you all night."

"I don't care. I've done it before," I said. "You can go back to the races, back to that girl, and back to leaving me alone. I'm done, and I'm not coming back to the garage either." Rage coursed through me. I wasn't going to play nice. Wasn't he the one who asked to see my claws? Well, I was sure as hell ready to use them.

I heard him rush up behind me. "No."

"What? Need to tell me what to do again? Maybe I can call Ryder to come to give me a ride."

"You're not walking home alone in the dark. It's at least ten fucking miles, Quinn."

"I can do whatever I want."

He growled behind me, "No, fuck no." He grabbed me, spinning me back towards him and bending over. His shoulder went into my stomach, and he stood, my feet leaving the ground.

"Did you really just grab me? What are you doing? Put me down!" I yelled, now slung over his shoulder.

"You are not calling Ryder to give you a ride home, and I am not spending my entire night hunting for you in these fucking woods."

He walked to the back of the car and set me down on the trunk. His hands moved on either side of me, caging me in.

"What are you doing? Let me go."

"I'm stopping you."

I pushed him back, trying to give myself some inch of space away from his deep scent that only made me want to wrap myself around him.

A laugh escaped me, "Because you don't want to wake up and feel guilty when my name is plastered on the news knowing you could have stopped it?" I asked, echoing the words he had said to me the first time he demanded to bring me home in the middle of the night.

"Yes," he said, his lips curving into a smile.

"Why did you hit your car earlier? I saw you hit it when I was across the track with Ryder."

"Because I saw the way you were looking at Ryder. It's the way you look at Fox. Like you think they are just so fucking sweet, like you think the world of them. I can't stand it."

"Well, I don't know much about Ryder, but Fox is sweet. I do think a lot of him. They are both full of charm, and it makes them easy for me to read and understand. But it doesn't mean I'm falling for their charm."

"And I'm not like that?"

"No, your face doesn't give anything away."

"You are not calling Ryder or Fox to take you away."

His voice was low, sending a shiver down my spine. "What if I want to?"

His eyes hardened as he stared down at me. "What if I change your mind?"

"I don't know. Ryder is pretty hot and did say he would take me for a ride."

"Fucking asshole. You're not going with him now or ever."

I laughed, knowing Ransom didn't realize I had said those exact words to Ryder myself. "Says who?"

"Me."

His hand wrapped around my neck, pulling me into him as his other hand pushed into my lower back, sliding my body across the trunk until I was against him. His lips crashed against mine, their angry warmth sending a shock of pleasure through me. I couldn't move, couldn't think of what to do next with his lips on mine.

One moment I was mad at him, and the next, he was kissing me.

I had dreamed of kissing Ransom, but it hadn't compared to the real thing. Pleasure hummed through my body, leaving every nerve on edge, each part of my body already begging for more of his touch.

He nipped at my lip before sliding his tongue against mine, exploring my mouth with a rough need that I found I could easily match. Years of need built up to one moment when he finally kissed me. My hips rolled, pushing into him as his hand tightened on my throat, forcing me to bare it to him.

He loosened his grip, pulling his hand away. The rough grip was replaced with teeth and lips, sucking and biting at my neck.

Every touch was setting me further on edge. I pulled him into me more and drug my hands down his jaw. The same jaw I had watched flex and clench all night was now working on kissing me like I had never been kissed before.

He kissed me with a fever I didn't know happened in real life. His teeth grabbed my lip again, biting it before licking, soothing the tender spot.

Of all the things I had expected him to do to me tonight, it wasn't this.

"You're not for him. You're for me."

His hand ran up my thighs, making me push my hips forward as he moved higher. It wasn't close enough, though. I needed more. I was so wet, the ache growing and making me desperate to soothe it. His hand teased, moving so high up my thigh but never touching the one place I needed him.

"Say it."

My back arched, and hands fisted into his shirt. I'd never felt so desperate for someone's touch who was already running their hands over every inch of me.

"Say what?"

"Say you're for me. Tell me that I could fuck you on the back of my car right now, and you would want me to."

"I would," I said, breathless, "you could."

His hand finally moved, running along my pussy, and even through my leggings. I moaned. The rough touch sent a wave of pleasure through me.

"I'm so fucking glad you're here," he said. "I've been dying to touch you for weeks." He scraped his teeth down my neck as his fingers moved back and forth along my pussy. Each touch more agonizing than the last, the pressure just enough to tease me but not enough to get me off.

"What about you, Quinn? Who do you want to be here with? Me or Ryder?" he asked, putting more pressure as he circled my clit. I knew how wet I was, and I wouldn't be surprised if he could feel it through my leggings.

His lips came to my ear, his warm breath sending pleasure down my spine. "Who did you hope would win that race?"

"You," I breathed, "I wanted you to win."

"Would you have gone with him if he had?"

"No, I told Fox I didn't want to, and he said I didn't have to." I sucked in a hard breath, needing more than what he was giving me. "Ransom." My voice was almost a plea.

"Kitten."

"Please," I begged, pushing my hips up and harder against his hand.

He moved, reaching to pull down my leggings as another car came down the road. In seconds I was being carried to the passenger seat and set inside before he jumped into the driver's seat, locking us in.

The car passed with a beep, and Ransom took a breath. "I'll bring you back home."

"What was that?"

"I didn't want someone to stop."

My heart dropped as tears caught in my throat. "I don't get it. You're that worried about being seen with me?"

He looked over, his eyebrows furrowed. "Seen with you? No? I thought you might appreciate not being seen fucking me on the back of my car in the middle of the road."

The words hit like a slap across the face. It was the truth, and now that he said it, I knew he was right. I didn't want to be seen like that, but after the video happened, the words took on a different meaning to me. Now I was so desperate that I needed to stop in the road and fuck someone? The worst part was I meant it when I told him he could and that I wanted him to.

"Got it. Thanks for not letting other people see me being a slut."

"What? That's not even close to what I meant, Quinn. I just

thought you would like your privacy for anything like that. Someone in that car could have stopped to record it, for all I know. I don't know who was in that fucking car, and I'm not letting them see you like that. That's none of their fucking business. I'm not some disgusting, evil monster. I was trying to give you some respect, even though I was one hundred percent trying to have sex with you in the middle of the road like an asshole."

I didn't know what to say. Didn't even know if there was anything to say. The car was quiet for a long time as he drove.

"Thank you."

"Are you okay?"

"Yeah, that was a lot. I haven't even kissed anyone since the dumb video, let alone gone farther than that. I guess I just freaked out, but thanks. I don't know what I would have done if someone stopped and saw us."

"It's almost been a year. You haven't done anything since then?" The shock in his voice was heavy, and I covered my face from the embarrassment.

"No. I haven't. It was so much I couldn't even think about doing anything like that. Who can be betrayed like that and trust someone not to do it again?"

"Shit. We shouldn't have done that."

"No, no. It's good. It's fine. I was a very willing participant and liked it."

"Liked it enough you would do it again?" His hand moved from the shifter to my thigh, his fingers moving in lazy circles.

"Maybe, but not in the middle of the road." I moved my leg, making his hand go higher, still needing to find some relief from all the teasing he had done.

He laughed, noticing my thigh moving under his hand. "You can do whatever you want, wherever you want with me. I'll make sure no one sees or bothers us."

"Whatever, wherever, huh?" I asked, liking the sound of that.

"Absolutely. Even in the middle of the road."

He groaned as we pulled into my dorm and stopped. I was surprised when he leaned over, kissing me again. "You can enjoy yourself, and I'll make sure no one bothers you." His lips stayed against mine as he said the words, and a wave of pleasure rolled through me, the promise of freedom and protection making me want to test my limits and climb on top of him right there in the car.

The thought made me snap back to my reality. He moved to kiss me again, but I pulled back.

Even if he did stop me from any embarrassment tonight, I had made out with him in the middle of nowhere in the road. That couldn't be what any girl trying to make a better future would do. I couldn't just fuck someone where ever I wanted. Fear rose up, taking over. I couldn't be the girl I had been, trying to find happiness and pleasure without giving a damn about the consequences.

He smiled, the wicked smirk reminding me that I was messing with the devil and he was better at this than I was. "I can tell you want to jump out of the car. I'll see you tomorrow."

I stared for a moment. "Yeah, right. I'll see you tomorrow. Goodnight." I got out, feeling like a zombie, as I pushed at every emotion that came. I didn't want them.

I made it a few steps until I heard his door open, and he stood. "I'll be thinking about you all night. Text me if you think about me."

"I won't." I said, my own heart dropping, "I'll see you tomorrow."

His car idled as I walked in, slamming the door behind me. The words were the truth. Even if I wanted to, I wasn't going to text him. My mind and emotions tangled like a web, and there was no way to unravel them. The crushing anger at wanting him and not wanting him all at once.

I turned my phone off as I made my way to my room. I wasn't going to text him, no matter how badly I wanted to.

FOURTEEN

QUINN

THE MORNING CAME, and I could barely register what time or day it was, last night leaving me feeling like I had a hangover. I had guessed I would have to find a job at some point and knew longer weekends would save me with studying and finishing homework, so I never signed up for any classes on Fridays.

I was still going to wait awhile to go to the garage, though, not knowing how to face Ransom after last night. The game he was playing was too much for me.

I wasn't in that league of head games, and I decided to pretend as though nothing had happened and move on. I didn't have time to play games with him.

I said those words over and over, hoping they would stick, but my mouth went dry the moment I walked into the garage and saw him, wondering how sweat and grease could look so hot. I came up behind him, the back of his gray tank top covered in dirt. His back muscles flexed as he worked on the engine in front of him.

I was surprised when I learned how in-depth they go on these cars. I assumed it was more of an oil change place, but they built entire cars. And after I saw the office, I was surprised at how well they were doing, gaining a name in the industry, but still needed a filing system. It was baffling and impressive all at the same time.

I stepped around him at the same time he turned, and a large wrench knocked down off the engine and fell, hitting my foot with a thud.

It hit my toes, the pain ricocheting up my leg. "Shit," I yelled, jumping back.

My boots did nothing to protect my feet. The sad leather had been worn in for years before I ever had them, but I had been lucky enough to find them on a half-off day at the thrift store.

Ransom grabbed my shoulders to steady me, his touch sending another shock through me, "Are you ok?"

"Yeah," I hopped forward once to hold on to him, not having a choice as I almost fell over from the sudden imbalance, "just broke a toe or two."

"Shit." He echoed my statement as his arms swept under my legs and picked me up, carrying me across the garage.

"I can walk, Ransom. Put me down. It was a joke. I don't think they are broken," I said, but I didn't know what broken toes would feel like. He seemed to think I had cut my foot entirely off.

He pulled open the office door, carried me in, and set me down on the couch.

"We still need to check them." Then he did something I wasn't expecting. He kneeled down in front of me and started unlacing my boot.

"What the fuck are these?" he asked, pulling one off. "Are these steel toes?"

I furrowed my brow, embarrassed at how old my boots looked. The leather almost looked worn through in some places. "I don't even know what that means."

"It means there is steel in the toe to protect them from things like this."

"Then no. At least, I don't think so."

"Shit, Quinn. You can't be wearing these around here. Some of these tools can cut off your foot if you're not careful."

"Well, I wasn't expecting you to throw a wrench at my foot."

"I had headphones in. I didn't hear you walk up behind me. There's no blood, at least," he said, inspecting my sock. He moved to pull it off, and I pulled my leg back.

"I'll do it," I said, not needing his hands on my bare skin any longer than they had already been.

I pulled it off. My toes were red but moveable. "See, not broken."

"Keep an eye on it. You need better boots."

"I need a lot of things. Better boots are not making the cut. I'll be more careful in the garage."

"No. You asked if there was a uniform, and that's it. Good boots." He stood to his full height and stared down at me. I couldn't take the gaze, the embarrassment turning my cheeks warm, and I knew he would be able to see how red they were now.

"Oh. Well, ok then. I'll grab them this weekend."

He nodded and rolled a chair over. "Stay off it today. There's plenty to do at the desk without running around." I nodded. He was still staring at me, his eyes dark and jaw tight. It seemed like he wanted to say something else, but didn't.

I wasn't going to offer up anything else, not knowing that there was anything to say when I was on the verge of crying from the pain and now embarrassment overwhelming me. He looked me over again and turned away, stomping to the door and slamming it behind him as he went back into the garage.

I didn't know if he was angry about the wrench falling, last night, or my boots, but either way, I could feel how red and hot my face was. The embarrassment made me feel like I was back in high school. Sarah and her group of rich girls made me feel like absolute shit for thrift store clothes. At some point, I learned to push back, making fun of their clothes and lives, not caring what they said about me. I went through all the tactics, but at the end of those days, walking into our tiny house that was falling apart, my mother gone or drunk on the couch, I'd cry.

She worked as a waitress, but there was never enough money left for me. At some point when I was young, I began selling her unopened alcohol bottles to other drunks on our street whenever I needed food or clothes. I learned how to hustle everything I could to make sure I could eat something. She never seemed to remember how much she drank, so long as I didn't take too much. A bottle here and there, a beer that would bring me fifty cents. It worked out. The other drunks didn't have to walk for another beer, and I would have enough to walk down and get dinner.

I felt like that little girl again, small and broke, not able to afford the clothes and things I needed. I knew he wasn't making fun of me. He only wanted me to wear the right boots to be safe. I could only imagine how expensive good work boots were, and knowing how little I could afford, even with this job, took the fight out of me for the day.

I went about my work, not realizing how late I had been there until Fox and Scout walked in. Fox fell back to lounge on the couch as Scout jumped up to sit on the now clean desk.

"If you told me a desk was under here before you started, I wouldn't have believed you," she said, laying back and smiling up at me.

"I thought the same thing. I really don't know how you guys have managed to run such a well-organized business with an office like this."

"Then I guess we're lucky Ransom found someone with beauty and brains to fix us up around here. We want to work on cars, not filing systems," Fox said with a wink, not an ounce of anger or annoyance at what happened last night. They both seemed fine, acting as though Ransom dragging me away was normal, and I was fine not going over it with them.

"Well, I don't know how to work on cars, so I'm fine sticking to the filing system."

"We can always teach you about cars if you want," he said, and Scout's eyes lit up.

"Yea! I can show you on my car. We're going to overhaul the engine, and I'd love having another girl around to do it with me. It'd be fun to work on the car together!"

"Hey," Fox said, scrunching his face, "I offered first."

Scout laughed, "Ransom would kill you if you tried to show her your car," she said, giving air quotes around the words.

"Is showing me a car some sort of innuendo that I don't know about?"

"For Fox, it is. The girls love it when he shows them his car."

"You're just mad the same line doesn't work on the guys. They tend to run off when they realize Scout's car is nicer and faster than theirs."

"Men," Scout said with a shake of her head, and I laughed, reaching out to pat her shoulder.

"You don't want any of those ones anyway."

"I know. If my car scares them off, they wouldn't last a day with this group."

"I doubt they would last an hour," I said, knowing how much they were to take as a whole.

"You about done here, Quinn?" Fox asked, looking down at his phone.

I knew it was late, but I was almost done filling the last of the parts orders and didn't want to stop now. "Not quite. I want to finish this pile."

"Alright, we were going to go out for a drive. Do you want us to wait till you're done?"

"No, not at all. I'll be fine. I just don't know how you want me to lock up."

Fox dug into his pocket, pulling out keys. "Ransom said he would be back, but that was a while ago, so I'll give you these in case." He handed me the keys and wrote down the alarm code, letting me know how to set it.

I held them in my hand. "You trust me with these? Are you sure Ransom would be fine with this?"

Scout nodded, and Fox laughed. "He won't mind as long as you actually lock the place. We have plenty of people that come snooping around here and will jump at the chance to get in here. Scout and I can drop by on our way back and check the doors if you want."

I let out a breath. "Yes, that would be perfect."

She jumped up. "I'll text you when we swing by so you know it's all good."

"Thanks," I said as she leaned down and gave me a hug.

"Lock up after us, so you're not alone in here with the doors unlocked. The garage doors are locked, so it's just this door."

I nodded. "You're sure Ransom won't care?"

"No, we all trust you here. I'm sure the only reason he hasn't given you one is that he usually won't leave unless you do. I don't know what he got up to tonight, but don't be surprised if he comes by."

"Alright, thanks."

"Anytime." He flashed a smile and walked out, Scout already in the car. I smiled as they pulled out his car drifting from the parking lot as Scout's hand popped out from the passenger side window, waving as they raced away.

I was glad I hadn't called in to report them for the statue. I could see why Ransom had worked so hard to protect them. They had all welcomed me in, making me feel like I belonged even when I didn't.

Fox, Jax, and Scout quickly became my friends while Kye and Dante were warming up to me.

A car raced by, and it made me wonder what Ransom was

doing and who he was doing it with, immediately picturing the girl from the races. I know he said I was the one he wanted there last night, but that was something people could say in the moment.

I slammed my head against the desk for a moment before turning back to the papers.

An hour went by as I reached the end of the pile.

The low rumble of a car sounded outside, and I strained to listen, wondering if it was Ransom. I was beginning to recognize each car and its sound, but none of them ever pulled into the garage that slow.

I peered out the window, not seeing anything, but I could still hear it. The engine cut, and my eyes jumped to the door. I still hadn't locked the door behind Fox, but ran to do it now. I could hear someone on the other side but couldn't see out unless I moved over to the large window again. The door pushed open before I could slide the lock into place.

I jumped back, letting the door hit the wall.

I stood frozen, as the figure pushed forward inside.

FIFTEEN

QUINN

"Ransom." I drew a ragged breath. "Thank god I thought someone was breaking in." Relief flooded me as I went to flip on the light. I turned back to him and froze.

It took me a second to take it all in, "Ransom," I yelled, moving over to him, grabbing the bag he held, and throwing it aside. "Why are you covered in blood?"

His shirt was ripped in so many different places I couldn't count, blood covering his arms and staining his green shirt so dark red that it was almost black in places. I grabbed his chin and looked over his face, watching him flinch as I tried to see where the blood was coming from. A dark bruise formed on his jaw, and blood dripped from his mouth, but it wasn't enough to cause all of this.

"I had a small accident," he said, blue eyes meeting mine.

"Car accident?"

"No. Not quite." He tried to pull away from me. "Need to clean up." He moved towards the small bathroom off the office, and I went after him, grabbing him as he swayed. I dropped his arm over my shoulder and pulled him the rest of the way into the bathroom, sitting him down as he leaned back and closed his eyes.

"Is this your blood?" I asked, pulling at his shirt, trying to peel the blood-soaked sections away from his body to search for cuts.

"Some," he said.

I found three smaller cuts before I found the source of all of the blood on his left side. Something, or someone, had cut from the middle of his shoulder going towards his neck before turning and cutting down into his chest. It was bleeding but seemed to have missed his arteries.

"You need to move to the ground. I need to clean this and stop the bleeding."

I didn't know how much he had bled, but the blood was still pooling at the cut.

"Yes." It was all he said as he nearly dropped to the ground. I thought it was good he was still moving, but it was obvious how tired he was, each movement slow and groggy.

"Wait," I said, grabbing him before he laid all the way down. I ran from the room, grabbing scissors and a pack of clean shop towels that had come in earlier.

He had propped himself up against the wall when I came back in, and I let him stay sitting as I started to cut at his shirt.

"Sorry," he said, his eyes trying to fixate on me, "I didn't know you would be here so late. Are you here alone?"

"Yes, and I'm glad I'm here. Did you think you were going to clean this up yourself?"

He shrugged and winced, "I've done it before."

"What happened?"

"Nothing. Just had to go to the other side of town."

"And what? There's a madman cutting people up over there?"

"Don't worry about it, Kitten. Why are you here this late alone? That's dangerous."

"You're one to talk." I had cut the shirt off, seeing the extent of the damage now, all while ignoring the fact that I was getting an up-close view of a bare-chested Ransom. One of the cuts had sliced through a tattoo, but it didn't seem too deep.

"I wasn't exactly a girl scout, Ransom. I never learned any first aid."

"Take a breath. It's ok."

"No, I mean, I know enough from TV to know how to clean it, but that's it. We should bring you to the hospital," I said, pulling him up, hoping to get him off the floor.

"No. It doesn't need stitches, just cleaned and put back together."

"You want me to put it back together? It's your neck! I don't think I can just put it back together." My breathing was heavy now, the reality of it was setting in, and panic was taking over, "It's skin! I can't just glue it!"

He smiled, making me curl my fists, "Technically, you can glue it. I've done that too. It doesn't need stitches, and it doesn't need glue. It's really ok. I checked the depth, and we can use butterfly closures. We have them in the kit."

I didn't move, "Are you serious?"

"Dead serious."

"Don't even say that word. You look like you should be dead."

"I'll be ok, promise." He winced as he adjusted, and I felt worse for yelling at him. He was keeping me calm while he was the one cut open.

"Tell me that after we get the bleeding to stop and this cut is closed."

I grabbed the first aid kit under the sink and tore into it, trying to find everything I would need.

"You're worried about me?"

"Of course I am. You're bleeding out on the floor."

He laughed and winced again, "It's not that bad."

"I don't know what level of knife fights you have been in, but this isn't good."

I cleaned the wound, drying it and putting as many butterfly closures as possible. He sat unmoving the entire time, even as I cleaned and prodded each cut.

"You're beautiful," he said with heavy eyes.

"And you're just being sweet, so I don't poke at your cuts more."

"No, I mean you're beautiful. I've always thought you were beautiful."

"Always, huh?"

"Yes," He reached up, caressing my jaw, "Always."

"You're delirious. How much blood did you lose?" He only groaned in response. The rest of the cuts were better, only needing to be cleaned and left to heal. I moved on, cleaning each one until I got him up, helping him move to the couch and out of the mess.

"I'm going to clean up the bathroom. Please don't move."

"I won't," he said, laying back and closing his eyes.

"You can't fall asleep either!" I yelled. The bathroom looked like a crime scene, my blood-smeared hands having left as big of a mess as his had.

It took me longer than I hoped to clean up before I dug for a clean hoodie for Ransom and some water. The one thing these guys did well in the office was keep the fridge stocked with every drink someone could want.

"Here," I said, setting the water down and reaching for his shoulders to pull him up. His skin was cold to the touch, "Sorry. I should have brought this sooner. Are you ok?"

"I'm fine." He lifted his arms, letting me help him slide the jacket over his arms and zipped. I handed him water and some pain pills I found in the kit.

"Thanks."

"What happened?" I asked again, wanting him to tell me the entire story.

"Did I bring a bag in with me?" he asked.

"What?" I glanced around, "Oh yeah, I took it when you came in."

"Can you grab it for me?" I rolled my eyes, he was avoiding the question, but I decided I would give him time for the painkillers to kick in before interrogating him more. I grabbed the bag, setting it in front of him, and sat on the other end of the couch.

"Open it," he said, looking at me.

"Me? Why?"

"It's for you."

"What?"

"Open it."

I grabbed for it, curiosity taking over as I looked into the bag.

"What are these?" I said in shock, pulling out the box of brand-new boots.

"They are steel toe. They might feel a little heavy at first, but you'll get used to it. Wear them when you are here."

"Why?" I opened the box and stared down at the black leather boots. They looked like the ones he wore. I had never had a new pair of boots. I had worn used shoes since I could remember. These looked perfect, the leather untouched and uncreased. Tears pricked my eyes, "You got me boots?"

"You needed them."

"I was going to go buy them myself."

He shrugged, "Now you don't have to."

"Wait? Is this why you got into a fight? Did you steal these Ransom?"

He let out a breath. "Damn, you don't think much of me, do you? I guess I don't have much room to talk when I come in here looking like this, though."

He pointed to the bag. "I didn't steal them, and the receipt should be in the bag to prove it, and in case you need to exchange them for a different size."

I pursed my lips, feeling like an ass for accusing him of stealing, but it was hard not to when he came back looking like he had been in a knife fight. I took his word for it, not wanting to be any ruder by looking for the receipt.

"Try them on." He murmured.

I didn't need to be told twice. I couldn't steady my hand as I reached down and slid into them. The leather was stiff, stiffer than my last few pairs.

"Ouch. How long does it take them to soften up?"

"It could be a while, but we can do a few things to help wear them in faster tomorrow. Have you ever had new leather boots?"

My head whipped up to him, he wasn't laughing, but I didn't know how honest I should be. I know Ransom knew about my struggles in High School, but talking about it was different. People were always quick to judge when you told them about how poor you really were. Too much information and they would pity you. Not enough, and they found you disgusting for not having money.

I didn't think Ransom would do either, but the knee-jerk reaction to want to lie took me a minute to stop. "No. I haven't even had new shoes."

He nodded as though he understood but didn't say anything else about it. "Do they fit?"

"Aside from needing to be worn in, they feel great. How did you know my size?"

"I checked earlier."

"Oh," I said. "Of course." The comments about needing new boots and I was worried about buying them. All while he had been planning to buy me new ones, "Thank you."

"Just tell me if you need anything else."

"No. I don't."

"Whether you like it or not, you're a part of our crew now.

So if you need something, tell me. Or Fox, I guess. You two seem friendly enough."

"Yeah. Fox has been great." His eyes found mine as he kept his head leaned back. "Thanks for the boots and the job."

"So you like it even though I'm here?" he asked, trying to give a smile but hissing at the pain.

"Aside from almost losing toes and cleaning up a ridiculous amount of blood, yeah, I like it. You, on the other hand." I shook my head, not knowing how to explain it.

"Well, hopefully, the boots can make up for some of my shit behavior." He reached for his jaw, the bruise deepening in color.

I jumped up, glad to have an out from the conversation, as I went for ice, bringing back a bag and handing it over. He didn't take it, though.

"I'll do it later. My arms are a bit...dead right this second."

I sat down next to him, too aware of how much of his body I had touched tonight and how close, and alone we were now. I set the ice against his face, watching his brows furrow at the sudden cold.

"Are you going to tell me what happened?"

"No," he said. His eyes were heavy as his hand reached out, resting his fingers on the back of my hand before running them up and down my arm. Chills went through me, the simple touch setting me on fire.

"Ransom," I murmured, not knowing if it was an invitation or a plea to stop. "It seems your arms are working just fine."

He leaned down, his lips by my ear, his soft breath caressing my neck before moving to my mouth. "No, they are still hurting. I'll still need you to hold that."

His hand made its way to the back of my neck, trying to pull me closer as his lips found mine. The kiss was slow until I leaned in more, and he took over. His tongue slid against mine, exploring my mouth with a revived energy he didn't have a second ago. I moaned into him. My body responded to his with a frightening speed, making me lose every thought that I shouldn't have been doing this.

My hands moved up his chest until they hit the bandage. He flinched, making me pull back fast.

"Sorry. I forgot," I said, looking him over, but he only laughed.

"Shh, it's ok. Come back here," he said with a growl, leaning towards me.

"But I–"

My words cut off as the back door flew open. Ransom was up before I could blink, moving between me and the door.

"Shit. What the hell happened to you?" Fox's voice echoed. I jumped up, moving around Ransom to stand on the other side of the office. Scout, Fox, Dante, Jax, and Kye piled in.

"She finally kicked the shit outta you?" Jax said, smiling over at me. "I'm impressed."

"Honestly, we all thought it was going to happen sooner," Dante said with a small laugh.

I held up my hands. "I tried to stop the bleeding, not cause it."

"What happened?" Scout said, sitting back in the desk chair. They all seemed so calm, and I wondered how many times a similar situation had happened here.

Ransom looked over at me, and this time, I could tell what he was thinking.

He didn't want me here for this. He wanted to tell them, but not in front of me.

No matter how much a 'part' of this crew I was now, I was still an outsider and wasn't allowed to know about what happened. I didn't say a word as I grabbed my bag, realizing the sleeves and front of my shirt were still splattered with blood.

"Oh," I said, pulling my shirt away from my skin. "I need to get home and take care of this, so…" I waved my hand over my shirt. "See you guys later."

I turned with a wave as I ran out the door. Ransom yelled out for me as I made it out of the parking lot, but he was moving slow, and would never catch up.

I turned the corner and ran, moving through the darkness and trying not to think about being alone out here in the middle of the night.

It wasn't until I reached the dorm that I realized I was still in the new boots, my feet aching from the stiff leather.

No matter how friendly Ransom was to me, I had to remember who he was and what they were doing. Whatever it was they were wrapped up in couldn't, and shouldn't, involve me.

No matter how bad I wanted to involve myself with all of them, I had to stop now before I lost myself.

SIXTEEN

RANSOM

I KNEW Quinn was mad at me. The way she stomped away last night made it clear that she knew I was leaving her out of this and wasn't going to tell her what happened.

I wasn't going to pull her into this problem. Slaughter and his crew were out for blood, and until they learned who wronged them, they would keep assuming it was us. I couldn't put her in the middle any more than she was just by hanging around us, even if it meant she was going to stay mad at me. I knew she would be even angrier if she knew what was happening.

"Ransom," someone yelled, snapping me out of my daze as Fox filled the apartment door.

"Shit. What?"

"We need to go down to the garage. Something happened to one of the cars."

I jumped over the back of the couch, knowing I could ask questions as we went. "Keys?"

"Got 'em. Just go."

We raced down to the car, and I hopped in with Fox, Scout already in the back.

"What happened?"

"Dante called. One of the cars was torn apart last night. Parts pulled off, but nothing on it wrecked."

"What parts?"

"He didn't say yet. Sounds like two or three parts that he noticed so far," Fox said.

"What car?"

"The one you've been working on," Scout said, and I knew she was thinking the same thing.

"That one is locked inside the garage."

"That's exactly why we are racing down there. We need to see if anything else was messed with or taken."

"I know I was a bit out of it last night, but didn't we lock up?"

Fox shook his head as we neared the garage. "I'm the one who finished locking up, and I could swear I didn't leave anything unlocked. I even checked the garage doors before we left. We've all been careful."

"Mistakes happen. It's not like any one of us hasn't fucked up locking up," I said. I could never be mad at any one of them for something like this, and I knew they wouldn't be mad at me. But, it didn't mean we all wouldn't take it hard if we fuck something up.

"No, I know. I don't think I messed up, though. I remember checking every door last night when I left Quinn there and then once again when we left. How could I have missed an unlocked door twice?"

At her name, my chest tightened. I didn't know if she would ever want to touch or even talk to me again. I made a clear line between us. She knew I was keeping her out, and I couldn't imagine it was going over well. I didn't know if I could go back to staying away, though. Now that I had a taste, I needed more.

Before I could think about it any longer, we reached the garage and all jumped out. The door was open, and Dante stood with Jax and Kye, who were looking over the cars they had been working on.

"What happened?"

"We just got here," Jax said. "Walked in to grab some tools and noticed the parts strung along the ground at your bay, Ransom. After we started looking around, we noticed parts were missing. We needed you to check everything that's gone, though. I only knew of two that you put on that are gone now."

I swore and headed to the car as Fox and Scout did the same to their bays and cars.

Scout bounded back over to me. "All good with mine."

"Mines fine too," Fox said.

"So they only went for one car? How does that make sense?"

Dante threw a towel down, running a hand over his face. "None of it makes sense. They came inside and took a few random parts off one of the cars? If this was the same people stealing cars, why wouldn't they have taken the entire thing?"

"You would think that they would after all the effort to get inside," Scout said, looking over my car. She had helped me install one of the missing parts and knew where I was at on the build. "Why would they take such random parts?"

"Maybe someone with a similar car needs stuff for it?" Kye shrugged. I hoped he was taking this seriously. It was so hard to tell with him sometimes.

"It was the more expensive parts. Maybe someone who needed cash," Fox said.

Jax leaned over the car with me, peering into the engine bay, "But Dante's right. If it's someone who's been taking the other cars, why not take an entire thing after you get in here?"

Kye walked over, and Fox turned to him. "What door was unlocked?"

"The side door to the garage. I was surprised it was unlocked after. I figured one of you was here already."

"Ransom, I know for a fucking fact I checked that door. It was locked."

"Nothing on the door was damaged when we came in. It was just unlocked."

"So, the person had a key?" I asked, running my hand through my hair. No one on our crew would take the parts. There was no need to, and I couldn't imagine anyone letting someone in to take things from us.

"Sounds like they would have had to."

"Luca is the only person with a key other than us."

Fox's face fell even more. It was hard to notice, but I'd seen it enough times before. "What?"

"I did give one to Quinn last night. We were leaving, and I told her she could lock up if we didn't come back before she was done."

I shook my head. "That's fine. Quinn wouldn't have done this."

"Hold on," Dante said. "We can't just rule her out. If she was just given a key, and this happened the same night, how are we not considering her?"

"He's right, Ransom. If you gave her one, and then this happened, we can't assume she didn't have something to do with it," Jax said.

Fox stepped towards me. "I wouldn't want to believe that, but we still have to ask her."

"I know Quinn wouldn't have done this." I didn't believe for a second that she would have done this to us.

"Just because you want her so bad doesn't automatically mean we should fucking trust her," Dante said. Heat burned as I filled my lungs and stalked over to him, ready to fight. We tried to never hit each other between the crew members, but now they were crossing a line.

"Fuck, dude," Fox said, taking a step between us. "Relax, none of us wants it to be her. We can't assume it isn't, though."

"Oh, come on. We all know that's why he's not considering it." Dante looked around, expecting everyone to back him up, and for a second, I thought they might.

"He's not considering it because Quinn didn't do this. She doesn't even know what half the parts are and wouldn't do that to us," Scout said, and I silently thanked her for being on my side.

"See," I said. "I'm not the only one who doesn't think she did it."

Dante shook his head. "Just because she doesn't know, doesn't mean she couldn't have had help. She needs money, doesn't she? So it's not that crazy of an idea."

"It's only something to consider. It's not like we are already blaming her." I looked at Jax, surprised this was coming from him. He always tried to stay at the edge of hard conversations, butting in here and there with a smart-ass comment, but never wanting to get involved much.

"Fuck off. All of you," I said. "we've all needed money at some point. That doesn't mean she set up this entire stupid thing to steal parts."

"Are you saying you've never stolen parts for cash before?" Dante asked, and I wanted to hit him again. He knew as much as any of us what I had done, what we all had done at one point to get ahead.

"That isn't fair."

Dante shrugged. "I'm not saying she's terrible for it. I'm saying it's not that crazy of a theory when we all know that she needed money for school. Maybe working here isn't enough."

I gritted my teeth. I was ready to go to war with my own friends for a girl who may never talk to me. I ran a hand through my hair, ready to pull it out. The worst part was he was right. It wasn't that crazy to think that she got mad at me last night, decided not to work here anymore, and took a few parts for extra money before the paychecks stopped. A pit grew in my stomach at the thought and the idea that she was only around me because she needed money.

"It wasn't Quinn. It can't be."

Kye shook his head. "You know we always try to be fair, Ransom. We all fuck up, but if Quinn did this, we need to figure that out."

Dante rolled his eyes with a huff. "We have to question her. I don't think you have a say in this when half the reason she is here is so that you can try to sleep with her."

I didn't stop that time. Instead, I charged forward and swung. Fox moved between us at the last second, my punch angling into Dante's stomach instead of his face. Scout yelled something as Jax and Kye grabbed for me, pulling me into the office.

"Enough!" Jax yelled. "We will talk about this and figure it out. Dante's right. You need to step back from this one. No one wants it to be Quinn, and if she didn't do it, she wouldn't mind us asking her," he said, slamming the door behind them as they left me alone in the office.

I sat back on the couch. I wouldn't be surprised if they were locking me in here now. We didn't fight, not like that. Now it was me who crossed the line. They were right. We had to ask her, but I didn't know what I would do if she confessed. I could feel every part of myself tighten, the all too familiar feeling of wanting to throw up creeping over me.

I tried to take a breath as I looked down, noticing the bag still from Quinn's boots. I still felt bad from when I yelled at her to buy new boots and saw her face twist in pain. I knew right then that I was going to buy her a pair. I didn't know which ones she would like, so I picked out the ones that matched mine.

I hated how happy that made me.

I groaned, not knowing what the fuck I was doing anymore. I'm thinking about Quinn when our garage had been robbed, and everyone seemed to suspect her. Maybe Dante was right. My judgment was clouded by whatever thing I had with her.

Scout walked in and shut the door. "You good?"

I rolled my head to look at her. "Yeah, fine."

"Sure, you sound it." She came over, bouncing onto the couch next to me. "I'm glad you stuck up for Quinn, though. We both know she wouldn't have done this."

"So you agree then?"

"Of course I do. Why? Are you second-guessing her now?"

"No. I'm second guessing myself and if Dante could be right."

"He's not. Quinn is great. Plus, she doesn't know the difference between a carburetor and a starter," she said with a smile. "She wouldn't have known what to take, why to take it, or how to take it off. Even if she did have some malicious reason to be here."

"Malicious, huh? Sounds like you're doing great in school then."

"I like reading," she said with a shrug. "That's where you learn the big words other than car parts and curse words."

"Ahh, so that's where I went wrong."

"It is, but you're not wrong about Quinn."

"Thanks, Scout. At least I don't have to sit here going completely insane now."

"Nope, just partially. Come on. We need to get this figured out and wrapped up so we can go."

"Go where?"

"The carnival. You all told me yesterday that you would go with me, and you're not backing out now."

I groaned. I had told her that, but that was when I thought Quinn would be going with us. Not that I didn't love Scout, but the girl was a viper at a carnival, and I knew we would be there all night. I'd usually bring a girl to distract me, but the thought of someone other than Quinn sounded worse than going alone.

"Fine. Let's go. I'm saying one more thing to everyone, and then if anyone says another word about this, I'm not going."

"Well, we know Jax's mouth. He can't control what comes out of that thing. Kye and Dante are going on dates tonight, so I'm not sure if they are coming, and I think Fox doesn't want to believe it was Quinn."

I stood and shook my head with a small smile before stepping into the garage.

"Listen," I said, all eyes turning to me. "I'm not going to say that I know Quinn didn't do this, but I don't want to believe she did. We are always fair with each other and our fuck-ups. No one gets to treat her any different, and I will talk to her about it." I took a deep, painful breath and looked at Dante and Jax. "I won't hide what she says. Good or bad."

"Then we will drop it for now," Jax said, and Dante nodded in agreement.

"Great," I said, no enthusiasm in my voice. "Then it's time to wrap this up and go to a damn carnival."

At least that part was over. Now I needed to get through the night without trying to go to Quinn.

SEVENTEEN

QUINN

I spent Saturday in bed, trying to forget about Ransom, and did everything I could not to text him to see if he was ok.

Scout had texted asking if I wanted to go out with them tonight, but I said no. I didn't need another reason to be around Ransom, and when Josie burst into the room asking me to go out with her and her new boyfriend, I didn't hesitate to say yes.

"He's so nice. Did I tell you he got me this bracelet? It's Tiffany's. I can't believe he got it for me after only two weeks." She sat back at her desk, telling me all about him, waiting as I changed.

"Yeah, that was so nice of him. Did he say why he got it?"

"He thought it would be right to buy me a gift to ask me to be his girlfriend." She squealed with pure happiness, jumping up from the chair and hugging me. "He's like Prince Charming come to life."

I sat and pulled on my boots, thinking that walking all night in them would help me wear them in without having to look like a fool in front of everyone at the garage.

"You got new boots?"

"Oh yeah, I got them the other day," I said, not wanting to go over how I got them.

"While they look so much better than your last ones, are you really going to wear them tonight?"

I was wearing a sundress that fell right above my knees. The yellow and black pattern was like watercolor sunflowers, and I thought the black boots went perfect with them. I ignored the little voice in my head telling me that they reminded me of Ransom. I had also ignored it when I picked out my dress, wondering if he would have liked it.

"Yeah, why?"

"It's just Brad, and his friend are a little more, um…worried about their appearance." This friend Josie said I would love and had to meet. She had asked to set me up with him, and I agreed, praying to the universe I would somehow fall crazy in love with him and forget about Ransom.

"Are you saying I don't look good or that I don't look rich enough?"

"You know what? Forget I said anything. We need to get going, anyway. I don't want them to have to wait too long."

"Alright." I grabbed my bag and walked out.

"Are you getting a jacket? Do you need to borrow one?"

"No, I'm good." The day had been unusually hot, and I figured the night would be the same. I hated being too hot and didn't want to carry one of her ridiculously expensive jackets around all night, worrying about damaging it. Josie grabbed a white furry jacket and slammed the door behind us.

"Ohh, you're hoping Brad's friend will want to put his arm around you instead?"

"Not at all," I said, wondering why the tightening in my gut made me feel guilty. The thought of another guy's arm around me sounded strange, wrong almost, even though there was no reason it should.

"Does Brad's friend have a name?"

"Clark, something? I don't know. All I know is that they are in the same frat."

"Oh. I didn't realize Brad was a frat boy."

She rolled her eyes. "Don't say it like that. He's a great guy, and even if you don't usually go for frat boys, it wouldn't be bad to branch off from the type of guys you've been around. Speaking of, how's the new job been?"

"Interesting, but good. They are a good group of people, and I am learning a lot," I said, meaning every word.

"Interesting is a polite way to put it, but a great group of people is a stretch."

I furrowed my brows. "No, they have been pretty great. I've felt comfortable working there. More than I thought I would."

"Well, that's good," she said, adding a quiet "I guess" to the end.

I tried to ignore it, realizing that maybe I was a little too close to the situation. She wasn't wrong in worrying. In a way, I had been worried about the same thing a few weeks ago.

A night out with other people would give me a better outlook on everything. I was around this crew of people that were considered degenerates, dangerous even, and Scout, of course. I couldn't lump her sweet face into their problems.

It could be good to be around the opposite type of people for a while.

Josie had ordered a car, and we sat in silence until it dropped us around to the carnival entrance.

"Ok, the guys said they would meet us by the Ferris wheel. Come on." She grabbed my hand, pulling me through the crowds until the Ferris wheel rose up in front of us. I loved carnivals, the bright lights, the games, and the food. It felt like a different world when you were there, but my nerves were getting the best of me now. Meeting new people I knew I wouldn't fit in with made me feel uncomfortable in my own skin, and I hated it.

Josie squealed with delight as a guy came towards her with

open arms and a big smile. He was the typical frat guy. Something about them came off like they belonged together. A guy I assumed was Clark came up behind him and smiled at Josie. He looked exactly the same. He had the same haircut, the same loafer shoes, and the sunglasses perched on his head, even though it had been dark for hours.

I stepped forward, scolding myself. This was a good guy, a safe guy. The secure future and once-a-week date night guy. The no tattoos and no race cars type of guy.

The word boring was added to the end of it before I scolded myself.

The type of guy I should go for when I was looking for a future that didn't involve drinking, illegal activities, or any other type of life that could leave me like my mother.

"Quinn, this is Brad and Clark. Guys, this is Quinn." She waved her hand over me like she was presenting me to them. They looked me over, their eyes approving enough until they reached the boots, their cocked eyebrows giving away their thoughts. They hated them as much as Josie. I almost laughed, their hard stares only making me like the boots more.

"Nice to meet you guys. I've heard a lot about you both," I said, my voice even, polite, and so unlike my own.

"And we've heard a lot about you. Josie goes on and on about her friends. I'm glad you could come out tonight," Brad said.

"Same to you," I said, trying not to cringe. I hated the way my voice changed when I was talking to them. The way I pinned my shoulders back and sucked in my stomach. It felt like some twisted interview that I already knew I was going to fail.

"So, what do you girls want to do first?"

"Ohhh. I want to grab some warm apple cider," Josie said.

"Good choice. I think it's on the other side, though. Come on, babe." Brad grabbed her hand, leaving me to walk alone with Clark.

"Hey," he said.

"Hey," I said back, trying to think of anything else I could say, but I was coming up with nothing. The conversation felt weird and forced, even when it shouldn't.

He was good-looking, his brown hair cut short at the sides and perfectly styled on top, not like Ransom's hair, which seemed to stay messy. Clark's hair was gelled and styled to perfection. He was pristine, too, his skin and clothes flawless down to his un-scuffed white shoes. I stifled a laugh. I had been worried about them judging me for my shoes, but they were at a carnival with white loafers. The dirty ground would have them turning gray before the end of the night.

The harsh contrast between him and Ransom was astounding up close, and I didn't know what to make of that. Part of me was yelling it was a good thing, and the other was laughing that I thought I should come out with him tonight.

I had spent the past two nights making out with Ransom, and now here I was on a perfectly respectable date with Clark. After Ransom pushed me away last night, I knew it was the right thing to do, but it still felt off.

He was cute, but nothing in me cared. Just the thought of Ransom touching me made me wet, but when I thought of Clark touching me, even the me in my imagination drew back. I internally fought with myself. Maybe I needed to start the rubber band trick, snapping myself with it every time I thought of Ransom. My wrist would be red and raw, but it might start to work.

Clark had been saying something I missed, but I didn't want to admit it. I couldn't imagine it was polite to be thinking of how hot another guy made you when you were on a date with another one.

"Oh yeah, me too," I said, nodding along even though I didn't know what.

"Really? With those boots, I wouldn't have taken you for a golfer." He gave a light laugh, the sound polite and rehearsed.

I faced away to hide my nose scrunching. A golfer? I just agreed I was a damn golfer? I didn't know the first thing about golf, aside from putt-putt, of course.

"Oh yeah, love me some golfing time," I said.

"What club do you usually go to?"

I glanced around, buying myself time. Did he mean golf club or country club? Was there supposed to be a difference in them, anyway?

"Oh, um, I have a few I bounce around to. What about you?"

"I mostly go to Montgomery," he said, an air of arrogance about his answer. I assumed that meant it was one of the best places.

"I've never been."

We were walking near one of the parking lots, and I could hear cars revving as they turned into the parking lot. With the food trucks blocking the view, I couldn't see what the cars looked like, and I forced myself not to peer out and check.

They wouldn't come to a carnival tonight of all nights, would they? Did street racer mechanics even come to stuff like this? I groaned. The thought of them seeing me here with Clark made my cheeks flame in embarrassment. Clark kept talking, and I had to turn my attention back to him as the cars shut off in the distance.

"You should go. Honestly, it's the best option out there. I would love to take you some time. We have a standing tee time of seven am each weekend, so you're welcome with us anytime."

People were nuts. Waking up at the crack of dawn to go hit balls. While I had never tried it, I couldn't imagine it was something I would jump out of bed for. Then again, I would have laughed at you if you had told me a few weeks ago that I would be looking forward to going to street races on a Thursday night.

"Yeah, sounds great," I said, my voice still ridiculous.

I said the words over again. This was for me, for my best interest, and for a better future. I needed a better life than what I had before. I needed a good degree, a good job, a good boyfriend, and, one day, a good husband. I needed a life that wasn't my mother's, and that's what Josie was here trying to help me do. I needed to forget chasing any bad boy type and stick with guys like Clark.

We turned a corner, and I squeaked. Fox was walking down the middle of the aisle, a girl on his arm and a giant smile on his face. Jax walked behind them, with Kye next to him. My heart sank for a moment, not wanting to see Ransom with another girl until I saw him come behind, Scout hanging on his arm. Relief flooded me, and then reality came back.

I was there on a date. A date barely one day after almost begging Ransom to fuck me on the back of his car.

Somehow I didn't think that would go over well with him, considering how well it would go for me if he had been there with another girl.

A string of curse words went through my mind. It didn't matter. I could be there with whoever I wanted since Ransom and I weren't dating, not even close, and we never would be.

I wasn't going to get hurt again, but that also meant I didn't have to confront the crew while I was here with Clark.

"Fuck," I mumbled as they came closer.

Clark seemed oblivious to my staring. I turned, pulling him towards Brad and Josie and using them as a wall, hiding and hoping the crew wouldn't see me.

Luckily, Brad and Josie had stopped, getting us all in line for apple cider and donuts, so my hiding in the middle didn't look strange.

Clark gave me a confused smile, but didn't say anything as the line moved. I tried not to look suspicious as I stole glances at the crew.

Fox had yelled something, making them all turn down the

row with a round of yells and happy whoops from Scout. She
jumped on Ransom's back, and he grabbed her, holding her there
as she yelled something else. Suddenly, the entire crew at the
carnival didn't seem strange. It honestly looked like fun. They
bounced to the next game, the loud, rowdy group looking like
they were having the best night of their life.

Part of me was dying to know what they were doing and
what was so fun and exciting because I hadn't seen or felt
anything like that tonight. I've been too busy pretending to know
about golf.

The line moved, and it was our turn.

"I'll take—" my words were cut off as Clark nudged me.

"Hey, don't worry about it." Turning back to the woman, he
said, "We'll take two apple ciders."

"Wait, I want a donut," I said, trying to nudge closer.

He stopped me. "A donut? Really?"

"Yea? Why wouldn't I? This is about the only place to get an
apple cider donut."

"Uhh, maybe you can do that next time? Those aren't good
for you, so maybe just the cider."

My mouth fell open, but I didn't politely hide it. Did this
man really tell me I couldn't have a donut?

Then I noticed Josie hadn't got a donut either. I rolled my
eyes. Were rich people too good for donuts now?

Clark paid and turned to me, offering me the drink as though
it was a diamond ring.

"Oh, thanks." I snapped, taking a sip as we moved on. I
debated going back to buy one for myself, but I knew how mad
Josie would be. Somehow my turning back to buy such a bad-
for-you-food would embarrass her and ruin the night. I gazed at
the trailer again. My stomach rumbled, but I knew it was too
late.

It was like a switch, and I was back to my grumpy self in

minutes. I didn't want to play polite anymore, even though I knew I should keep trying, for Josie's sake.

We walked more as I persuaded them to go in the opposite direction of the crew. The carnival wasn't that big, though, and I worried I wouldn't be able to avoid them all night.

Clark said something, and I realized I was supposed to laugh as Josie and Brad broke into a fit of giggles. I forced a laugh as Clark watched me. I could see the approval in his eyes, the appreciative look as he stared. I was playing the part and doing a good job, even when I hated every second.

I looked down and pursed my lips.

Was this what I wanted? To play a part with someone, not be myself, or laugh even when their jokes weren't funny? Or not get a donut when I wanted one? God forbid I want a cookie next time.

And I couldn't imagine what Clark would say if I lost my temper one day. I pictured him getting mad, angry that I would have the nerve to talk back. When I pictured losing my temper with Ransom, I could only imagine his smirk, his irritating fucking smirk, and his soft tone before clothes were ripped off.

I groaned, trying to focus my attention back on Clark. I had been here all of thirty minutes.

I took a deep breath. I was going to have to give him a chance, a real chance.

It took less than two seconds, and my mind already wandered back to Ransom. Would he have got me a donut?

I groaned again. I needed the rubber band on my wrist to snap.

EIGHTEEN

QUINN

WE WALKED FOR ANOTHER HOUR, but it felt like days.

My brain was turning to mush, and my eyes were glazing over every time Clark opened his mouth.

Minute after minute of the dullest conversation ever, until I knew everything about him. Golf, frat houses, his finance degree, even the BMW he was given as a birthday present. He spoke about the car as though he built it himself. Working at the garage filled me with shock at his audacity to act like he worked as hard on it as the guys did on their cars. He hadn't even worked hard to have it. We both knew he wasn't fixing anything on the car with his own hands.

It made it worse when I realized he hadn't asked me much more about myself, choosing to ask if I agreed, and when I nodded, he would move on to the next dull topic.

We were supposed to stay for another two hours, the car picking us back up at eleven, and I questioned if I could make it that long as Clark's date.

Could I pretend to pass out? Would Ransom figure it out and come help me? I let my imagination run wild as Clark went on and on about some party they had this weekend.

"Hey, guys!" Josie yelled to us, snapping me out of my trance of boredom, "We're going to make out in the funhouse." She wiggled her eyebrows. "Want to come?"

"Not a chance," I yelled out with a laugh before I realized what I had implied. "Not that I have a problem with you. Just that I didn't want to do....that." I said, waving my hand at the fun house as I rambled.

"No, I get it," he said.

Josie ran inside with Brad, and Clark stepped closer. I tried not to make it too obvious as I took a step back, but he didn't seem to care, moving towards me again.

"We might not be at the make-out-in-the-fun-house stage yet," he ran up my arm, "but how do you feel about a kiss out here?"

"Umm, not quite there yet either," I said as sweet as I could, a sudden worry upsetting him might cause a scene. A loud enough one that the entire crew might see it.

He wrapped his fingers around my wrist, moving down to grab my hand, but I pulled it away, trying not to scrunch my face.

"Really? I was there the moment I met you."

"Really?" I mimicked back. "I thought the boots threw you off." I laughed and took another step back.

"They did, but I guess the rebel thing has grown on me now that I know you."

"What does that mean?"

"It's just...I get it. The world we live in can be a little stuffy. It's nice to rebel sometimes. Even if it's only with some boots."

"I don't think you understood that I don't come from your world, so there's no need to rebel."

"What? I thought you and Josie came from money?"

My eyebrows shot up. "Um, no, Josie does. I do not. I come from dirt, dirt poor." I laughed, trying to let go of any judgment I had for myself. I really didn't care if Clark was ok with it or not.

"Oh well, that explains some things then."

My nose scrunched at his tone. "What things?"

"Josie had mentioned you had a rough time earlier this year and needed a nice guy. That's why I chose to come, because I am a nice guy."

I laughed at his ego, but stopped as he took another step closer. I knew what a guy who called himself a nice guy meant. "Clark, seriously, enough."

He grabbed my wrist hard, forcing it over to him. "It's ok, Quinn. We can do anything you want. I won't hurt you or post it online, so you can relax." He pulled my wrist up towards his lips. I wasn't hiding it now, the action so forced and creepy that I couldn't hide my face twisting in disgust at his words. So he knew about the video then.

It always seemed to bring out the maggots.

"Get off of me." I tried to yank it away, but his fingers gripped harder, ripping me forward.

"Relax, Quinn. I know girls like you want a guy like me. I'm making it easy for you."

My stomach churned, and I almost puked as I pulled back hard again, my skin twisting until it burned.

His mouth puckered as he leaned in just as an arm snaked around my shoulders. I jerked away but stilled when I noticed a set of boots that matched mine perfectly. I looked up, Ransom's eyes fixated on Clark.

"Oh," I said, the shock in my tone making Clark's eyes open. He stood straight, finally noticing Ransom and his protective arm around me.

"Hey, Kitten, who's your friend?"

Clark and I were both stunned. For a moment, I couldn't even think of what to say until Clark's hands finally let go of me.

"Ransom, this is Clark. Clark, this is my friend, Ransom."

Clark's eyebrows shot up. "Your friend?"

"Yeah," I said again. Clark was looking him over, and it took everything in me not to follow his gaze. I knew what Ransom looked like to Clark, though, and I knew the calm glare that could make anyone uncomfortable.

"And your name is really Ransom?"

"Is that a problem?" Ransom said, his tone polite.

"No, just—" Clark leaned towards me, "Are you seriously friends with a guy like this?"

I couldn't take it anymore. I finally looked up at Ransom. The bruise on his jaw had spread and turned a deep purple. The cuts on his arm were still fresh, and I could see the bandage wrapped along his neck just above a tattoo I knew stretched across his shoulders. He looked dangerous, eyes darkening and body so beaten and raw.

He looked like every sin I wanted to commit.

"Friends, people who work together, all of it," I said as Ransom pulled me in closer. He smelled so good, the musk scent of his cologne making me want to take a deep breath and lean into him.

"Well, nice to meet you, Ransom," he said his name like it was beneath him, "I didn't realize you worked. I thought you were a student."

"I do both."

He gave a sharp nod, his lips so pursed I thought they would turn purple soon. "Well, not to be rude, but Quinn and I need to go back to our date now."

Ransom wasn't much taller than Clark but commanded so much space that it didn't matter. He looked down at him. "No," he said. The word was confident and final.

"No?" Clark repeated.

"No," he said again.

"And why not?" Clark said.

"Because I'm ready for my date with Quinn to start."

My eyebrows shot up, and I froze.

"You have a date with this guy?" Clark said, and I realized it was now my decision. I could pull out of Ransom's grip and stay here to deal with Clark alone, or I could agree and say I did have a date with Ransom, getting out of here without wasting another minute with Clark.

It wasn't a hard choice.

"Yes. I do."

"But you still came out here with me to what? Be a tease? Are you some sort of —" Ransom stepped forward, his arm around me falling.

"Finish that sentence, and I'll break your fucking jaw," he said, his arms relaxed at his sides. His whole body seemed calm, but I knew he wasn't lying. If Clark finished what he was about to say, Ransom would hit him.

I thought of all the movies I saw where the girl begged the guys not to fight. They would cry that it wasn't worth it, that she didn't want him to get hurt or get in trouble.

For a second, I wondered if I should pull him back, stop him and ask him not to fight, but I didn't.

I wasn't worried about playing that part. I was fine if he wanted to hit Clark for me. I wanted to hit him myself. And I definitely wasn't worried about Ransom getting hurt. Even with his cuts, I knew he would win any fight with someone like Clark. Part of me liked the power, knowing someone would protect me without a second thought. It wasn't right, but I still reveled in it for a minute.

I waited, ready for Clark to say the next word. The guy had been giving me the creeps for the last hour, and now I wanted him to get away from me.

"You know what?" Clark said. "Fuck you then. Fuck you both. This isn't worth a night with a girl like her." He glared over at me, but I was looking at Ransom.

His nostrils flared, and he charged forward, but Clark was already scurrying away.

I stood, stunned at his words, stunned at Ransom's protection.

So Clark was using me for one night. The guy that was supposed to be sweet and secure, safe even, was trying to use me for sex and force me into touching him. And the guy that was supposed to be hurting me was protecting me. Using his already broken body to make sure I wasn't called names. Coming to rescue me from the creep the moment I needed him.

I reached for Ransom's hand, and he gave it willingly, coming with me as I pulled him along.

NINETEEN

QUINN

I PULLED him through the crowds and around into the dark shadow of the funhouse, not stopping until my back hit the metal wall. His hands braced on each side of me as his head leaned toward mine.

He was so close, but still didn't lay a finger on me.

"Thank you," I whispered.

"So you did want me to come for you?"

"Did you think I wouldn't?"

"I didn't know. You seemed like you were enjoying yourself the first time I saw you when we came in. Then you were alone together, and he was grabbing at you." He took a deep breath. "I wanted to come over and punch him in the face, but I thought you would rather me give you the choice." His dark hair fell across his forehead, and I reached up to move it, needing to touch him. He didn't move, just waited for my answer as his eyes burned into me.

"I wanted you to come. You could have come earlier, even, and I would have been relieved. That was one of the most boring dates of my life."

"You saw us come in then?"

"I heard the cars and then saw you."

"You didn't want to say hi to us?"

"No. I was embarrassed."

"And why's that?" he asked, his tone so low and dark that I shuttered.

"Because that guy is a tool, and I was supposed to be here on a date with him."

"So I can assume the date went bad?"

I gave a strangled laugh. "You just threatened to break his face, and I was happy you did. I'd say it was a bad one."

"You hate me so much you wanted to go on a date with someone else?" His words were so quiet, and for a second, I thought he was hurt.

"I thought he was the type of guy I needed."

"And I'll never be the type of guy you need." It was a statement, one I didn't know how to answer. I knew Clark wasn't the guy for me, but that didn't mean Ransom was all of a sudden.

"You were what I needed tonight. You were there when I needed you." It was all I could offer him, and I didn't know why that made my chest hurt.

"I will always be there when you need me."

It was statements like that which made me wonder what he was doing. They sounded so long-term, like he would be there for me forever, but I knew he wasn't that type of person. I never knew him to have a girlfriend. If he did, they weren't together for long, as far as I could tell.

"Yea?" It was the only thing I could say as he moved closer, his body only inches from mine.

He leaned down and nuzzled into my neck, making a burning heat shoot through me. All I could think of was wanting more, needing more of him.

He tried to move back. I wrapped my arms around him to try

to pull him hard against me, but he was unmoving. His hands stayed on each side of my head, and I wanted to rip them off the metal and put them on me.

"Did you think of me at all when you were with him?" he asked, his lips so close to mine they were almost touching. I leaned in until they were letting my tongue run along his bottom lip.

I could barely hear the words. I wanted him all over me, but he was still holding back. I pulled at his shirt, trying to bring him closer. The desperate need for his hands was leaving me speechless. I needed him to get the hint, but he still didn't move.

He wanted an answer first.

"Yes," I said. "I was comparing him to you all night."

"And?"

"And you're the one I decided to pull back here with me."

"I love knowing you think about me as much as I think about you," he said. "I've been dying all night knowing you came with him." He bit hard at my neck, making me arch against him with a gasp. "I wanted to kill him. I wanted to punish you. I don't think I can handle seeing another guy's hands on you ever again."

"I'm sorry," I said, meaning it. "I don't know what I would have done if you were here on a date."

He growled against my ear, "Are you saying you would have been jealous?"

"Yes," I said the words so fast they came out like a breath. "I thought you were for a second and was ready to burn the place down."

He laughed against my neck, his breath sending an agonizing shiver down my back. "Then you can understand why all I've thought about tonight was killing that guy and tying you to my bed."

I moaned at the thought, "Will you please do one more thing for me?"

"I would do anything for you right now." His voice was raspy and low, making me wonder how he was still able to hold back.

"Can you please put your hands on me now?"

"I don't know. I do still want to punish you, Kitten. I don't ever want to see you out with another guy, especially one who thinks he can touch you like that. Maybe me not touching you right now would help you remember that."

"I would deserve every second of punishment. I didn't want to be out with him. I don't know what I would have done without you here."

"I have no doubt that you would have kicked his fucking ass," he said with a quiet laugh, "but if I ever have to see you go on a date with another asshole, I'm not going to wait for your call before I beat the fuck out of him."

"I would prefer to never go on another date with an asshole."

"I would prefer you never go on another date at all." He grazed my neck with his nose, and I could feel his warm breath tickling my skin.

"Please, I think I've learned my lesson." I pushed my hips towards him again, but he inched away.

"I don't know. You haven't convinced me."

"Ransom, if you don't take care of this problem for me. I will go find someone who will."

He growled, his hands sliding down my body, grabbing my ass, and picking me up to pin me hard against the wall. My legs wrapped around his back. One of his hands roamed until it reached my breast, cupping it and moving his thumb over my nipple until he pinched it.

"Always trying to taunt me," he said.

His hands moved back to my throat, wrapping his fingers around it but not squeezing. I was already so wet, his touch making me ready to beg for him to fuck me right there. I didn't care what came next. Right now, I wanted it all.

"Ransom," I murmured.

"Anything," he said, his voice breathless. His teeth found my neck as he scraped down it toward my chest, licking and kissing every inch of skin he could find. The feel of it sent shockwaves to my core, every desperate touch sending me spiraling into a deeper need. I moaned, thankful that the noise of the carnival masked every sound.

"More," I demanded.

I ground my hips against his stomach until he lowered me. I could feel his cock push hard against me through my wet panties. He slid me down until one of my legs was back on the ground. He kissed down my body, and I could only hold my breath, waiting as he inched closer and closer to the one spot I needed him.

"Are you kidding me?" he asked with a small laugh. His fingers stopped on my thigh, way too close and too far from where I wanted them.

"What?"

"You're so wet it's dripping down your leg."

"Sorry," I said, not knowing what I was apologizing for. His fingers were so close I wanted to force them higher.

"Sorry? That's not something to be sorry for. It makes the not having sex with you part a whole hell of a lot harder." His other hand reached for mine, moving it over his jeans until it rested on his hard cock. "I've never been so hard in my life. Every time I think of you, it's fucking agony."

Finally, his hands moved until he hit between my legs. My back arched into him as I moaned. The contact was almost enough to make me come right then and there.

"Please," I begged.

"Do you want to come on me?"

"Yes. I need you."

His fingers circled my entrance and back to my clit, teasing and torturing me.

"Say it again."

"I need you, Ransom."

He groaned as his fingers plunged into me. The palm of his hand grinding against my swollen clit. Tears pricked my eyes at the overwhelming pleasure. He pushed hard, pulling out his drenched fingers and slamming them back into me again and again. My legs clenched around him as the pleasure built.

"Are you close?" he asked, and I nodded. "Look at me."

I did, meeting his eyes in the dark, the carnival giving off enough light to see him. The intensity of his gaze made me hotter.

The world shattered around me, the waves of pleasure racking my body as I rode his hand. I moaned again, and his lips covered mine, muffling the sound.

"So good," he whispered, "So, so good."

My chest heaved as he pulled his fingers from me and held me against the wall. He licked and sucked at the two wet fingers before kneeling in front of me, spreading my legs and dipping his head under my dress.

"Ransom, I can't," I said as his tongue ran up my thigh, licking every inch.

"You can and will."

His tongue moved higher, moving my underwear out of the way to lick and suck every inch of me. My legs shook, every part of me sensitive and aching from him, for more of him. "If you don't stop, I'm going to come again," I said, pulling at his hair.

"That's the point," he said, laughing against my pussy, the vibration leaving a tingling sensation through me. His tongue moved against me until he reached my sensitive clit, sucking and licking until my body spasmed. I pushed my lips together as I tried not to scream. The world exploding around me as I came again.

"Ransom, please." I panted, pulling at him. "I'm not going to be able to hold myself up in a minute."

"I just didn't want to leave you unpresentable," he said, kissing my legs as he pulled off my now-soaked underwear.

"Wow," I breathed hard, trying to steady the beat of my heart, "what a gentleman."

"I'm glad you think so. Of course, some would argue doing this behind a fun house at a carnival isn't a gentlemanly move, but I wanted to do things that were so much worse."

"So then, why aren't we having sex?" I asked, remembering what he had said.

"I'm pretty sure I can't have sex with you behind a fun house at a carnival."

I couldn't hide my laugh. "Wow, never thought I would be disappointed to hear that sentence."

"Well fuck. I'm about ready to stay on my knees and beg you to come home with me so I can."

"Mmmm," I said, looking down at him. "I'm about ready to agree."

He pulled off my underwear. "You're a bad influence, Kitten, and I think these need to go."

He stood up and stepped against me, letting me know he was still hard. I trailed my fingers along his cock, lost in my own head on if I should tell him to take me home. With just his hand gave me one of the best orgasms of my life. I wanted to know what sex with Ransom would be like.

Before I could think of how to say it, he pulled me off the wall and into his arms, pressing his lips to mine.

"You look beautiful tonight. You wore the boots even on a date with that guy," he said.

I nodded again, embarrassed at how much I had thought of him all day. "I thought they worked great with the dress."

He leaned down and kissed me again, this one softer as he held my hips. "They do."

"What about you?" I asked.

"Me?" he asked, nuzzling into me again. "What about me?

"What about you...getting off?" I asked, wondering how I could be embarrassed to say the words out loud after what he had just done to me.

"I'm already worried about you regretting all that. I don't think we need to add it."

"If you thought I was going to regret it, why did you do it?"

He leaned down, whispering into my ear, "Because I'm bad, remember? The worst, and I was entirely selfish in wanting you all to myself for a moment when you were ready to give something. Whether you decide if you regret it or not, I'll be thinking of that moment right then. Your face when you came. I could get off thinking about what just happened forever."

His words stopped me. "What if I don't end up regretting it?"

"Then please, please tell me the moment you want more."

A wave of pleasure rolled through me at the thought of having more of Ransom. He was right, though. I could wake up tomorrow and regret it.

I pushed the thought away because, for tonight, I didn't.

"Aren't you cold?" he asked.

The wind had picked up, bringing in a colder breeze than I was ready for. He didn't wait for my answer and pulled off his jacket, sliding it around me. It fell almost to the length of my dress and smelled like him.

"What do I do now?" I asked. "I don't think I can go back and face Josie after this. She's going to be pissed."

"The crew is around somewhere. Come hang out with us."

He was already walking us out from behind the fun house, holding onto my hand and pulling me with him. "Fine, but you guys can't let Josie see me."

"Not a problem."

We wound through the crowd, and he didn't let me go. My head was a mess of him, his touch turning the world around me to dust as I thought of his hand in mine.

We turned the corner, and I could see the crew scanning the

crowd for Ransom. The thought of them being able to tell exactly what had happened between us made me drop his hand and take a step away from him.

Even not touching him, I still felt branded, like they would be able to read it clearly across my face.

"Quinn," Scout said, running full speed towards me and jumping into my arms. I lost my balance, and Ransom caught me holding us both up.

"Damn, Scout, give people a warning," he said.

"I got excited. I didn't know you were coming here! Why didn't you have us pick you up?"

"Quinn was here with her friend but wants to hang out with us."

"Who wouldn't?" Scout said with a smile, dragging me over to the guys.

"Damn, Quinn." Fox said, his arms still around the girl I had never seen. "you look hot." The girl looked up at him, her face showing just how pissed off that comment made her.

"Uh, Fox," Scout said. "Probably not what you should say in front of your date."

"Well, I have eyes, don't I? She looks hot, right Ransom?" His eyes shined, and I could feel my face burning. Did Fox already know what we had done?

I pleaded with Ransom in my head not to say anything. I was too worried that one wrong word was going to give it away.

For once in his life, he didn't keep quiet. Instead, he threw an arm over my shoulder. The casual touch set me on fire. "You know what, Fox? She does look hot."

Fox nodded. "Fucking finally, dude," he said with a shake of his head and leaned down to say something to the girl on his arm. His charm worked, and she smiled back up at him.

"Alright, weirdos," Scout said, "I have two more rows to go, and unless you want to be standing here all night, we better get moving." She jumped to the next stall, this one a game of darts to win a prize.

Ransom's arm was still around me, making my entire body hum, but I tried to look calm. Fox put his arm around me all the time, and that was normal, right? No one thought twice about that. I didn't know why this felt like a secret on display for everyone to see.

"What does she mean?" I asked.

"Scout has a carnival addiction," Jax said. "She has to play every damn game here, or her head might explode."

"Hey," Fox said, grabbing our attention, "we're leaving, and one of you is bringing Scout home." He waved, not waiting for an answer as the girl giggled on their way out.

Scout yelled in excitement, throwing another dart.

I thought about how I was getting home now. I wasn't going with Clark or Josie, and I still didn't want to waste money to pay for a cab.

"Ransom." I whispered, "Can you give me a ride home?"

He smiled but didn't answer, getting lost in a thought he didn't seem to want to share.

"Ransom," I said, angrier now. "Are you giving me a ride home, or do I need to find someone else too?"

He laughed, leaning down to my ear, "Always with the threats. Of course, I'm driving you home. Do you think I would be stupid enough to let you find a ride from someone other than me when I still have your underwear in my pocket?"

I smacked his chest. "You're the worst."

"I think we both knew that, but I'll keep taking every second I can until it really sinks in."

We played more games as Scout won, trading her prize until she ended up with an alien that was twice her size.

Ransom's words weighed on me. Was he the worst? The way he was treating me was the best I had ever been treated.

Two hours later, we all loaded into the cars, Scout riding with Jax, and I was once again alone with Ransom.

He reached over as he pulled onto the main road, grabbing my hand and wrapping it around the shifter. His hand blanketed mine as he shifted.

"Wow," I said as he moved it again. I wasn't driving, but I could feel the power of the car and his ease at using it.

We drove in silence, but I kept my hand on the shifter as he told me what to do. Soon, I was shifting when he told me to. His hand was still over mine, but I was controlling it.

"That is fun. Much better than my old car."

He laughed. "That's one reason we do it."

We pulled into my dorm's parking lot, and I was surprised that I was sad the night was over.

"Don't hate me in the morning," he said, pulling my hand up to kiss my palm.

"I don't want to."

"But you will." He leaned over, pulling me in for another kiss. He didn't wait as he nipped at my bottom lip and started moving to get closer. I put my hand on his chest, stopping him.

He was right, and I had to stop this before I fell any further.

If that was even possible.

"Goodnight, Ransom."

"Goodnight, Kitten."

I jumped from the car and went inside, turning to watch his car peel from the parking lot and jump forward, speeding off into the dark.

It was the same scene as when he dropped me off the first night. It hadn't even been a month, but everything was different. There was no changing what happened between us now.

I hated that he thought I would regret what happened tonight. I hated it even more, that I would probably regret it in the morning.

It wasn't what happened, but knowing I couldn't let myself get close to him now. I knew he had secrets he didn't want me to know.

I couldn't get close to the fire again and risk getting burned, even if I wanted to.

TWENTY

RANSOM

MONDAY CAME FAST, each day a blur of cars, parts, and now having to go over and then back over who could have come into the shop to take the parts.

I had ordered replacement parts, but the thought of it happening again had me on edge. I also ordered another camera after finding out our setup missed the angle of the door perfectly. Someone had known what they were doing and had a key. I told everyone I would tell Quinn and ask about her key, but I hadn't done it yet, needing to wait until I could see her again.

It was another hour before she walked in. She never came through the garage anymore, and today was no different, but I always listened for the front door to the office to open and close. I hadn't seen her since the carnival, and each second that went by set me further on edge. I didn't know if she regretted it now or wanted more like I did. She could hate me again for all I knew. I stopped at the door. My cock was getting hard at the thought of touching her again, getting the chance to taste her again. I felt like an idiot.

I stepped inside, and she turned, freezing like a deer in headlights. Her shirt was cut into a deep V, giving me a perfect view of her breasts, and she wore the same type of tight leggings as race night, along with her boots. Similar outfits had seemed to become her work clothes, and I wondered if she knew how crazy it drove me. I couldn't catch my breath as I looked her over. She was a dream come fucking true, and now she was in my garage every day. Weeks of torture came to a head at the carnival when I couldn't stay away any longer, and I still couldn't now.

I took a chance, taking three large steps and grabbing her, wrapping my hands around her thighs and picking her up, setting her on the desk.

"Wow. Hi," she said, her voice quiet. I remembered her saying my name in that same tone as she came, and I wanted to hear it again. I searched her face, trying to see any hint that she wanted me to move away, but there was nothing.

"Hi."

Her hand came up, running along my jaw until she threaded into my hair, pulling me close with one yank.

It was all I needed.

I pulled her in, slamming my lips onto hers, biting and licking until I drove my tongue into her mouth. I needed her closer. I needed less clothes and more skin.

She leaned back, and I followed, coming over her on the desk. I reached for every part of her, stroking her sides and palming her breasts.

"Ransom," she moaned as I slid a hand along her thigh, going up until I ran a finger over her pussy.

"Mmm. I like when you say my name like that."

"Someone could see us here."

"Then I think you need to be wearing another dress to make this a lot easier."

She laughed and pushed me back an inch, her eyes heavy. "Oh yea? New work uniform?"

I nodded, "Mandatory." I leaned in, taking her mouth with

mine again. "Does this mean you aren't completely full of regret?"

"Yes. Well, I mean, not right this second, no."

Her hand slid under my shirt, running over my stomach and chest. Her touch sent ripples of pleasure through my body, and I couldn't hide it. I took a deep breath, her soft hands on me filling a need that I didn't know I had.

She smiled, moving her hands again, trailing back down my body until her fingers hooked into my pants.

I groaned, "Quinn."

"Yes?" Her voice was so sweet as her fingers dipped down further.

"Not only has it been a while since I've had sex, but it's you, so I might lose my mind and, more importantly, my self-control if you go any further."

Her hand stopped, "Oh. So I guess we're ruling out sex on the desk then too? Wow, I would have guessed Ransom Ward was more adventurous than this. No carnival sex, no office sex. I'm shocked."

I laughed and pushed into her again. Her fingers slid farther into my pants at the motion, and it forced her further onto the desk until she was almost on her back.

"Are you taunting me?" I growled, prowling over her. "Do you want me to fuck you right here on the desk?"

Her eyes went wide, but she didn't say anything. I leaned down, pressing a line of kisses over her cheek and down her neck. "Want me to rip these right off of you?" I pulled at her leggings. "Fuck you hard until you scream my name? I liked when you did that. I bet you'll like my cock even more than my fingers. Make you scream even louder." I whispered into her, dipping my hand into her leggings until her legs clenched.

"I–." Her words dropped off as she pushed her hips up, "Yes. I want –."

I laughed. "I wasn't ruling it out for my sake. You say the word, and I will lock that door."

She glanced from me to the door, and my heart stopped, wondering if she was actually considering it, but like switching off a light, her face fell, twisting with pain and disgust. It was the wrong thing to say.

"No. No, definitely not. Move back in case someone walks in," she said.

The surprise at her change made me drop my hands and step back. "Are you worried about being seen with me in particular or being seen at all?"

"Ransom, I've been put on full display before. I don't need it to happen again."

I reached out, grabbing her hips, and she jerked back.

"No, stop. We can't do that again."

"Relax, I was getting you down." I pulled her onto the ground and started to fix all the shit she had so neatly organized before on the desk.

"That's all wrong."

I shook my head. Her snippy attitude was never-ending. "Fine. I'll sit over here and watch as you fix it." I went over to the desk chair, leaning back and watching her as she watched me.

"I told you, Quinn, there's no trap here. Even if someone had walked in and seen us, they would have laughed and closed the door. We might not hear the end of it," I said with a smirk. "But no one outside of this crew is going to know what happened if we don't want them to."

She stared at me in silence. I couldn't even start to guess what she was thinking, and I wasn't going to try now. She moved, organizing the desk in whatever precise way she had.

"Quinn, you didn't answer me. Are you afraid to be seen or just seen with me?"

I could see tears filling her eyes, but she stopped them before any could spill over. "I don't know. Both? If I'm seen with you, people will treat me worse. They will assume I'm sleeping around. I think everyone here knows you don't have relationships, and you have no idea what people said to me after the video. I don't know if I can add fuel to that fire."

A knife sliced through my chest, but I leaned back, not letting it show, "Well, I do like that you're honest."

Her lips pursed, and she crossed her arms, giving me an annoyed look. I shifted, hiding how much it was turning me on.

"I can stop anyone from saying that shit to you. I can make it easier if you let me."

"You can't stop everyone."

"I will," I said, meaning it. I'd tear apart anyone who wanted to talk to her like that. "Would that help you not hate me?"

"I don't hate you."

I laughed, "You don't exactly like me."

"I don't know how I feel about you."

Now she was twisting the knife. "I know how I feel about you. If you are ever ready to find out, let me know."

I didn't want to talk anymore about how much she hated me or how embarrassed she would be to be seen with me. We had worse things to talk about anyway. "Do you still have the key Fox gave you?"

Her eyebrows furrowed before she went to her bag, digging inside and holding it up, "Right here, why?"

"Someone broke in the other night after we all left. They took a few parts off the car I'm working on. Fox swears the door they came in was locked when he left, so the person would need a key."

Her eyes went wide. "Ransom, I didn't do it! I don't know anything about these cars, and I didn't give the key out to anyone. I would never -"

"Take a breath. I know you didn't do it. I was making sure someone didn't swipe your key."

"Oh." She took a deep breath, her chest heaving once, "Okay, good."

"That leaves us right at the beginning, then. I don't know who would have done it. Even if someone on the crew took the parts, we would see them when they installed them on their cars."

"That's true. And why steal parts? I've seen the papers, and you guys seem to buy enough parts for your own cars. It doesn't look like any one of you is lacking the parts you need."

"Good point. So we need to assume someone picked the lock because everyone has their key."

She shivered. "How invasive."

The door swung open, and Jax walked in, stopping as he saw us. There was an entire desk between us, but Quinn still jumped away from me.

She just kept twisting that damn knife into me.

"What's up?"

"It can wait. Just needed your opinion on something." He looked between us with raised brows, but I stood up before he could say anything else.

"No, it's fine. I'm coming out. We're done here." He nodded and turned back, heading into the garage but leaving the door open.

"Ransom, I think this has to be done for good. Whatever make-out party we keep getting into can't happen again. It can't go any further."

It was my turn to stare, my mind going into overdrive but not finding anything to say. Maybe she was right, at least until I got this Slaughter thing figured out and figure out who the fuck got into our garage. I stopped next to her and grabbed the back of her neck, pulling her into another kiss. I heard her suck in a breath as my lips came down on hers.

"We can be done for now. Not for good, though."

"We have to be."

"I see the regret has finally set in."

Her eyes were wide, but I didn't say another word as I left, walking out into the garage and shutting the door behind me.

Whatever the fuck Quinn Carter hated about me was still there. Whatever part of her that thought Logan, or apparently Ryder, was a better choice than I was, seemed to still be stuck in her mind.

It didn't matter what I did or didn't do for her. In her mind, I was the enemy. The bad guy in all of this, and it didn't feel like that was changing anytime soon. Maybe she did like touching me, but she didn't want more than that, and most days, barely even wanted that.

I was the monster. I could do everything right, and to her, I was always going to be the devil that would ruin her.

As much as every moment of doubt from her hurt, I wasn't done with Quinn, and I worried I would never be.

TWENTY-ONE

QUINN

THE NEXT FEW days were filled with classes, homework, going to work at the garage, and avoiding Ransom at all costs. He had given me my space, not pushing me to even talk to him after Monday in the office.

I was supposed to be relieved, especially after telling him we couldn't let that happen anymore. The other part of me was annoyed, wishing he would come and kiss me again. Wishing I could agree to do it again as easily as I would have before the video.

I walked in on Wednesday, expecting the same as every other day this week, but the door to the office was locked in the front, forcing me to walk through the garage. I had done so well at avoiding Ransom all week that I had to stop and take a deep breath as I stepped inside.

I walked straight to the office door, trying to avoid meeting his eyes.

That door was locked, too. I whipped around, panic ripping through me. Was this how they were telling me I was fired?

Fox, Ransom, and Jax walked over, circling me.

"Scout locked herself in there an hour ago," Fox said.

"We tried talking to her, but she threatened us if we tried to go in," Ransom said.

"She's never done this before," Jax said.

All three of them were baffled, not knowing what to do next.

I knocked, and something shattered against the door. I jumped back, but the guys didn't move. "I don't know what the hell she is breaking in there, but that's the third time that's happened," Fox said.

"Scout." I said, knocking again. "It's Quinn. Can I come in?"

The entire garage fell quiet, waiting for an answer.

"Fine, but if any of those boys show their face, they are getting a dart in the eyeball."

"Fair enough," I yelled and turned to them while I waited. "What the hell did you guys do to her?"

"Nothing." They all said in unison, throwing up innocent hands.

"Oh, right? I'm sure she locked herself in here for nothing."

I pushed inside, locking the door behind me, leaning against it, and taking note of the room.

It wasn't much of a mess other than the mugs that had shattered against the door.

"Scout?" I said, not seeing her. She stepped out of the bathroom, her eyes and nose red from crying.

"What's wrong?"

She ran over, pulling me into a hug. I hugged back, knowing what it was like to cry alone. "What happened?"

"I went to school and," she sucked in a deep, crying breath, "the girls made fun of me for wearing a dress. They, of course, know who I am and who I hang out with, but I just wanted to be seen like a girl today. Not the little girl who works on cars with all the scary guys. The bitchy girls made it such a spectacle all day, though. I felt so stupid for trying to dress like this. Then," she sucked in another breath, "the guy I liked sided with the mean girls, saying I looked strange in a dress. So then I come here, and all the guys ask why I'm wearing this and why I'm dressed so girly. Kye even told me to go put on some pants, and Ransom agreed with him. I wanted to feel pretty for one damn day," she said, crying harder into my shirt.

"Scout, you are beautiful in the dress. You always look beautiful," I said, meaning it. Scout hit the good looks jackpot. The perfect body, face, lips, and even her hair did everything she wanted it to. She worked on cars all day and still looked adorable every single time.

"No, I'm little and young, and people treat me like a child. Guys, don't look twice. It doesn't help that I hang around five scary-looking guys that will beat the shit out of anyone for me. People know it, the rumors of them have been around for years, and I'm stuck in that shadow."

She wasn't wrong. People were scared of this crew. It made up half the rumors at school when they were there, and I believed her that the rumors still made their way inside the school for Scout to deal with alone. Kye was in school too, but since he didn't go half the time, I couldn't imagine it bothered him as bad.

It wasn't any wonder why guys would stay away from Scout. She came with bodyguards that are rumored to kill people.

I pulled her back. "You're gorgeous, Scout, and all those guys out there know it. That's why they worried when they saw you in a dress. They don't know how to keep you safe and keep the guys away from you when you look so pretty. In this dress? You'll have guys lining up to be beaten up by this crew to get a chance at you. And as for the bitchy girls at school, don't even worry about them. You will graduate and never have to see them again. I dealt with the same thing. It all changes once you're out."

She laughed, a sob coming with it, "Why didn't the guy I wanted to pay attention to me want to then?"

"Because he's stupid? Most high school boys don't know a thing, including when a girl likes them. And you want a guy who isn't afraid of those guys out there. One who isn't afraid to stick up for you and isn't intimidated by how smart you are and how good of a driver or mechanic you are." I pulled her to the couch, and we both fell back, my arms still around her. "And those boys out in the garage aren't much better than high school boys. Freaked out or not, I can't believe they said that to you. Especially Ransom," I said. He seemed to like my dress a little too much, but couldn't compliment Scout for dressing up.

"Wait," she said, pulling back, "Why 'especially Ransom'?"

"Nothing. Just…nothing. Can I yell at them yet?"

"Yeah. I guess that would be good. All this crying has me wiped out."

I smiled at her and then pulled the door open, stepping into the garage.

All eyes turned to me.

"You all need to listen closely. Scout is a girl. An extremely pretty one at that, and if she walks around here in a dress, you compliment her. You DO NOT make fun of her, tell her to change, call her names, insinuate she isn't pretty, or anything along those lines, you assholes," I said, pointing to each one. "She already has to put up with all of you when she's here and has to walk around with every guy, knowing she has an army of bodyguards. Do you know what rumors go around about you guys? She carries that around with her at school all alone. She doesn't need you all making her feel like shit."

Quiet filled the garage until Fox smiled, "You got it, boss," he said, thinking his charm would get him back on my good side. I flipped him off and turned to Ransom. "You," I said, and he raised his eyebrows. "Outside."

A chorus of ooh's filled the room. "At least someone is in more trouble than us," Jax said, turning back to the car he was working on.

Ransom walked out the back door but glanced over his shoulder at me. I pushed against his back, picking up the pace. The door slammed behind us, and I turned on him.

"How could you make fun of Scout for wearing a dress and telling her to put more clothes on?" I yelled, "That's quite hypocritical of you when you didn't mind me in my dress the other night."

His eyes darkened, and he gave a small smile as he leaned against the building, unmoved by my yelling at him.

"I would keep your voice down a bit, Kitten. The garage doors are still open." I looked over the back garage doors that were maybe twenty feet from us and wide open.

I growled as he tried to hide his laugh. "Why did you say that to her?"

"Because I know how pretty she is, and she doesn't. I also know what goes through a guy's mind when he sees a pretty girl in a dress like that." He pushed off the wall and stalked towards me, grabbing my hips and pulling me in. "I know because those thoughts were running through my mind the minute I saw you the other night, and I only got to do a fraction of what I had been thinking about."

I swallowed as he leaned down, his nose running along my jaw. It was a light touch, but it sent a shiver through me as warmth spread between my thighs. It wasn't right that such a small touch ruined my control of my own body.

"I guess that's fair, but she doesn't know that."

He smiled against my lips. "You can explain it to her," he said, knowing the explanation would require me to tell what happened. No one here needed to know that anything had happened between us.

"I am not going to do that."

He stepped away, dropping his hold on me, but I wanted it back. I lifted my hands to grab him, but stopped.

"Scout is like our little sister. I've known her since she was five and have felt like her big brother since we met. All of us feel that way. It was a shock to see her grown up and," he scrunched his face, "wanting any male attention."

"It doesn't matter how you see her. You can't make fun of her for wanting to dress like a girl. She's getting enough shit at school because of you guys. We all know the rumors you and everyone here have attached to you and, by extension, Scout. The only difference is you guys had each other at school. She's there alone. Now the guy she liked started going after the mean girl instead of her."

Ransom's face hardened. "Who's the guy?"

"I'm not telling you his name. Rumor or not, I know you guys will beat him up or at least scare him to death."

He bit his lip as though he was going to deny it but changed his mind. "I know. I'll apologize to her. We all will."

"I wouldn't do it yet. She's still pretty upset. That's the only reason I was allowed to be the one to come yell at you. She's too tired from crying."

"Shit," he said, running a hand down his face and reaching into his pocket. "I hate her crying. Knowing it's our fault is the fucking worst. Here," he said, digging in his pockets and handing me keys and a few hundred-dollar bills. "Will you take her out? Go do girl stuff or something that will cheer her up?"

"Girl stuff or something?"

"Yeah. I don't know, movies or shopping? Go out to eat? What do girls like to do together?"

I shrugged, still confused at the contents of my hands. "I don't know. All of that, I guess."

"Okay, here. This should cover anything you two want to do." He added more hundred-dollar bills, which had to be closer to a thousand dollars now in my hand.

"What am I supposed to do with all of this? What keys are these?" I said, my heart hammering in my chest. Had I ever held this much money at once? Sure, I had it in my bank account here and there, but holding this much money? I didn't think I had.

"Take my car and bring her out. Cheer her up. Buy her stuff and go out to eat."

"Where am I supposed to go out to eat with this much money? The Ritz?"

"Sure, if that cheers her up. It's not like we can ever do this with her, and there's no one at home to do anything for her. We've never had another girl around here to take her to do stuff, and her dad is an asshole. Us taking her shopping includes us waiting in the parking lot while she grabs whatever she can in ten minutes. It's never seemed to be a problem, but now I'm wondering if it's been bothering her. What are you doing? Put that stuff in your pocket, Quinn," he said, looking down at my still-open hand. My body was frozen in place.

"I don't know what I'm supposed to do with this. We can't spend all this money. I can't take your car." Panic was sweeping through me.

"You know how to drive. I saw you drive to school all the time, and you seemed fine. Do you not remember?"

"I mean, I got my license, and I remember, but I don't do it often anymore. Ever since I started college, I haven't driven anywhere. I left my car with my mother." I wasn't going to add it was sold off by now, and I never saw a cent.

"Then you remember how, so you're good."

I rolled my eyes. "This is your car. Your car, Ransom. What if we got into an accident or something happened to it?"

"Then Fox and I will come to get you."

"Come get me, like kill me?" I said with a small, nervous laugh.

"Kitten," he said, "just make sure you and Scout stay safe and help her have fun. Maybe try to convince her that we don't suck."

"Yeah, okay. That will take more than one night. We don't need all this money. What are we supposed to buy?"

He laughed, pulling me into a hug, resting his chin on my head. "Whatever you want. Anything you or her want. I'll give you more if you don't stop asking what to do with it."

I pushed him back, horrified. "What? No, please, I don't want anymore."

"Tell her we're sorry. I'm sorry to you too."

"For what?"

"For upsetting you so much the other day that you don't even want to talk to me."

"That's nothing for you to apologize for. I'm having a hard time with all of this. It's like I can't stand not touching you, but know I shouldn't. Then you hide things, and I don't know how to trust you if you keep such big things hidden."

"What more do you want to know about me? I've never let anyone aside from the crew this close to me. Hell, I've never let anyone else drive my car, and I just handed you the keys."

"Tell me what happened the other night when you came in here beat up."

His jaw twitched and tightened. "No. I won't do that," he said. "Come on. You two need to go. She needs a break from us."

"I think we both do."

He gave a small smile, "Understandable."

I was mad he wasn't telling me, wasn't letting me in, even though I knew I was pushing him away. It still kept me from grabbing his hand when he offered it.

I went inside, the money and keys in my hand, now even more confused about what was happening between us. Was I keeping him away or pulling him closer? What was he doing? Pushing me away but handing me keys to his prized possession, trusting me to take Scout out and cheer her up.

I knocked on the office door, which had been re-locked.

"Scout. Your bodyguards have been set straight, and now we get to go out for a girls' night." I yelled. Silence filled the room as everyone waited.

The door ripped open, Scout on the other side with a huge smile on her face, "None of these chumps?"

I shook my head, holding up the keys. "Just you and me, babe."

TWENTY-TWO

QUINN

THE LOOK on Scout's face when she opened the door was enough to make me get over driving Ransom's car or using his money. It was all for her, and that made it so much better. I hadn't seen her so excited since I met her, which was saying a lot.

Her eyes flew to the keys in my hand, and her mouth fell open. "Are those Ransom's keys?"

Ransom leaned against the car, watching me, his face calm but unreadable.

"Yes?" I stammered out the words as everyone in the garage turned to look at me. Heat rose up in my cheeks, and I turned back to Scout. "We needed a car, so we could go out." I was unsure of every word I said now.

"Damn, dude," Fox said with a big smile, "It just gets worse and worse for you, huh?"

I glanced back at Ransom again, not knowing what Fox meant. He hadn't moved, though, his face still cold and hard, not giving anything away.

"You've never let me drive your car!" Scout yelled. "I've asked and asked."

"And you're not about to start. Quinn can drive. You've had a rough day, and we decided you need to get away from us."

"We could get away faster if I drive," she said, a hand on her hip.

Ransom shook his head. "Maybe another day. Can you please go do girl stuff and forgive us?"

"Fine, but I'm only giving in because I want to go out with Quinn."

The other guys came over, each one wrapping Scout in a hug and apologizing. Ransom leaned over to me, "Please buy her things until she forgets I'm never letting her drive my car."

I gave a quiet laugh. "I think I might need a few more hundred to do that." He moved to reach into his pocket, and I stopped him. "I'm kidding!"

"Please don't wreck my car," he said, his mouth close enough that I could feel his warm breath on my ear, and I considered throwing out my current decision of staying away from him, wanting to pull him in and feel his lips on mine.

"You can have the keys back."

"No, you two take it. Don't worry. There's some selfishness in there too."

"How so?"

"Watching you drive off in my car might be the hottest thing I have watched this week, including watching you come on my hand."

My mouth fell open, and I turned to him, glad no one else could hear us. "Ransom." I said with gritted teeth. "Don't say things like that out loud."

"Why? Are you wet? Need me to clean you up?"

"Oh, my god," I said, mad because I was getting turned on. "Scout, are you ready?" I yelled, shaking my head at Ransom. He smiled and walked out, bringing me over to his car to go over all the buttons. Scout knew most of them, so I was glad I didn't have to remember all by myself.

Luckily, I knew how to drive a stick shift from my old beat-up car. I wasn't the best at it, but I knew I wouldn't ruin his car completely, at least. He buckled me into the harness, his hands lingering as he clipped it.

"Be careful. It goes fast without a lot of pressure on the pedal."

"Are you sure about this?" I said, sitting in the driver's seat with Scout next to me.

"You'll have to learn at some point. Why not today? Have fun."

He shut the door, and Scout looked over at me. "Oh my god, what the hell is going on between you two?" she asked, swatting at me with a huge smile.

My heart hammered in my chest, "If you can help me get out of this driveway without wrecking or looking like a complete idiot, I will tell you anything you want to know."

"Deal." She walked me through the steps until I pulled to the edge of the parking lot with grace.

"Want to really freak him out?" She looked over with a mischievous grin.

"I mean, yes, but not at the expense of wrecking this thing."

"When you pull out, hit the gas a little harder. Then, when you hit the pavement, the tire will swing, and you'll correct it by turning the wheel the other way. Then straighten out and keep going."

"And if it doesn't correct the right way?"

"Ransom will run over here to kill us both."

I laughed. If he was going to let me drive his car, I might as well have fun with it. I did as she said, letting my body follow the fast direction she yelled out as I went. The car hitched and swung before I turned, correcting it and getting it straight down the road.

"I did it!" I yelled. Scout whooped and hollered, leaning out the window to yell to them. I dared to look back. The group of them all yelled and cheered me on, except Ransom, who stood shaking his head and crossing his arms. A smile grew on my face. I felt so light, so free with the power of the car under me. I was in control this time, and I loved it.

We drove to the mall, both of us deciding a movie sounded boring, and the mall had both restaurants and shopping.

"I've never been shopping with a girl like this before," Scout said, jumping from the car.

"I've never driven a car like this before." I took a deep breath as I grabbed my bag and got out. The ability to move so fast and accurately was exhilarating. I felt like I was flying, and I didn't want it to end.

"You did great. Seriously, I can't believe this was your first time driving anything other than that clunky car you had."

"Does everyone remember that horrid thing?"

She shrugged. "When you're in the car world, you start to remember people's cars more than their names or faces. Plus, Ransom had to comment every single day how much he hated your car."

"What?" I said, taken aback.

"Yeah, he hated that thing. I don't know why. It wasn't much different from anyone else's. Apart from ours and the rich kids, of course."

I pulled out my phone, ready to ask, when I saw four texts from him already waiting.

> Ransom: You are trying to give me a heart attack.

> Good job, though. That was perfect

> And so fucking hot

> Worth every second of panic. Might go get off to the thought right now. Tell me when you get where you're going so I know all three of you are at least in one piece.

I rolled my eyes as my body betrayed me, warmth flooding between my legs at the thought of him going to get off to me. It was a thrilling thought that I needed to not think about right now.

Scout pulled me over, wanting to start with a coffee and then head to a new store she had heard about.

I texted Ransom back as we stood in line.

> Quinn: You better knock it off or I'm not returning the car. We're here, and all THREE of us are fine.

Good.

> Why did you hate the car I used to drive?

What?

> Scout said you hated the car I drove in high school, and you commented on it earlier. Why?

Shit. I forgot you two going out would involve Scout telling you things about me.

That didn't answer my question. Dots formed and disappeared until a response came after we ordered.

You deserved a car like ours. Better than the piece of shit you had. I always figured you would come to our shop or buy a better one based on how often you stared at ours.

> I wasn't staring at the cars.

The texting made me feel brave and more honest, which was dangerous.

If you say you were staring at Fox I'll go fight him right now.

I laughed, knowing he was joking but realizing how much I loved this side of Ransom. The joking, the honesty, it was everything I hoped he would be like, but I knew there were two sides to everyone, and I worried I would hate the other half of him, the half I knew he was hiding.

> It wasn't Fox. Don't fight him. He has too pretty of a face.

And I don't?

> Have you seen your bruise? It's just now starting to heal.

So if it wasn't Fox, you were looking at me?

> Every day.

I had so much I wanted to say, so many questions that I needed answers too. I wanted to know if he hated me in high school, what he really thought now. I didn't know what that truth would lead to now, though. We were on some sort of edge, and I was worried at any point, I would fall off.

I can build you a car.

I shook my head. He had given me boots and money for us to shop. Now he was offering me a car? I hoped he was joking, but I was coming to know better.

> Very funny. I'll text you when we're done so you know when your precious car will be returned.

It wasn't a joke

I looked up finally, Scout staring at me with an open mouth. "What?" I said, looking around.

"You're texting Ransom! And before you deny it, I already saw his name. You are flirt texting with Ransom!" she said, louder this time.

"Will you quiet down, please? Why do you assume I'm flirting?"

"I saw that smile. That was a flirty smile. Is he flirting back?"

"Back? You think this is my fault? He starts it! He flirts and backs off every damn day."

"And you don't?" she asked, calling me out.

"Ok, maybe I do the exact same thing, but I have good reasons."

"Hey, I don't blame you. Ransom's a difficult one. Don't get me wrong. I love him to death, but damn, he needs to ease up on the glaring."

I couldn't stop my laugh. "I can never tell what he's thinking with that glare."

"Each one of those guys is the best and the worst," she said. "Oh, I want to go into this store!"

We went in, trying on outfit after outfit as I doubled over in laughter. Scout was hilarious and easygoing. Being around her felt like we had been friends forever. It made me realize how different Josie and I were becoming. Every time I had been around her, felt like a race to keep up with her money and idea of cool. Like I wasn't the person she wanted me to be, and I was desperate not to disappoint her again. With Scout, though, I felt relaxed and happy.

I realized I was starting to feel that way around Ransom, too, the entire crew even.

Scout stepped out in a floor-length, glittering gown. The green was a perfect shade for her eyes. "You look like a movie star," I said, star-struck for a moment and surprised she put it on. "What's this one for?"

"We have a homecoming dance on Halloween weekend."

"Next month?"

"Yeah. I was thinking of going, but didn't have anything to wear."

"Well, this dress is perfect. You look amazing."

"Now that I have the dress on, I realize I don't have anyone to go with."

I rolled my eyes. "I'm pretty sure you have a garage of good-looking guys who would love to be your date."

"But none of them are in high school anymore. There is a guy I kind of like at school, not the one who was mean to me."

I shrugged. "You could always show up with the hot older guy. Make those mean girls jealous," I said with a smile. "Who's the guy?"

"Someone I don't talk to, but he likes cars and goes to the races sometimes. Like I said, though, I've never talked to him."

"You could always try talking to him? I know for a fact you will regret not at least trying. I never talked to Ransom and wondered about it all the time."

"But what if he's like the other ones there? They can be ruthless."

"Then you take your pick of one of the hot guys who will do anything for you. Any one of them would suck it up and go for a night," I said. "And again, they are all hot enough to make the mean girls jealous, and maybe that guy will think twice and talk to you."

She huffed, "Maybe you're right. Maybe I should talk to him once."

"I didn't talk to Ransom, and I spent way too many days wondering what would happen if I did."

"I can't believe you never did. We would have been nice."

I cocked an eyebrow.

"Ok, I would have been nice. Do you really think I could ask a guy to go with me?"

"Ask him in that dress, and he will do anything you want him to."

She turned and looked in the mirror. "You think so?"

"I wouldn't tell you if I didn't think so. I'm here as your friend, not to make you look like a fool. Ask him, and if he says no, you can take your pick of your crew. I suggest Fox. Hot and something resembling good enough manners to get through the night."

Her smile grew again. "Good point. Then onto the next problem for now."

"What?"

"This dress is four hundred dollars, and I would still need shoes."

"Oh, problem solved," I said, pulling out the cash Ransom gave me. "Ransom's treat. Well, probably more like every one of those guys treat for being so rude to you, but Ransom said we can buy whatever we want."

"What?" Her mouth fell open like mine had. "And he handed that to you?"

"Yeah, it was something like please take Scout and buy her everything she wants, so she forgives us." I smiled. "But that means you can buy the dress and a killer pair of shoes to go with it."

She was still staring into the mirror. "They have taken care of me since before I could remember."

"Yeah, Ransom said you guys have been like family for a long time."

"Every time I needed clothes or shoes or anything. One of them would drive me to the store and tell me to run in and grab it, handing me money or cards after they were old enough. I never really went without because of them. I only work there a few hours a day, and they give me so much. My dad's a drunk, and mom is gone, so there wasn't anyone to take care of me besides them."

I smiled at the similarities between us. "I get that. No dad and a drunk mom here," I said, raising my hand. "You were lucky to have them."

"I know. I see how lucky I still am. Who raised you?"

"I did, I guess? I didn't have anyone that stepped up to help me, so I figured it out. It was the world's biggest shock when Ransom got me new boots. I think it was an even bigger shock when he handed me all this money today."

"I thought I saw a new boot box in the office. Didn't know which one of the guys' feet suddenly shrunk."

I laughed, "Yeah, it was nice of him."

"They are pretty nice." She turned to me as though she was reading my mind. "They seem like a bad group, but they are a bunch of suckers. Look at me. I'm here in the most beautiful dress and found out I can buy it because they feel bad that they upset me. Big. Fat. Suckers," she said with a loving smile.

"So, are you taking one of them then, or are you going to ask your mystery crush?"

She huffed, blowing her hair out of her face. "Let's start with getting the dress, then the shoes, and then we will talk about who I'm going with."

"Fine," I said, jumping up as she changed. "I'm just happy you're getting it."

"So what are we getting you?" she yelled from the dressing room.

"Nothing? I don't need anything."

"You've got to need something."

"Not really."

"Come on, Quinn. We've got money to burn. Let's burn it!"

I shook my head with a smile. "You're a bad influence, Scout." I took a deep breath, knowing she wouldn't let up now. "Fine. If I find something that I want, I'll tell you."

She whooped again from the changing room before coming out with the dress. We checked out and then moved on to finding shoes before standing outside one of the shops and looking in the windows.

A leather jacket sat in the window, the leather the same shade of black as my new boots. "Is that what you want?"

"What? No, that's way too expensive."

"No, it isn't. I can see the tag from here. It says $150. We still have that."

"But I should give something back to Ransom."

"Na," she said with a shake of her head, "I'm still mad at them. Let's go."

She pulled me in and didn't stop the flurry of movement until I stood in front of the mirror with the jacket on. It was beautiful, the leather soft enough to be comfortable but still brand new.

"Ok, we're getting it." Scout said, "It matches the boots!"

"No. No, no, no, no," I said.

"Come on. Ransom will love it." I looked over, and she knew she had me. "You look great in it. You deserve it the way you handled them all today."

"I feel pretty great in it."

"Then it's settled. Just like I had to buy the dress and handle the guy. You have to buy the jacket and handle Ransom."

"Handle Ransom?"

"I know something is going on, and when you two are ready to face it, you're going to want to look good to deal with him. The boots and jacket will help."

I don't know what it was, but I didn't fight her on it anymore. Checking out with the jacket and letting her pull me into more stores. We even stopped to buy new underwear. I hated to admit how badly I needed a new bra and underwear. The money I had been earning went right to my college payments, but I felt a lot more comfortable now buying myself a few things.

We walked out to the car, bags weighing us down and smiles stuck on both of our faces. "I can't remember the last time I had this much fun."

"Me either," Scout said, "Don't get me wrong, I love racing and hanging out with the guys, but this was perfect. I hope we can go again sometime."

"Maybe go out at least every other month?"

"Yes!" she yelled, moving closer to put her head on my shoulder for a minute. We turned down the parking lot aisle to see two men leaning against Ransom's car.

My heart jumped at the thought that Ransom and Fox had come to check on us since we had been gone so long.

When we moved closer, though, the overhead lights shining down on the faces glaring back at us, panic washed over me as I realized that it wasn't them.

TWENTY-THREE

QUINN

"Hey," Scout yelled, reaching down and grabbing a knife out of her boot without hesitation. "Who the hell are you? Get off the car."

"What the hell, Scout? Where did that come from?"

"My boot. You don't have one?"

"A switchblade? No, I didn't think I would need one to go shopping."

She reached into her bag, pulling another one out, and handing it to me.

"What the hell are you guys wrapped up in?"

"There's been a bit of a problem lately, so I've been over-prepared."

We came closer, and the guys pushed off the car. "Well, neither of you looks like Ransom. Where is he?"

"Ryder?" I said, recognizing him from the night of the races. He didn't look quite the same now. His eyes were a little more wild. Everything about him more unhinged now than charming.

"Ransom? Who is that?" Scout said, her voice so sweet and innocent.

"You know damn well who Ransom is, you little bitch, and we know this is his car. Where is he?"

"Not here. Now move out of our way," Scout said. Her voice was even and calm, as though the confrontation was normal.

"Well, we know who you are." The larger one said, pointing at Scout, "but who is this? Did Ransom find himself a girl?" I held the knife tight in one and reached for the keys with the other.

"Nope," I said. "Now move." I steadied my voice, trying to keep it even.

"She's lying," Ryder said. "This is the girl I used to make Ransom race me. He was all pissed she was talking to me and said we could race for her."

"If you guys don't leave, I'm calling our entire crew, and I think we both know they can get here faster than yours," Scout said with a smile, crossing her arms. They walked forward, getting close enough that I could smell the beer and weed on them.

"Make sure you tell them we are looking for them. I would love to have a talk with Ransom or Fox. I'll take either."

"Go away, Slaughter," Scout said to the big guy, and I looked over at her. It sounded like a name a guy would pick out for himself to sound tough.

He leaned down towards me, and I leaned back. "And so nice to meet you," Slaughter said.

Ryder stepped closer to me, and I almost gagged at the smell. "Nice to see you again. That offer for a ride still stands. Anytime you want one, sweetheart." He winked, but it wasn't cute. Of course, after a few beers, nothing was as cute as they thought.

They sauntered off, walking into the darkness and leaving us in an eerie silence.

"Move," Scout said, running towards the car, "Unlock it and get moving."

I listened, unlocked the door, and jumped in, throwing all my stuff into the back as I fired up the car.

"Just go. Move as fast as you can."

"Why? Are they coming after us?" I asked, putting the car in drive and taking off.

"I don't know, but I wouldn't doubt it. Better to get out of here before they do."

I sped off, reaching the highway in record time.

"I don't see them. I think we're good."

I let out a breath. "What the hell was that?"

"That was Slaughter. A different crew leader. I didn't know Ryder was with him now. That's going to piss off the guys. Quite the nice bunch."

"Why are they after the guys? Are they the reason he was beaten up the other week? Ryder is an enemy now?"

"I want to tell you, but I think Ransom should. He has to have his reasons for not saying anything yet. As for Ryder, that's as shocking to me as it is to you."

"Yeah, well, I think all those reasons just went out the fucking door when people threatened us."

"I agree."

I flew down the side roads until we reached the garage. I could see the lights were still on and the doors were open.

He was waiting.

I turned the car in, throwing the car in park before Scout could say a word. Ransom and Fox walked out, smiles on their faces, until they saw me.

"Shit, dude, you're in trouble," Fox said, walking over to Scout.

I was seething as I stalked towards Ransom, anger rolling off me, making me sick.

"Why the fuck was I just threatened by a guy named Slaughter when we were walking out to leave? And why is Ryder with him?"

"What? What happened?" he asked, looking me over and then at Scout and the car.

"We walked out of the mall to find Ryder and some guy leaning against the car asking for you. Both of you."

"Slaughter?" Ransom said, directing the question to Scout.

She nodded. "Him and Ryder were waiting for us."

"Waiting for us, threatening us, trying to find you. Lucky for us, Scout here had some switchblades, but nobody told me I needed to be ready for a fucking knife fight when we were going to the mall." My chest heaved, the adrenaline of being threatened and not knowing why still rushing through me.

"Quinn. It's ok now. Calm down. I'm sorry. Are you ok?" Ransom said, coming forward.

"I'm fine, but I think I deserve to know what the hell is going on now?" I took a deep breath, trying to steady my breathing, but it wasn't working.

"Can we have a minute?" He nodded to Fox and Scout. They nodded and went inside, not looking back at us.

He walked around me, turning off the car and shutting the door.

"Did you have fun?"

"Before or after, some idiot named Slaughter tried to scare us?"

"Before," he said, his voice so soft and calm.

"The most fun I have had in a very long time."

"Good." He leaned down and kissed me, the gentle touch making my knees weak. He tasted like mint and coffee, the flavor intoxicating. It wasn't urgent or demanding, just comforting.

My body betrayed me again as I leaned into it, and his arms wrapped around me, covering me in quiet protection.

"I'm sorry I wasn't there," he said, kissing me again.

His lips were so warm and inviting that it took everything in me to pull away. "That's enough."

"I know you said this can't happen, but I can't help it. Anytime you're close, I need to kiss you. I'm glad all three of you are ok." He smiled, looking down at me, and there was something in his gaze I couldn't place.

"Enough, Ransom. You need to tell me what is going on," I said, breaking apart from him.

"I know. I wish it wasn't going to make you mad."

"I don't know if it will or not, but you need to tell me now, regardless."

"Yea, I know you're right. Come on."

We walked into the dark corner of the back lot, and he shined his phone flashlight onto some car parts.

"What?" I said, not understanding.

He let out a heavy breath. "About three or four years ago, me, Fox, and Jax had all started here with Luca. Dante wasn't with us yet. We weren't mechanics then, but we were quick learners, and all loved cars. After a few months, we realized that Luca wasn't doing so well. The business was going to shit, and he told us we would be out in a few months. We had nowhere else to go after this place, so we chose to do something about it."

My stomach was turning to lead, the sinking feeling making me want to puke. "What did you do?"

"We stole cars. Not a lot, but we stole some mid-level race cars. We brought them back here, tore them up, and sold the parts to buy cars legally and create race cars."

"I thought you said you weren't a chop shop," I said, trying to keep my emotions in check.

"We aren't. We haven't done anything like that for years, not after Luca found out. Slaughter and his crew caught us with parts from one of their cars. Luca smoothed it over but told us we either stop or get out. At that point, things were getting better around here, so we stopped."

"How many cars did you take?"

"Thirteen."

"And I assume the value of that is high."

"They would have all added up to a few hundred thousand dollars. Money we've worked to give back when we could."

"Shit, Ransom," I said, taking a step back, not even comprehending that type of money.

"After we stopped, things cooled off, but now it's starting again."

My heart dropped, wondering if they really could be doing that again. Is that where the money he gave me was coming from?

"And?"

"And Slaughter went right to blaming us. We tried to tell them it wasn't, but they didn't believe us after what we did. He knows I started it last time, and he's right. I'm the one who even suggested it. We all participated, aside from Scout. She was younger, and we knew she wouldn't like what we were doing. Kye was in on it, though, which I regret. Scout and him are the same age, but we let him help. That hasn't helped him now since he seems to be getting in trouble every month with something new."

"But it isn't you this time? You guys aren't doing this?"

"No. I promise it isn't us. We've been on the right track since the day Luca gave us the ultimatum."

"And you don't know who is taking them?"

"No, we have been looking for weeks while worrying we would be next. Some of these shops had three or four cars taken in one night. It's not an easy task to do unnoticed. It would definitely take someone who has done it before, and I know it could wreck a business to take that many at once."

"So that's why they would assume it's you?"

"Yes."

"Why didn't you tell me this before?"

"At first, I figured you believed other rumors and would hate me again for this. Then I didn't know if you would believe me if I told you the truth. It's like you would see all the worst parts of me, and I didn't want to give you another reason to hate me. Then I didn't want you wrapped up in our problems. As you can tell, they aren't happy, and it's becoming more dangerous for us all. We've been trying to stay together a bit more, but sometimes it's unavoidable. I think they keep pretty good tabs on us when they can."

"And that's who attacked you the other day? When you came back here, all beat up?"

"Yeah, a coincidence that they caught me out. At least, I think it was a coincidence."

I didn't say anything. The entire day of classes combined with a night of Scout and then all of this. I was starting to feel like I could fall over from exhaustion.

"Are you upset?"

"No. I mean, yes, but not…not really." I shook my head, each thought a little too foggy to make sense. "It's been a long night, and I don't know what to think right now. Can we talk about it tomorrow more?"

"Yeah, come on, I can get you home."

"No, it's fine. I'll ask Fox."

"No, let me. Please." He grabbed my hand and pulled me towards the car.

The quiet plea made me give in and let him pull me along.

Scout ran out, throwing her arms around Ransom, "Now that that's all over. I wanted to say thanks. I had a great time and got a new dress."

Ransom groaned, "Another one."

"It supposedly covers everything," Fox said, leaning against the wall.

"Ok then, let's see it."

She pulled the garment bag from the car and unzipped it, holding up the shimmery green dress for us all to see.

"It looks beautiful on her," I said.

They both had their brows furrowed. "And why did you need such a…beautiful dress?" Fox asked carefully.

"Well, I decided that I will be going to homecoming this year."

"What?" they both said in unison, "With who?"

"No one yet."

"I was thinking one of you should take her," I said, turning to them both. Their faces gave away enough to know they did not want to go to a high school dance ever again.

"Isn't Kye still in school? Couldn't he take her?" I asked.

"I would rather you go with Kye than any of those dumbasses at your school," Ransom said, and Fox nodded in agreement.

"I know what happens at homecoming. You're not going with any one of them," Fox said.

"You guys?" I hissed, stopping them before they went too far.

Scout looked over at me, her lips tight. "I'll see. It's up to me who's going with me, though," she said, pointing to each one of us.

"Come on. We need to get you home." Fox grabbed the bag with her shoes. "You got a tiara in there, too, princess?"

"No, but that would have been a smart thing to buy." She zipped up the dress before hugging me. "Thanks, Quinn."

"Thank you back."

"Oh, and Ransom," she said as she slid into Fox's car, "I made Quinn buy a new jacket. She claimed she didn't need anything, but she needed it. Make sure she shows you." Scout slammed the door, and they were off.

Ransom shut the last garage door and locked it. "Well, I'm waiting?"

"Waiting for what?"

"To see this jacket."

I huffed, walking around and waiting for him to get in the car, but he stayed put on the hood.

"Fine. It is a nice jacket, and I will pay you back every cent."

"I don't want any money. I just want to see you in it." I reached into the car, pulling on the bag, before standing up to face him.

He smiled. "You look amazing."

"Amazing?" I rolled my eyes. "You're just trying to suck up to me now."

"You look like you could drive my car and kick someone's ass."

"So I look like you?" I scrunched up my face.

"No, not even close. You look so much better." He came closer, starting to reach out to me, but stopped. It was like he was waiting for my permission, and I gave it, reaching out and fisting my hands into his shirt, pulling him against me.

He grabbed me, picking me up and setting me on the hood of the car. "Your jeans are a little harder to get into."

"That was the point," I whispered, kissing him.

His tongue flicked out, running along my lips, and I moaned.

"You can't look like this and make those noises. I want to strip you down and take you right here. I've been hard since I had to watch you drive out of here like you knew what you were doing."

"I did know what I was doing."

"Sure, Kitten," he said, pressing his lips to mine before trailing a line of kisses down my jaw and neck.

His hand slid between my legs. "I need these jeans gone."

"Trying to give me an orgasm isn't going to make me forget what just happened."

"Oh, I wasn't just trying."

The thought of him admitting to stealing cars came to mind and how that was now putting them, and me, all in danger. I pushed him back an inch. "Maybe you should take me home," I whispered.

"Can I take you to my home? You'd love my bed, I promise."

The thought made my stomach jump. Ransom's home, his bed, him naked in it. The idea of it sounded like heaven.

"You're thinking about it, aren't you?" he asked. "Are you going to admit you want to go home with me? Get into bed with me?"

"I'm not admitting to anything, and I'm going to say no. Take me to my home." He groaned over me, pulling my body close and picking me up as he stood. "You're killing me. Are we still going to talk tomorrow?"

"Yes," I said as he buried his face in my neck, carrying me to the passenger side. I could feel how hard he was, and it was making me reconsider going home with him.

"What time are you coming over?"

"What do you mean?"

"It's the first Saturday of the month. All of us get together to do a cookout. Didn't any of us tell you?"

"No. Should I really be coming?"

"Why wouldn't you?" he asked. "You're a part of us now. Seems whether you like it or not based on how much Scout likes you."

Scout was the only one he mentioned, not adding his name to that list. I knew he wanted to sleep with me, but I wasn't sure what was going on past that.

"What time should I be here? Am I supposed to bring something?"

He slid me down his body and helped me into the car, going around and getting in. The car started up, and I was surprised at how comforting the sound was now.

"No, you don't need to bring anything, and whenever you can. We start around one or two, but you can get here whenever."

We drove to my dorm in silence, and he stopped at the door.

"Alright. I'll be there. I still don't know how I feel about all of this, but thanks for telling me the truth."

He nodded. "Thanks for not running away immediately."

He watched as I pulled my two bags out from the back, one that held the jacket and the other one he grabbed out of my hands as it went by.

"What is this? I know what store this is," he said, looking up at me with a mischievous smile.

"Hey, that's private." I reached for the bag containing one new bra and five new pairs of underwear that I made sure to buy with my own money.

Ransom reached in, pulling out my favorite pair of panties I had bought, the lace fabric a beautiful red.

"Fuck," he said, leaning his head back. "Please, please forgive me for everything I have done and any reason you hate me, and let me see these on you."

I grabbed the bag and the underwear, jumping from the car.

"I guess we'll see how I feel tomorrow," I said, shutting the door, but he rolled down the window.

"You better be there early. I need you to figure out exactly how much you want me before the party starts."

I turned back and smiled before shutting and locking the dorm door.

Ransom was going to be the death of me.

TWENTY-FOUR

QUINN

SATURDAY MORNING, I woke up and immediately groaned. Everything that happened yesterday still felt like too much. My mind was overloaded with everything he had told me.

Part of me didn't want to care anymore about Ransom and his past. I didn't want to worry about who it looked like he was and trust in who he was showing me he was now.

The other part of me, the part that still hasn't gotten over what happened to me, sent off blinding sirens telling me to run from another bad boy. But I didn't know if Ransom was anything like Logan. The difference between the two felt like night and day now.

I turned over, looking at the clock. It was already ten in the morning, so I had two or three hours before heading to the garage.

I got up, deciding to clear my mind with some homework. Josie still wasn't home, and I guessed she would be at Sarah's for the day.

I tried to fight it, but my thoughts came back to Ransom.

There wasn't anything standing between us now. The secrets and hidden past were gone. It felt like that was enough for me to take a chance, but I didn't want to be someone he slept with and left. I didn't want to lose the crew and spending time with him just for some sex.

Every moment with Ransom, and the crew, was changing who I thought they were and who I thought I could be. I needed and craved this new part of my life that made me feel more like myself.

Even being at the garage had become a comfort. The loud noise of the garage, the scent of oil and dirt, and the crew made me feel safe and at home each time I walked in. I knew I could tell Ransom I wanted to stick around and be more than a one-night thing, but that seemed like just as much of a risk. I didn't know if I could face him again if he told me I wasn't worth anything more. I could never go back again.

I had wanted Ransom since the moment I saw him, and getting to know the real Ransom was only making the wanting worse. What if all of this was a trick, though? A ruse to make me think he wanted something long-term when he didn't. Or worse, he was setting me up only to tear me down.

It was an endless loop of terrible thoughts that I couldn't shut off.

The worst part of it was that I knew the only way to shut up that voice inside me. I had to risk it all and ask Ransom what he felt.

I got ready, still not knowing what I should say to him, but knowing I had to say something.

My hands shook as I left the dorm, running through scenario after scenario of ways this could go. He could fall to his knees or laugh in my face, letting me know he wanted this for real or was just hoping to get in my pants.

The garage came into view, and I could tell most of them were there, their cars lined up in a perfect row. It made my chest tighten. I didn't want to lose this.

I hadn't been this nervous to walk into the garage since my

first day. I went into the office, setting down my bag and trying to take a deep, steadying breath.

I was going to do it. I was going to ask Ransom about all of this. If he thought he wanted a relationship or a fuck buddy. He said he wanted to talk, and I was finally ready to talk.

I walked through the door and scanned the backyard. Kye was stationed at the grill, another guy next to him that I didn't know, and a small fire pit next to them where everyone else was sitting. I stepped next to Fox. "Hey, what's up?" I asked.

He looked down at me, panic coming over his face as I recognized the back that was to us. Ransom sat in an oversized chair, a girl with long dark hair snuggling up on his lap. She giggled and whispered something into his ear. The world dropped around me, and I felt like I was about to throw up.

It was happening again. I was blind to the truth about what had been going on, but Ransom was making it clear now. Flirting with me, touching me. It had been a game. I came with questions, and they were all clear now.

Dante saw me and smiled as he glanced from me to Ransom. "Quinn, you're here!" Ransom's head whipped over, his face falling and eyes wide. Did he think I wouldn't be here yet? Or maybe he had hoped he would have time to finish with her before I showed up.

Scout ran up next to me. "Oh shit, Quinn," she said as everyone stood frozen.

I stared at Ransom, not able to look away from him or the girl. She didn't seem to notice or care what was going on around her.

"Quinn, wait," he yelled, but I was already spinning around. I had no reason to be here. Even if I did work with them, I wasn't one of them, and I didn't need to be here to hang out.

I made it back into the office before Ransom caught me.

"Quinn, wait."

"All this time, I've been waiting for the truth to come out.

For whatever game you were playing to come to light, and here it was. I should have known this was what I thought it was. I should have learned my lesson the first time." I was holding back tears, my chest feeling like it was caving in on itself. This was it. Everything I was just given in life was already taken away.

"It's not like that at all. There's no game. I was telling her to get off of me. I don't even know why she is here."

"No, you just planned on her being gone before I got here," I said. "You're fine, Ransom. It's not like we're together, right? You can go around fucking whoever you want, which you apparently are."

"I'm not sleeping with her or anyone else, Quinn. Please, I wouldn't do that to you."

"No? Not fucking the girl who seems to show up around you all the time? Isn't she the same one who wanted to fuck you at the races? Now what? She just mysteriously shows up here too? Why would I believe you now?"

"Because I'm not lying," he said, trying to stay calm. "I've only wanted to be with you."

"No," I said, stomping towards him. "you do not get to mess with my head more. You've messed with me enough. All to what, say you got to fuck me too? Need to make a video while you're at it? You're just like him, aren't you? You want to fuck every girl that comes around, no matter what it takes. Sorry, I didn't make it easier for you. That's what you like, though, isn't it? When they put up a fight? Isn't that what happened with the girl in the library? You corner her, fucked her, and left her crying in the library?" I froze, my mouth dropping at my own nasty words. I never believed the rumor, but somehow I was now using it as ammunition.

His lip curled, and his jaw tightened, making me take a step back at the vicious look. "How fucking dare you, of all people, accuse me of something you only heard as a rumor of being true. Do you know that she was crying in the library because her boyfriend had cornered and threatened her? I happened to hear it and got involved until he ran out. She walked out crying because of that, not because I hurt her. I can't believe you would ever even think I would do something so disgusting." His voice was low. "And then you want to compare me to him?" He looked down, anger so evident in his eyes as his lip curled again. For a moment, I was stunned. I thought all those times he looked at me before I saw hate, but it wasn't.

This was what true hate looked like on him.

"I— I meant that—"

"No, I know what you meant. It doesn't matter what the fuck I do for you or how I treat you, does it? I've only tried to give you fucking everything since the moment you walked in here, and you still think I'm the same fucking asshole that Logan is, worse even. I've never pushed you for sex. I've waited as patiently as I could because, yeah, I have wanted to sleep with you, not because I'm trying to make some fucked up video or just have sex. I've wanted you." He was yelling now, the words so deep and laced with anger that I couldn't move. "I've only wanted you. I've never hurt you, and I would give my entire fucking life to not let anyone else hurt you, but it's not enough. For once in my fucking life, I've wanted a relationship, and it's with the one girl who seems to think I'm a monster. If you think I'm so fucking terrible, why the fuck are you here, Quinn? Why the fuck have you let me touch you and kiss you all the fucking time if you can't stand me?"

"That's not what I meant."

He stalked towards me, and I stepped back again.

"Did you hear what you just accused me of? Do you know what the fuck you just said to me?"

He was so close I could touch him now, but there was no invitation to do that.

I shuttered, "I didn't mean that. I just...I meant I don't need to be messed with. I don't need to be another girl that you fuck and move on. I was coming here to tell you as much, but then that? I can't play this game."

"And I can't have someone here that thinks so little of me when I'm trying to give them everything. Get out, Quinn. Leave, and please, don't come back here."

My eyes went wide as it settled in. Somehow, he was breaking up with me when we never dated and firing me all at once. Not that I could blame him. I had been debating for the last month if he was a monster, and now, after everything, I was standing here accusing him of being one and realizing I never truly thought that to begin with.

I grabbed my bag before turning back and heading to the door. Tears welled, and I wanted to turn around, but I couldn't. If he was going to show up here with another girl, I didn't need to stay any longer. There was nothing here for me.

TWENTY-FIVE

QUINN

I GRABBED MY PHONE, sending a quick text to Scout to update her and another to Josie to ask what she was doing.

Scout texted back first.

> Scout: Do you want me to come to you?

> Quinn: No. I'm going back to bed at this point. Maybe the day will reset.

> I wish. I hate to be the one to say this, but I think you should come back. We can still have a good time, and she's been kicked out. Ransom doesn't look happy.

> I need a break from all of this, and Ransom told me not to come back again. Even for work.

> What? Are you serious?

> That's what he said.

He didn't mean it. Just let him calm down. He doesn't usually get mad, but when he does, it's a lot.

Either way. I don't think me coming back right now is a good idea.

Ok. Let me know if you need anything. We're still best friends!

Josie's text came through next.

Josie: What's up? You good?

Quinn: Problem with Ransom. Can we hang out?

I thought you weren't getting involved with him? I knew you lied to me.

I didn't mean to, and it's done now anyways.

Fine, we're going out tonight. Come with?

Yes, please.

I still stared at my phone. I was hoping that Ransom would text me and apologize, even though I knew that I had plenty to apologize for myself.

I thought of that girl all over him. I know he said he didn't want it and was trying to get her off him, but it sounded too good to be true. I knew if it sounded like that, it was usually because it was.

I couldn't be with Ransom, and he made it clear that wasn't even an option anymore.

I needed to forget about him. Distance myself and find a soft, easy-going guy without a crew of misfits, one who wouldn't throw me away.

I could do that. Clark wasn't the right one, but it didn't mean

I couldn't find the right one. Josie seemed head over heels for Brad, and maybe he had better friends than Clark.

I laid in bed for a few hours, staring at the ceiling, wondering what mess I had found myself in before getting up and looking in the mirror. I didn't look terrible, but I still had to fix my hair after laying on it for hours.

I would go tonight and change my life. I took a deep, steadying breath. I could have a Cinderella moment and dance the night away with a prince, right? A guy that would sweep me off my feet and be there for me while not letting girls all over his lap.

Because I didn't believe him.

I repeated the words, hating the fact that I actually believed every single word he said. Even worse, I felt like shit for making him think I did believe any rumor about him. He was sitting there believing that I really did think he was a monster that would hurt a girl because I knew now he wouldn't. He was right. He had been giving me everything I wanted and then some without pushing me too far. He was the one who stopped it from going too far each time because he was worried I would regret it.

I shook my head, pushing the thoughts away as I looked down with a huff. Maybe I wasn't entirely Cinderella because the idea of taking off the warm boots for something less comfortable sounded miserable.

I tapped at the app, needing a car to come to pick me up. The address that Josie had sent over was too far to walk to. I had finally begun to build my money back up as my paychecks had come in, but I realized there wouldn't be any more paychecks. I groaned.

I wasn't canceling the car, though. No, tonight, I was going to enjoy myself, and tomorrow I could face reality.

A reality that no longer included Ransom, the crew, or the garage.

I texted Josie I was on the way, and she returned a smiley

face. I was glad she was always there for me, even if I was going to get another massive lecture on staying away from Ransom and boys like him. She hadn't batted an eye when I told her Clark was an ass, only saying I shouldn't worry and that we could find another guy.

The car came, and we took off. The guy was chatting politely, and I sat there, silently begging him to stop talking as I looked down at my phone again.

Nothing had come in, and it started to set in that it was done. Ransom wasn't coming for me and told me not to come back for him.

It was over, and not only had I lost the guy I'd been dreaming of for years, but I had also lost a group of friends that I had come to love.

I smiled, a half laugh-half cry escaping my lips, but I only clicked my phone to silent.

I needed to forget all about Ransom tonight.

———

THE HOUSE WASN'T anything like I expected from a party Josie would show up at.

The older home sat alone on a corner, lights and music filling the area. It wasn't the worst part of town, but it wasn't great, either. I hesitated as I pushed open the car door.

The driver must have noticed. "Are you sure you want me to drop you off here? I will bring you home for free if that's an issue."

"No, it's alright. My friend is inside, waiting for me."

"Alright, be careful then, and have a good night," he said. The words were like an omen as I stood on the sidewalk, and he pulled away.

I took a deep breath, heading inside to find Josie, and I assumed Sarah would be with her tonight.

The crowd of guys on the porch looked me over and took way too long, staring at my bare legs. They definitely weren't friends Josie would hang around. I shuffled inside, looking everywhere for her. She hadn't texted more than the smiley face, but I had assumed that meant she was here or about to be.

I moved to the kitchen, where another large group of guys stood around a keg. I pushed through too far, though, until I was standing in the middle of them.

"Hey." A few of them said, "Do we know you?"

"Uhh, I don't think so. I'm a friend of Josie's."

"Who?" Confusion covered their faces. They didn't know Josie, and that was obvious.

"Um, Josie and Sarah?"

"Nope, not ringing a bell. Sounds like you might be lost." One of the bigger guys said with a creepy smile on his face. "That's alright. You can stick with me." His hand wrapped around my wrist and pulled me close. I wasn't ready for it and stumbled, which only helped him drag me closer.

"It's alright. Relax babe. You're in good hands." One of the other guys said, reaching out and running a hand down my cheek.

I pulled back. "I'm going to go find my friends," I said, trying to slip out of his grip, but his hand clamped down harder.

"No, it's alright. Stay here. Maybe they'll come around."

"Don't I know you?" One asked, "I feel like I've seen you somewhere."

"No. I don't think so."

"I know her." Another guy perked up, but I didn't recognize him. "She looks like that girl who sent out the sex video of her and that guy, Logan."

Shit. Shit. Shit. I watched as all their gazes changed. The video out in the world was like a green flag for perverts to think they could do whatever they wanted, and it didn't fail to get all around town.

This wasn't good.

"Is there a bathroom around here?" I asked.

"Right there," he said, pointing to a door right next to them. "Going to get cleaned up?"

I nodded, knowing I was going to be climbing out the window.

"Hey, wait," another one said. I turned my back against the bathroom door, looking back at the crowd that was gathering.

"I do know you."

It was then that I realized I knew him, too.

It was Ryder.

"This is the girl I raced Ransom for. She ended up going home with him."

"Ryder? What are you doing here?"

"What?" One of the others said, their face changing from creepy to shocked.

"Yeah, and she was the one driving Ransom's car the other night too. Seems like things worked out pretty well after our race, huh?"

My hands shook, and I flung the door open, slamming and locking it behind me.

"Someone go outside and block the window. Make sure she doesn't climb out," Ryder yelled out.

I couldn't stop the panic bubbling up, taking over and making every part of me shake.

I tried to call Josie, but she didn't pick up.

I stared hard at my phone, trying to stop it from shaking in my hand. It's not like I had a long list of friends I could call.

At this rate, my only friends were Josie and Scout, and I wouldn't risk Scout coming in here to help me. I had no one else. Especially someone who I would ask to come get me here.

There was only one person I could call, only one person who might walk in here and help me.

TWENTY-SIX

RANSOM

I TRIED NOT to look at my phone or think of her, but it was impossible.

The look on her face when she walked in and saw Brooke sitting on me and then running before I could even get her off me. She didn't know Brooke had been drunk, stumbled into the party, and immediately sat in my lap as though I had asked her to. I was already pushing her up and telling Fox to call her a ride, but Quinn walked in before she moved.

Quinn had looked so pretty and perfect that I froze, not believing this girl was hanging around us, around me.

The thought of fucking that up pissed me off.

It didn't seem to matter either way, though. She said what she really thought about me. She thought I was horrible, that I was a monster, and even after everything I had done for her, she didn't think any different of me.

How could I apologize to her about Brooke on my lap when she was yelling that I was horrible either way?

I needed to fight someone, race someone, do something other than sit here watching the fire.

Fox stalked over, and I could already tell I didn't want to talk to him.

He stood over me. "Is Quinn coming back?"

"No."

"Why?"

"Because I told her not to."

"You fired her?"

"I told her if she thinks I'm so fucking terrible, then she doesn't need to come back."

"And you didn't think to run that by me? Have you thought about the fact that having her here has made all our lives easier?"

"Not mine."

"Five out of six of us. I thought I had a say in things like this. I understand why you didn't say anything about hiring her, but to fire her without even talking to me? To any of us?"

"It's not like it was planned. Plus, you have barely wanted any part of the business. You never care about these decisions."

"Yes, I do. You just take it upon yourself to make them before talking with me."

"Because when I talk to you about it, you say you don't care and for me to handle it."

He shook his head. "You know I like Quinn being here. We all do, and you didn't even think to ask any of us. You would flip out if any of us dated and let that relationship get in the way of work, but you're allowed to?"

I stood. "I wasn't dating her. And do you think I wanted her to see me as a monster? That I wanted to have to tell her to go?"

Everyone turned to me now.

"No, but that doesn't give you a right to make these decisions without me. Without any of us."

"I think I can decide without asking when it's about something important."

"No, that's exactly the time you have to ask us. I don't care whose name is on the papers. We all own this business."

I shook my head, sitting back down, the fight leaving me. "Sorry that for one fucking day, I put myself before the business."

"That's your choice! You leave me out of everything you can. Somehow you think that's better for all of us, and I'm sick of it."

"I do it because I didn't think you cared about those parts of it all." I could barely care. It seemed that everyone thought I was the worst, my friends included.

"No, I care about it all, and you're going to have to start realizing that. Starting with getting Quinn back."

"Alright, you two, calm down. Fox, I'm sure you two can talk about this later when he's not so upset," Scout said. "Ransom, you don't have to handle everything on your own. We are all on board to make decisions and get things done. Stop acting like you have to do it all. Now," she sat down next to me with a thud, wrapping her arm around me, "are you ok?"

"I'm fine."

"Come on, Ransom. All this started because of Brooke on your damn lap."

"But I didn't invite her. I didn't ask her to jump all over me. I haven't texted her in months. Let alone invite her over. What the fuck is my luck with Quinn that something always gets fucked up? And why the fuck does she think I'm so bad?" I could hear my rant, hear the desperate anger in my voice. But how the fuck could I care when every moment I had liked Quinn was met with me being not good enough to get her?

Now the moment she may have changed her mind and somehow the world still aligned to make her think I was truly a terrible person.

"Maybe she will —"

I cut her off, "Not now, Scout. It's fine. The universe has no plans to let me have what I want, and I accept that. And I told her not to come back."

"So you do, or did, want Quinn then?"

I looked over at her, surprised at the question. "Was that not clear?"

She shrugged, "I mean, not really? I knew you liked her and liked having her around, maybe even liked messing around, but I figured it was like any other girl you mess with. I didn't realize it was more than that."

"It's more. It's a lot more, and it's been a lot more for a long time."

Jax sat down. "What has?"

"Nothing."

"Who invited Brooke? I thought that was done and over?"

"It was. I don't know why she was here or knew to come."

"Strange. It's been a week of weird things, hasn't it?"

"Yeah, it has, and we need to figure out why."

My phone started ringing in my hand, and a picture of Quinn popped up.

"Fuck," I said, staring at her picture and deciding what to do. I could pick up and see what she had to say or block her number and try to forget everything.

"Is it her?" Scout asked, making the rest of the crew turn.

"Yea."

"Pick up. See what she has to say," Scout said, but I shook my head. "Come on, Ransom, just see. The worst thing is you hang up on her."

"Fine," I said, jumping up and walking away from everyone. They didn't need to hear every detail of my life.

"Quinn." It was all I could say without spilling my guts again.

"Ransom. I'm sorry. I'm so sorry." Her voice was a whisper.

I let out a breath, not knowing what to say. I wanted to tell her it was ok and to come back, but how could I when she hated me? Then something crashed in the background.

"What was that? Why are you so quiet?" I didn't know what

it was, but I froze, waiting to hear that she was just in bed or trying not to wake her roommate up.

She sucked in a shaky breath, and I realized she might be crying. "I need help. I need you. I need —." Her words cut off with a squeak, and I could hear thuds and a guy's voice over the phone. "Get out, bitch. Let's send a few pictures to your boyfriend. Maybe even a new video. Where is Ransom anyway?"

I started back towards the fire, the crew all turning to me. Something must have shown on my face, because Fox stood up.

"Quinn, what's going on? Where are you?"

"Ransom." Her voice was louder now, but still a whisper. I could hear the fear in her tone, and a cold sweat flushed down my back. "Can you please come get me? I know you're mad, and you can keep being mad, but I don't know who else to call, and they aren't letting me leave."

"Yes. I'm coming. Where are you?" My heart raced, not caring where she was or our fight. I needed to get to her. I looked around, grabbing my keys and nodding to the rest of the crew. They needed an answer, but I couldn't give one. It didn't matter. They were already moving, pulling out keys, and heading to lock the garage without any questions.

"I have my keys. We're coming now. Tell me where you are."

She was quiet, but I heard more yelling and thumps in the background. I couldn't breathe. "Quinn, what's going on?"

"Hold on."

"I sent it," she said with a deep breath.

My phone dinged with an address from her, and I stopped to send it to the rest of the crew.

"Quinn, you have to tell me what's happening."

"I went to a party, and Josie was supposed to be here, but she's not, and then... It's Ryder. He's here. They have me trapped in the bathroom."

Fuck. If my heart wasn't racing before, it was now. This had to be a heart attack. I struggled to pull enough air into my lungs.

I hit the door, slamming it behind me as everyone else came around. "Ryder has Quinn trapped at a party. We need to go."

They raced to their cars and started them up as I closed myself into mine, trying to keep my hand steady as I turned it on.

"I'm coming. Take a deep breath. I'll be there in a minute." I looked down at the GPS. It said 15 minutes, but I could beat that.

I set the phone against my ear and peeled out, everyone following close behind me. I'd never been more grateful for people who wouldn't ask questions and just go, all while being able to keep up. I pushed the car faster.

"Are you locked in the bathroom?"

"Yeah, but they are right outside the door. There's some outside the window too."

"Ok. I'm coming. We'll get you out."

"There's a lot of them, Ransom. I'm so sorry. I don't know how I can get out of here. I didn't mean what I said."

"It's ok. And I didn't want her near me. I wanted you," I said. "Don't worry about any of it now."

She squeaked again. "Ok. Alright."

My voice shook. "I'll get you out. Take a breath."

I'd kill every single one of them to get her out.

TWENTY-SEVEN

QUINN

SOMEONE KICKED AT THE DOOR, splintering a hole through it, and I screamed. Laughter and shouts of encouragement filled the house.

"Quinn. What happened?" I tried to focus on his voice, and the roar of the engine in the background, the calm sounds helping me breathe.

"They kicked a hole in the door."

"Are you wearing your boots?"

"Yes," I whispered.

"If they make it in before I'm there, start kicking. Kick as hard as you can and don't stop till you see blood."

"How far are you?" The words were shaky as they kicked at the door again.

"5 minutes, Kitten. I'll be there in 5 minutes."

Five minutes felt like a lifetime. The room went quiet until they threw something against the door. Glass shattered as it made it inside and hit the mirror, but the door still held.

"Ok." I held back a scream as the door finally gave, the wood splintering.

"I'm sorry, Quinn. I'm sorry."

I slid down the wall, thinking I could kick better if they couldn't grab onto me. I held the phone with white knuckles as two of them broke in through the pieces of wood, reaching out for me.

I pulled my foot back before kicking one in the face. Blood splattered around the room as it sprayed from his nose. I gagged at the sound and blood, but kept my eyes open.

"What the fuck, you fucking bitch!" he yelled, moving from the room.

"Whatever you did, do it again," Ransom said, "You're doing great. I'm almost there."

The other one came closer as more crowded into the small bathroom. I kicked him hard between the legs. He doubled over, a string of curse words coming from him.

"Good. Keep going," Ransom said. I tried to tune out their swears and curses as four of them piled in the room.

"Grab her fucking feet," the one who I had kicked in the face said. I put the phone in my pocket before they got closer, hearing Ransom's muffled yells on the other end.

Two of them grabbed my arms and two on my legs, making me laugh. "How many of you is it going to take to grab me?" I asked, the nervous energy and pure panic bubbling up and turning me into someone I didn't recognize.

"Shut up, bitch."

"Is that the only thing you can call me?"

"What would you prefer? Ransom's fuck bunny?"

I laughed again, the sound desperate to my own ears, "It's 'buddy,' you idiot, not bunny."

He looked at one of the other guys with surprise on his face. The other guy nodded. "She's right."

"I thought it was like a puck bunny? You know those hockey groupies?"

"No, dude," his friend said.

"What the fuck are you guys doing?" Ryder said, "Stop talking to her and put her over there."

"Then what?"

"Fucking hold her, you idiots."

"Then what?"

"Fucking hell, you two. Call Slaughter and tell him, then maybe send a nice picture to Ransom." He grabbed my face, squeezing my cheeks in his hand. "Think he'll come find you?" Ryder said, "Think he'll risk walking in here?" Two guys held my arms now, pushing me back against the chair, but their grips loosened as Ryder grabbed at me again.

Ransom had to be close now.

I didn't say anything, and he must have taken that as my defeat, but I was too busy sliding down my chair, trying to move my leg into a position I could kick again.

He was facing me, leaning back against the table they had in the middle of the room. He was looking at his phone now. I assumed he was calling Slaughter, but I didn't care. It was my opening.

I pulled my foot back, aiming to slam it right at his face. The door crashed behind him right as I lifted my boot and kicked. His head turned at the sound of the door crashing in, giving me a lucky shot to hit his jaw.

The heel of the boot hit. I could feel the moment it collided. I squeezed my eyes shut as blood splayed again, hitting my white dress and jacket.

"Eww," I said, looking down, the thought of some random guy's blood on me making my stomach churn.

Ransom and Fox stormed into the room, Jax and Kye right behind them. I was relieved to see that Scout didn't slip inside, but I was surprised Dante didn't come in.

I looked at Ransom, his face stone as he glared at Ryder, not daring to look at me.

"Oh hey, Ryder, looks like we're late to the party," Fox said, looking him over with an easy grin.

"You got a little something right here, Ryder," Jax said, pointing to where I had kicked him.

"You fucks think it's funny?" Ryder stood back up, wrapping his hand into my hair and pulling. I yelled as Ryder forced my head to the side and into the back of a chair. My vision blurred for a moment before it cleared again. I looked at Ransom again. He looked like he could murder, and I wondered if he was debating it.

"Fuck you, Ryder," I said, trying not to move, each shake of my head pulling hair out.

"If you insist," he said, looking at Ransom. "What do you think? Should your girl become my girl?" Ryder pulled me up against him with a knife to my neck, forcing me forward until my hips hit the table.

"We could try it out right here," Ryder said.

Ransom moved quick, the glint of a knife in his hand catching the light. His face darkened, and I had never seen such a murderous gaze. "I'll kill you."

Ryder laughed, "Not with this knife to her throat, you won't."

The knife pressed in harder, and I winced, the blade pinching my skin. I knew Ransom would come for him, I could tell by the deadly look, but nobody was going anywhere until the knife came away from my throat. Fox, Jax, and Kye were frozen behind Ransom, their eyes scanning each guy in the room. They were outnumbered. There had to be at least ten of these guys. I had broken one of the guys' noses, so hopefully, that brought the number down to nine.

I had taken self-defense classes during my orientation week at school. It was something they offered free to anyone who wanted it, and I went, learning the basics of what to do. Ransom's face twisted with pain and anger. The fact that he even cared to show up spurred me forward, ready to get to him.

I picked up my foot and slammed it down, landing on enough of Ryder's toes for his arm to drop with a curse. I fell to the floor, scrambling under the table to Ransom, who held out a hand and pulled me up, pushing me behind all four of them.

Everyone froze as Ryder stared daggers at Ransom, the balance of power shifting as I got away. We were still outnumbered, but I looked at each of their faces, and none of them seemed worried. Fox even looked thrilled.

"We didn't take Slaughter's cars, Ryder."

"I don't believe you."

"That's not my fucking problem. If you touch her again, I'm going to kill you. I don't care how many guys you have around you. I will fucking kill you. We didn't steal your cars, and she sure as hell doesn't have anything to do with this."

A hand came around my wrist, and I flinched until I saw it was Kye. He jerked his head, looking towards the door. I stepped back once before Ryder smiled, looking right at me.

"I can't help it if your bitch comes to my house begging for my dick."

The room went silent before Ransom moved, jumping over the table. The rest of the room erupted into chaos. He swung out an elbow, hitting Ryder in the same place I had kicked him. He yelled, but Ransom was on him again, hitting the same spot with his fist. Ryder fell to the ground, and Ransom was on top of him, hitting him over and over.

I couldn't take my eyes off him. He was violent and wild. I was right all along. Ransom was dangerous, and he was the first place I had ever found safety.

Jax and Fox were already fighting with the others. Kye kept them back from me, pushing me towards the door, but I yelled, "Stop! We have to help them."

"No. We have to get out of here. They will be right behind

us." He put his hands on my back, trying to push me forward, and I grabbed the doorframe to stop him.

"Are you sure, Kye?"

"We will drive the damn car into the house if they aren't out in one minute. I was told to get you out, and I'm not fucking with him now."

He pushed me forward. "I'm holding you to that."

We made it to Ransom's car, and he opened the door, pushing me into the passenger seat.

"Clip in," he said. I pulled the harness down but didn't clip it yet, needing to be ready to go back in. I watched the house, holding my breath as seconds ticked by.

Finally, I saw movement. Fox jumped over the patio, Jax right behind him as they ran to their cars.

I held my breath, waiting for Ransom to come out.

"Kye." He was standing guard next to me. "It's been a minute."

"Hold on."

He yelled something to Fox, and Fox nodded, getting in his car and revving it.

Kye slammed my door with me inside and went to his own car as Ransom ran down the steps, sliding to a stop at the driver's side. Three guys ran from the house, but he was already in, starting the engine and sliding the car across the damp grass. We hit the pavement, and the car took off, kicking into gear as Ransom fell into line with the others. I realized Dante's car was with us and looked at Ransom.

"We made him stay in the car with Scout."

I nodded, realizing his harness wasn't on. I leaned over, pulling it over his head and snapping it into place.

He smiled down at me. "Worried?"

"Considering it says we're going ninety, and there is blood on your face. Yes."

"I don't think it's mine. Ryder tried to headbutt me but missed. I think it's his."

"That guy just had to get blood everywhere."

Ransom laughed and shook his head. "What an asshole."

I laughed and smiled back. "I'm shaking."

"Keep taking deep breaths. We will slow down in a minute, but they are going to follow." We hit the highway, and everyone split off. Forming a line across the empty highway before each one started taking different exits.

"What's happening?" Fear gripped me again as I looked back, expecting to see Ryder and his friends behind us.

"It's pretty easy to find us as a group. We will all take different routes back."

I leaned back, trusting their plan, and took a deep breath. The adrenaline was wearing off, leaving exhaustion and panic in its wake. He reached for my hand, and I let him take it, my fingers still shaking.

"Are you ok? Do you want me to stop?"

"No, I'm alright. Go where you need to."

The car was silent as he drove, heading down the highway before he branched off and pulled onto a side street, slowing down to a normal speed.

"Thank you," I said, my voice quiet, not registering what had happened. I couldn't have been there more than thirty minutes, but it felt like a lifetime. I couldn't understand how things could go so bad so quick. Tears welled as the night replayed. "Thank you for coming for me. I didn't know who else I could call."

"You can call me anytime you need me. I will always be there if you need me." The last words were quiet.

"Even if we're fighting?"

"Apparently."

"I didn't know exactly how serious you were about always being there for me."

"And you know now?"

"Yes. It's just saying something, and following through on it, are two different things. You could say sweet things to me all day, but bail when things are rough. Obviously, you didn't."

"When you called, did you doubt that I would come?"

I thought back to the moment I reached the bathroom, knowing there was no one else who would come for me. I couldn't imagine anyone in my life who would be willing to go into a house filled with people who basically wanted to kill them, all for the sake of rescuing me.

"No. I didn't. I knew I would be safe as soon as I called you." I gave a tight laugh. "I didn't know everyone would be coming with you, though. I can't believe they came to help."

"If one of us needs help, we are all there. No questions asked. At least not until everyone is out. Then there might be a few questions."

"I take it that you have questions, then?" I asked, staring at him in the dim light of the dash. A radio crackled, and I shot up.

"Not right now. Let's just get you home." He picked up a walkie-talkie-looking thing and waited, voices coming over it saying they were clear. Ransom said it back and set it back on the hook on the floor. I hadn't noticed it there before, but then again, I had been too worried about Ransom in the car or trying not to crash.

"What is that?"

"CB radio. We installed them so we could talk. It's easier than trying to text everyone or call while you're driving."

"So that means everyone is fine?"

"Yeah. All clear. No one is following any of us. At least not anymore."

I was quiet for a minute, not knowing if I wanted to know the answer to my question. "What now?"

"Get you home, clean up, calm you down." He had turned onto the road of my dorm, and I could see the building looming in front of us.

He pulled in, throwing it in park at the front of the building.

I thought of going back to my room, the cold concrete walls and empty bed. The possibility of facing Josie and finding out what the hell happened to her and how I ended up there.

"What is it?" he asked, his fingers running along my jaw, the light touch nearly making me cry. I undid my harness, hesitating as the tears welled.

I took a deep breath, climbing over the shifter until I straddled him, my back against the steering wheel.

"I'm sorry. I know you're probably still mad, but I'm sorry for what I said, and thank you for saving me. You're not a monster. You're a hero. That was one of the scariest things to ever happen to me, and I knew you would come for me no matter how many of them there were."

He didn't move. His eyes watched mine, but he didn't say anything.

I ran my hand along his jaw. It was strong and sharp, and all I wanted to do was kiss him. I didn't care about the girl on his lap. I didn't think he was terrible. He was everything I had dreamed he would be and more. Strong and scary, soft and sweet. He was all of it, and I wanted every part.

He still hadn't said a word, so I pushed forward, "I know we're fighting, I know you didn't want to see me again, and I know this is a lot to ask for, but for tonight can I go back to your house? I mean, can I come home with you? I don't want to be alone in my dorm. I don't feel safe and….and I'd rather be with you."

The admission was hard. Telling someone that I didn't want to be alone and didn't feel safe being alone, especially after that person told me not to come around again. Not only that, but I didn't want to be away from him. His calm strength might be the only thing keeping me together at the moment, but telling him that was like handing over my heart at a time when he could crush it in seconds.

He reached for me, his warm fingers laced in mine, solid and steady. The same hands that had just beaten Ryder because he hurt me.

"I'm sorry too. I didn't want her there. I was waiting for you. And yes. Yes, fucking, please come home with me. That sounds a lot better than sleeping in my car."

"Sleeping in your car?"

"If you think I wanted to drop you off and leave you here alone tonight after all of that, you're out of your mind. I was going crazy thinking about it. I didn't know, though, with every-thing that happened, I didn't know if you would come with me."

Every knot that had tied in my chest unraveled. I grabbed his face and crashed into him. His lips were hot and as needy as mine. I didn't care if it was only for tonight or a thousand more. I needed him.

"Can we go home now?"

He gave a deep laugh. "I've been ready to hear you say those words for weeks, but I think you need to move back to your seat first."

"Oh, right." I pulled away, sliding back over to my side.

He didn't say another word, just grabbed my hand and kissed my knuckles before turning my hand over and kissing my palm, each touch of his lips sending a burning need through me. The car raced down the road, and for the first time, I wasn't second-guessing if I should be there with him in the car or, this time, going home with him.

TWENTY-EIGHT

QUINN

HE DROVE another few minutes past the garage until we reached
a tall, older brick building. There were three large garage doors
at the bottom, and he hit a button to open one and pulled in. I
recognized everyone's car as he angled next to Fox's.

"So, what? You all live here?"

"Kind of. Scout and Kye still live at home. Dante stays here
sometimes, but most of the time at his own place. It was an old
firehouse when we bought it. We've been fixing it into apartments. Fox and I share the next floor up from here, and Jax is on
the top floor. There's one empty apartment on the second floor
that will probably be Scout's. Kye is redoing the attic to be his,
but like Scout, he won't stay here permanently until after gradua-
tion. He's here most nights, though."

I nodded, knowing Scout's home life was probably pretty
similar to what mine had been.

"This place is amazing."

He led me up a flight of stairs into a small hallway with two
doors. There was a second set of stairs leading up to another
landing. Ransom opened the one on the right, the door already
unlocked.

"You don't lock them?"

"No, the entire building has a security system, so we don't need to lock our doors. Would you feel better if I locked us in tonight?"

I nodded, feeling stupid, but I had always locked my door. Whether I was at my mom's or my dorm, I locked my door every night since I was tall enough to reach the handle.

"It's ok. No one else needs to be here tonight."

"Thanks."

We walked in, and I stopped. The place was huge, the main room holding a kitchen, a table, and a giant living room with a couch so big I felt like I could live on it. It was obvious that they had built the bedroom off to the left, along with another room, which I assumed was the bathroom. The oversized window looked out over the small downtown with more windows up higher, unreachable but able to bring light in when the sun was up. He hadn't decorated much, but the worn couch was oversized and cozy, and the kitchen seemed used enough. The table was piled up with mail and car parts.

I laughed. "Can't get away from the cars, can you?"

"I would bring one in here to work on at night if I could," he said with a smile. "We are still working on the place. It's a big project, but it keeps coming together."

"It has to be nice, all being so close."

"Yeah, it's been pretty great."

I wrung my hands, nervous that we were so close and alone. "You guys don't get sick of each other?"

He laughed and leaned against the back of the couch. "All the time. That's why we decided to convert the place into apartments instead of one big studio. The first year of living here, there were no walls. There was one big bathroom, one kitchen area, and four mattresses on the floor. The place had gone to auction, and Luca helped us buy it for cheap. After we paid him back, we poured money into material and immediately split the place up. I love everyone, but we are a difficult group of people, making walls very necessary."

"Considering what you had to do to get me out of that place, I can't be one to talk about being difficult."

His head fell, and he shook it. "I'm sorry you've been pulled into this. I never wanted that. I was trying to keep you out of it. That's why I didn't tell you about it in the first place."

"You didn't bring me into it."

"You had to fight for your life because a guy wanted to get to me. You have blood all over you. How did I not bring you into this?"

"I didn't go to that house because of you. It's not like you led me there or knew what was happening. There was no way you had anything to do with what happened. I still would have been there if you weren't around. They didn't do anything because they knew, or at least hoped, that you would come. I was safer with them knowing I was with you than if I hadn't been."

He went into the kitchen and started messing with things. "Why were you there?"

"I was supposed to go out with Josie. I guess she gave me the wrong address or something because she wasn't there, and it wasn't her type of people."

His brows furrowed, but he didn't say anything, and I was thankful he didn't. I wasn't ready to look closer at the coincidence that Josie sent me to Ryder's house, of all places.

"Come on." He spun me around and pulled off my jacket. "We need to clean you up."

He took a wet washcloth and started to clean my face and chest.

"You left before I could tell you how beautiful you looked." He ran the cloth down my neck. "I was looking forward to seeing you all day."

"So was I until I walked in and saw another girl cozied up in your lap." I nudged him back, grabbing the towel to wipe his face.

"If you had stayed a second longer, you would have seen how I was pushing her off me. She showed up and seemed drunk. None of us know why she was there. She has never even been to one of our cookouts. We usually keep that to close friends only. She came acting like I had invited her, but I didn't. I keep asking her to leave me alone. I can prove it on my phone right now. I'm sorry either way, though. You shouldn't have had to see that."

"No, I'm sorry. I shouldn't have overreacted like that. To say those things to you wasn't right. It's not like we're together. You have every right to be with whoever you want. I didn't like feeling like I was being messed with again."

His fingers trailed down my jaw, and all I wanted was to wrap myself around him.

"You're the only one I've wanted to be with. I'm not messing with you. I've been trying to get you from day one."

"No, you weren't."

He gave a small laugh. "I mean pretty damn close."

"You look at me like you hate me. You always have."

He sighed, "Because you give so easily to everyone else. To Fox, to Jax, to Logan. Hell, you even did with Ryder. You smile at them like you think the world of them like they can do no wrong, like you're comfortable around them, but you don't look at me like that, and I've been going fucking crazy trying to figure out why. Fox can put his arm around you, and it's fine, but I do it, and you freeze like I'm hurting you. I wanted to know what they gave you that I didn't."

"Oh," I said, shocked at his honesty. "I don't like them more than you, at least not in the way you think. I know it's weird, but when they touch me, there's nothing there, so I relax, but when you touch me…Every single time you touch me, my body reacts, and then I want more of you, all of you. It's a lot to take."

"Back there in the car, you finally looked at me like that. I feel like I've been waiting my whole life for that."

"Your whole life, huh?"

He blew out a breath. "It feels like it."

I ran the washcloth over the side of his face, cleaning off the last of the blood, and was happy to see it wasn't his.

"I was so mad you told me to never come back."

"What a ridiculous thing of me to say," he said, leaning into me. "I'll have to show you how bad I lied and how much I do want you around."

His hand wrapped into my hair, pulling it back and kissing my lips in a frenzy. The chill that had come over me disappeared as his tongue moved against mine. My body melted into his, and arms wrapped around his neck, bringing him closer.

His dark hair fell against his forehead, and his blue eyes were heavy as he pulled back. "Does staying here tonight mean you want to sleep in my bed or on my couch?"

"Bed."

"Thank god because I didn't know how I would stay here with you without you next to me."

"I didn't say that I wanted you in the bed with me," I said, biting my cheek to not smile.

His eyes flew to mine, and it took him a second to catch on. "Oh, you think you're funny? When you're in my bed, I make the rules, and the first rule is that you will not be in it without me."

He stepped forward until my back was up against the counter, pushing my knees apart and pressing close between them. He dipped his head again, kissing my neck as his hands moved around my back, pulling the zipper of my dress down until the entire thing fell to the ground.

"Shit." He fell to his knees, kissing from one hip to the other, following the edge of my panties. "Did you wear these for me?"

"Maybe."

His hand trailed up my thigh and stopped. "Just maybe? I guess I'll stop here then." His hand dropped.

"No," I yelled, "I did wear them for you. You said you wanted to see them."

He smiled up at me, and I was ready to come undone. This dark god was at my feet, and I didn't care what he wanted from me anymore. He could have it all.

"Good girl."

He leaned forward, and his mouth came down over my clit, the lace fabric feeling too thick, leaving too much between me and his mouth. He sucked once, and I shuddered, a ripple of ecstasy running through me.

"Off, Ransom, take them off." I breathed, the words almost begging.

"In a hurry?" His hands circled one of my thighs, trailing down until he took off my boot and then moved to the other.

His fingers traced back up my body, blazing a trail over my sensitive skin until his lips met mine again.

I grabbed his shirt, pulling it over his head. The cut had healed more, but it was still an angry red. The rest of him was all in one piece. My hands splayed on his chest and ran down, reaching for his belt.

"Please tell me now if you don't want this to go any further. Tell me my limits because I need you and don't want you to regret one fucking minute tomorrow."

There was a moment left for me to turn and leave, a moment where he wasn't touching me, letting me decide what would happen next. I couldn't stop now, not after wanting him for so long and having him so close, especially finding out he wanted me just as badly. Something I thought was a faraway dream was now my reality.

"No limits. Give me everything."

He didn't hesitate again, wrapping his hands around my legs and grabbing my ass as he lifted me up, carrying me into the bedroom. Our lips met, the fire blazing through me again the moment they did. I wouldn't regret a single second of him touching me.

Setting me down on the oversized bed, he watched as I reached out to feel the soft, dark gray blankets and sheets beneath me. With his eyes fixed on mine, he began to undress, taking off his clothing until every inch of him was revealed in all its raw, unfiltered beauty. All that was left was a pair of boxers. Tattoos trailed down his body and started again on his thigh.

"You're beautiful," he said, covering my body with his.

"I was thinking the same thing about you," I said.

"I've never been called beautiful before."

"I don't know why. When I first saw you, I thought you looked like a Greek god. Hades, of course, but a god none-theless." He laughed and kissed me again.

"I've never been compared to a Greek god. The devil maybe, but not a god."

"I said Hades, so it's close." I joked. His fingers trailed up my thigh, hooking my underwear and pulling them down.

"Ransom." My voice was breathless.

He groaned as he kissed down my stomach and back up. "I love hearing my name on your lips. I love hearing you want it to be me here touching you and not someone else." He came up to kiss me and then ran his nose down my jaw. "Someone more perfect."

"You are perfect. Just because I've been running away doesn't mean you aren't."

"I know that's not true."

"But it is. Aside from your perfect face and body," I said, running my hands over his arms and back, reminding me just how perfect his body was. "You're sweet and caring and gener-ous. More than anyone else that I know. So dedicated and vicious to protect the ones you love," I pulled up his now swollen, red knuckles and kissed them, "and protect me."

"You deserve someone a whole hell of a lot better, and we both know it. You believe that yourself."

"No, I deserve someone I can trust. Someone I know will come to save me when I'm scared and locked in a bathroom. One who buys me new boots when I need them and makes sure his friends are always happy and safe. Someone who gets me off at a carnival but doesn't take advantage of me even when I was begging for it." I laughed, "I'm starting to think I deserve someone like you," I said, not realizing how much I meant them until that moment.

I deserved an amazing guy, that's what I have been looking for, but I was looking in the wrong direction. I deserve someone who gave a shit about me and would do something about it, even if people thought he was dangerous or wild. Maybe he was from afar, but up close. He was perfect.

"Ransom," I said again, his fingers running along my thighs and stomach, touching me everywhere except where I needed him.

"Yes, Kitten?"

"Stop teasing me."

"Tease you? I would never." His fingers circled my core, and I couldn't hide my moan.

I pulled at his boxers, moving them down his legs until his cock was in my hand. "You're teasing me now, and I don't want it. I've been waiting weeks." I pushed, and he rolled, letting me move on top of him.

"You're greedy," he said with a smile, pleasure in his eyes.

I rubbed his cock along my wetness, his groan spurring me forward. He reached up, unhooking my bra and pulling my nipple into his mouth. He nipped and licked, his fingers rubbing my clit at the same time. The sensation was too much, and I was ready to come before he was even inside me.

"Fuck me." I breathed, "Please." He flipped over, pinning me to the bed.

He bit and licked at my neck once. "You kill me," he said, and then he placed his cock at my entrance. He pushed in, slamming to the hilt as I stretched around him.

"Oh, my god." I breathed, gripping his shoulders.

"I'll be your god," he said as he pushed inside of me further. "I'll fuck you until you see stars. I'll make you the goddess that I worship. I'll rip apart anyone who tries to hurt you."

"Ransom." I couldn't take his words, each one turning me on more as his cock filled me. Tears pricked my eyes at the thought. This is what I have wanted for so long, and it was even more than I had dreamed.

He kissed every part of my neck and chest. "I can't stay in control when you say my name like that."

"I want you. I've wanted you for weeks. I want you to fuck me until I can't think of anything but your name."

"Fuck," he said, pushing harder, driving his cock into me.

My nails dug into his back as I moved against him. He was hitting every perfect spot, and my body was knotting and tightening, ready to break me. "More." I breathed as he leaned down.

"I knew you had claws," he whispered, moving faster now. Every stroke harder and more desperate until he was pounding into me.

The world came undone, my body shaking as I came around him. I yelled his name, but my thoughts weren't coherent anymore.

I laid out, trying to catch my breath as the world came into focus again. "That was…" My words trailed off.

"I'm sorry. Did you think I was done with you?" he asked with a deep laugh. His hands wrapped under me, flipping me onto my stomach and pulling me back until I was on my knees, my face against the bed. His hand wrapped into my hair, holding it back just enough to keep me in place.

"It's not over that fast. I think we are going to go again."

In a moment, he was back inside me, pushing and fucking

me as my body responded. The orgasm coiling in every part of me as my body tensed. "Again?" I breathed, not able to believe it. Could I come that fast a second time?

"Again," he said, moving faster, his hand wrapped around my stomach until he reached my clit where he rubbed light circles. My body answered for me, tensing before stars burst, blurring my vision as waves of pleasure rolled through me. I couldn't believe the satisfaction that filled every inch of me. I could only grab onto the bed, holding on as my body bucked and writhed in ecstasy beneath him.

He flipped me again, sliding back in and watching me. I think I could come again without my body melting away. "I can't. I can't take another."

"Yes, you can. Such a good girl. You're taking it perfect."

His pace slowed, and he kept his eyes on me. I was so turned on by his gaze that I moved harder against him. He understood and thrust into me again, slamming against me so hard it should have hurt, but the feeling only made me hotter.

"Quinn." He murmured, his body shaking with his own release. His body shuttered, and I ran my hands down his back.

"What. The. Hell," I said, trying to catch my breath. He laughed but stayed inside me, dragging in deep breaths before he rolled to my side.

His hand reached over, running up and down my stomach and chest, his lazy touch comforting, and I moved closer.

"What the hell what?" he asked, laughing against me.

My body relaxed into the bed, and he pulled me against him. I couldn't even think of what to say. My brain mush. Every part of me was useless. I tried to find the words. "How did that just happen? What just happened to me?"

He laughed into my neck. "Say the word, and I'll give you more."

I couldn't think, couldn't move as he held me. I don't know

when I started to fall asleep, but soon I was drifting, the world fading away.

I felt Ransom stand up and grab a towel, cleaning me up and helping me into a shirt before I fell back again.

He wrapped his arms around me, pulling me into his chest.

"Goodnight, Quinn."

"Goodnight, Ransom."

"I knew I would get to say that to you in bed together one day."

"Mmm," I murmured with a smile, already falling asleep.

His lips came to my ear. "I love you," he whispered, but I couldn't tell if I was dreaming or just hoping for the words so much that I made them up. I didn't have time to think about it more as I fell into a deep sleep.

TWENTY-NINE

QUINN

THE SUN CAME through the windows in the morning, hitting me in the eyes and making me groan awake. I felt Ransom move behind me and froze, looking around the room.

"Oh my god," I murmured, rubbing my eyes. Everything that happened last night came back to me, "Oh my god." I mumbled again.

"Mmm." I heard Ransom groan behind me, "Which part of yesterday are you referring to? The part where you kicked a guy and broke his face or the part where you begged me to fuck you?"

"Ransom." I groaned, pulling a pillow over my face.

He pulled it off. "Would it help if I begged you to fuck me this time? Because I will absolutely fall on my knees and beg for more." He kissed me, the soft touch there and gone as he lifted my head and put the pillow back underneath me.

"Actually, yes, because you aren't going to let me live it down if you don't."

"Oh, I'm not going to let you live that down either way. I liked it too much. Changed my whole life the moment you asked for it." He kissed me again, and I groaned.

"Yesterday was the weirdest day of my life."

"Yeah, I probably won't let you live down fighting off a group of men that could have killed you. You looked like a little warrior last night. It took four of them to hold you down. I knew you had claws, but I was wrong. You're not like a kitten. More like a wild lioness. I think you broke more bones yesterday than me."

I groaned again. "I can't believe I did that. I'm a horrible person."

"By whose standards?" He sat up, and I realized he was still naked. I reached out, tracing every scar and tattoo with my fingertips.

"Everyone's?"

"You're a fighter. You were fighting for your life and should be fucking proud of what you did. Do you remember what you said to those guys when I was on the phone? You were making fun of them. I had never been so scared in my life, but I couldn't stop laughing as you made fun of them. I mean, I yelled for you to stop, but still, I was laughing."

"That was stupid of me. I was making them angrier." He shrugged, playing with my hair splayed out on the pillow.

"Probably, but sometimes you can't control those things when adrenaline kicks in. You were a badass, Quinn. Be proud of yourself. You fought back and won."

"Only because you guys showed up."

"And we will always show up. No matter what, I'll be there for you. Do you know how mad everyone was I told you to leave? They will always be there for you, too."

I turned to him, my breath catching at his face. The perfect jaw and blue eyes could knock me over. He was so beautiful. He must have been hit yesterday because a bruise was forming near his temple. I ran my fingers over it. "Sorry you were hurt."

"It's not bad. I've gotten hit a few times lately."

"Apparently."

"What do you want to do today?" he asked.

"Together?"

He laughed, "Yes, together. Are you ready to run out of the door? Do you not want to spend the day with me?"

I thought it over. I was a little bit ready to run. The thought of fleeing to my dorm to hide away was better than risking this going bad. Then again, Josie would be there.

The idea of spending the day together, though, sounded better than all of that. Getting Ransom to myself for an entire day when I could touch and kiss him was a dream come true.

"No, it's worth the risk. I want to."

"What risk?"

"The risk of this going bad."

He nuzzled into me. "I'll do everything I can to make it not go bad."

"And if I'm the one to mess it up?"

"I don't think that is possible. You're perfect." He nipped at my ear. "I've waited so long for you. I want to spend the entire day with you."

He rolled on top of me, pulling off the shirt I had slipped on in the middle of the night, kissing and touching every inch of me until I was lying in the middle of the bed, satisfied once again.

"Was your idea of spending the day together in bed?" I asked, somewhat hoping he would say yes.

"No. We will obviously get up and shower." He flashed a wicked grin. "But I thought I could take you out. We've never gone on a date."

I shook my head. I knew Ransom had a sweet side. He's shown it so many times, but being in a world where I was having sex and going on dates with him felt unreal.

I turned to watch him as he got up and got ready.

"Hey," I yelled as I grabbed my dress and looked it over. "I need to grab clothes before I go anywhere. I think my dress is ruined."

He came out of the bathroom. "How are we going to grab your clothes if you don't have any to begin with?" He smiled, kissing me like it was the most natural thing to do.

"Do you have anything that would work?"

He walked into the living room and came back with a girl's pair of leggings and then pulled a hoodie out of his closet. "Here, and before you kill me, the pants are Scout's. She comes over here and does laundry. She sometimes forgets things in the dryer and hasn't been over to grab these."

Lucky for me, Scout wore close to the same size as me. The leggings were a little tight but fine to wear for now. I shut the bathroom door, needing a second away from him.

I showered and cleaned up, Ransom's soap the only thing to use, making the scent of him fill the steamed bathroom around me.

Afterward, I leaned my head out of the bathroom. "Give me one of those tank tops you are always wearing."

His brow furrowed as he grabbed one from the dresser and handed it to me.

I pulled it on and then the hoodie, looking in the mirror. A memory flooded back as I remembered this exact hoodie. He had been wearing it one day at school, and his car must have broken down because I remember him bent over the engine, the car's hood up, and he had pulled this hoodie off. His t-shirt had come off too, and it was the first time I had seen the tattoos on his side. I couldn't look away that day as he stood bare-chested, not seeming to care as he kept fixing the car without a shirt. I had almost passed out from watching him and wanting him so badly. I smiled.

At the time, I struggled to make out what the tattoo had been, but I knew now. I had seen every part of him up close.

I still hadn't confessed my crush on him and how long it had been going on. The thought of telling him made me want to die from embarrassment. I couldn't face it today of all days. I just wanted to enjoy the day without any more fights or confessions. I walked out, finding him in the kitchen.

"Hey," I said, sliding between him and the counter.

I pulled him down, running my hands into his hair and kissing him. Thinking of the moment of him at school in this hoodie. How badly I had wanted to touch him, and now I was wrapped up in his arms in that same hoodie with his lips on mine.

He pulled back, lifting me onto the counter, "Are you ok?"

"Very ok. Why?"

"One minute, you're locking yourself in the bathroom trying to avoid me, and the next, you're all over me. I'm worried I won't be able to keep up."

I smiled, "This is just hard to get used to."

He nodded, "Whatever you need, then. I'm used to it now. Come on. Let's go. A date might help. Unless you run off in the middle of it." We grabbed our stuff and headed to the car.

"Can I drive?" I asked when we reached the doors.

He stopped, and the driver's side door opened. "You liked driving it?"

"More than I thought."

He looked at the car and then back at me, "Alright. You drive there, and I'll drive back."

I bit my lip, the thought of trying to drive with him the car was more daunting now, but I still wanted to do it.

"Deal." I ran around, grabbing the keys and getting in. We drove around, him teaching me how to listen and feel the car to know when to shift it better. It wasn't anything like my old beat-up car. I was getting the hang of it as I drove us to my favorite diner.

"This is where you want our first date?"

"Is there a problem with it?"

"Not at all. I love this place, but we can go anywhere you want. Seriously, anywhere."

"Ok, then I want to go here." The diner was on the edge of town, the small building up on the mountain a bit, giving the old restaurant one of the best views in town.

We walked in and sat down. "I've sat here a lot of nights alone," I said.

"Yea?"

"One of the waitresses that used to work here lived by us. I would ride with her and sit in that corner, reading, doing homework, and hanging out until she brought me home. It was always a nice break."

"I can imagine. I started going to the garage as soon as I could walk there."

"Bad home?"

"Two parents who hated each other and were dirt poor. It was always a fight around there. My dad died, and my mom moved away. I haven't seen her since, which is best for both of us."

"I'm sorry," I said. "I know the feeling."

"Yeah, but look, we got out and changed things. I'm happy now. Now being the last twelve hours," he said, smirking.

We ordered and waited as the food came, moving from comfortable silence to talking about cars, music, and my classes. It was so easy, everything so normal, that I felt like I could do this every day with him.

"You know, I thought I heard you say something last night, but now I'm not sure."

He leaned back against the booth, watching me.

"Do you mean when I said I loved you?" His words were so calm, like it was something he had told me a thousand times.

My breath caught, and for a moment, I couldn't say anything. "Yes, that."

He sipped his coffee. "Yes, I said it." His eyes didn't change this time, and neither did his expression. He was completely serious.

226226226226

"And you meant it?" My face scrunched, not understanding how he could mean it.

"I wouldn't say that without meaning it."

"And how are you so sure that you do? Enough to say you do?"

"I've known since I met you."

"That doesn't answer my question."

He huffed and leaned forward. "I can give you one example, but there's a thousand now. Yesterday when you called, the panic in your voice made me panic. I'm not one to freak out, even in the worst of fights or races. I usually keep a clear head, but I thought the worst and couldn't get a handle on myself as we drove over." He took another sip of coffee. "Then something I didn't even think possible came true, and it truly was the worst. When you stopped talking on the phone, and they took you, I thought I was going to show up to you dead. Then I thought I'd been a terrible enough person that they would do it in front of me. Like a cruel joke from life taking everything I wanted away in front of me. But you, you just fought. You slammed his face and foot, got away, and came under the table to me. I couldn't take a fucking breath until I grabbed your arm and pulled you behind me. I was worried I loved you before. Then I knew for sure because I would have done anything, fucking anything, to get you out of there safe. From the moment I saw you, I thought I would do anything for you, and now I know that's true."

He was so calm and assured at his words, like they were pure fact. There was no question about it. To him, it wasn't a heartfelt speech, it was just the truth, and I knew that made it more meaningful.

Tears threatened my eyes for what felt like the millionth time in 24 hours, trying to take in everything he said. "I've never had someone that fully loved me. Not like this. I don't know what to do with it."

"I get it. I've never loved anyone like this before. It wasn't until the crew came together that I figured out what it's like to have people around who actually care. It's a weird feeling when you realize that there are other people who give a shit about you. You have that, too, now. Like you saw last night, nobody hesitated to come for you."

I dropped my face into my hands. "I'm an ass. Everyone got back okay? I know you said they were fine, but I figured you were just trying to make me feel better."

"They are fine. I texted last night telling them thanks and that we would be busy."

"You did not say the word busy, right?"

His smile widened. "I did."

"Oh, my god. So everyone knows about this?" I said, waving a hand between us.

"They've known for weeks. I think you're the only one who wanted to avoid it. Why? Trying to keep me a dirty little secret?"

"You're the worst. No, that isn't what I meant," I said, standing up to head to the bathroom. "Although, now that you mention it, maybe —"

He caught my wrist, cutting me off to pull me down and kiss me. My body almost melted right into his lap.

"No secrets," he said.

"I really don't think you can kiss me like that in public."

"I'll do it again if you think I'm not going to let everyone know you're mine. Does this mean you are ready to go?"

Warmth spread through me, knowing exactly where we were going after this. "Yes. Yes, I am very ready to go."

THIRTY

QUINN

I RAN to the bathroom and back out, way too excited at the thought of going back to his bed.

I turned, running right into someone as I did. I went to apologize before shock and anger hit me.

"Move Tyler," I said, trying to nudge my around him to see if Ransom's back was still towards me.

"Wow, Quinn, what are you doing out here? Did Josie tell you to come out?"

"No."

He ignored me as his mouth twisted. I knew he was ready with a nasty reply. "Well, I can give you a ride if you want. Sarah and Josie are at my house. I'm out picking up some food. I'm sure they would love for you to come." His finger hooked into the hoodie's front pocket, making me stumble forward as he laughed, the deep sound letting me know what was coming. "And maybe all of us can film movie number two."

There it was.

"Fuck off, Tyler."

He laughed again. "You know, I wondered what I was

missing ever since that video. Logan always said you did pretty good in bed. I'm ready to find out."

The words were so low only I could hear. He knew his manners, and when he could cross the line, consequences never came for him if no one else heard.

My eyebrows furrowed. I was a consequence, though. What did Ransom call me, a wild lioness? I fought those men off me last night. If I could handle them, I could definitely handle Tyler, right? For the first time, I wasn't going to let Tyler bother me.

I looked over as an arm snaked around my waist. "Who's your friend?" Ransom asked.

"Ransom, Tyler. Tyler, Ransom."

"I know who you are," Tyler said, his lip curling in disgust. He couldn't hide the step back he took from us, though.

"I don't know who you are, but I'm glad I caught the end of that conversation," Ransom said, his tone bored and annoyed, but I knew better now.

I smiled up at Ransom, anger coursing through me. I was sick of Tyler always whispering these things to me, making sure no one else had heard. I was ready to end it. I didn't want to be bullied by him anymore.

And now I was out for blood, the taste of fighting back still fresh in my mind that I wanted more. I wanted Tyler to be afraid of me, like he was Ransom.

"Oh, sorry. Let me introduce you properly. Tyler is one of the perverted assholes who helped Logan orchestrate releasing a tape of me. He was asking if I wanted to go with him and the girls to film movie number two." I smiled at Tyler, knowing what those words would do to Ransom. I was thrumming in anger, and he would be too.

Ransom sucked in a deep breath, and Tyler crossed his arms. Part of me was happy. I wanted Tyler to pay for all the terrible things he had said to me over the years, and I knew Ransom could make him pay for that. I knew he would make him hurt and never want to see me again.

"Did you just ask my girlfriend to have sex with you? And you thought, what? I wouldn't do anything about it?"

Tyler's eyebrows shot up, and eyes went wide as he glanced from me to Ransom. "Girlfriend?"

"Yes, girlfriend," Ransom said, his stare deadly. I leaned into him, wrapping my arm around his back. "Didn't know you were a part of the first video. Funny how your name wasn't brought up before."

"Tyler likes to pretend he didn't help, but he was there. Now he's been making my life hell ever since and never misses an opportunity to beg me to have sex with him."

"What, you think you're going to be all big and bad, beat the shit out of me too?" Tyler asked. I could hear his voice crack before he tried to puff up his chest.

"I'm considering it." Ransom said, his face giving nothing but hatred away. He looked down at me once and must have seen the same. "Then again, she can do that herself. Maybe I'll just be her getaway driver. Again," he said the last word with such an emphasis Tyler would know it wasn't the first time. "Imagine the shame that will come if she is the one who beats the shit out of you," he said with a laugh.

"Yeah, right. What are you and your fucking freaks going to do? Hold me down while she slaps me?" Tyler asked. He tried to sound relaxed, but it was too hard to hide the edge of fear in his voice.

"I'm pretty sure there's still blood on her boots from the guy's face she fucking broke last night."

Tyler's eyes dropped to my boots and snapped back up.

"What's your problem, Ransom? You do all this just to have a chance at her? Wanted in her pants too? Bet you liked that video a little too much and had to try it out yourself."

Ransom stepped closer, dropping his arm around me and saying something I couldn't hear to Tyler.

Tyler stepped back. "Fuck both of you." He pointed a finger at me. "Josie's going to be pissed that you're slutting around again. Especially with him."

He was running out as he said the words, almost tripping over his own feet to reach the door.

Ransom let out a breath. "Fucking hell, is that what you have been dealing with? I didn't realize he was involved in all that."

"Every. Single. Time," I said. "I guess he blocked the door so no one would interrupt. Every time I run into him, he gets worse. He's the reason I left that party the night I ran into the street. I wasn't even thinking when I stepped off the sidewalk. I was angry and hurt. What did you whisper to him?"

"Just what I would do to him if he ever talks to you again. The rumors about how horrible we are make it easy for people to believe every threat you give them."

He pulled me in and kissed my head, "And you say the word. We will give Tyler a visit. Imagine all of us pulling up in our scary cars to his house. We can make him cry without laying a finger on him."

I laughed, "You are a scary group."

We walked out, "Sadly, you're going to have to realize you're a part of that group now, Kitten. You do actually still have blood on your boots and don't seem to mind giving out threats like candy. I know exactly what you did back there."

"What do you mean?" I said, trying not to sound too guilty.

He pushed me up against the car, dropping his forehead to mine as his fingers traced my jaw. "Weren't you trying to provoke me? Telling me all the little truths, hoping I would hit him? Admit it. You wanted me to beat the shit out of him. I could see it in your eyes."

I took a deep breath. "Yes. Yes, I did. I'm sorry. I've wanted him to pay for what he's done to me, and I know I couldn't do it myself."

He grabbed my hips, pulling me into him until my lips crashed against his with a bruising force. "Mmm," He scraped his teeth down my neck, "You don't have to apologize." He bit at my lip. "My body is all yours. For fighting, for fucking, for anything you need it for, it's all yours. I'm all yours."

The words sent a shiver of pleasure through me. I moaned into him as he trailed a finger down my hips and then once over my pussy.

"Anything you want. I'll go after him now if you say the word."

"No, don't. I mean, I do, but please don't," I said, pulling my head back from him. "I am sorry. I wanted blood, revenge even. I liked the power of it last night. And the thought of being able to do that again sounded like a relief."

"That's why I offered to watch as you did it again," he said with a quiet laugh.

"I can't believe I liked it," I whispered. "I liked all of it, being brave enough to hit Ryder last night, provoking you today, and you telling Tyler how strong I am. I liked that I could stand up for myself and have a voice. I liked it and hated myself for it."

"Mmm," he said with a shake of his head. "Welcome to the dark side, then."

"Why do I like it? I shouldn't."

"Says who? You're not doing anything wrong," he said, pulling open the door and waiting for me to get in. "We all get sick of getting pushed around at some point. You're sticking up for yourself. It's not your fault if someone takes it too far and needs to be kicked in the teeth. Tyler and Logan took it too far. Ryder and his fucking idiots took it way too far. You're not out looking for blood, just aren't afraid to spill it now."

"You make my sudden lust for blood and revenge sound great."

He laughed, "Well, all that matters is that you're happy. Are you happy?"

I thought it over. I had Ransom and a group of friends now. Friends I liked and seemed to like me. I was standing up for myself, still acing my classes, making money at a job I enjoyed.

I smiled, "I'm really happy."

"Then I don't think there's much to worry about as long as you don't take it further than it needs to go. It's not like you're going around trying to boot-stomp people. You're standing up for yourself and what you deserve."

I kissed him once before getting in and settling into the seat. Even with Tyler making those comments, I was ready to stand up for myself, and now I didn't have to do it alone.

I realized I had never been happier.

"Since I can use your body for anything I want, and I don't want you to go after Tyler to fight, maybe we can use it for that other thing you mentioned."

The car roared as he pulled out, "Hmm, I don't remember what I said now," he said, his smile growing.

"Yes, you do."

He shrugged. "But I like hearing you say it."

"Take me home and fuck me," I said, my hand running down his arm and resting it over his on the shifter.

He groaned and pushed the car forward, getting us home and back in bed in record time.

THIRTY-ONE

RANSOM

I PULLED her into me as we sat back on the couch, fully satisfied and showered after I spent the last few hours licking and kissing every part of her.

"You know, you never explained why you went to the party yesterday. I know for a fact you weren't big on parties after everything that happened," I said, trying to tread lightly around bringing up the video.

"I was going to go out and find someone else that could hopefully make me forget about you," she said, making me jerk back and turn her to face me.

"Damn, I deserve that, but punch a guy in the face next time instead. It would feel better. All because of one fight?"

"One huge fight where you told me to never come back. I figured the best option was to go find somebody else or at least get you off my mind."

"Yeah, have I apologized for saying that? I went too far, and I'm sorry."

"You already did. A few times, actually. What I said was wrong and unneeded too. You had every right to tell me to go for how I was treating you, but I'm glad you didn't mean it."

"So you went to the party to forget about me then?"

"I thought if I found someone else, I would stop thinking about you so much."

"How did that go?"

She gave a tight laugh. "Somehow, I ended up at your house after a huge fight broke out. It definitely went according to plan."

"So you going and kicking some guy's ass and having me pick you up was all a part of the plan?"

"Yep. All according to plan to get you into bed."

"I feel so used," I said with a scowl.

"Oh babe," she said, the words making me hold onto her tighter, "I'm so sorry. I swear it won't happen again. I promise I will never use your body for my own pleasure ever, ever again." She couldn't hold back her laughter any longer, and the sound filled the room. The sweet tone made my chest ache.

I smiled, picking her up and flipping her back onto the couch, coming down over her. "And you call me the devil? You know that's not an option. You've given me a taste. I need you to continue using my body."

She laughed again, and I couldn't help but lean down and kiss her more. The fact that she was finally here, wrapped up in my arms, in my apartment, in my shirt - it all felt surreal.

"I want to kiss you all night."

"Then I won't get any sleep."

"I'll buy you the biggest coffee I can find in the morning. Please stay."

She groaned, "Don't say please like that. It makes me want to give in."

"Please," I said, kissing down her neck. "Please." I worked my way back up. "Please." With that, I bit her neck, loving how her body arched as she pulled me closer.

A knock came at the front door. "What?" I yelled.

The door burst open, and I pulled Quinn up, knowing she

wouldn't like it looking like we were just about to have sex. Again.

Fox walked in first, grinning at us as Scout went to the fridge, grabbing drinks and carrying them over. Jax jumped over the back of the couch, spreading out on the opposite side of Quinn and me.

"Sure, yeah, everyone, come on in," I said, putting a few inches between Quinn and me. As bad as I wanted to, I was hesitant to wrap my arm around her. I watched as she smiled at everyone, relaxed and calm beside me as her hand wound around my bicep, and she closed the distance I had put between us. She wasn't shying away from touching me in front of them and then looked up at me, her smile growing as her eyes met mine.

She was happy to be there with me, and in that instant, I did feel like a god.

Quinn fucking Carter was finally looking at me the way I always hoped she would and doing it in front of everyone, not only when we were hidden away. I wrapped an arm around her and kissed her head. I wanted them out.

I wanted to take her to bed and keep those eyes on me as I made her come again and again.

"Why are you guys here?" I snapped.

Fox and Scout sat down.

"Hey, be nice." Quinn hissed. "They saved me too."

"Fine. What's up, guys? Why are you here right now?" My nice tone too fake to be taken seriously.

Fox's grin grew wider, and I wanted to punch it off his face. "Look at you, such a pleasant host all of a sudden."

"And you, such a pleasant uninvited guest."

"Hey, be happy we waited this long," Scout said. "I told them we should have come over right away."

"Right away? What's wrong?"

"Someone tried to get into the garage again." Fox pulled out his phone, hit it, and flipped it around to show me. The new cameras we installed over the door had recorded a guy walking up, messing with the door, and unlocking it. I couldn't see his face, hidden by a dark coat, hat, and mask.

"He does have a fucking key," I said, watching as the door opened and the new alarm started going off.

"Yep. The alarm must have spooked him enough because he disappeared inside for a second before hauling ass back out," Fox said, and I watched as the guy ran back into the night.

"Do you know which way he went after that?"

"Into the patch of woods across the street. From there, there's no way to know where he went."

"Why didn't my phone go off?" I looked around, trying to figure out where I had left it, when I saw it on the counter in the kitchen. I wouldn't have heard it after going into the bedroom.

"Pretty sure you were otherwise occupied," Jax said, his eyebrows wiggling.

"Shut it," Quinn said, throwing a pillow at him. He caught it laughing, and I laughed too, surprised Quinn was the one to speak up.

"So he didn't steal anything, then?" I turned my attention to Fox. "What time did this even happen?"

"After we all got back. Around one?"

"We got back here around midnight," I said.

"And Scout slept on my couch," Fox said.

Jax raised his hands. "I went right to bed."

"Are we really suggesting the options are now Kye or Dante stealing from us?" Scout asked.

"Or they stole another key from one of us at some point, but we literally just had them changed, so it would have to be someone close. Or one of us." I said.

"I would rather believe that someone grabbed one again." Scout huffed.

"It's not hard to grab and copy one, though." Quinn said. "They could grab your keys, copy them, and have them back to you in an hour or less. You would almost have to rule out anyone that has come and gone from the garage." All eyes turned to her.

She shrugged, "What? You get locked out enough or have the locks changed. You learn how to pick them or swipe the key pretty fast, especially when it's cold. And no, to be clear, I didn't do this, but if they knew you changed the locks, they could grab one again. I didn't think of it before because you thought a key was stolen, but they could do it without anyone noticing."

"Your family would change the locks on you?" Scout asked.

"Yeah, not exactly to kick me out. Just too drunk to know where she left her keys and then too drunk to remember to give me a new one. I'd break in and then make myself a set."

"Shit," Fox said, "Sounds like you should have joined this misfit crew a lot sooner."

I pulled her tighter into my side, whispering into her ear, "Sorry you had to deal with that alone."

She shrugged. "We all deal with some sort of shit alone at some point in life. Let's hope I got mine over with early."

"You did," Scout said, reading my mind. "You're stuck with us now and don't have to deal with anything like that by yourself. None of us do."

"I think I learned that last night," Quinn said. "With the break-in's though, I wouldn't jump to conclusions about any of us yet. It's too easy to copy a key."

"I agree," I said. "We can change the locks again if we want, but also put in a better security system. And maybe more cameras."

"Let's fucking hope because having to call Kye or Dante out for this would kill me," Fox said, and we all nodded.

Losing someone you've grown so close to would fucking suck, but if one of them was stealing from the garage, we couldn't trust them to work there anymore.

"Alright, I'm having the locks changed again tomorrow. It's

cheaper than losing more parts or even cars," Fox said, and everyone nodded again but didn't move.

"Meaning we have this figured out, and everyone can leave right now." I snapped. Fox, Scout, and Jax just looked at me, still not moving.

"Get out!" I yelled with a laugh. They moved, grumbling as they went to the door, and I followed.

"You'd think you'd be a little happier finally getting…." I slammed the door in Fox's face, not letting him finish the sentence. I locked it, knowing Quinn wanted to go to her dorm tonight, leaving me with only a few hours alone with her.

She laid back on the couch, watching me as I came back over, falling over the back of the couch and grabbing onto her.

Every moment with her felt so fragile. It was like this was a temporary life I got to live, not knowing when it would end. It made me wonder when she would pull away, when she would regret being around me and try to run off and find a better guy again.

The knife twisted in me. She had run twice now. Once with that Clark guy and again the other night, even though I knew that one was all my fault. I knew it would happen again. She would realize she wanted different and go again, or I would fuck up, and she would leave.

If I was only going to have a few days with her like this, I wasn't going to waste them. I held onto her, taking in every second as she lay against me, and tried to stomp out the anger that someone else would have this with her forever instead of me.

THIRTY-TWO

QUINN

AFTER SPENDING a few more hours at his place together last night, Ransom dropped me off back at my place. I needed to come back to the dorms for clothes and all of my things for classes.

He had offered so many times to bring me to class if I stayed the night, but I didn't know if my willpower was strong enough to leave and actually go to class.

I made it through each one, somehow finding the focus during class to not miss each lecture, but I felt electric by the time I turned the corner and saw the garage.

I nearly ran, trying to control myself as I made my way inside. I went over to Ransom's bay, seeing him underneath one of the cars on a rolling creeper.

I grabbed his foot, pulling him out without a word. A tool dropped from his hand, and a smile grew when he saw me. He grabbed my hips and pulled me down until I was straddling him, his hands pulling me hard against his already rigid cock. He didn't say a word as his lips met mine and didn't stop until every other coherent thought in my mind was gone.

"Oh, gross," Scout said, walking in. "Is this really what I'm going to be subjected to now?"

Ransom pulled back, his blue eyes bright and happy. It was a beautiful sight, the angry glares gone and replaced with a calm happiness I knew reflected in mine. I got back up, using the car to steady myself. He groaned, sitting up and grabbing my hips, which were right in his line of sight.

"Get up." I hissed.

"Oh, I already am," he said. "I think I'll stay here for just a minute."

Fox and Jax had walked over. "So this is finally a thing now?" Fox asked.

"Finally?"

"Well, yeah, it's only been —."

He stopped as Ransom interrupted, "I told you, everyone else has known for weeks that I was trying to get you."

"Yeah," Fox said. "Why do you think I wasn't hitting on you every second you were here? Although I'm always here if you get sick of him." He jerked a thumb at Ransom with a wink.

Ransom jumped up, pushing against Fox, who then reached to put him in a headlock. They moved out into the parking lot, pushing and grabbing at each other as Jax followed, riling them up more.

"So you two are going to stay together, then?" Scout asked, as we watched them.

"It seems that way. Also, thanks for coming the other night."

"Anytime. You're ours now." She wrapped her arms around me, and I held onto them. "I was mad they wouldn't let me out of the car. I had my knife with me. I heard you kicked ass, though."

"Yeah, I guess I did."

"I'm glad you and him worked it out. I don't think I've ever seen him smile so much."

"He said he loved me." I blurted, needing to tell someone.

Scout nodded like she was expecting this. "I figured the guy has had it bad."

"And I just what? Didn't notice?"

"Maybe you didn't want to notice," she said, knocking into me. "But it seems like you might feel the same. I like having you around, though. The other girls they have dated, if you even want to call it that, never liked me and never stayed around long."

"And I will be?"

"Oh, yeah. You're hooked. Line and sinker, you love us all."

"That's true. As far as a package deal, you guys are like hitting the lottery. I don't know how anyone wouldn't like you."

"Just, please don't judge all of us on any of Ransom's dumb decisions."

"Deal," I said, laughing as they walked back in.

Ransom came over, giving me another kiss as Fox walked away. A chorus of gross and get a room being called out.

"What do you say? Want to get a room? I know of a private one, and it has a nice bed there."

"I have work to do, and so do you."

"Want to stay late with me?"

"Depends. Why are you staying late?"

"I'm trying to wrap this car up and could be done tonight if I'm not too distracted or if I have some help."

"You want me to help you? On a car?"

"Yes. I may need help doing a few other things, too," he said with a wink.

"If I answer now, I'm just going to say yes. Come grab me at five, and I'll let you know then."

He let me go, and I disappeared into the office as the garage filled with the sound of tools and music. The sound had become soothing to me, making me feel a sense of calm every time it started up. I looked around. I had changed so much in the office we now had a whole second room cleaned that could be used.

Right now, it was filled with parts ready to go on cars, but you couldn't even get inside it a month ago.

Until now, I had never realized how much of my life was spent trying to survive. Finally, having something more to look forward to was a strange feeling that I was coming to love.

When the clock hit five, everyone left, leaving Ransom and me alone. I closed the laptop and waited, watching the door to see if he would come to me.

Finally, I heard the overhead doors closing, and then he walked into the office, his jumpsuit rolled down to his hips again, a dark shirt. The shirt was ruined, covered in grease and oil, and he pulled it off and threw it aside as he walked in. He was all scars, tattoos, and muscle, and knowing what those muscles lead to was already making warmth flood between my thighs.

He crossed the room, walking past me to lock the main door and then turning his fevered gaze on me.

I didn't think the determined set to his jaw would ever stop being a turn-on when I knew now what he was determined to do. He picked me up from the chair, not saying a word as I wrapped my legs around him and let him carry me into the garage.

"I thought you had to work late."

"I'm changing my mind."

"I thought you wanted to finish this car."

"Fuck it. I've been out here for hours knowing you were on the other side of the door, and I've been hard thinking about you on top of me earlier. I would have fucked you right there on the ground, but this will do for now," he said, setting me down on the car's hood and kissing me.

The thought of him out here hard and waiting for me was like a drug. That he wanted me, needed me like I needed him all day. I played with the zipper on the jumpsuit. "I've wondered what you wore under here since the moment I came in to get my phone."

"You were thinking of me naked that first day?"

I almost said long before that, stopping myself before the secret slipped, "It's pretty hard not to when you look like this." I splayed my fingers on his chest and drug them until I reached the zipper, pulling it down and seeing only boxers underneath.

"Mmm, I was hoping for nothing, but I guess that will work," I said, smiling when I heard him laugh. I slid down the car's hood until my feet hit the ground. I reached into his boxers, pushing them down as I pulled out his hard cock.

I sucked in a breath and slid the rest of the way down until I was on my knees in front of him.

"Quinn, wait, you don't have to do that here," he said.

"But can I?"

"You can do anything you want with me. I meant it when I said I'm all yours. Are you sure?"

"Very, very sure." I could hear my voice go lower, but I couldn't help it. I wanted to taste and please him like he had for me. I wanted to know what it felt like to control his body with my mouth, like he had done.

I reached my tongue out, licking at the tip of him. I knew the general idea behind a blowjob, but I had never done one. The act of it felt so intimate I had never wanted to. I knew what to do for the most part. Obviously, I had googled it enough times and heard plenty of stories, but I was still nervous.

"Ransom," I whispered, looking up at him.

"Fuck," he said with a groan, looking down at me. "You're a fucking dream come true."

"I've never done this before. I don't want to mess up."

He stilled, "Never?"

I shook my head, "No."

His hand moved through my hair. "You won't. You're fucking perfect. Anything you do is perfect."

I wrapped my lips around him, flicking my tongue to lick the tip. I slowly slid him in, keeping my tongue pressed against the underside of him. I sucked harder as I took more and more of him into my mouth. It wasn't what I had thought it would be. I thought I would feel dirty, maybe even wrong, but I didn't. Instead, I felt powerful, I felt in control, and I liked it.

He ran a hand down my jaw. "You look so pretty with my cock in your mouth."

Each word spurred me on more, and I kept going until he hit the back of my throat, making me gag.

"Fuck, you're amazing. Taking it so perfect."

The encouragement was all I needed to do it again, pulling him out and taking it all back into my mouth again, letting it hit the back of my throat. My tongue explored as I pulled him back again, and I dared to look up.

His eyes were on me, watching as I took his cock again. His hips moved, and I moved with him, taking as much as I could each time. Something darkened in his face, an unhinged look making my thighs clench together. I dropped my hands, his gaze too much for me to handle as I unzipped my pants, pulling them down enough to dip my hands in.

I pulled him deeper again, hitting the back of my throat, and I dipped my fingers into myself at the same time, rubbing my clit and trying to soothe the ache that was growing. Every time I thought of giving head, I thought it was something to get over as quickly as possible. Something for his pleasure, not mine, but I was wrong.

I was so wrong.

I was already so wet and turned on that the sudden touch of my fingers was enough to make me moan as he filled my mouth.

I looked up again and could see Ransom noticed what I was doing. His mouth fell open, and his hips moved as he fucked my mouth, hitting my throat as I kept my mouth tight around him.

"You feel so fucking good. I'm going to come already." He groaned as he pulled back, but I pushed forward, taking him deeply again, and I sped up my fingers.

I felt his release on the back of my throat, and then I was lost to my own, my body shaking as waves of pleasure rolled through me. His body jerked and pushed into my mouth once more before pulling out completely.

His hands came down my body, grabbing me under the arms and dragging me up against him. I tried to catch my breath as he set me back on the car.

"Kitten," he said, his breathing hard, "How in the fucking world was that the first time you have done that?" He kissed down my neck and then back up to my lips.

"So it was ok?"

"It was more than ok. It was fucking amazing. I don't know what I did to deserve that. To deserve you."

I smiled, "Good."

"Good is an understatement," he said, leaning towards me. "Really, what did I do to deserve you?" He reached for my shirt, pulling it up and over my head. "It's your turn now."

I laughed as he kissed his way down my chest. His phone rang, but he ignored it, continuing to kiss his way down my body.

The phone rang again. "Maybe you should pick it up."

We both looked down, seeing Kye's name, and he clicked to connect the call, "If this isn't an emergency, I'm going to key your fucking car." He kissed my shoulder again as he listened.

"Where?" he asked.

"Alright. I'll be right there. I have to drop Quinn off on the way."

I knew our night was done. I grabbed my shirt, and he helped, slipping it back over me.

"Kye and Fox are out and got a flat tire. I need to bring them another one."

"Alright," I said, kissing him as I zipped his jumpsuit back up and tied the arms at his waist. "I guess I should go home and finish some homework."

"Ok. Will you spend the rest of the week with me at my place?"

"It's only Monday. The rest of the week would be the entire week."

"Yes, exactly," he said, grabbing up the tools he needed and waiting for me to grab my bag before heading to the car.

He reached for my hand and started kissing it, "I can't get enough of you," he said, "And after you give a guy a blowjob like that, he will think twice about letting you out of his bed ever again."

"Really?"

"Really." He was quiet for a minute. "I don't know if I'm going to like the answer to this, but why haven't you done that before?"

"I've never wanted to. It seemed too intimate, and I was right. I never cared about giving someone pleasure when they didn't care to give it to me. I didn't think I would like doing it, but I was definitely wrong about that part."

"Alright, I did like that answer, but now I want you in my bed tonight even more than I did before. I don't know if I will survive a relationship with you."

"So it's a relationship, then? Like, we're doing this?" I asked as he pulled up to the dorm.

"Yes, we definitely are. I'll text you later."

I kissed him and jumped from the car.

I was on a cloud, life better than it ever had been, until I opened the door to my room to find Josie sitting there, ready to explode.

THIRTY-THREE

QUINN

"WHERE HAVE YOU BEEN?" Josie said, sitting up in her small bed.

"At work, around, why?" I realized as soon as I saw her face that I was still angry. She never checked in with me after the other night or even wondered why I hadn't shown up. I had let it go, but wondered if that's why she looked so upset now.

"Tyler told me what happened, Quinn. He told me you were out at the diner with Ransom."

"So?" My heart sank as hope left me. She wasn't even thinking of the other night.

"So? He said Ransom threatened to kill and have him beaten up. Then he said, you're dating Ransom? I told him that was ridiculous. What is going on? Why did Tyler say that?"

I rolled my eyes. "Tyler came up to me, like he always does, and started making fun of me and starting shit about the video. Telling me that he and I should make one. Ransom told him to knock it off. I'm allowed to defend myself if someone is saying horrible things about me to my face."

"Tyler wouldn't say that. He's dating Sarah."

"Well, he did. Do you think I'm the one lying?"

"No." She blew out a breath. "I'm sorry. I was so surprised at the things Tyler was saying, I freaked out. I know Tyler doesn't always treat you the greatest."

My brows furrowed, and I shook my head. That was an understatement. "Well, you're going to love finding out that it's true. I'm dating Ransom now."

Her face turned to disgust. "I figured you were messing around with him, but dating seriously?"

"Yeah, dating. He's my boyfriend."

It was the first time I had said it out loud. The first time I had really considered it, but a shock of excitement went through me at the words. I couldn't stop the smile from spreading across my face.

"Do you think that's a good idea? You do know what happened with Logan, right? I thought you were going to try to find someone better like —"

"Like Brad or Clark?"

"Well, yeah. Brad's perfect. Rich and funny. His family has a lake house right down the street from my family! Isn't that funny? We were all going to go this weekend. I was going to see if you wanted me to set you up, and you come with us, but now this?"

I thought it over. Even if I wasn't dating Ransom, spending a weekend with people who wouldn't like who I am sounded horrible. I would have to pretend and fake my way through every interaction and then be set up with another Clark at the same time.

Now my face twisted with disgust, "No, I don't want to go to any lake house, and I don't want to be set up."

"But Ransom? Really? I know you had a crush on him in high school, but how are you not growing up and getting over that yet?"

"Not growing up? What is that supposed to mean?"

"It's like you're living out your high school fantasy now, and it's sad to watch, Quinn. Like Tyler was telling us, and all I could think about was how pathetic it all sounded."

I snorted, "Sad? I'm the happiest I have ever been, and as for pathetic, maybe you should think that about Tyler, who almost fell over trying to run away from us."

After watching what the crew could do, I was seriously starting to consider sending them to scare Tyler off.

"I mean, I get that. I'll say it's a little pathetic, then. It's like you haven't moved on from high school. Ransom isn't exactly the dating type, and we all know it. You can't stand there and expect me to believe he wants to date you. Are you even his type? And not only that, do you want to date him? He's poor, Quinn. You've lived such a hard life. I don't want to see you end up in the same situation."

My jaw dropped. She couldn't be serious. I wasn't even going to mention that Ransom wasn't poor. I didn't care, and neither should she. I planned to make my own money. I didn't need him to have it, but that's half of what she was judging him on. The other half was that he couldn't possibly be interested in me.

If I said he had money, would she like him then, or would it not be enough? Would she care if they worked hard for their money while Brad's money belonged to his parents? She would probably assume any money he did have was stolen.

"Josie, I'm exhausted and have early classes tomorrow. Can we please talk about this later?"

Her lips pursed. "Yeah, but I want you to know I care about you. I don't want anything bad to happen, and it seems to happen with guys like this." I nodded as though I agreed.

I changed and got into bed, staring up into the dark. I wanted to ask Josie about the other night. The thought of how she would get an address so wrong and not call to check on me had nagged at me since it happened.

By the time I had gained enough courage, she was snoring.

The loud sound made me throw a pillow over my head. I wonder how Rich Brad was going to like that this weekend. I tamped down my snark and rolled over.

The last thing I remembered before falling asleep was that I could have been in Ransom's bed and arms, avoiding all of this.

———

I WOKE up to my phone going off. Josie was still asleep. Her snoring still filling the room.

I looked down. Texts and calls had been coming in for the last twenty minutes. The first one from Scout.

Scout: Call me

Scout: Now

Scout: Are you home?

Scout: I'm so sorry, Quinn.

My heart dropped, worried something had happened to Ransom until I saw the next one.

Scout: I know he wouldn't do this.

What the fuck? I clicked open the texts from Ransom.

Ransom: I don't know what happened

Ransom: Call me

Ransom: I DIDN'T do this and don't know who did.

Ransom: YET.

Ransom: Call me please, Quinn. Please don't think I did this.

My heart raced as I opened the next one from an unknown number. A photo of me on the car last night. My shirt was off as Ransom kissed my neck. The next was a 10-second clip of him grabbing my breast as I leaned back, giving him more of me.

A sob caught in my throat as I went online, seeing the photo all over, my name tagged in it, but Ransoms wasn't. His face had been covered, but my pleasure was on full display.

Embarrassment and shock made me freeze in place. There wasn't any way this was happening again, right? This thing couldn't happen to someone twice in her life.

"What the fuck?" I yelled, throwing a pillow across the room.

Another text came in from Ransom.

> Ransom: I'm coming over

Josie had shot up. "What? What's going on?"

I was already up, grabbing bags and shoving clothes in. I didn't know what to pack. Enough for a week? Maybe a month?

I knew when to fight, and I knew when to run, and I was going to run.

The last time this happened, I tried to face it head-on. I even went to school that Monday. It had been bad, so bad that I didn't go back for a week after. I knew I wasn't going to make that mistake again.

I grabbed both suitcases, stuffing them full and grabbing my backpack.

"Quinn, what's happening?"

"I need to get out of here. Do you have your car back?"

"Yeah, I got it yesterday."

"Can you bring me to your lake house? I need somewhere to go for a couple of days."

"I guess," she said, her brows furrowing. "Will you tell me what's happening?"

"In the car. Grab your keys. Come on." I pushed her out the door, still in pajamas, and to the car. She hopped in and left.

"Isn't that Ransom?" she asked, watching as his car sped towards us. He was heading to the dorms. I ducked down as his car went past. There and gone in a second.

"Fucking hell. Does he always drive like that?"

I didn't say anything, watching in the mirror as he drove away, feeling like an idiot that part of me wanted to stay and be comforted by him.

The photos and videos repeatedly played in my head as I tried to make any coherent thought. Would Ransom really do something like this to me? He was always trying to protect me, but it didn't mean he wouldn't ever hurt me.

Then, another text came in from him, and it was like he was reading my mind.

> Ransom: I meant it when I said I love you. I wouldn't hurt you. I would never share you.

Would he come after me if he had been the one to do it? Logan had laughed in my face when I confronted him. He didn't come after me, but Ransom was now.

"Why are we driving away from Ransom so fast if he's your boyfriend now?" I could hear her trying to hide her smug tone and failing.

"There were pictures of us posted online last night. Intimate photos and a clip." I forced the words out, and with them, I started crying, the tears falling fast and hard. "I need a minute before I talk to him."

I could hear Josie's curses in the background, but my ears roared with tears as my chest heaved, the sobs making it harder and harder to breathe.

How could the same thing happen to someone twice in their life? Not only twice in their life, but twice in not even two years. At least this wasn't a full-blown video and only a few pictures, but it was enough. I would never live down the assumption that I was sleeping around and vying for attention when this time, it was with Ransom, of all people, on a car. People knew his reputation just like they had known Logan's.

I cried the entire drive until, forty-five minutes later, we pulled into her parents' empty lake house.

I jumped out, gulping down breaths of fresh, crisp air. The days had turned cold, and I hadn't noticed. Fall was fading, and winter would set in soon, leaving the lake house and most of the ones around it empty.

The world was quiet, and Josie came around the car, pulling open the door, so I could get my bags.

"I can't believe you fell for Ransom and let this happen," she said, anger lacing her voice. "I told you not to be so stupid, and you went and did it, anyway. How did you let this happen to you again?"

"I didn't let this happen. I don't know who did this. How is it my fault? I was in a place alone with him. It's not like I was in the middle of a crowd," I said, taken aback at her harsh words. Josie had always been a little blunt, but this wasn't just being blunt. This was cruel.

"No, Quinn." She turned and pointed a finger at me. "You did this. I've tried to help and help. Sharing the ugly ass dorm room with you instead of finding an apartment, I almost didn't rush for the sorority because I felt so bad for you. Luckily, Sarah talked me into it. Then I try to set you up with a nice guy like Clark, and he tells me you ran off with Ransom. To what? Fuck him in his car? Admit it. You like sleeping around, you like these shitty guys, and you like the attention. Are you hoping to end up like your mother? Because if you didn't, you would have learned the first time this happened. I put the video out there for you to learn a lesson, and you didn't because, look, it's happened again. So you're either that stupid or you like it. Which one is it?" Her face fell for a second before recovering.

I pushed my bags back, taking a step towards her. My voice was low. "What did you just say?"

"I said you are either stupid or like the attention," she said, a smirk on her face as she crossed her arms.

"No, you said you put the video out." Disgust churned in my stomach as reality fell around me like broken glass, our friendship shattering as easily as a mirror. "You put the video out there?"

She froze, deciding what truth to go with. "I did. I did it for your own sake. It worked, didn't it? You broke up with Logan for good and calmed down. Before the video, you kept going back to him, thinking it would fix the problem, that you wouldn't want him or Ransom anymore, but it wasn't happening. You were going to end up just like your mother, so I did something about it. You got back on track with school, and we got into the same college."

"By sharing a sex tape with everyone we know? You thought that was the right thing to do as my friend?" I wanted to scream, I wanted to fight, but I knew I couldn't kick her teeth in, which reminded me of Ryder.

"Did you send me to the wrong house on purpose the other day?"

She huffed, calculating her next step again. "There were rumors that the Ryder guy was looking for Ransom and his friends. He sold drugs to some of the frat guys and was asking if anyone knew the girl Ransom was with. I happened to be at the right place at the right time and overheard their conversation. I guessed it was you with how distant you've been and being at work so much all of a sudden. I knew if you saw what Ransom was into, you would stop talking to him. At least I thought so, but again, I underestimated how stupid you are when it comes to any poor guy with a fucking tattoo and a dick."

All I could think of was the fear I felt that night and the entire crew who risked their lives for me. With each emotion echoing through me, I pushed her chest, throwing her hard into the car, and she hit with a scream.

"You bitch, Josie. You almost got my friends, and I killed. Do you know what they did to me? Do you even care that they held a knife to my throat and threatened me? That they cornered me in a bathroom and kicked the door in?"

"Well, I didn't know they would be that dramatic. Ryder just said he wanted to use you to bait Ransom and all of them."

"And you thought what?" I asked, my hands moving faster than my words as they shook, "That you would trust a fucking drug-dealing asshole? And you have the nerve to call me stupid?"

"You know what, Quinn, fuck you," she said, trying to look down her nose at me. It wasn't superiority in her eyes, though. She was scared of me now. Her chest rose and fell fast, and I was so shocked I laughed.

I moved towards her again, and she jumped back, a squeak of panic coming from her.

"You're a horrible person," I whispered, shaking my head. "I can't believe I trusted that you were my friend."

"I was your friend. I was trying to help you stop this obsession with destroying your life with these horrible guys. You're not like them. You could be better than them."

"No, I'm better than you. I am one of them. They know who I am and love me for it. Whether I'm rich or poor or happy or vicious, they love me, unlike you. You only love me if I pretend to be who you want me to be. They got me away from someone trying to hurt me. They didn't lure me in and lock the fucking door." I yelled now, the sound echoing in the empty lawns around us.

She huffed a laugh. "Keep telling yourself that. But don't call me when you're broke and have nothing left. When you are so washed up that no guy wants you for anything but a quick fuck.

When no one wants to be around you because you're so pathetic."

"Get the fuck away from me, Josie. Never speak to me again." I stepped towards her again, ready to hit her this time, but she ran, reaching the driver's door before I could get to her.

She turned the car on and rolled down her window, feeling braver with a door between us now.

"I'm calling the cops in an hour, and you better not be here. We don't need trash littering the lawn," she said, the tires screeching as she tried to peel out, but almost hit the ugly fountain they had in the middle of the driveway.

I sat down on the front steps, minutes ticking by as I tried to find a breath. My lungs couldn't handle it, though, the weight on my chest crushing me.

I realized I was running out of people who could save me. It had already been on my mind that Ransom didn't post the photos, and now it seemed like I might have my answer, but I still didn't know if I wanted to call him. I needed a friend, but didn't have many of those around. A cab ride back to the dorm would be crazy expensive, and then what do I do? Live with Josie until I can change rooms? The semester was half over, and I doubted they would let me change rooms now. Even if she did move out, I couldn't even begin to afford a double room by myself. My world was falling apart, and I couldn't catch the pieces fast enough to even attempt to put them together.

I clicked through my phone with a strangled laugh that came out more like a sob. I knew who I wanted to help me, surprising myself when I scrolled and found his name.

THIRTY-FOUR

QUINN

"Fox?"

"Hey, where are you? Are you ok?" The concern in his voice almost made me cry more. "Ransom told me about the photos and shit. He has been looking for you."

"I don't know if ok is the right word, but yea, I'm alright enough. I need a big favor."

"I'll help with almost anything, but if it has to do with getting Ransom to calm down, then I'm out. He's been going crazy all morning."

"No, nothing to do with Ransom. Don't let him know you're talking to me."

"I'll try, but I think we're one broken window from him checking our phones," Fox said with a light laugh. "What do you need?"

"I had Josie bring me to her family's lake house to get away, but we got into a fight. I'm stuck here, and I don't think I can afford the almost hour drive back by cab."

"Yea, of course, I'll come get you. I can leave right now if someone doesn't stop and ask me a hundred fucking questions." I could almost hear his eyes roll.

"Really, you'll come?"

"Of course. Send me the address and please let me know if anyone that wants to kick my ass before I make it there. The other night was fun and all, but I've been dealing with Ransom for hours now and am not ready for a fight."

I laughed, loving Fox for his easygoing nature like nothing rattled his humor or charm, and his ability to make a shitty situation so much lighter made me glad I called him.

"No one to kick your ass, just me and my pathetic self. Oh, and the cops, if I'm not out of here in about an hour."

"Well damn. I'm hurrying. Text me the address, and I'll keep you updated."

"Alright, thanks." I went to end the call, but heard Ransom in the background.

"What was that? Is she calling you now? You can't seriously be making a move on her already, Fox," Ransom said, his voice somewhere between anger and pleading.

My heart wrenched at the pain in his voice. A pain I didn't think deserved to be there if he did nothing wrong. But I still couldn't bring myself to text or call him yet.

Fox laughed. "Shit, chill out. I have a part ready to pick up. I'll be back later. Can you get a fucking handle on yourself? We can't afford to replace any more windshields."

"Oh fuck off," Ransom said.

"You know Quinn won't be happy dealing with all that ordering and organizing." It must have shut Ransom up because it went quiet, and I ended the call.

He wasn't wrong. If he made a mess of the garage, he would be cleaning up his own mess. I had enough to clean up on my own.

Based on his texts, I had forty-five minutes to figure out my life before Fox got here.

I laid back on the cold stone. I had to figure out where to live, where to work, and who to trust now.

It brought me right back to working at the garage and to Ransom. I didn't think he helped in this whole photo thing, but what if the worst came true and he did help? I never thought for a second Josie would do that to me, and apparently, she was the mastermind. What if Ransom hurt me too? Like an out-of-control car, my thoughts kept rushing, wondering what I could afford to live in for the next three months now that I couldn't go back to my dorm and live with Josie. There had to be rooms for rent I could afford.

I screamed, my mouth closed, so no one called the cops any faster. I couldn't believe what my life was coming to.

The moment it felt like I was building it back up, it was ripped from beneath me.

The next forty-five minutes were a spiral of me crying, laughing, cursing, and trying to tell myself I could do this.

Finally, I heard Fox's car coming down the road. He pulled in, the yellow of his car shining in the fall sun.

He parked and hopped out, looking every bit of the golden hero that I knew he was.

"Aww, Quinn," he said. Seeing my red eyes and slumped head, he came over, wrapping me in a hug.

He was so tall and big that I burrowed into his arms. The warmth and affection were the most comforting feeling after this day. "Thank you for coming."

"Anytime. Whether Ransom wants to be an idiot or not, you're a part of our little misfit crew now. We've all liked having you around. You bring some balance to the group. Not only that, but most days, it makes Ransom tolerable." He laughed. "I'm guessing you don't want to sit around here longer. You ready to go?"

I nodded, and he grabbed my bags, the big suitcase looking huge next to his car.

"Were you packing to leave the country?" he asked, stuffing it into the small backseat.

"I'm not sure. I was debating on heading to the Bahamas based on the ridiculous number of bikinis I brought or maybe the other side of the country."

"Shit, if you want to head off to the Bahamas, I'll come with you. I would look hot on the beach, have myself a surfboard and a nice tan. Girls would love it."

"I bet they would," I said with a laughed as I got in.

He started the car and left, leaving a lot more gracefully than Josie had.

"Alright," he said as we reached the main road. "Time to tell me what happened."

I started from this morning, telling him about seeing the texts and photos, running out with Josie, and then everything she said when we got here.

"So she posted the video the first time?"

"Yeah, it sounds like she thought up and organized the whole thing."

"And then last week she met an angry street-racing drug dealer and thought, wow, I should lure my friend to his house to show her how awful this guy Ransom is?"

"That was her genius plan."

"What an absolute bitch," he said, and I smiled. There was something about Fox that, even angry, brought a light in the darkness. "How the fuck could you do those things and still look that person in the eye? Still act like you care about them and live in the same room as them?"

"I don't know. I don't get it. We've had our fair share of fights, but I thought all friends did. I didn't realize she was trying to ruin my life and do whatever she felt was right with no regard for me."

"Friends fight, but that wasn't a fight. Those things were full-on sabotage. What would she have done if Ryder had hurt you? Or even killed you? Ransom will be pissed that he didn't find out she was involved in the video."

"What do you mean?"

"Has Ransom told you anything from before you started working with us?"

"No? Well, I mean, he told me about you guys stealing cars and Slaughter and stuff."

"But he didn't tell you about anything else?"

"Oh god," I said, throwing my head into my hands. "What else is there?"

"I told him to tell you. I told him you needed to know, and he said he would tell you at some point."

"What, Fox? Just tell me what it is."

"Ransom has liked you since the first time he saw you. I mean, the guy has been half in love with you for years."

"What? When?" My heart pounded almost painfully in my chest.

"Since high school. I think it would have been your sophomore year and our junior year. I want to clarify the only reason I know this story is because he told me about it after I put things together and figured out what was going on. I guess you pulled in and hit the gas, swung your car into the parking lot, and almost hit some dude on a skateboard. The guy was pissed and started slamming on the hood of your car, but you got out and yelled at him back. Ransom said he almost came over to help you, but you jumped back into your car and threatened to run the guy over if he didn't move."

"I remember that. It was our first week back at school.

"Apparently, Ransom was done for then. He had seen you around enough and had some sort of crush on you. He thought you were perfect. He was ready to try get your attention until I pointed out that you were too good for him. At first, I was just messing around because that's what we do, and I didn't think it was serious. We were never really serious about the girls we liked, but then he kept watching you. I knew you had a hard time at home, and we were still stealing cars at that point, and I told him you didn't need his shit added to your plate."

My jaw hung slack. All those times I thought Ransom had been glaring at me, all the times I told myself he wasn't looking at me, just annoyed by anyone looking at him.

"He was looking at me all those times?"

"Oh yeah, every day we would sit by our cars, and I think half the reason he did it was to watch you pull in every morning and then leave at the end of the day. He didn't tell anyone else that. Everyone but me thought we were only hanging out, but the guy was going crazy. The day I told him about you not needing his shit added to your plate, he went and confessed to Luca what we were doing and asked how to get out of it. He wanted to know how to get him and all of us on a better path. I think he thought that would help him feel good enough to go after you, but by then, some nasty rumors were going around, and when he came and talked to me about it, I said the same thing as I had the first time. You didn't need his bad choices making your life harder."

"Oh." It was all I could say as I took it all in. Realizing all of Ransom's little comments, flirting with me so fast, saying he had already loved me for so long, why he was treating me like he did.

"I'm sorry, Quinn. When I saw you and how hard you had it, I don't know. It made me feel like how I feel about Scout. It makes me feel like I'm the older brother, and I wanted to look out for you. I thought Ransom in your life would make it harder back then. Not now, but then."

I reached out for him and patted his arm. "No, I get it. I appreciate it."

"I was worried you were going to be pissed. I think he felt like I kept you from him for so long. He was always so pissed when I said to leave you alone, and I think he blamed me a bit when he lost his chance to Logan. I know he's happy now that he stayed away because he's not such a mess now. None of us are."

"I can't believe he even noticed me. I thought he hated me."

"What? Why?"

"Because he was always glaring at me. I could never tell what he was thinking, but it always looked like he hated me. He would basically curl his lip at me when I pulled in and met his eye."

"I think he probably did hate you for a while. He wanted you so bad I used to make fun of him." He laughed. "It's like no other girl compared to you for him. He was always hung up that you were the best and no one else could measure up. I mean, not to be too blunt, but he's messed around and dated other girls, but something stuck for him that none of them were as good as you."

"I know the feeling."

"What?" he asked, his eyebrows shooting up. But I didn't say anything, realizing it wasn't just hard to admit to Ransom. It was hard to admit to anyone.

"Come on. Now I have to know what that means."

"I've been pretty much in love with Ransom since the first time I saw him. At least in a very hard lust." I laughed at the words, "Like I tried to date Logan because I thought I needed to get over wanting a 'bad boy.' I was under the impression that all girls wanted one at some point, and I needed to get it out of my system, but damn if I didn't think of Ransom half the time I was around Logan. The guy was a fucking prick, though, so some-where along the line, I assumed Ransom would be too. It made not getting to be around him so much easier. I would break up and get back together with Logan on a monthly basis because I kept in this cycle I thought would have to break at some point."

"No fucking way."

"Yeah, I hoped I would just forget about Ransom at some point. Then you guys graduated, and I didn't see him much anymore. From there, I got worse. I was sick of it all and sick of comparing these guys to a guy I had never even talked to. Not that it was his fault, but I spiraled with everything going on in my life."

"And you haven't told Ransom this?"

"No! I thought I would sound like a lunatic."

Fox laughed. "You two are ridiculous. He thought the same thing. He thought it would scare you off. Since I'm spilling all of his secrets, though, there's one more thing that seems relevant right now."

I held my breath, waiting, "Ok?"

"Ransom beat the shit out of Logan after the video."

"What?" I yelled, and Fox jumped. Of all the things I was expecting him to say next, it wasn't that.

"The night of the party when the video came out. I guess he saw the parts of the video and then watched you run out."

"Watched me run out?" I laughed. "He literally yelled at me to leave. I thought he was giving me shit about being a slut like everyone else was that night. I was getting called so many names, I thought he was adding to the pile. I started to hate him after that."

"No, he told you to leave because he was going after Logan. He pulled him behind the house and went off on him. I've never seen Ransom lose control like that during a fight, but he couldn't stop it. We had to pull him away when someone else saw what was happening, and it took me, Jax, and Kye to get him off of Logan."

"I remember. They brought Logan to the hospital. He had some broken ribs, and a broken nose. He was bruised and messed up for weeks. I thought it was just karma. I didn't realize it was because someone else also thought he deserved it. No one else seemed to think he deserved any punishment."

"Ransom told him if he ever saw you to run the other way or he would come after him again. Logan was so scared after that, I think he listened."

"That's why I never run into Logan? I would rarely see him at school, and he would turn the other way when he saw me. I just assumed he didn't want to face what he did."

"Maybe, but I would say Ransom had a lot to do with that."

"I didn't want to leave the house for weeks after the video, but hated being home. I started going to school and going out and realized I wasn't running into Logan anywhere. I always thought it was weird but didn't want to question it."

"He wants to give Tyler a visit but said he won't without telling you first now."

"Fox," I yelled, the shock of everything making me freeze as I turned in my seat to look at him.

"Yeah, it's a lot. That's why I wanted him to tell you, but with what happened last night, I didn't know if you would believe him if he came clean now."

"No, I'm glad you told me. I should have told Ransom my feelings sooner. I was planning, too, the night at the cookout, but obviously, the night didn't go as planned."

"Listen, I know I could be biased because I've been friends with Ransom for a long time now. He's like my brother, but I know he would never do that to you. He doesn't betray the people he cares about. Ever. And after everything he has gone through and done for you, it doesn't make sense for him to have someone take photos and spread them around online. I can't even figure out what he would gain by doing that. Pretty sure he would do anything to keep you safe and happy. He wouldn't go beat the shit out of the people who did it the first time just to turn around and do it himself. Plus, if we're being honest, I think the guy is too jealous to share anything about you like that. We both know he even hates me touching you, and he trusts me with his life."

"I was already skeptical he would take and send out those photos, but with Josie's confession, how could I think it wasn't her and Tyler?" I shook my head. "I don't even know what to think right now. It's like my whole life blew up right in front of me. I feel like someone hit me with a truck."

"I bet. I feel it for you." He turned off the main highway, bringing us to our part of town.

"Where do you want me to take you?"

I groaned, "I don't know. I can't go back to my dorm and be around Josie. Ever again."

"I don't blame you. I would bring you to my apartment, but I like having a door." He turned towards their firehouse. "How about we put you up in the empty apartment upstairs? Nobody goes up there, and there is a bed and couch. We also have Wi-Fi, and you'll be left alone. I won't tell anyone you're there. You can do that when you're ready."

"Really?"

"Yeah, then if you decide to make up with Ransom, you know where he is, and we can all have some peace and quiet."

"I don't know what I'm going to do yet, about anything, but a hot shower and some time alone to think sounds good. Thanks, Fox."

"Anytime." He pulled into the garage and helped me carry my things upstairs.

"You were going for the long haul, huh?"

"I didn't know what I was going for. I don't even know what's all in here."

He opened the door and set my suitcase aside. "I have to get back to the garage, but are you good here? Do you need anything?"

"No. I think I'll order some food and hide away."

"Alright, here's the key to this apartment. If you want to have anything delivered, go to the front door. We try to keep the garage locked up." I nodded, pulling him into another hug.

"Thank you." He kissed my head and squeezed me once before letting me go.

"I'll always be looking out for the both of you, but I think you should talk to him tonight. He won't know you're up here, but you know where he is. See you later."

I waved as he left, looking around the apartment. It was similar to Ransoms, but less cozy and lived in.

But for once, I had somewhere safe and all to myself.

THIRTY-FIVE

QUINN

THE REST of the day moved in slow motion. I had nowhere to go and nothing to do other than eat and clean up. To avoid thinking about the photos, I didn't dare to go online to see the comments. Worry was gnawing at me at the thought of the original video resurfacing now.

Night had fallen outside, and I watched the dark streets, wondering if I would still be awake to see Ransom come home. Fox's car had pulled back in, and so had Jax's, but his still hadn't.

It was ten o'clock before I gave up and went to bed, wondering if he was coming home at all. The worry that he could assume this was over and go find the girl from the other day and stay with her or sit in the garage all night.

I rolled over and let out a groan of frustration. The bed was tiny and scratchy, and the sheets felt like they were made of sandpaper against my skin. I couldn't get comfortable, no matter how much I tossed and turned.

I heard a noise outside and jumped - the room was so big that every little sound echoed, and it gave me the creeps.

I had never been scared of the dark, but my body had learned it couldn't sleep when it wasn't safe. The nights of random people coming in and out of our house kept me awake and on guard. I knew the building was safe, and the guys were here, but each sound made me stiffen.

I turned over again, the sheets scraping against me, sending a horrible shiver through my body, the feeling grossing me out. It was cold too. I didn't know if this place had heat, but with the temperature dropping outside, it was getting colder and colder inside. The bed only had one quilt, and I hadn't brought any more.

I hit the bed and sat up. I wasn't going to be able to sleep here.

What I wanted was downstairs.

Ransom's bed was a cloud, the sheets soft and luxurious and his blankets big and fluffy. I was sleeping on straw compared to his bed.

Of course, it didn't hurt that his bed usually had him in it.

As soon as I saw him racing past us earlier, I knew I wasn't mad at him and that he wasn't involved in whatever was going on. I sighed, grabbing my phone and slippers before sneaking down to his apartment and sending out a silent thank you that they didn't lock their doors.

I opened it and peered in, hesitating to step inside. The apartment was dark, and I left it that way, shutting the door and shuffling through the dark into his bedroom.

The lights stayed off while I set my phone down and slipped into bed, shimmying my body deep under the covers. I took a deep breath of his scent, the deep musk all over his sheets, "Mmm." I let out a sigh of contentment as I burrowed deeper into the warm, cozy bed. It was the most comforting thing I had felt all day, and my body was finally able to relax. Closing my eyes, I let myself drift off to sleep.

Sometime later, the apartment door opened and closed. I was awake immediately, too scared to check if it was Ransom or, worse, check that he was alone.

I pulled the blankets over my head, feeling my face turn red with embarrassment. The room fell silent for a moment until I heard the sound of boots hitting the floor and keys being dropped on the counter. He finally walked into the room and headed straight for the bathroom.

He flicked on the lights but hadn't turned towards the bed yet. I was just happy he was alone. From my cocoon of blankets, I watched as he turned on the shower and started undressing. Even from here, I could see every muscle in his body working as he stripped off his dirt-covered clothes and stepped into the shower.

I waited as the water continued to run. I even considered joining him in the shower for a moment, but before I could make up my mind, the water shut off.

He stepped out, and I smiled, enjoying the sight. He wrapped a towel around his waist, but I still took my time looking over every inch of his wet chest and body. My breath caught in my throat as I stared in disbelief. Was this really the guy who loved me, protected me, and the one I trusted with everything?

I trusted he wasn't the one to do this and that he would help me find who did. I trusted him with my heart and every other part of my body.

The realization was like being hit by a truck all over again, and I didn't think my body could take any more shock.

I froze as he reached for his phone, his face pinched as he looked down at it.

It hadn't occurred to me that Fox wouldn't have told him what happened today. He didn't know anything. I was so wrapped up in my world crumbling, and he only thought that I hated and blamed him for the photos. He didn't know about Josie or that I knew how long he had liked and even loved me. Or how long I've felt the same.

His jaw twitched as he typed before hitting the phone once and setting it down. My eyes flew to my phone sitting on the nightstand, and I realized I hadn't silenced it.

The text notification chimed, and his eyes jumped up, looking out into the bedroom. I was still burrowed down in his bed, the covers up to my nose, but I knew how wide my eyes had gone.

"Quinn?" he asked, running over and dropping to his knees next to me. "What are you doing here?" He was all over me, pulling the covers down as he frantically ran his hands through my hair and down my jaw. "Are you okay?"

"I'm okay," I said, my voice quiet and small.

"What are you doing here?" It wasn't anger in his voice, though. It was relief.

"I was cold, and the sheets on the bed upstairs are scratchy. I couldn't sleep. Then I wondered where you were. I figured I could use your bed since you weren't."

His head came down with a breath as it fell against the bed, deep breaths making his body shake. My hand snaked up, covering his hand, still cupping my jaw.

He finally lifted his head again. "I was at the garage. Hoping you would come there. Hoping I would find out where you went. I never thought in a million years you would be waiting here in my bed."

"Me either."

"Do you want to tell me how you ended up here?"

"Maybe."

"Quinn, I didn't have those photos taken or post them. I would never do that. I would never share any moment you give me. I wouldn't want to share them. I'm too selfish and want those moments to myself." He gave a small smile, looking over at me, "I hate that anyone else has seen you like that without your permission. I'm sorry it happened, but I will find out who did it. It will never happen again. I'll make sure no one ever —"

He was stumbling over the words, the rushed rant growing frantic. "Did you think that the first time?"

"The first time?"

I nodded against the pillow. "The first time this happened, when you beat Logan up?"

He rocked back on his heels and sighed, running a hand over his face. "You found out it was me?"

"I found out a lot."

"And that led you to my bed?"

I thought it over. Everything that had happened today led me here, but not in any way I could clearly explain. "Kind of."

"Does that mean you are upset about the stuff with Logan?"

"No. I was surprised to find out it was you, of all people. I never understood how he happened to get beat up the same night the video came out, and no one confessed to it. That night, I thought you were on his side when you told me to leave. I thought you wanted me out of there because you thought the same horrible things everyone else did."

"I wanted you out of there because I was going to kill him, and didn't want you crying at me to stop." He admitted, "I was going to hit him, and I would have died right there if you stepped up to defend him. I needed you far away from it."

"I'd like to think I wouldn't have defended him, but who knows, I was a mess that day. Now though? I'm glad he got some sort of punishment. No one else ever held him accountable for it all. Thank you for doing that."

"You're okay with it, then?"

"Sticking up for me and making sure I never had to deal with Logan again? Yes, I'm okay with it. With everything I learned today, I think you were the only one on my side back then, too. Thank you for what you did."

"What about the other guy? You're not mad about that either?"

"There was another one?" I asked, trying to think back.

"Shit." He mumbled.

"No, tell me."

"There was that football player. He was fucking with you and trying to get you to sleep with him for money. You hit him, and I was so fucking proud of you, but you walked away, and he said some other shit to his friends. I hit him and one of his football player friends. I didn't want them to bother you anymore."

I gave a small laugh. "That was you?" I looked up at the ceiling, remembering that day. "I couldn't figure out how my little punch broke his nose and gave him two black eyes, but wasn't going to question it when they were finally leaving me alone." I turned back to him, "Always my protector, even when I didn't know it."

"You didn't answer me, though. Are you mad I did that?"

I shook my head against the pillow. "No, not mad. Actually, I'm a little relieved. All this time, I thought I was alone in this fight. I mean, Josie was always around, but it's not like there was anyone there to stand up for me, defend me. I always felt so alone, and now I figure out you were following me around trying to do that. I'm not mad at all. I think you're pretty amazing for doing that."

He ran his hand down my face again, and a smile broke on his face. "I think you like it when I'm vicious for you."

"I don't think I should like things like that, but I do."

"I'll always do those things for you."

Warmth flooded me, making my toes curl. "Will you get into bed?" I asked, wanting him next to me.

He got up and grabbed a pair of boxers before turning off the lights and changing.

"Hey," I said. "Why did you turn the light off?"

"I didn't think showing you that my dick was already hard

was the gentlemanly thing to do," he said. I could feel the bed move as he climbed in next to me. Getting under the covers and getting as close as he could without touching me.

"Were you watching me when I got home?"

I stifled a laugh. "Yes."

"You watched me undress and shower?" My lips pushed together, but a laugh still escaped.

"Yes."

"You are a very dirty girl."

"I can't help that I was lying here, minding my own business, and this hot guy started to change and shower in front of me. What was I supposed to do? Look away? You're the one with a hard dick already."

"Mmm, are you trying to tell me you aren't wet? Not even a little turned on by watching me shower?"

"I'm not answering that."

He laughed, "You are something else."

My eyes had adjusted to the darkness, the streetlights bringing in enough light to see him turn to face me.

"Not that I am complaining, Kitten. I'm relieved you're here, but why are you? I spent the whole day believing you hated me again. You wouldn't text me back and weren't at your dorm when I went. I was debating going back over tonight to try to see you."

I took a deep breath before telling him about the morning and what Josie had done.

"Fucking hell. Are you serious? Your own friend did that?" He hadn't touched me yet but finally pulled me close now. My body melted as his leg wrapped around mine, and he buried his head into my neck. I snuggled in closer, needing everything he was giving me.

"Fox told me something else today, aside from you being the one to hit Logan."

"What did he tell you?" he whispered into my ear, a shiver of pleasure running down my back.

"He told me that you have liked me for a long time. Since we were in high school."

The room was quiet for a minute before he confessed, "Yes."

"Yes?"

"I've liked you since the moment I saw you. It got worse over the years. Fox told me to stay away, and I did, but you were always on my mind. When we graduated, I hoped to forget about you and chalk it up to a high school crush, but I still saw you around. Then at the party with the video, it all came to a head there. I knew I was in love with you. I tried getting you to come to the garage once in high school."

"What?"

"Your car was acting up, and I had Fox offer to fix it. I was hoping you would come and I could see you, fix your car, or hell, give you one of our cars. I just wanted you to come see me. To give me one single sign that I had a chance, and I was going to jump at it."

"Oh yeah, I forgot about that. I wanted to so badly when I realized you might be there, but I couldn't afford to pay you guys for anything and wasn't going to embarrass myself like that."

"I told him to tell you we would do it for free."

"He did, but that was hard for me to believe. By then, I knew the world wasn't friendly, and nothing is ever free."

"That's true. There were strings attached to it."

"See."

"Like talking to me and me trying to keep your car as long as I could. Maybe me offering to drive you to school. Now that you mention it, there were a lot of strings attached to that offer."

I pulled back, "Really? You thought about those things?"

"Yes, really. It was the only thing on my mind for a week straight until I realized you weren't going to take him up on the offer. You wanted to come when you thought I would be there?"

I took a breath, knowing it was my turn to confess, "I have kind of had a crush on you since the first time I saw you, too. But," I added, "I thought you hated me."

"Hated you? Why would you think that?"

"You were always glaring at me. I hoped at first it was because you liked me, but then I realized that the glare wasn't a friendly one."

"Oh," he said, "I was pretty angry for a long time. Not at you. Well, maybe a little because of you. I wanted you, and you were too good for me. Fox always reminded me of that. Then I would be mad I couldn't be near you. Then you started dating Logan, and I was just flat-out pissed. The guy was an asshole, and I thought I was at least better than him."

"You're a lot better than him. Here's a part you really might not like," I said. "I think part of the reason I dated Logan was because of you."

He pushed back a bit. "You think what?"

I explained fast. "I thought I only liked you because of the bad boy syndrome. You know where girls go through a bad-boy phase in life. I thought dating Logan would make it stop, and then I wouldn't be comparing every single guy to you when I didn't even know you."

"You're saying if I had asked you out, you would have never been with Logan?"

"I don't know. Maybe? It's why I broke up with him so many times and still tried again. I kept thinking, alright, that should be enough now. I'll forget about Ransom and find myself a nice guy to date, but then I would see you, and somehow you would look hotter than last time. Then you would glare at me, and I would get pissed, so I would try dating Logan again. It was a horrible cycle. He was never you, though. I sound insane, I know. That's why I didn't tell you."

"That's why I didn't tell you," he said, running a hand down my body. "I thought of you all the time. Wondering if you tasted as sweet as you seemed."

"And the verdict?"

"So fucking sweet," he said. "The sweetest, most vicious lioness I've ever met."

I pushed against him further, finding his lips in the darkness. He was warm and safe, everything I needed after one of the worst days, and now I knew how much he had my back when others wouldn't.

THIRTY-SIX

RANSOM

MY HAND TRAILED down her spine, and I didn't miss the small moan as her body pressed into mine.

I'd been hard since I realized she was in my bed, and her pressed against me wasn't helping.

"You thought of me a lot?" I whispered into her ear, loving the shiver that ran through her.

"Yes."

"Tell me," I said, wishing I could know every single time she had thought of me, wondering if I had been thinking of her then, too.

"One time, I saw you working on your car in the parking lot. You had taken your shirt off, and I could just start to make out the tattoos on your side. I was surprised you had so many, and I wanted to know what they all looked like up close," she said, running her hands over those exact tattoos, "Then I wondered what your hands would feel like after you worked on your cars all day, if they would be rough against my skin, how it would feel when you kiss me. I thought about how bad I wanted you to bend me over your car. I wanted to know how hard you could fuck me, and I went home dreaming of it."

"Mmm, all I want to hear about from now on is every fantasy you had about me." I bit at her shoulder as she laughed, "I can assure you, I've had the same fantasies about you."

"Oh, yeah?"

"You were like a fucking star. I wanted you so bad for myself but couldn't have you. I thought about you constantly, wanting something that good for myself. You never seem afraid to stand up for yourself, even if you don't see it. I always thought you were perfect for me, so pretty and vicious. I just never thought I would get it. You'd come to school in those fucking skirts but looked so mean, and it took everything not to drag you to my car and fuck you till you looked at me like you do now."

"Mean? How did I look mean?"

"You think that little scowl you have doesn't look like you want to rip someone's head off?" I asked with a laugh.

"I didn't know I looked mean. I thought you were the one who looked mean. Maybe I was a little pissed about you not coming and grabbing me."

"I'm an idiot," I said, rolling on top of her. "I promise not to make the same mistake twice."

She reached up, running her hands through my hair and pulling me down to kiss her. I would kiss her every second she wanted me to. I wasn't going to make the mistake of letting her go or not letting her know how much I wanted, needed, and loved her. Years of wanting her, and now her body was mine to take. Now I just needed her to fall as in love with me as I was with her.

I undressed her in a frenzy, her pace matching mine until her naked body pressed against me.

"I think I owe you something," I said, sliding down, leaving a line of kisses until I reached her thighs, kissing each one. I slid my tongue in lazy circles as I moved along the edges of her pussy.

She pushed her hips up into me, and I laughed. "Trying to get more already?"

I licked along her once more before rolling off.

"Come on." I pulled her over me.

"What? That's it?"

I could hear the annoyance in her voice and laughed more. "That's it unless you come to straddle my face," I said as she sat over my hips.

"Your face?"

"Yes, get up here." I pulled at her as she resisted.

"I'm not sitting on your face!"

"Yes, you are. You were just trying to grind your pussy into my mouth, and now you're going to do that again. Get up here."

She looked at me but started to move. I coaxed her more until every perfect inch was right above me.

I was too excited, too lost to her to wait any longer. I grabbed her hips and pulled her down, her wet pussy filling my mouth as I pushed my tongue inside.

"Ransom!" she yelled, losing her breath.

I lifted her up, running my tongue from her ass to her pussy until I reached the clit, sucking and holding her tight on top of me again. I wasn't going to let up until she relaxed, until she took over, and enjoyed the pleasure. Her body was still tense, and I knew her face would be red with embarrassment.

"Can you even breathe?" she asked, panting as her hips started to grind against me.

"Yes, and if I pass out by some chance, keep going. I'll come to sooner or later." Her hips bucked as I sucked hard onto her clit again, flicking my tongue against the sensitive spot. "I won't stop until you relax, Quinn."

She moaned as I pushed my tongue back into her and pulled out, moving to her ass and pressing my tongue against her. I felt starved, needing more. Like a damn miracle, she finally relaxed and ground down on top of me harder.

She grabbed my hair, forcing my mouth back to her clit, and I listened, pushing two fingers into her as I sucked.

She fell apart, almost falling off me as her body shook. I flipped her over, crawling over top of her.

"You taste so good," I said into her ear, waiting as she caught her breath. "Are you still embarrassed?"

"Of course I am."

"Well, you better get over it fast because I'm going to lick and fuck every inch of you, and it won't be the last time."

I pulled her legs up, throwing them onto my shoulders as I pushed forward until my cock pressed against her entrance. I ran it through before pushing inside. I could feel her body stretch and hear her moan as she gripped my shoulders.

I'd had plenty of sex, but nothing like this. Quinn was something more. She was everything to me. My chest tightened, knowing I couldn't live my life without her now.

"Quinn," my voice strangled as I pushed further, losing every thought to her, "you feel too good. I can't last much longer with you gripping my cock like that." I pulled back out before slamming into her again with a groan.

Her legs stayed up, and I lifted her hips until she gasped, "Yes, more." I grabbed her chin, making her look up at me as I slammed into her again.

"Is this what you wanted? All those times you thought about me, did you want it like this?"

"Yes," she cried. "Yes, I wanted it fast and rough until I couldn't move. I wanted you to grab me and fuck me like this."

I moved my hand around her neck, giving a light pressure as her pussy clamped down onto my cock again. She cried out as her orgasm crashed into her. I thrust once more before I let go, my body shaking, finding my own release along with her.

I didn't move as I caught my breath, pulling her legs down and falling next to her on the bed.

"That was—"

"Amazing," I said, cutting her off. "Fucking amazing."

She laughed, "I was going to say unbelievable, but that works too."

We laid there in silence until I grabbed her, dragging her against my chest. "Are you going back to your dorm?"

She froze, "Tonight?"

"No, you have no choice on staying tonight. I would do unspeakable things to force you to stay tonight," I said, kissing her head. "I meant after tonight. Are you going back?"

"I can't. I can't manage to live with her or even see her. She's moving out at the end of the semester and into her sorority house, but I don't know what I'll do in the meantime."

"Why don't you just stay here?"

She laughed, "I can't live with you, Ransom."

"Why not? I have plenty of space here. Please, Kitten, stay here with me."

"I feel like that's a pretty quick jump from not dating to kind of dating to living together."

"Fine, but then move in upstairs. There's an empty apartment, and Scout won't mind sharing. Then you can sleep here all the time."

"And if you get sick of me and want me to move out?"

"Quinn, that's not happening," I said. Just the thought made my stomach churn, "I've waited literal years to have you here. I don't, and won't, want you to leave, ever. I meant it. I love you. I don't want you going anywhere."

She turned into me, putting her head on my chest, "Thank you. This has been a lot today."

"I know. Get some sleep. We'll sort everything out tomorrow."

I could feel her nod into my chest and waited as her breathing slowed, turning into a light snore before I pulled her in closer.

I laid there wide awake, wanting to take in every second. I

was already worried about what came next. I thought I had lost her earlier, and the world had dropped out from under me.

Suddenly, nothing but her had mattered. I had wanted to burn the life I had worked so hard to build right to the ground when I thought she wouldn't be in it anymore.

Now she was back again, and every part of me hoped she was staying.

It didn't matter, though. I would give Quinn every part of me over and over again. She could break me into a thousand pieces, and I would still hand her my heart and watch her do it again.

THIRTY-SEVEN

QUINN

I woke up to an empty bed.

"Ransom?"

A second passed, and he walked in, bare-chested, in a pair of sweatpants that hung off his hips. I groaned. How could I want him naked next to me while also wanting to stare at him standing there like that for hours?

"Yes?"

"What are you doing?"

"I was trying to make something to eat."

"Trying?" I said, smiling as I watched him from the bed.

"I remembered I am a mechanic who races cars, not a chef who cooks delicious breakfast, so now we have warmed up pizza."

I laughed, "That will work."

He walked back in a few seconds later, a plate of food and coffee in his hand as he sat down next to me, handing me the cup.

"What are you doing today?" I asked.

"I have to go to the garage for a while. Someone is coming to pick up their car, then I should probably grab us some food because we now have none here, and then I can spend the rest of the day with you if you aren't busy."

"After we left yesterday, I told my professors I wouldn't be in this week, so I have nothing to do. I was thinking about cleaning up the apartment upstairs if you guys are actually ok with me staying there for a while. I don't want any problems to come up that get me kicked out."

"I'm sure we can give you some guarantee that even if we fight, I'm not kicking you out. God, not that I could ever fucking do that to you. Keep your space upstairs and then please, please stay with me all the time," he said, nuzzling into my neck as I took a bite of pizza. "Don't they charge a shit ton of money for living in the dorms?"

"Yeah, thousands extra each semester, but I couldn't live with my mom, so I didn't have many options."

"Now you do. No rent, tons of space, close to school and work." He kissed me. "Me right downstairs."

"Oh well, now I'm sold," I said, laughing.

"Good, and when Scouts is ready to move in, you can move in with me."

"Wow, you really have this planned out."

"I do, and just so you know, plan B still includes tying you to my bed. I've waited years, and I'm trying very hard not to fuck this up or let you get away."

"You're terrible."

"Oh, it gets worse."

"How's that?"

"It's going to take a little bit to make the upstairs more livable." He moved the cup before rolling on top of me. "So I think you're stuck with me until we finish it up."

"Oh no, how am I going to bear living with the hot guy who gives me orgasms?" I said, falling back. "You know, most people make it to the second date before they move in together."

He laughed. "Second date or not, you can stay here as long as you want. Even if you decide you never want to move in upstairs and just stay here. It seems our circumstances have changed our dating timeline. You can clean the place up, and we'll start fixing the rest of it."

"Well, it sounds like I'm moving in for now. But I still want a second date."

"Then we'll go tonight. Anywhere you want."

I pulled myself up and leaned back. "Ransom, I need to figure out who took those photos and posted them."

"Would you want to ask Josie? I can go with you."

"And what? Be my backup in case she jumps me?" I laughed. "I don't know if it was her. How would she know we were there? And she was surprised when I told her we were, in fact, dating, so I don't know if she would have known to come and try to ruin my life again. Then again, Tyler found out right before this happened, which is too much of a coincidence."

"So you told her we were dating?" he asked, his face unreadable.

The shock felt like a heart attack. "Um, well, I thought we were, but I don't have to say that, of course. Like, I don't have to call you my boyfriend or anything. I thought —"

He cut me off as I panicked. "Quinn, I'm just happy to hear from you that we are dating. You didn't seem to be into it the other day. I've told you I loved you and asked you to move in with me. I'll give you whatever you want or need. Obviously, I would want to do all of that as your boyfriend, if you wanted me."

"Well, how am I supposed to know?" I asked, throwing up my hands. "I can't figure out what you're thinking half the time. I thought you hated me when, all this time, you liked me. You're infuriating sometimes. Plus, let's be honest, Ransom, you don't come off as the dating type."

"Oof," he said like I'd hit him, "That hurts."

"How many people have you dated?"

"Including my kindergarten girlfriend or not?"

"Not."

"Then one."

"You've only dated one other person?"

"No," he said, getting out of bed and turning away from me, "No other person. You'd be the only person I've ever actually dated."

My jaw fell slack. "Ransom," I said, throwing my head back. "You're really proving my point here."

"Hey, it's not my fault. I've basically been in love with you for years. I can't help it. I didn't want to date anyone else."

"No, you just wanted to sleep with them."

"I'm not going to lie and say I haven't slept with anyone else. We both have, but it seems like we had each other on our minds most of the time, anyway." He leaned down and kissed my forehead.

"I guess that's fair."

"And to be even more fair, I've been in this one hundred percent since the night you walked into the street. I've pushed to be with you. You're the one that's been running."

"Ouch, I guess that's also fair."

"I may not be well experienced in dating, but I know I'd do anything for you. I'll try to figure this all out and be a decent boyfriend. I hope that's enough." His head fell slightly.

"It's more than enough," I said, meaning it.

He laid over top of me, spreading soft kisses over my jaw and nose. "Good, you're mine now. No one else will ever get to see those perfect lips wrapped around their cock."

"Oh, yeah? And what if they do?"

His hands wrapped into my hair and pulled me up against him. "Trying to provoke me so early in the morning? Don't forget that I have a group of friends who would absolutely help me bury a body and give me an alibi." He gave me a wicked smile, making me question how much he was joking.

He bit hard at my neck, making my head fall back, the rough touch blazing heat through me. "Aren't you supposed to be heading to the garage?"

"I'm caring less and less about it. Ready to get rid of me already?"

"No, but you better leave before we stay in bed all day," I said, and he let me go with a groan.

"And people say I'm the devil? You're driving me into madness. Making me want to murder people I don't even know and fuck you until you could never think of another guy. Then you tell me to go to work. I'm going to lose my mind."

It was my turn to grin. "Just remember, you're the one who wanted to date me so bad. You asked for it. Also, I wish I had a car. I'll need to grab a few things for upstairs, even some cleaning supplies."

"You can take mine if you want to drop me off and grab me from the garage when you're done. Then, we can go grab food together after."

"For being a boyfriend for the first time, you really make all of this so easy. I need a place to live. You have the answer. I need a car," I snapped my fingers, "poof, done, I have one I can use."

"It's an easy solution."

"It's fine. Between the three of you, I'm sure one of you has some cleaning supplies hidden away. I'll text Fox and Jax. Go do your stuff, and I can go on a different day."

"You know, you're my girlfriend now," he said, walking out of the bathroom a few minutes later, dressed and ready. He was wearing dark jeans and a t-shirt, but it didn't matter what he wore. There was always an edge to him, a dangerous look that felt unpredictable. It was such a contrast to the other side of him that I knew now.

"Yes, I think I figured that out, but I suddenly don't mind hearing you say it."

He smiled, "I mean, you're my girlfriend, and you are a part of our crew now. It only makes sense you have a car. And I mean an actual car like ours, not that beat-up shit you used to have."

"You mean a ridiculously fast car that's only good for street racing?"

"Exactly."

"I don't have money for a car like that."

He shook his head. "Have you seen the garage? We have enough parts there to build you a car."

"I can't take something that expensive."

"Then we'll build it together. You can do the work and put one together. Then it's not any handout, and it's pretty fucking awesome to drive something you built."

I thought it over, but he wasn't giving me a chance to say no.

"You know what? It's a new requirement to work there. You have to have a fast car," he said.

"Why are you pushing so hard for this?"

"Because I saw how happy you were when you drove mine. And as much as I love seeing you drive it, and to be very, very clear, you can drive it whenever you want to. I think you would like the freedom of having your own car, and a nice one at that."

"I guess it would be nice to go where I want, when I want, and not worry about it breaking down every five seconds. Alright, fine. I want to build a car." I shook my head. "That's six words I never thought I would say."

"But I am so glad you did. I'll start getting ideas."

He grabbed my hands, dragging me against his chest. "You'll be here tonight again, right? You're not going to run away?"

"Yes, of course, I'll be here," I said with a huff. "I've run out of other options."

"Rude," he growled as he picked me up, carrying me with him into the living room and he grabbing everything he needed. He set me on the counter and kissed me once before pulling away.

"I'll text you when I'm done, but should be back by three or four."

"Ok, see you later," I said as I went for another cup of coffee. The door caught before it slammed, and he stuck his head back in. "I love you."

I rolled my eyes with a small laugh. "See you later."

THIRTY-EIGHT

QUINN

THREE O'CLOCK CAME AROUND without a word from Ransom. He had texted me around noon that he missed me, but that was it. I was fine until four came and went without a response still.

I called Scout. "Hey, are you at the garage?"

"No, I'm home now," she said, and I heard someone yell in the background.

"Are you ok?"

"Yeah, that's normal." I could hear the eye roll, but I knew how much it sucked firsthand.

"I get it. You know, as long as you're good with it, I was going to move into the apartment upstairs. Would you be allowed to move out sooner if you lived with me here?"

"You're moving in?"

"Yeah, I need a place to stay now."

"I heard from Fox. I'm so sorry, Quinn."

"It's alright now. She was kind of dead weight as a best friend since I got a better one recently."

"Me?"

"Of course, it's you." I laughed, "But you could say you're

staying with me now instead of a house full of boys. Maybe that would help your dad drop it?"

"Maybe," she said, "It's not a bad idea. He was pretty pissed about it being all guys there. There has been plenty of name-calling for always hanging out with them."

"I'll meet him if you want. Tell him we want to move in together. I've dealt with my mom my whole life. I can deal with him."

Her voice sounded lighter, like there was hope coming sooner than she thought. "It would be worth a shot."

"Alright. We'll figure out a time to try it out."

"Why are you looking for Ransom?"

"I haven't heard from him, and he was supposed to come back to pick me up."

"When I left, he wasn't at the shop. Fox said he was out grabbing parts, but that was like two hours ago."

"Alright, thanks. I'll call Fox." I told her to set up the best time, and we'd try to get her out of there before clicking off and calling Fox.

He didn't pick up, making panic bubble in my throat. It was almost five now. They should all be finishing up for the day.

The garage wasn't far, so I grabbed my shoes and started towards it. Worst case, I would see one of their cars coming down the road.

No, the worst case was something terrible happened. The thought weighed on me as I reached the garage, seeing Fox and Jax's cars still out front.

I almost ran inside. They both stood looking something over on a car. The garage was half closed down, and I knew they were finishing up. "Have you guys seen Ransom?"

"No, he said he was running to grab parts and pick some stuff up before heading to get you."

"When?"

"A few hours ago."

"Ok, how long does it take to pick up parts and go to the store?"

Jax looked at Fox like it was a trick question. "An hour or two."

I huffed, "He's not answering me back. I haven't heard from him in hours."

Fox's face changed, making me panic more. "What? What's that face for?" I asked.

"I don't know. I've just had a bad feeling today, and now it's worse. I thought it was nothing, so I ignored it, but now, I don't know."

"Oh great," I said. "Would Slaughter, Ryder, or whoever go after him?"

"There was another round of cars stolen this weekend. If they really think we are doing it and catch Ransom out, yeah, they would."

"Especially after the way you humiliated them the other week," Jax added. "I'm sure they are pissed that we beat on them a bit."

Fox smacked him in the stomach. "That doesn't help."

"What are we supposed to do?" I asked, trying to take deep breaths.

"Relax, Quinn. We can't freak out. Let me try to call him."

Fox walked away. His phone pressed to his ear.

"What about the radio thing? Wouldn't he have that if his phone died or something?"

"I'll try it," Jax said. He ran to his car, messing with his radio.

"Didn't pick up," Fox said.

I waited, tapping my foot as Jax came back over. "Nothing."

"What do we do now?" I yelled this time.

"Jax will stay here in case he gets back, and we'll go see if we can find him anywhere. He told me his stops, so we can retrace his steps."

"Ok." My hands shook as I reached the car, fumbling for Fox's door and getting inside.

He yelled for Jax to keep his phone on and slammed his door. The car revved to life, the sudden noise and power making me jump.

He reached out, patting my leg. "Take a breath. We'll figure out where he is."

"I'm putting trackers on all your cars."

He laughed, "I think you might get bored watching us go from the house to the garage to the races day in and day out."

"Fine, a crash alert system."

"That's a little more reasonable. I don't think Ransom would crash, though. You know he's a good driver."

"But you have a guy named Slaughter after you guys. Nobody wants to acknowledge the concern there?"

"Ransom and I just talked about it. He thought we should skip the races this week."

"What? Why didn't he say anything to me?"

"Pretty sure he was a little more worried about keeping you. Although, I'm glad you took the hint and headed for his apartment. I wondered if you would make it the whole night up there."

"You put me up in that cold room and a horrible bed on purpose?"

"Of course I did. The place has no heat, and that bed needs to be thrown out. Ransom's happy with you. I had to help my brother out, and I like you being around." His smile was golden, the twinkle in his eye obvious in the fading sun.

"You're the worst," I said.

"Wow, what a way to thank a guy. I'm pretty sure it worked out perfectly."

I thought about last night and how perfect it had been. How good it felt to hear how he had felt for so long from his lips.

"Shit," Fox said, speeding up.

I yelled the moment I saw it. Ransom's car flipped over on the side of the road. The driver's side door was open but crushed in, the roll cage the only thing holding it all together.

Fox was already calling everyone, telling them to come.

I jumped from the car the moment Fox slowed, running to find Ransom, but all I found was blood smeared along the side.

There was no one. The woods around us were quiet, without a house or car in sight.

"Fox," I whispered. Needing to hear him say something.

He was walking around the car, looking it over. "I don't think it was an accident. I think he was ran off the road."

"How do you know?"

"The back passenger side is crushed in. I'm guessing Ransom would have been speeding down here, and they caught up. Smashed into his side, forcing him off the road. It's not the most unique of tricks." He bent down and reached into the car. Pulling out his phone, "Here, hold on to this. He'll want it back."

I tried to take a deep breath, but a sob escaped me instead as I grabbed the phone. It lit up as I touched the screen and could see the notifications of missed calls and texts, but the photo behind it caught my eye. I swiped them out of the way and stared.

It was a black-and-white photo of me standing with his car. I was looking away from him and hadn't noticed he had taken the picture. I was laughing about something as I leaned against the car. I looked so happy and relaxed.

I remembered the day and realized it had been at least two weeks ago now. Before we even slept together.

I couldn't believe he took the photo and now even had it as his background. It was something so small and trivial, but it felt like someone had punched me. Now he was dead or hurt somewhere, and I couldn't just reach out and touch him. I might never be able to again if Slaughter really did find him.

"Fox." I said again, not knowing what else to say. "I do love him and never said it back."

He pulled me to him. "It's ok, we're going to go find him, Quinn. He knows. Take a breath. As soon as Kye and Jax are here, we're going to get him."

"What do you mean? Where is he?"

"My guess is at Slaughter's garage."

I wanted to throw something, hit something, anything to gain an ounce of control. Instead, I kicked at Ransom's car. "Slaughter is a stupid fucking name."

"Yeah, it's a bad one."

We weren't far from the garage, and it didn't take long for Kye and Jax to show up. They looked over the car as I paced, ready to throttle each one of them, wanting to leave and go find him.

"You guys are wasting time."

"We had to figure out how to get in there."

"In where?"

"If Ransom is in the garage with them, we can't just drive up and walk in. They are going to be expecting us to come in. We need to give some element of surprise."

"This isn't an action movie. Don't one of you have a gun? I know how to shoot. I'll go in with that."

Jax raised his hands. "While I love the enthusiasm, that's not happening."

I crossed my arms, glaring at him, "Why not?"

"One, we don't fuck with guns, and two, you could shoot Ransom if you're going in blindly shooting, and three, we need to do this without going to jail, but again, love the enthusiasm."

I growled, kicking his car again and pacing as they talked it over.

After what felt like hours, they turned. "Ok, Quinn. We have a plan."

THIRTY-NINE

RANSOM

<u>Earlier That Day</u>

I stalked into the garage to hunt Fox down and found him standing next to his car. I pushed him, making him step back.

"What the hell?" he asked with a smile.

"I can't believe you told Quinn I liked her in high school."

He started laughing, almost falling over as he moved away from me and to the other side of the car. "Hell yeah, I did. You should have done it before. What girl isn't going to be happy to find the guy she liked actually liked her back?" He shook his head. "Got a lot to learn if you're trying to keep a girl. Sounds like she came to talk to you, didn't go too well?"

"No, it went great, but that doesn't mean you had to tell her."

"I'm the only reason she came to talk to you, so you should be thanking me. Who went to pick her up and deliver her to your door? Me. Try saying thank you next time."

"Try not making me sound like a lovesick puppy next time."

"You were a lovesick puppy. I couldn't lie to Quinn. And she felt the same, so it was a win-win."

I wasn't actually mad at him, but damn if he didn't make me

sound ridiculous. "Well, thanks then, because it did go well, and Quinn will be staying."

"No shit. Looks like I did something right then," Fox said.

"You act like this was all your doing. Do I not get any credit?"

"Nope, this was all me. And you're welcome."

"The fucking worst," I said, shaking my head with a laugh. "I'm heading out to pick some stuff up, and I'm done for the day."

His eyebrows wagged. "Of course you are."

I didn't even respond, knowing any smart-ass comment he had wouldn't make me happy. I didn't need his comments. I needed to stay on this high of happiness, in my own world and away from any reality.

Driving was second nature now. I didn't even need to think about it as I moved through the gears and hit my favorite road. The twists were always enough for me without being completely deadly.

The music played loud enough that I didn't hear the other car next to me until it hit. The front of their car smashed into the back of mine, knocking me to the side into the dirt as I tried to straighten it out. I was already being hit again, though, the angle and rocks flipping me before I had any chance of regaining control.

My head still hit something, making my vision burst as glass shattered everywhere.

I had flipped a car once before, my stupid mistakes making me turn and roll, but this wasn't my doing now.

I heard voices coming closer, and I moved quickly, undoing my harness and kicking through the windshield to pull myself out.

It still wasn't fast enough. My head exploded. I stood as two hands wrapped around to hold me, and an elbow collided with my face.

———

WHEN I WOKE UP AGAIN, I wished I hadn't. Every part of me was either aching or screaming in pain. My hands were chained, and I could feel blood dripping down my face.

Slaughter and Ryder stood in front of me, and I smiled. "Finally caught one of us, huh? Driving down the road is a crime to you now?"

"No, stealing our shit is."

"I don't want your shitty cars. I can build better ones myself." I said, keeping as calm as possible.

"Fuck off, Ransom. We want our cars back, or we want to be paid for the stolen ones."

"Then go find the guy who took them. I'm sure he could help."

"There's no one else. It had to be you and your little fucking crew of idiots."

"Aww, Ryder, you're just mad my girl fucked up your face," I said, my chest tightening.

My girl.

Quinn had to know by now something was wrong. I told her I'd be back hours ago based on how dark it was. We were supposed to be having our second date right now. I groaned. I could have Quinn naked in bed right now. Instead, I'm chained up in this shitty garage for something I didn't do.

"Fuck you, you fucking prick," Ryder yelled, and Slaughter knocked him back.

"Shut up, both of you."

I pulled at the chains they had wrapped around me, trying to wiggle them loose enough to slip out of, but nothing moved.

Slaughter laughed, "You're staying here until I get my money or my cars. Let's hope your crew isn't as stupid as I think they are, and they show up with one or the other soon."

It was cruel enough to have my car wrecked and body beat,

but to know the universe kept trying to ruin any chance I had to keep Quinn was just fucked up. I couldn't imagine her happy about any of this. She was going to freak out and run, deciding once and for all I wasn't good enough for her.

I groaned and pulled again, but Ryder hit a button, making the chains pull up and over my head in one quick movement as my shoulder popped.

I groaned as pain exploded again, my shoulder no longer where it was supposed to be.

"I said shut up," Slaughter said. I looked up as his fist pulled back, watching helplessly as it smashed into my jaw, and the world went black around me.

FORTY

QUINN

BOYS WERE RIDICULOUS SOMETIMES.

It was the only thing I could think about as we parked the cars four blocks from Slaughter's garage.

Their big plan was to sneak in the back and bring Ransom out.

That was it.

That was the entire plan.

It took them ten minutes to come up with it, which somehow won out to my going in shooting plan.

I took a deep breath as we made our way to the garage.

I realized this was how Ransom must have felt when I was in that house, and how he had so much restraint was beyond me. I was about to burn the entire building down.

Anger boiled over. I just got him, and he was gone again.

"I know I don't get a gun, but do I get any weapon?"

They looked between them, making a silent decision, before Fox pulled another knife out of his car. "Here, try not to use it."

"Sure," I said, a sarcastic edge to my voice like I wouldn't hesitate to cut through each and every one of them in there.

"Come on," Fox said, nodding towards the garage. We

walked through the night, and part of it felt wrong. The quiet streets were calm compared to the fear that was taking over every part of me.

The garage was lit up with one of the doors open.

"Fuck," Fox said, "I bet that's the only unlocked door."

"What?"

"There's not going to be an unlocked back door. They knew we would come after him. They want money or these cars back. I wouldn't be surprised if they are out a hundred thousand dollars. They knew we would come and thought we would pay them in exchange for Ransom. I was worried this would happen."

"Who has that kind of money?"

"The person who stole the cars," Jax said.

"Your timing for smart-ass comments is impeccable," I said, shaking my head at him.

"Sorry," he said, squeezing an arm around me before letting me go.

Fox only stared at the building. "We don't have that much money to give away for something we didn't do."

"But it's Ransom," I said.

"And we will get him out the way we always do."

"Which is?"

"Kick their asses and pull him out of there." Fox shrugged. "It worked last time."

We laid out a new plan, one that would include Ransom out safe and leave all of us safe too.

I took a deep breath. "Ok then. Time to go."

I moved before they did, heading straight for the garage door, my courage coming from the three guys behind me and the one inside that had come for me. He didn't care who had been in the house. He only cared about kicking the door in and getting to me. He didn't shy away from any fight for me, and while I couldn't fight off a group of grown men, I could still help get him out.

Eyes turned as I walked in, realizing the guys had spread out, hiding in the shadows as I walked in, so everyone on the inside only saw me. I wasn't worried, though. I trusted each one of them behind me. I knew it only looked like I was going in alone.

It was a weird feeling to trust that they weren't abandoning me. They weren't running to hide or cowering away. That if I needed them, they were going to run in here and save me. They were giving us the best chance to win, and I trusted them.

"Where is Ransom?"

There were only seven of them tonight, but some of the faces looked familiar. I wondered if there were more around. It wasn't a big building, but there was an office to the left and a massive sliding door to the right.

It was Ryder who stepped forward. "Wow. Of all the people I expected to walk in tonight, it wasn't you." He smiled, the twisted curve of his lips making me gag as he came towards me.

"Eww," I said, looking him over and taking a step back.

"That's not what you'll be saying later," he said, and the others laughed. The simple comment felt like someone slapping me, the sexual taunts happening over and over again in my life, and I hated it. I was done with them.

Images of Logan, Tyler, and even Josie flashed through my mind. And then it was Ransom telling me that I was allowed to kick people in the teeth if they went too far. I was allowed to be angry and fight back if they came at me. Ryder was coming at me, and I was ready to kick him in the teeth.

Again.

I smiled. "Didn't you learn not to mess with me the first time, Ryder?"

He laughed, "The difference is you had Ransom to back you up last time." He peered around my shoulder into the dark night. "Looks like you're all alone now."

"And it looks like you're surrounded by the same idiots who couldn't stop me before."

"Admit it. You came back for me." He laughed, and the rest of them laughed with him, "Wanted what I was offering last time. Ready to scream my name loud enough for Ransom to hear?"

I smiled, "You know what, Ryder? I will be screaming your name that loud."

"I knew you would come around."

I stepped forward, pulling the knife out of my pocket and pointing it at him as I curled my lip. "I'll be screaming it when I push my knife deeper and deeper into your fucking neck."

He smiled, "You wouldn't dare because if you do that, they'll kill your boy." He looked around the room, and I did, too, watching as everyone nodded.

It was standing there holding the knife that I realized this was who I was. I wasn't lying when I said I would do it. I would stick Ryder with the blade if it meant we were all safe. It wasn't a pretty side to me, but I didn't hate it anymore.

I fought to survive, to stay safe, I fought to get ahead and out of the bad parts of my life. I would fight just as vicious as Ransom did.

I fought for what I needed, and right now, I needed Ransom.

I would draw blood if that's what someone like Ryder needed, and I wouldn't stop to feel bad about it.

"He didn't take your cars, Ryder."

"I wouldn't expect him to tell you about it, so save your breath. Ransom's going to stay here until you give our cars back or until you pay for them." Ryder said, but he made a mistake.

He didn't notice what he did. The motion was so natural no one else around caught it.

He had nodded to the large sliding door off to their right when he said Ransom's name.

That was my part to play in the plan, find out where Ransom was in the building and then give Fox a signal. Then I find him while they hold off the group.

I remembered where Ryder had held the knife to my neck before, where the small cut had healed, so I stepped forward. He was having too much fun to stop me, letting me press the cool metal under his chin as I pushed the blade into the thin flesh in the same place he had done it to me.

"Thanks, Ryder," I said so sweetly as I pushed the knife up, drawing a small line of blood as I lifted my other arm. It was Fox's signal.

The room erupted as the guys threw in the thick smoke bombs Kye just so happened to have in his car. After learning more about Kye, I could only figure that he stole them from somewhere, but I wasn't about to complain to him now.

Boys were ridiculous, and sometimes that was the best thing in the world.

I ran to the sliding door, pushing it open enough to slip in and pulling it closed, looking for anything to hold it shut behind me. I found a bar and shoved it onto the locking hook before turning back to the room.

I almost screamed when my eyes landed on him, but I held it back until it was only a whimper, not wanting to bring any more attention to myself.

"Ransom," I whispered as I saw him across the garage bay.

Tears filled my eyes as I got closer. His arms were chained above him, holding him up until his feet were almost off the ground, and his shoulders weren't sitting right. They had to be almost dislocated if they weren't completely. His temple and jaw were already turning purple, where he must have been hit hard. He was a mess of blood and dirt from his face to his stomach. His body was littered with small cuts, but I couldn't tell where all the blood had come from.

"Ransom," I whispered, reaching up to his face and neck, making sure there was still a pulse. I could feel his warmth, his heart still beating. The silent tears came harder as I tried to figure out how to get his hands down. The chains were wrapped tight around his wrists, and there was no way for me to lift him up to take the pressure off enough to unhook them. I pushed up onto the tips of my feet, reaching for him, pressing my lips gently against his. "Ransom." I whispered again, trying to wake him up.

"Kitten?" he asked, his voice strangled and dry.

A sob escaped me as I tried to focus. "Yes. I don't know how to unchain you."

"Engine lift, button." He croaked. I looked around the contraption, looking for a button. I felt everywhere until I reached the back, two buttons showing up and down. I hit it, hoping it wouldn't drop him to the floor, but I did not have time to test it. It came down, his arms going with it, dropping another foot. It was enough as I grabbed a bucket to stand on, untangling the chains from his wrists.

"Kitten," he whispered again.

"I'm here. I'm getting your hands free." One came loose, and I wrapped it around my neck. "Try to hold on to me. I need to get the other unchained." It came free, and his arms dropped, his body almost dead weight as he fell onto me.

He groaned from the movement, but tried to hold on and keep himself upright.

Tears fell from my eyes. He was in bad shape. His car had flipped, and then he was chained and beaten. I didn't know how I would get him out of there, let alone make sure he was ok. I pulled him towards the nearest car, propping him up against it.

I grabbed my shirt, wiping at his face and trying to wipe away some of the blood and dirt before looking over him for more injuries. His nose didn't look broken, but it had been hit at some point.

"I'm so sorry," I said while I worked. "I should have told you how much I love you. I shouldn't have waited. I should have gone with you today." I reached up, placing light kisses across his lips and jaw.

"Love you too. Didn't know I had to be beaten up for you to say it back." His words were quick and hoarse.

"I shouldn't have waited. I've loved you for so long, and it scared me to say it."

"It's okay, Quinn. I already knew. There was no time limit for you to say it back."

"Can you walk? We need to get you to the car."

"Just need some help."

I wrapped my arm around his waist, and he winced, but there weren't many places I could hold on to that weren't bruised or bloody.

We made it to the back door, and I kicked at it, trying to hit the latch without needing to let him go. It caught, opening enough for me to shove my boot in and start getting us through.

He leaned over, his head rolling onto my shoulder. "Mmm." He murmured into my ear, "My wild, wild lioness come to rescue me?" He sounded drunk, the words quiet and tired.

We made it outside, and I leaned him against the wall. The guys were supposed to have made it back here by now, but I didn't see them. I had worried something would go wrong, and they gave me a key to one of the cars in case.

To make it four blocks carrying Ransom seemed impossible, though. I turned, ready to grab him again, when a figure came around the corner. I stepped closer to Ransom, who reached a hand onto my hip.

The figure came into view, and relief flooded me.

"Dante?"

FORTY-ONE

QUINN

"Hey, there you two are." He started forward.

"He can help me. You get to the car," Ransom croaked from beside me.

"What?"

Dante had been close enough to hear, "I'll start getting him closer if you bring the car around. Where did you guys park?"

I ignored them both. Every hair on my body raised like hackles as Dante stepped closer. I don't know what it was or why, but something was wrong. I slid the knife out of my back pocket, and stepped in front of Ransom.

"When did you get here?"

"A few minutes ago."

"Quinn," Ransom said. I know what he meant. I needed to stop asking questions. "We need to go," he said, the words so quiet and weak that I knew he needed help, and fast.

My heart twisted. We needed to get out, but everything felt off. I knew Dante was their friend, and I didn't know why he was making me nervous now.

"Go on, Quinn. Get the car. I'll bring Ransom around." He

took a step forward, and I stepped back, not wanting him to get closer to either of us.

"Quinn," Ransom said again. This time, it was a warning. I didn't want to make him stand there any longer, and I had never been good at reading people, but at some point, I had to listen to myself. I shouldn't feel a need to protect us from his friend.

I was questioning myself. Not knowing if I should trust my own body screaming at me to run, not that I could, at least not fast enough, with Ransom.

"Please, back off, Dante," I said, my teeth clenching together.

"What are you doing?" Ransom asked as I stepped back against him. He sounded more coherent, more alive.

I turned to whisper to him, "I don't know, but something isn't right."

Dante took another step forward, and I pushed back harder against Ransom. We were getting trapped in the corner.

"Go around and see if the coast is clear," I said to him, wanting him to leave.

"No, I'll help Ransom get to the car. What's your problem, Quinn? What are you doing?"

Sweat beaded down my back, the adrenaline from getting to Ransom replaced with a deeper need. I wasn't going to ignore myself. I couldn't when all Ransom had been telling me to do was stand up for myself. I had to start trusting myself. Dante wasn't going to come near either one of us now.

"Back off, Dante," I yelled now, holding the knife up towards him like I had to Ryder.

"No, Ransom needs help, and now you're fucking this all up. Do you not see how bad he is?"

"Yeah, I do. I'm the one who came and got him. You were nowhere to be found."

"Is that what this is about? You're pissy because I didn't come fast enough when called? Get over yourself. We don't all want to be up each other's asses all the time, and I didn't see all the messages right away."

Ransom hadn't said anything, and I didn't blame him. He had to be so mad at me at this point. His hand was on my hip and gave a weak squeeze.

"Dante," Ransom growled from behind me, tapping me to step aside, but I didn't move. "It's been enough tonight. She's had enough. Can you just go grab your car?"

He was giving him a chance to both help us and back off at the same time.

"Please, Dante," I begged again. "Move out of my way and get the car. I'll help him," I said, already knowing I wasn't getting in any car with him, and neither was Ransom. Not tonight.

"What the fuck is wrong with you? Do you not care if he dies? He could be bleeding out right now. Whose side are you on? I knew something was wrong with you, but this seems like a stretch."

Ransom made a move to step forward, but I stood my ground, not letting him.

I didn't realize I was still holding the knife up at Dante until I took a breath. That question was enough to know I was making the right decision. They say cheaters will blame you for cheating on them, and I think this had the same effect.

"Are you on our side?" I asked. The knife still raised at throat level.

"He's coming with me whether you get in the way or not, Quinn, so don't be stupid."

"No, he's not, and if you move any closer, if you try to touch him, I'm going to start using this knife."

"You bitch. It was supposed to be over tonight. They were going to believe you guys stole these cars. Then, I could stay out of it, and then they would leave me alone to take the cars and money. If you take him, they are going to keep looking. You guys have to stay and pay them back for the cars. It's all your guy's fault, anyway." His words were a whine, each word like a child stomping their feet.

"Our fault?" Ransom said, his voice barely loud enough to hear.

"Yeah, I needed money, and you wouldn't help me. You help everyone else, even her. Why not me?"

"We gave her a job, just like we gave you a job. How is that not enough?"

"Because you pay me scraps. I had to go out and get these cars like you guys used to do. I had to go out and make more money because you all didn't want to give me a bigger cut of the garage's profit."

The confession knocked me back. I don't know what I was expecting, but it wasn't this.

"We are here to get Ransom home. None of them are going to confess to this."

"You know, Quinn, I was so excited to see you join the crew. I needed parts and couldn't find a way to take them without raising suspicion. I thought it would be easy to get them to blame you for breaking into the garage, though. The new girl, the odd one out. How could they be loyal to you? I thought I could make them think you were the one doing all this, but no, everyone was more than happy to have your back. I thought inviting Brooke would run you off, and then I could put the blame on you, but no, you still come around. Finally, I had to post those photos thinking that would get you to turn on them, but still, you stuck around, and they had your back."

"You're the one who invited Brooke over?"

"Wait, you posted those photos? It wasn't Josie?" I asked.

"Yeah, I invited Brooke over, and I don't even know who Josie is. I thought you would learn your lesson after your photos got out again. You would stop coming around, and I could put the blame on you, but you came right back. What is it with this guy? Is the sex that good? Do you like humiliation?" He rolled his eyes. "It was only a matter of time before they realized it was me taking parts. After the photos were out and you were still around, I knew they were never going to blame you for the break-ins, and I knew they wouldn't stop until they found out who it was. I'm sick of you all hanging around like you're a damn family, but don't want to help me. No, that's where you draw the line."

"So your plan is wrecked. What now?"

He gave a strangled laugh. "Now? Now, I'm going to take you with me, Quinn. You're coming with me, and I'm not letting you go until they confess and pay off Slaughter and his crew." His words were desperate, and the thought of him making up this disgusting plan was making me sick.

"You're not touching her," Ransom growled.

"Shut up," Dante yelled, "like you could do anything now? I came to you and asked for money, and you said no. You'll give everyone else what they want, including her, but I asked for extra money, and you guys said no. I was forced to go out and find another way to get it, so you're taking the blame now. It's your fault, so you have to fix it. I know you're obsessed with her. You do what I want, and she won't get hurt."

"If you touch her, I'm going to kill you." The words were low, the threat so honest that I wondered if Ransom would really go that far to keep me safe.

Dante was already stalking forward, but I knew Ransom was in no position to fight. I had to figure out how to stop him myself.

He was finally close enough that I swung out the knife. It hit his arm, but he was still too fast. His fist connected with my face before he pushed me out of the way.

I had been punched in the face before. A few times.

But a hit from my drunk mother was a lot different than getting hit by a full-grown, coherent man. My head spun, and white stars exploded in my eyes. I could only hold on to the ground, waiting to see if I would be able to see again.

If Ransom had been hit like this for hours now, I didn't know how he was still managing to talk.

I looked back. Dante was on top of Ransom, who was fighting back, but I knew he couldn't go on too long. It felt like any hit could be his last.

I moved, jumping onto Dante's back and trying to get my knife to his neck. He reared back, slamming me into the back of the garage and pinning me there. His hands swung around, trying to hit me off, but I held on. I still couldn't angle my knife to his neck, his arms stopping me, but I could reach his other arm. I pressed the blade hard against his bicep, trying to push through his jacket as he swung around to get me off.

Ransom had moved, getting us out of the corner and turning Dante into it. Dante hadn't noticed, though. The only problem now was I didn't know how to get off without Dante throwing me.

I heard shouts from behind us, but I was only focused on holding on and holding the knife.

He finally stopped thrashing. "Get the fuck off me, Quinn."

It was enough of an opening. I pulled the knife back and shoved it hard into his arm. It only went in about an inch, but it was enough for him to roar in anger, reaching for the knife instead of me.

Hands wrapped around my waist, pulling me off his back and dragging me backward. Dante fell to the ground, yelling and grabbing at his arm.

Fox held me, half carrying and half dragging me as he ran. "You ok?"

"Yes, fine, Ransom?"

He pointed ahead into the darkness, Kye and Jax carrying him to the cars. "Other than trying to stop us and yelling to get you, he's ok enough to get to the car."

"They chained him up."

Fox grabbed my hand, squeezing it as we ran through the streets. "It's ok. We'll all be ok."

"It was Dante, Fox. He did it all, even the photos."

"Well, that explains you stabbing him." He grinned as we reached the cars. "Quinn, get in the back of my car."

I listened, climbing in the small back as they helped Ransom in. His head and half of his body were on me, and the rest of his body angled so he was lying down, his legs in the front seat. I wrapped my arms around him as best as I could. He didn't look comfortable, but he was out of it, his eyes opening and closing as he tried to look at me.

Cars roared around us, and Fox peeled out, getting us out faster than I had ever seen him drive.

I looked down, "Ransom." I whispered, tears falling again. I tried to wipe them off before they dropped onto him.

"Wild wild lioness." He mumbled, "Saved me."

A sob escaped me, "Yes, always."

"Love you."

I leaned closer, making sure he would hear me. "I love you too. So much. I love you."

"Mmm," he said, a smile trying to form on his split lip. "I want to hear all about your rescue mission."

"You can have anything you want if you stay awake. Anything. You've offered me everything, and I've offered you nothing. I'm sorry. I don't have anything to offer you, Ransom. I'm sorry." I kissed him again. "Anything you want."

"You. Just want you."

"You have me."

He gave a half smile again, and I pressed a soft kiss on his lips. By the time I sat back up, he was completely passed out.

"Fox, he's out."

"I'm going." He sped the car through town, getting onto the highway.

"Where?

"The hospital."

I breathed in relief, hoping I wouldn't have to fight him to go. These weren't exactly injuries I could fix in the garage bathroom.

Fox was weaving through traffic, Jax ahead of him on his right and Kye ahead on his left. For a moment, I almost yelled at Fox as he stayed behind them, wondering why he couldn't go faster until I realized they were making sure he had a safe, clear path for us.

"You guys are amazing," I said, looking down at Ransom, trying to brush more of the dirt out of his hair.

"We just like keeping each other alive."

I gave a strangled laugh. "That's amazing enough. We'll focus on that for now."

We reached the hospital as they lined up in front of the doors. Jax jumped out and helped Fox get Ransom out while Kye ran in, yelling for help. I helped them, lifting his head up and out of the car, hoping we weren't too late.

FORTY-TWO

QUINN

I FELT helpless as they carried him in, my heart tightening in my chest until it felt like it could burst.

Kye ran back out, "I'm going for Scout, be back." He ran to his car and took off. Another sob came as I thought of Scout, wishing she was there now.

I stood there, frozen and watching as nurses grabbed Ransom, laying him down and checking his vitals. In the cold lights of the hospital, he looked worse.

Cuts and red marks covered his body, the dirt covering half of them. I couldn't even believe what he had been through. Fox talked to one of the nurses before turning back to us.

He wasn't looking great, either. I looked at Jax and then down at my own clothes. We all looked pretty rough. I was covered in Ransom's blood, and it seemed like the fight in front of the garage had been a little brutal.

Fox's lips were pulled into a tight frown. He was always so calm and happy that his sudden seriousness worried me more.

"What did they say?"

"They are going to start tests to check for the worst and let us know when we can see him."

"How long?"

"At least a few hours," he said, taking a deep breath, "Kye?"

"Went for Scout." He nodded and pulled out his phone. "I'll tell him to bring us all clothes."

"And food," Jax said. I gave him a warning look.

"Listen, we fought off some nasty fucking dudes. You cannot tell me you're not hungry. Ransom will be fine, Quinn." He knocked against my shoulder. "The guy will make it through by sheer stubbornness to spend more time with you. He was like a schoolgirl today, smiling and talking about you two being together. Trust me, he's not leaving you yet."

I stared at Jax for a moment before pulling him into a hug. "That might have been one of the nicest things I've heard you say. Even though I'm telling Ransom that you said he was acting like a schoolgirl," I said with a smile.

"Good try. He'll be so drugged up when he wakes up he won't remember," he said, pushing at me, a smile still covering his face.

Fox fell into the chair on my other side. "I wouldn't count on it. That's a hard one to forget. At least he won't be able to catch you for a day or two."

"If he gets out of here in a day or two," I mumbled. I just wanted to know if he was going to be okay and that he wasn't bleeding internally or anything deadly serious.

"Ransom will be out tomorrow," Fox said it like it was a fact.

"How could you possibly know that?"

"Because the guy hates hospitals. Can't stand them. He panics at the thought of going to one. I never understood why. It's like claustrophobia or something. Why do you think he had you fix him up at the garage? He'll be leaving as soon as he wakes up from whatever tests or surgeries they have to do on him."

"I don't know if that makes me feel better or worse." I leaned back, sitting in silence between them as the minutes ticked by.

My adrenaline had worn off, and I realized how sore I was. The chairs in the waiting room were not helping.

Fox shifted and threw an arm around me, trying to get comfortable as he stretched out his legs. But, with a muscled frame and six-foot-something body, these chairs were even worse for him.

I smiled over at him, but it fell the moment I saw his arm. "Oh my god, Fox." I pulled it closer. "You need this checked out." A deep cut was across the top of his forearm, blood still pooling around the open wound.

"No, it's fine." He swatted me away, but I jumped up, going to the closest nurse.

"Excuse me. My friend needs someone to look at his arm. I think he needs stitches."

"Quinn." He groaned from behind me.

"Shut up, Fox."

The older nurse looked me over. "You're here with," she hesitated, looking all of us over, "that boy that just went back?"

"If you mean Ransom, then yes, we are. Now, can you help him with his arm?"

"We're pretty busy. I don't know how long of a wait it would be."

I looked around. It wasn't that busy. "Listen, he needs stitches. Can't someone help?" I knew I was most likely overreacting. My words were more threatening than pleasant, but I couldn't handle any more blood or open wounds. I needed everyone taken care of and safe.

She jumped at my words. "Fine," she hissed. "But you are all going back to the room. We've had two different people complain about you three."

"Fine, but I want to be in the room that they will be bringing Ransom in."

"Fine."

I scrunched my nose and walked back to Fox and Jax. "Come

on. We're getting your arm checked, and we can wait in the room for Ransom."

"Really?" Jax asked. "How did you manage that?"

"Apparently, people are complaining about us," I said, grabbing at Fox and following another woman through the doors. "I don't know why. We've been quiet."

"We look like trouble, Quinn. You're going to have to get used to it."

"Oh," I said again, remembering what this group looked like from the outside. I remember being scared to walk into the garage. My anger and interest in Ransom were the only things keeping me going inside. I was a part of that now. Covered in blood, pulling up with my bloodied unconscious boyfriend, the race cars, and the crew. "That part didn't occur to me."

Because from the inside, it was the safest, most loving place I had ever been. The only place I had ever belonged. Even all beat up, dirty, and bloodied. I couldn't imagine sitting here waiting with anyone other than Fox and Jax. I couldn't wait for Scout and Kye to get here, either.

They stitched Fox's arm, and we waited. They tried to keep me distracted as I sat on the bed, watching the clock change from minute to minute.

Kye and Scout got there, clothes and food in tow, and we took over the small room.

"I really want to hug you," she said, handing me a pile of clothes, "but I'll wait till you change." She smiled and pushed me towards the bathroom.

I stared in the mirror. I looked rough. Blood was smeared on my face and lips from where I had kissed Ransom. My shirt was torn across my stomach and coated in blood and dirt. I pulled off my clothes and tried to wash up in the sink as much as possible before pulling on the clothes she had brought. A pair of leggings and one of Ransom's shirts.

I took a deep breath of him, silently thanking Scout for

bringing it. She had also grabbed a zip-up hoodie, a change of shoes, and clothes for Ransom. I grabbed everything up and went back, hoping they had brought him to the room, but it was still the rest of the crew, everyone spread out, lounging on every piece of furniture in the room as they ate.

"Alright, Kye is a terrible storyteller. I think I got like three whole sentences. Can someone please tell me what happened?" Scout asked.

I stopped at the door, watching them talk as Fox told Scout what had happened. Her eyes went wide with each part he shared. I could only watch as my heart beat wildly, loving each and every one of them.

I begged the universe to bring me Ransom back, begging for more of this life with him. The more time I spent with this family I found, the more I wanted to keep them. It was a life I felt like I had just been given, and I wasn't ready to give it up yet.

I sat back on the bed next to Scout, listening to them talk, their voices growing quiet as the night wore on.

I pushed closer to Scout, wrapping my arms around her as she did the same. She was there as I fell asleep, safe for once in a room full of people who would do anything for one another - including me.

FORTY-THREE

RANSOM

THE SMELL HIT ME, the thick industrial cleaner waking me up from a dead sleep.

Then it was the honeysuckle sweetness of Quinn. I nuzzled closer, hoping her scent would wash away everything else.

I heard a beep, and my eyes opened, remembering where I was and why.

I could see Kye and Scout on a small couch and Fox and Jax in chairs. Slivers of light cracked between the curtains, and I was surprised it was daylight. I tried to find a clock and laughed as I took another look around the room. It was so small that it looked ridiculous with all of us in here.

Quinn felt me move and bolted upright with a squeak.

"Shh," I said, pulling her back down to me. My arms shook in protest at the sudden movement. "Everyone is still sleeping."

"You're here. You're awake." She pressed her lips gently to mine, and I tried to move, my body groaning in protest.

"Alive, and think I am in one piece, even if it doesn't feel like it."

"Nobody woke me up. When did you come in?"

"A few hours ago. Jax was the only one awake."

"How did I get into bed with you?"

"Jax helped." I wasn't going to tell her about the fit I started to make in my drugged state, demanding they put her next to me.

At the time, she felt like the only thing tethering me to the living. The drugs were putting me in such a fog I thought I was truly dying and needed her to hold on to. I sure as hell wasn't going to tell her that, even without the drugs, I was still feeling that way this morning.

"What happened? What did they say is wrong with you?"

"Aside from the nurses telling me I had a bad attitude. I have a broken arm, my shoulder was dislocated, a few broken ribs, and a lot of cuts and bruises."

"That's it?"

I laughed and put her lips against mine again, needing the touch. "Is that not enough?"

She tried to move back, but I held her in place, and she didn't fight me. Instead, she stilled, her voice so quiet and soothing. She hadn't left or run away.

"No, no, that's more than enough. I mean - it was so bad. I thought it would be worse. Oh my god, your arm was broken, and they hung you up like that."

"Let's not go into details." My body tensed on its own, remembering every second of pain. "I'm glad you're still here."

"Where else would I be?"

"At home, packing bags, wondering how you could run from me."

"Run away? Because you were attacked?"

"Run away because you would have one more big reason to think I was no good for you."

"Ransom, I don't think that at all. I won't lie and say I didn't before, but I know better now. You're perfect for me. Every vicious, sweet, scary part of you is perfect for me. I'm sorry I didn't tell you before. I love you. Every single part of you."

"I love you too." It was all I could think to say when it felt like my heart was exploding. Quinn wasn't running. Even after seeing the worst of me, she wasn't leaving.

"I'm sorry," she said again, trailing kisses across my mouth to my jaw and down my neck.

"Kitten," I groaned, "please don't do that."

She jerked back, her eyes wide. "Does it hurt?"

"Yes, it hurts my cock when you kiss and touch me like that, and I don't think I can take care of those issues right now, considering we're in a room full of our friends."

"Oh." She kissed me one more time with a quiet laugh. "I don't think there's much you could do even if we were home alone in bed."

"I can promise you I will figure something out."

"Did they tell you when you go home?"

"I'm going this morning. I'm not staying a second longer in this place than I have to."

"Yeah, I heard you hate hospitals."

"Like my own personal form of hell. The smell, the sounds, it's the worst."

She looked me over, the hospital gown covering bandages, but it was obvious I was still covered in dirt and dried blood. "I guess that's fine. I would hate to stay and let someone else give you a sponge bath."

I groaned again, my cock responding before I could try to stop it. "You're killing me."

Her hand slid under the blanket, running a finger down my cock and pulling away. I tried to take a deep breath and get it under control, trying to remind myself we were in a room full of our friends, in a hospital, but somehow it felt like weeks since she had touched me, even if it hadn't even been a day.

"You're both killing me," Fox said, pulling a hoodie off his face as he tried to stretch.

"I second that," Jax said. "If I hear one more flirty comment, I'm separating you two."

"You are not separating us." Her hand tightened on mine, her tone so sharp and commanding that I smiled. It felt like Quinn had been unleashed onto the world and somehow became a champion for me in the process. All the days that I wanted her to like me, and now she loved me, my fierce lioness that would bring out her claws to save me. I nuzzled against her, kissing her neck.

Fox laughed, closing his eyes and leaning back. "Calm down. After what I saw last night, you can bet your sweet ass I am not trying to get between you two."

"You can't talk about her ass," I said with a light laugh, anything more sending pain through my chest.

"It was a compliment. You should be proud, Ransom. You got a girl with a sweet ass that ran into Slaughter's garage alone to save you."

Jax leaned forward. "She also held a knife to Ryder's throat. Which, a round of applause to you because I was pretty sure he was scared there for a second."

"I wasn't alone. You guys were right behind me."

"They didn't know we were right outside. I was a little star-struck there for a minute when you threatened Ryder. I think I fell a little in love with you a bit myself," Jax said with a wink, and I tightened my arm around her.

"Oh, me too," Fox said with a smile. "I liked that part. You're a bit violent, Quinn. Seems like you fit right in with us."

"And reminded all of us not to get on your bad side. Speaking of," Jax said, "what are we doing about Dante?"

The room fell quiet, "I called and had the locks changed again on the garage and house, so that's done. I also called Slaughter," Fox said, his tone holding regret. "I didn't want to, but we couldn't have him come after us again. I told him Dante had taken those cars. I said he could follow him and probably find the cars, or at least what's left of them."

"And?" I asked.

"And I told him we weren't associated with anything he was doing. So he's cut from our crew. Slaughter said he won't bother us again if he finds the cars or proof Dante did it."

"And if he doesn't find it?" Quinn asked.

"Then this could start up all over again," I said.

"Let's hope he finds them, and if not, we'll have to double down on being more secure until we can prove it," Fox said. "We can't afford anyone else to get hurt."

They all nodded, and Quinn sat up more, wrapping her arms around me. Her fingers seemed to mindlessly run through my hair, calming every aching part of my body.

I knew Fox was right. We had to make this stop. I couldn't imagine any one of them having to face what they did to me, and I knew Quinn and Scout would be high on their list if they wanted to get our attention again. I was glad they found me first. I couldn't live with myself if they hurt Quinn again.

Scout and Kye had finally roused from all the noise.

"Look who's still alive," Kye said, trying to uncurl himself from the small couch.

Scout smacked him in the chest. "Not funny."

"It is now that we know he is still alive."

I shook my head. I loved the crew, but damn, they were a lot to handle after you've been beaten and drugged for the last 24 hours.

"Alright. Everyone needs to get out. I want to change, go home, and apparently need to hear all about what the hell happened last night," I yelled.

No one objected, each one of them as ready as I was to leave the cold, smelly hospital.

Quinn got up, and I grabbed her arm before she was out of reach. "Where do you think you're going?"

"You told everyone to leave the room."

"That will never include you. You stay with me. I'll need

some help getting dressed anyway," I said, giving her a wicked smile.

"Hmm, I might be able to help with that."

"You know, no one has told me how rough I look after being beaten up all night. I'm starting to worry since no one made any jokes. Can you still stand to look at my face?"

She laughed, each sound from her making me feel more alive, pulling me from the fog of pain and drugs. "Don't worry. You're still as handsome as ever…kind of."

"Oh, you're going to regret that," I said as the nurses walked in. They unhooked me and went over the paperwork before I could leave.

The door shut behind them, and she turned to me with a smile. "I'm going to regret that? How? You're laid up in a hospital bed. You can't do anything about it."

"No? You don't think I can find ways to punish you from here?" I asked. One arm was numb and wrapped in a cast, but I still had one good one. I could sure as hell find ways to make her scream my name.

"Nope. But I think I can find ways to punish you."

"Punish me for what? I'm an angel?" I asked, putting the sweetest smile on my face that I could with a split lip.

"An angel?" She shook her head. "The devil, remember? And you scared me to death."

"I know. I'm sorry, Kitten. Thanks for coming to save me," I said, my heart stopping as she climbed into the bed and straddled me.

She came to me, she saved me, and somehow it made me love her more. I didn't know how I could love someone with every part of myself and still find ways to love her more.

More importantly, I didn't know how I could be laid up in a place I hated more than anywhere in the world and only be thinking of driving my cock into her again.

I tried to push my hips up, but pain ricocheted through me.

"Fuck, Quinn, please don't tease me right now. Everything hurts."

"Then be a good boy and stay still," she said, her voice so low and demanding that I froze, the command turning my cock to stone.

She was already moving clothes out of the way, and I could barely process what was happening. I reached up, tugging her down to kiss me, but she moved my hand back.

"Are you sure you want to do this?" I was ready to follow that up with some serious begging to keep going.

She laughed, pulling out my cock and positioning it at her entrance. "Ransom, I don't want to be anywhere else. This is the only thing I want to be doing right now. You are the only one I want to be doing it with. Now, stop talking."

"You think you're going to take control of me?" I asked, reaching up with my good hand to pinch her nipple.

"I already am," she said as she swatted my hand away.

She moaned my name as she sunk down onto me. I loved hearing it, the simple word making my cock twitch every time it passed her lips. She wasn't wrong. She had control of every part of me, and there was nothing I could do about it.

"Fuck, Kitten, get off on me. I love the way you use my cock for your own pleasure."

"Ransom," she growled, her hand reaching out and wrapping around my throat. I laughed against it, watching as her head rolled back and her lips pushed together. Her face twisted in ecstasy as she tried to stay quiet. I could feel my own orgasm build, loving every wild inch of her that she was finally letting out.

I grabbed her ass, holding her in place as she sunk down, taking my cock again in one quick motion. She started to move again, but I gripped harder, stopping her.

"What's wrong?" she asked, looking down at me with wide, worried eyes, "Are you hurt?"

"Nothing. I'm okay." I said, pulling her down to kiss her. "I just needed a second to feel you. I love you." I said again, wondering how I came to say the words so easily, but it became harder and harder not to say them around her.

"I love you too."

"Good. Remember that because I'm not going to forget every moment of torment and control you think you have. You better watch out, Kitten, I'll be giving it back double once I'm better."

FORTY-FOUR
QUINN

HIS THREAT MADE my body shake, my mind already thinking of every delicious thing he would do to me.

I got off him, fixing my clothes and trying to keep my legs from giving out, "Then I guess I better enjoy every second of owning your body until you're healed."

"Fuck, that sounds like heaven. I'm ready to go."

"No more wasting time, then. The crew is waiting out front."

"Yes, that's a great idea. I'm glad you agree," he said, smiling as I helped him up and started to dress him.

"To rest, Ransom."

"Fine, fine." He relented as a nurse walked in. She grabbed a wheelchair and took him out, his protests loud enough to echo down the hall. He shut up quickly when he had to slide into the car, wincing with each move.

I sat with my arms around him from behind, enjoying the feel of his heart beating under my hands.

Finally, we made it back and upstairs. He was already trying to move around, grabbing things from the kitchen and groaning every time he tried to bend even an inch.

"Just sit on the couch now," I said through gritted teeth. "Please, relax."

"Fine, but can we please order some food? I'm starving."

"Of course, if you sit still."

He looked over at me, a smile growing on his face. "You're loving this power trip, aren't you?"

"Yes, but only when you listen."

"I don't know. I liked my punishment earlier."

"Sit!" I yelled, trying not to laugh as I sat down, waiting for him.

He finally listened, sitting back as his dark hair fell into his eyes. He winced as he raised a hand to move it, but I was faster, running my hand through his hair to push it back. His eyes closed, and he leaned his head back, so quiet and calm that I did it again.

"That makes me feel much better."

I laughed as he melted, his head falling deeper into my lap as he got comfortable. "Oh, yeah?"

"Very much. Keeping your hands on me will cut my healing time in half."

"How am I supposed to get food if I also have to keep my hands on you?"

The door burst open as I said it, but Ransom didn't flinch as the crew came in, a flurry of talking, footsteps, and laughter.

Kye and Jax filled the kitchen, pulling food containers out of bags and filling drinks as Fox and Scout delivered everything to the coffee table. They were already handing things to Ransom and me as I helped him sit back up.

I had wondered why Ransom had such a big couch when it was only him, but I saw why now as everyone piled into the living room and flipped on the TV. There wasn't a question of if anyone was staying awhile or who was doing what. They all piled in, knowing they needed to be together, even wanting to be together.

Everyone started to eat in a happy silence until Ransom's eyes changed, and he groaned, "No one's mentioned my car." He looked around the room, seeing who would talk first.

Jax sucked in a breath. "Yeah, we were trying to avoid that subject."

"Shit," he said, leaning back and trying to take a deep breath that seemed to hurt, "that bad?"

"Completely totaled," Fox said with a grim face. "It's back at the shop already, so you can go look it over tomorrow."

"Or maybe the next day," I offered, worried about him trying to go out tomorrow.

He turned his head, kissing my cheek, "Unfortunately, you won't ever be able to keep me away from my cars."

I groaned, "Fine, but no racing for at least two weeks."

"Without a car, I can agree to that."

I shook my head, but knew it was as good as I was going to get.

"Looks like we'll be building two cars now. Shit, they will look so good together." He smiled over at me, the excitement radiating off of him.

It was so cute I couldn't look away.

"Two?" Scout asked.

"One for me and one for Quinn," he said, and Scout's eyes lit up.

"Well, that officially puts another girl into the crew."

I laughed, "So I haven't been a part of the crew yet? I kinda figured, but ouch."

"No, of course you have, but it's different when you drive with us. You'll see what I mean after you have your car." She beamed.

Even after everything that had happened within the last day, everyone, including Ransom, was smiling.

"Can we watch the movie now and deal with all of this tomorrow?" Kye asked.

"Absolutely." Fox grabbed the remote and hit play, the room quieting as the music started.

Ransom turned, "I love you." He whispered as a movie started to play.

"I love you too," I said, leaning to kiss him as a round of groans came. I laughed, "It's going to happen again, so you better start looking away."

The world had fallen into place, and after years of wanting and loving Ransom, I found out he loved me too. I looked his face over. Cuts and bruises were already forming, but he was still beautiful, especially when he smiled at me like that.

It was everything I had dreamed about and more.

FORTY-FIVE

QUINN

<u>3 Months Later</u>

Ransom rolled on top of me as I tried to stop him. His cast had come off last month, but part of me was still worried about what he could do. He had tried to convince me it was fine this morning, putting his fingers to good work as I tried to keep any coherent thought in my head.

He waited until I was about to come apart before rolling on top of me. "See? I'm fine."

I tried to protest again, but he pushed inside of me, making me forget my words. I wrapped my legs around him and pulled, urging him harder.

I had been on top of him for two months now, not letting him use his arm, and as much as I had come to like the control to move and use him how I wanted, I loved this. He slammed into me until I couldn't take anymore, my body tightening around him, my nails digging into his back as I yelled out his name. It was seconds later when he came apart above me.

A shiver went through me, still not believing I was with him and that it was still working out for us after everything we had to deal with.

He collapsed on top of me, and I sighed, the weight of him a comfort. He leaned on an elbow, kissing me. "I told you I was fine, and it's just been too long since I felt those claws." He growled low in his throat, dragging me against him as he rolled to his side.

"We need to go," I said, looking at the clock. "We said we would be there by two, and it's ten till."

"Will they really miss us?"

"Probably not, but we would never hear the end of it."

"Fine, but then right back here."

"Deal." I jumped from the bed, getting ready.

It was the first Saturday of the month, which meant the garage was having its cookout. It was cold out, but we set up the tables in the garage. I saw these people daily, but something about the Saturday cookouts felt comforting. Like a family dinner, I could sit around and hang out with all the people I loved that loved me.

Ransom drove us down. Even with an arm in a cast, he kept driving after the first few days, and with all of this downtime, he made sure we started to build our cars.

"Wow, so great of you two to show up," Fox said, sitting down at the table.

"Seriously, are you guys not sick of each other yet?" Jax asked.

"Not even a little bit," I said as Ransom pulled me onto his lap.

"You know, you guys," Ransom said, "I can't wait till you find a girl you actually want to stay with for more than a few hours. It's going to be a punch to your fucking face."

"Nope," Fox said, "I've seen the way you pined after her for years. It was torture to watch. You think I would be dumb enough to fall for that?"

Jax stayed quiet, his eyebrows jumping, but there was no smart-ass comment. I narrowed my eyes, but didn't question him further.

Ransom pulled me closer, ignoring him, "You hear that? I wanted you for years. Couldn't get you out of mind."

"Wow, what a coincidence. I wanted you too."

"Oh gross, you two," Scout said, walking out of the office.

Everyone stopped, looking over to stare. "Scout, you look beautiful." She was dressed in her green dress, her hair down, and a ray of confidence she finally had any time she dressed up. After missing the homecoming dance because of Ransom's attack, she decided to still go to their winter formal.

"Great, because I feel like a fool." She stalked over. "Can you put some of this makeup on before he gets here?"

"Of course."

She sat down in front of me, and the guys circled around, watching as I did her makeup. I was no expert, but I knew the basics.

"Why didn't you want to do this at the apartment?" I asked, trying to do her eyeliner.

"Because isn't it like true crime number one that you don't have the guy meet you at your apartment?"

I groaned. "You've been listening to way too many podcasts. And yes, that is the general idea, but I don't know how much it matters when it's a high school boy, and you have an entire building of guys who already want to beat him up for dating you."

"We aren't dating!" she yelled quickly. "It's just a dance."

"Well, whatever it is. Call me if you need a ride from the after-party. You're staying at the apartment tonight, right?"

"If you're staying there, then please, no guys over," Fox said, trying to look relaxed, but I could see the concern across his face.

Scout put her hands on her hips. "I can do whatever I want. You have girls over when you want to."

"And I'm no longer a teenager, so I can do what I want. When you're eighteen, then I won't say a word."

"Yeah, right," she said, rolling her eyes.

After we all moved past the entire Dante thing, and I moved past the Josie thing, we were able to convince Scout's dad to let her stay with me more often. We didn't mention it was an apartment building filled with those same guys he wanted her to stay away from. We only said that she would be spending the night at my place a few times a week. Living with Scout had been like truly living with my best friend, even if I did spend most of my time at Ransom's apartment.

A car that looked similar to all of theirs pulled in, and a guy jumped out. He was cute and only a little bit nervous as he walked up.

"Hey," he said, looking around. The guys all grumbled their hellos, and Scout jumped up.

"I think that will be enough conversation. We will see you guys later," she said, grabbing the guy's hand and pulling him back to his car.

"Hey, wait!" I yelled, "I don't even get to meet him?"

"Nope, not this time. Have fun without me, even though I know how hard that will be!" She jumped into the passenger seat, giving wild hand gestures to the guy to leave.

I smiled. After everything with Josie, I thought it would be hard to have a best friend again. That wasn't the case with Scout. It was always easy to love and trust her.

Plus, she was there every step of the way when I went to the police to tell them that it was Josie and Tyler who put the first video up. They were charged, and the videos were starting to come down everywhere. With all their families' money, though, both only had to pay a ton of fines. It wasn't exactly fair, but at least it was something. She was still living her life in their sorority, but at least she left me alone, and I didn't have to live with her any longer.

I tried to go after Dante for what he did too, but because there was no nudity, and it was technically taken with the garage's security camera, there wasn't much to do about it. At least that video wasn't nearly as embarrassing and was with Ransom. I could handle the second one floating around as long as the first video was gone.

And it's not like Dante got off completely.

After Slaughter and Ryder found their cars in Dante's secret garage, he was beaten up, and they pressed charges to get paid for the cars. Seeing Slaughter dressed up in a courtroom had to be the funniest thing I had seen in months. Dante was currently going through the court process, and we could all only hope he would be found guilty and not bother any of us again.

"Quinn!" Ransom's voice broke through, and I turned back to him.

"Yes?"

"Are you coming out back with us, or are you going to stand there and stare until she gets back?"

"Maybe stand here and stare? I'm just so happy for her."

He came over, wrapping his arms around me. "And you? Are you happy?"

"Very happy."

"Not sick of me yet?"

"Not even close."

"Going to fully move in with me yet?"

I smiled. He only asked me on a weekly basis, "Maybe. Soon."

"You can't play hard to get when I already have you. Have you and plan to keep you."

I leaned into his chest. "Good, because I wasn't going anywhere."

We walked outside, and he sat, pulling me into his lap. I looked down, his blue eyes clear as he looked back at me.

They weren't hard to read now. I knew they were full of love and always had been, but the line between love and hate can be blurred so easily.

THANK YOU!

Thank you so much for reading Quinn and Ransom's story!

If you enjoyed Heart Wrenched, please consider leaving a review! Support from readers like you means so much to me and helps other readers find books.

Ready for more of the Hollows Garage series? Don't miss Fox's story next in *Wrecked Love*!

Printed by Amazon Italia Logistica S.r.l.
Torrazza Piemonte (TO), Italy

58845898R00198